Is that

a moose in

your pocket?

Is that a moose in your pocket?

~~~~~~

kim green

DELTA TRADE PAPERBACKS

IS THAT A MOOSE IN YOUR POCKET?
A Delta Book / November 2003

Published by
Bantam Dell
A Division of Random House, Inc.
New York, New York

Book design by Laurie Jewell

Library of Congress Cataloging in Publication Data is on file with the publisher.

ISBN: 0-385-33717-5

Delta is a registered trademark of Random House, Inc., and the colophon is a trademark of Random House, Inc.

Manufactured in the United States of America
Published simultaneously in Canada

RRH   10 9 8 7 6 5 4 3 2 1

For my parents,
Steve and Shelley Green

〰〰〰

Who showed me that
pretending to be fearless
is half the battle

acknowledgments

A book isn't something you create alone. *Is That a Moose in Your Pocket?* would not have been possible without the support, guidance, and enthusiasm of my agent, Victoria Sanders, who kept things just risky enough to be fun. I also thank my editor, Jackie Cantor, whose editorial vision, discriminating eye, and conversational brilliance are unmatched. Thanks to assistant editor Abby Zidle, who answered my endless questions with patience and wit, and to Bantam Dell's knockout production and design team, particularly Anna Forgione, Laurie Jewell, and Marietta Anastassatos. I'm grateful to Kathy Lord, whose attentive and inspired copyedit made this a profoundly better book.

Deepest thanks to my readers and supporters, family and friends, who went to "Mantana" and back with me: Susan Williams, B. J. Green, MiHi Ahn, Amy Adair, Pat O'Brien, Kathe Sweeney, Graciela Villarreal, Jennifer Bush, and Melanie Wasserman. The support and interest of the Wasserman family, the Gibrat family, and all the Greens and Millers meant a lot to me. Special thanks to Mike Wood and Dana Green for showing me "the full Montana"—any mistakes are mine alone.

And, most of all, thanks to Gabe Wasserman, my good guy, whose imprint on my life remains magical and sweet.

Is that

a moose in

your pocket?

prologue

january 2001, san francisco

It started with an e-mail, as things often do these days.

You see, I never intended to move to Montana. Or fall in love with a guy who thinks crème brûlée is men's hair gel. Or get caught in flagrante delicto with my ex-boyfriend by, of all people, my parents. Or commit industrial espionage. (Okay, that one had crossed my mind on occasion.)

In fact, the spring of my thirtieth year, getting away from it all was the last thing on my mind. My job as a Web-site editor was going well. I had lots of friends and a nice apartment, and, having been raised in Miami, where the unceasing sunny days and rows of scorched backsides tend to give one a permanent headache, I was looking forward to a typically bracing, fog-shrouded, tourist-lamenting San Francisco summer.

My stats: Name: Jennifer Maya Brenner. Born: Miami. Live: San Francisco. Surrendered virginity: Fort Lauderdale (embarrassing, but true). Provenance: Eastern European Jewish-American with a dash of French Catholic—just enough to cause me to turn up my nose at a youngish Brie, but not sufficient to know how to tie a scarf with panache. Family: Quite mad. Siblings: Karen, 38, and Benjamin, 34. Parents: See *Family.* Age: As I said, 30. State: Relatively, if inconsistently, well preserved. On my best days, I've been known to get carded for buying cigarettes. (Yes, I used to smoke, back when it was socially acceptable in California.) On my worst days, I can sometimes score a senior discount at the movie theater. Therapy: Most definitely. Light therapy: Probably not. Massage therapy: Whenever and wherever. Exes: Too many for sainthood; too few for a memoir. Interests: Writing, editing, drinking red wine, drinking white wine, killing green plants, extracting twenty-dollar bills from ATMs, stalking attractive fellow gym-goers, buying red shoes, yoga, and feeding the poor (okay, once, but I intend to repeat the act next Christmas, so I'm claiming hobby status in advance). Things I would never say in a personal ad, even though I enjoy them: Walking on the beach, seeing movies, cruising to Mexico, dining at fancy restaurants, watching sunsets, and doing it in hot tubs.

So there I was, in a nutshell.

If not perfect, my life was at least bearable and, on paper, even a little impressive. Okay, I cried on the stair-climber once in a while and ate whole pints of Ben & Jerry's New York Super Fudge Chunk in one sitting and dreamed about chucking it all and having tantric sex with my Indian ob-gyn, but basically, life was tolerable.

Then I got the e-mail and everything changed in a heartbeat. Sure, it all worked out great in the end, but it took a lot to get there.

ex marks the spot

six months earlier

The e-mail arrived in my in-box as I was killing time adding books and CDs to my Amazon wish list that I would never buy. *Starting a Dialogue with Your Inner Child's Child* and *The Best Latin Dance Party Hits of 1980–1990* ring any bells?

To: Carl Hanson
From: Nancy Teason
Subject: Department changes

C,

I've been giving the changes we talked about some thought, and the topline is, Jen's just not ready for this kind of responsibility. She has tons of talent, and with the right kind of mentoring, I think she could be a managing editor in a year or two. Irregardless [sic] of the current budget freeze, I think we need to look out of house on this one. We can talk about it more but this is really my gut call.

p.s. Steve and I have tickets to the Giants game on Sunday. Interested in making it a foursome?

Nance

Nancy Teason, Director of Product Development
Technology Standard / TechStandard.com

I read it through several more times, heart pounding. My college roommate, who is now a practicing personal coach with two homes (Laguna Beach, California, and Old Saybrook, Connecticut) and two ex-husbands (both in L.A.), says that the important thing in times of stress is to isolate the thought attack and put it away in your "negativity closet." I have tried this method several times and have found that it is nowhere near as satisfying as imagining backing an SUV slowly over the backstabbing turncoat who has wronged you.

For about six weeks now, I've been going through the humiliating process of applying for my own job. Why do I think it's mine? Well, for one, my former boss, Jem Abbott Pierce (yes, that's really her name—Mayflower forebears), had the temerity to go have a baby and leave me stranded with her work. Not that I mind, since her job is infinitely more interesting than my own, what with the trips to L.A. in spring, New York in fall, and free shwag up the wazoo.

It just stands to reason that I, Jem's Fully Anointed Protégé, am supposed to take her place when she invariably decides that darning pashmina shawls, painting landscapes of rotting barns, and nurturing her blue-blooded progeny are more important than covering high-tech news in Silicon Valley.

One Internet hiccup, and a message I was never intended to see found its way to my in-box. This happens, what, once every five years or so? Twenty? As there was something omenlike about this, I grabbed my spongy carpal-tunnel wrist ball and squeezed obsessively while staring out at the parking lot, hoping for a divine or at least everyday revelation. I considered my options: Forward dreaded message to Carl and cc Nancy Teason (Treason?) with a kind *fyi* at the top, and pretend ongoing ignorance while conducting a quietly dignified job search, which would hopefully offer me 387,000 instantly vesting stock options and an all-straight-male staff? Delete dreaded message and sublimate my rage into therapeutic massage and book club? Reply to dreaded message using colorful expletives, stomp over to Carl's office, urinate on the copier, and fling my meager belongings in a box?

In the end, I did what I always do when I'm panicked—I called Robert.

He answered before the first ring ended.

"O'Hanlon." Robert always sounds incredibly butch on the phone.

"It's me. You are not going to believe this."

"Try me." Keyboard clacking.

"Somehow an e-mail from Nancy to Carl was misrouted to me. They're not going to consider me for Jem's job." Tears at the back of my throat threatened to choke me. This only happens with Robert and my mother.

"Holy shit."

"Yes," I whispered.

"Hang on."

I can hear Robert ordering his minions around in a charming, drill sergeant-esque kind of way. Robert is creative director at a trendy advertising agency in The City, and that, in addition to his brilliant wit, ridiculously handsome black Irish looks, and ambiguous sexual orientation, has everyone from junior copywriters to VPs in a constant dither to get his attention.

"Okay, I'm back. What are you going to do, lovey?"

"I don't know. I've worked hard for this, and I deserve it! It sucks, it just sucks..." Then I ranted a little more.

"Okay, what time is it?" he asked when I was done. I held my tongue on this one because most of Robert's non sequitur remarks end up somewhere good.

"Three forty-five."

"Leave. Leave right now and meet me at work."

"I can't. I have to finish editing this week's bullpen and call some of the freelancers and—"

"No. Drop everything. It is absolutely essential that you leave immediately and take the special O'Hanlon job-fuck treatment."

Treatment?

Which is how I ended up puking in a gutter at three A.M., the *Meredith Gazette* editor's business card crumpled in the back pocket of my favorite jeans.

DK is one of those revoltingly hip bars where San Francisco's yuppies and fashionistas can, for the price of a few highballs, pretend that Manhattan has nothing on the Left Coast in matters of personal style and price gouging.

When I walked in at exactly 5:35 P.M. on Thursday afternoon, the dim space was mostly empty, with the exception of a couple of precious dyke girls with chin piercings and a tatty-looking guy with a skateboard talking to the bartender.

After guiding my battered VW Fox through seemingly endless traffic on Highway 101, I just had time to throw on my Lucky Brand jeans and a black turtleneck (professional mourning) and run some pomade through my short, curly hair in order to make it to the bar by 5:30. I had successfully talked Robert out of making me meet him at Kleiner Price by reminding him that their mailroom clerk, Andy, had a crush on me. What would it do to the poor boy's universe to see me looking like Bette Davis in *What Ever Happened to Baby Jane?*

Naturally, Robert was late, so I grabbed a barstool and ordered a Sierra Nevada and a couple of shots of Cuervo Gold. I'm really not too much of a drinker, but there is something so clichéd about the experience of getting dicked around by upper management while you toil haplessly away in cubeville that it seemed to demand an equally clichéd response.

By 6:05, I'd killed the Sierra, three tequila shots, a handful of

green olives, and was starting on my second Cape Cod. The bartender, a really nice guy named Zurik—like Switzerland!—was
getting cuter by the minute, and the dyke babies in the corner
weren't looking too bad either.

Robert finally walked in at 6:15, his overcoat flung over his
arm, leather bookbag strapped across his very attractive chest. He
threw everything in a heap under the bar and pulled me into
his arms. It is at moments like these that the phrase *gay husband* leaps to mind, a concept that every woman over twenty-one
living in an urban milieu should embrace and promulgate with
fervor.

Finally, the dear man released me and did that head-nod
thing that had Zurik in front of us in two seconds flat.

"What can I get you?"

"I'd have what she's having, but I want to be *alive* tomorrow,"
Robert said. "How about a vodka tonic? Stoli, please." Zurik nodded and sidled over to the part of the bar that housed alcohol that
didn't taste like it came from Hawkeye's tent.

"How are you?"

"Okay, I guess. I just don't understand how they think I can
stay if they don't promote me, which leads me to believe they
don't want me to stay."

Robert made affirming noises, and we talked for a while
about the feasibility of chucking everything and buying a charming villa with sex-crazed houseboys included in Cabo San Lucas
(low), enrolling in a graduate program on a Caribbean island that
is conducted entirely in English (slightly better), and ending up
homeless and disease-riddled as we troll the sidewalks outside of
our former offices (best). We sipped our drinks in silence for a
minute.

"Robert O'Hanlon?" I glanced up to see a little gnome of a
man in a horrible brown suit place his hand on Robert's shoulder.

"Bernie!" Robert jumped up and hugged the little guy like he
was his long-lost dad (which he could have been, given the proclivities of Robert's gin-loving mother).

"It's been—how long?—six, seven years?" Robert pulled out a stool for the gnome.

"More like eight, I think." The gnome took off his brown polyester jacket to reveal a funky stars-'n'-stripes-motif short-sleeved shirt with a bona fide pocket protector.

"What are you doing here? I saw Nate Beckham at a conference about a year ago and he told me you were up in South Dakota or something," Robert said.

"Well, you're looking at the editor-in-chief of the *Meredith Gazette*. You probably didn't know I was from Montana, did you? We went back a couple of years ago when my mother took ill. Elaine wanted to get out of the city, and the kids were all gone away to college anyway." The gnome had a raspy, cigarette-cured voice. He looked a little like Harvey Keitel, but after a few drinks, who didn't?

"Amazing. I didn't know they let short Jewish guys into the state," Robert said.

The gnome laughed. "Oh, sure. But only if they can prove their parents are first cousins and they know how to shoot a moose at a hundred feet."

I leaned over and pressed my leg against Robert's under the counter. Robert turned to face me. "Oh, sorry. Bernie, this is my friend Jen Brenner. We worked together a couple of jobs ago here in San Francisco. She's an editor for the Tech Standard down on The Peninsula. Jen, this is Bernie Zweben. He was the managing editor at the *Manhattan Business Journal* when I was a copywriter there. We all worshiped Bernie. The man is an institution. His *breakfasts* are an institution." At this, Robert and Bernie slammed their glasses down hard enough to lose liquid and had a good laugh.

Robert wiped tears out of his eyes. "The *Journal* was famous for its blowout dinners with the financial folks. I mean, the guys from Morgan Stanley and the other Wall Street firms would drink like fish, and most of the reporters couldn't keep up the pace. Bernie would insist that we all be at work at the usual time the next day no matter what time we got home. But he'd always have a big eggs-and-sausages breakfast waiting for us when we got there."

"I still do it, you know, but it's caribou and venison instead of pork." When Bernie smiled he looked just like Harvey Keitel in *Reservoir Dogs*.

At this point, Robert and his new old best friend Bernie Zweben got into this deep conversation about: (1) old times; (2) drunk old times; and (3) drunk old times when you were on deadline. It was all pretty interesting, but I was feeling a little parched, so I called on Zurik again.

"Zurik!" Oops. Too loud. I leaned across Robert's lap. "Sorry, Bernie. I'm just trying to get our old friend bartender Zurik over here." Bernie nodded like he was right there with me. I really liked this guy.

Turned out Bernie was down for a conference of local newspaper editors in Oakland. He was staying with friends in The City, which is how he ended up at DK, which he had mistaken as the local dive bar (don't tell the fashionistas).

"So, Jen, Robert's been telling me you're having some problems at the Tech Standard. I'm looking for city reporters at the *Gazette*. Any interest?" Bernie asked.

"Are you guys thinking of relocating to, um, somewhere with sushi?" I parried.

"I hear they have sushi in Sun Valley, Idaho. For all the movie stars that are moving in, you know? That's only about seven hours' drive from Meredith." Bernie showed me his fangs.

"But seriously, it's a bitch recruiting talent up there. We've got the kids coming out of college in Bowman and Missoula, and a few escapees from the big city, but by and large it's a mom-and-pop operation. We've got one columnist who has been writing an unsyndicated etiquette column for forty-seven years. Can you imagine? I don't have the heart to let Madeleine go, and, truthfully, her column is pretty popular with the locals."

By now the potent blend of disappointment and alcohol had

me ready to say yes to a street-sweeping gig in Tulsa, just so I never had to see Nancy and Carl again.

"Why don't you take my card and call me after you've had a chance to think it over?" Bernie dug a slightly dog-eared business card out of his pocket protector.

Robert chose that moment to leap up and stand between me and the door.

"What are you doing?" I asked him, ducking under his arm.

"Er, incoming. Door. Damon." Robert jerked his head toward the door.

Ah, Damon. Damon Sanchez is my ex. Ex-what, you ask? Answer: Ex-everything. We both grew up in Miami. I guess you could call us college sweethearts, but that would mean negating the many nights we flung bilingual insults at each other and sought refuge from the other's angst in everything from food and booze to blondes and bungee jumping. We moved out to San Francisco together and tore our way through four more years before survival instinct kicked in and we parted ways. Oh, there was also Kristina, whose sleek honey-blond ponytail and sleeker legs had Damon dreaming of a Cuban–Swedish merger even while he traded bonds on the stock-exchange floor where they both worked for Paine Webber.

Don't get me wrong—there were many good times too. Nights when we had just arrived in San Francisco and huddled together under our first down comforter, lulled by the fog and wind and fantastic multiethnic food that felt so foreign to us, weaned on the warm embrace of Miami.

Two years out isn't so long, is it? His smooth olive face and sweet grin could still stop my heart, and on the few occasions I'd seen him in public, my instinct was still to meet his eyes across the room and smile warmly at him. Generally, this feeling faded after a few moments and was replaced by thoughts like, *Does Kristina still go to advanced step every day at the YMCA?*

When a six-foot-two, black-haired hunk in a Zegna suit leaps wildly in front of his woman friend in a bar full of malnourished boys in capri pants, it's bound to attract attention, and Damon spotted us as quickly. Frantic, I tried to raise my attractiveness quotient by swiping at my mouth with lipstick and tucking my shirt in over what was surely a gross display of plumber's crack.

"Robert." Damon shook his hand firmly. "Good to see you."

"Dame. How's finance?"

"Oh, same old, same old."

Was it my imagination, or did Damon's usual ebullience seem muted? Were those shadows under his jade eyes? A twinge of melancholy at the corners of his mouth? So many years of loving him had created a caring habit that I feared was lifelong, like brushing one's teeth or stepping over cracks in the sidewalk.

"Hey, Jen," he said.

Then I was folded into the warmest, most sincere embrace I'd experienced in at least six months. Damon's hugs were always one of the best things about him. In that regard we were equals, his large, stereotypically exuberant Cuban-American family a match for my own small, stereotypically exuberant Jewish-American clan in hugs, eating habits, and histrionics.

Damon was not classically handsome but possessed the kind of maleness so rare these days outside of a few maximum-security prisons and the rodeo. Starved for the feel of a man's back under my fingers, I clung desperately to his button-down shirt as he eased away.

"How are you?" he asked.

"Good," I said firmly, placing my wayward hands in my lap. Was it his business if I was clinically celibate and my wobbly career had given me a one-way ticket to Tulsa?

"How about you? Are you still at PaineWebber?"

"Yeah, still 'in Paine.' Still working New York hours, working toward the prize." He smiled, and my heart tripped. Damon always said he wanted to retire when he was thirty-five. In West Coast finance, that meant getting up at four A.M. daily, shepherding inebriated corporate clients on weekend golf binges, and kissing older traders' asses for a decade until you had earned the right to sit on the throne yourself.

"How are Ramona and Papa and everyone?" I asked. Ramona, Damon's mother, was a librarian from Havana who wore feathered mules with three-inch heels and flaunted her cavernous cleavage in magenta, orange, and canary-yellow wrap dresses à la Diana von Furstenberg. Everyone called Damon's father "Papa," perhaps because of his way with children, at least two of whom always seemed to be nestled happily in his lap as he played cards with his *compadres* in their shaded courtyard. Papa was at least twenty-five years older than Ramona—they were married when she was a teenager—and he loved her with the blind passion of a man who had lost everything before he was old enough to vote and rebuilt his life piece by piece, starting with the slats of the raft he had used to traverse that choppy ninety miles to the United States.

"They're good. Mom's the same as always, a real firecracker. She's volunteering at the *Médico Clinica* three days a week. Papa's had a few minor health problems, but Frank and Nona are there to help out. How's your family?"

"Oh, Mom's doing a piece for *Condé Nast Traveler* on spas, so she's happy as a clam. She was in Tucson last week; I think she'll be in Santa Fe next. Dad's just plugging away at the hospital. Oh, Ben and Julie broke up. It was really sad, Dame. It just about killed Ben. It's hard to get him to talk about it now."

"I'm sorry to hear that," Damon said.

"Yeah, well, breaking up. It's what people do." I swigged some beer for courage. "Speaking of significant others, how's Kristina?" Now, why did I say that? I mean, did I care how Kristina was?

"Fine. Kristina's fine."

Awkward silence.

"Well, I'm meeting some people, so..." Damon gestured toward the back room.

"Good to see you. You interested in playing fall league, Dame? We need people," Robert said.

"Sure. Call me. Bye, Jen, Robert." He waved as he floated away. I could almost smell the American Crew gel he used to comb his thick black hair into crisp waves.

Breakup lore has it that you "get over" people. That the one who once made your stomach tense and your palms moisten and your heart flop around won't provoke these animal responses in you anymore. That you'll be safe to roam the world once again, unafraid of seeing him at the video store, the movies, or the frozen-foods aisle. Maybe these things are true. Maybe it hurts long after it has to because we *want* to feel pain. Because we fear the slow, shuddering shutdown of ourselves as we disengage from the daily tonic of living with and loving another person. I don't know.

Three drinks and one heaving session in the gutter later, I still didn't know.

CHAPTER 2

the world of hurt

To: jenb@techstandard.com, ohanlon@kp.com,
maya@jpb.com, George.Pitt@cityofsf.gov,
traitor@dnai.com, skelman@earthlink.net,
wendyj@asiapacific.com
From: Els_Janssen@ucsf.edu
Subject: friday night

Hi, Friends.

Friday night is ON. If you want something to drink, bring it with you,
otherwise expect dinner and dessert and exceptional conversation.
Swing by around 7:30 or so. Jen—will you bring that big platter?

thx
els

My otherwise gentle father's best turns of phrase were reserved
for the times when Karen, Ben, and I drove our parents over the
top with our brattiness: "I'll give you something to cry about" and
"You're going to be in a world of hurt" are two I remember quite
well, having had them directed at me every couple of days for the
better part of the 1970s.

Well, I was finally there, and Dad wasn't even here to see it.

When I woke up on Friday morning, the wreckage of my life poured in like toxic sewage in a Rio shantytown. My turtleneck was still on, but bunched up around my neck. Mouth cottony, eyeballs parched, head pounding rhythmically against the walls of my skull. I felt like those gnarled, blackened mummies you sometimes see in touristy pseudomuseums that everyone says are fake but you just have to wonder.

It had been years since I'd drunk enough to be sick. Like the good Jewish girl that I am, I first checked to make sure my chastity and purse were intact before attempting to achieve vertical stature. Sadly, all was well in the chastity department—jeans still on, buttons cutting into my bloated stomach.

"Ahhh!" I moaned, collapsing back into my IKEA pillow set. Welcome to the World of Hurt! Dad was going to be so pleased—all those years of parental permissiveness were not to go unpunished.

After about an hour, things stabilized somewhat, and I was able to ease myself shakily over to the bathroom. Like La Streisand says, the mirror has two faces—and neither one of mine was fit for public consumption. My dark curls stuck up in matted clumps, and my normally olive skin was pale and blotchy, dark blue-gray eyes moist and red-rimmed.

I trudged over to the phone to call Nancy, praying for voice mail. Taking pity on the hideous among us, Goddess answered my prayers this time when Nancy's recorded nasal tone kicked in. I gave her my regrets and then stumbled back to bed.

The bleeping of the phone pierced through my subterranean coma at six o'clock in the evening. I had slept the entire day! I groaned and slid the earpiece off the nightstand, knocking off a pile of jewelry, receipts, and Claritin tablets.

"Hello?" I croaked.

"Hallo, Jen, is that you? You sound horrible."

My friend Els Janssen is many things good, but diplomatic is not one of them. She likes to say that she gets her big hands, big tits, and no-nonsense conversation from her German mother—and her big hands, big hips, and no-nonsense conversation from her Dutch father. At five eleven, with a head full of springy blond curls, Nordic bone structure, denim blue eyes, and a rack that belongs on a St. Pauli Girl, Els is more often taken for a supermodel than the brusque pharmacology student she is. We met two years ago when I was doing background research for a story on pharmacologists gone bad who operate crystal-meth labs in their dorms.

"I was out drinking with Robert last night. I'm not feeling well today," I said evenly.

"You're still coming tonight, right? I need to borrow that large platter for the hors d'oeuvres." Els pronounced *hors d'oeuvres* in that charming European way that implied—correctly, in this case—that she was equally at home speaking French, Italian, or Cantonese.

"What time is it? Oh, God, it's after six. I just need to jump in the shower and throw on some clothes. I'll be over in forty-five minutes."

"*Ja,* okay. See you later."

"Bye."

"Bye."

I hung up and surveyed the clothes situation. I had two choices: dress like I felt, which would be somewhere between sinner monk in hair shirt and crack ho, or dress for bravado, which would require a little more strategic planning.

One of the worst things about being single in a town full of couples is that you are made to feel like you're not really trying if you are not constantly ready to meet The One. Being ready, as far as I can tell from my many conversations with the gainfully attached, means maintaining a repository of scintillating conversational gambits ("Can you pass the cocktail napkins?"), maintaining that delicate aesthetic look I like to call executive-aerobi-gamine-whore ("*Love* those capri pants with that jacket and G-string"), and wearing lipstick at all times ("You know, my husband always says it was my Viva Glam that drew him to me during that five A.M. swim class at the Y"). You are also not permitted to skip parties where straight quasi-functional male hominids might be in attendance, throw away the Learning Exchange catalog, or go to more than three women-only affairs per year (you try to find a woman over thirty at Lilith Fair). The rules get even tougher after the big four-oh. I once heard of an attractive forty-ish woman whose mother hit her in the face with an iron (yes, it was on) when the daughter refused to go on an arranged date with her first cousin. I looked for that one on the urban legends Web site but—horrors!—couldn't verify its falsity.

Rummaging through The Pile was too painful to contemplate, so I honed in on the part of the closet that housed things that were too small, too 80s, or clean. I settled on a pair of clingy black bootleg pants, a charcoal form-fitting three-quarter-sleeve button-down, and my best platform mules. The perfect outfit—slip on a white collar and I could go from tart to nun in a heartbeat.

After a blissfully hot shower, I rubbed on some face lotion and glittery eyeshadow, applied a little cherry Blistex, and squirted myself all over with vanilla aromatherapy oil to neutralize the alcoholic fumes I feared were still emanating from my pores.

I grabbed the platter for Els, a bottle of red that someone had left on my table at the last party, and my short black trench coat and headed out.

Els lives in a nondescript cinder-block building near the university, in a foggy, predominantly Asian part of San Francisco called the Sunset. When I arrived, she buzzed me up to the second-floor, three-bedroom apartment she shares with two other students. Richard, a sweet guy with a pompadour from New Jersey, is premed and is never home. Evangeline, a massage-therapist-cum-psychologist, once told me that her clients tell her all their problems anyway; she might as well get paid a hundred dollars more an hour to listen to their shit.

"Hi, Jen," Els yelled from the kitchen in her lilting English. When Els says my name, it sounds more like *Yen* than *Jen*.

I dumped my coat and purse on Els's bed and followed her voice to the kitchen, which looked like a cross between Bosnia and Beirut. Cocoa powder dusted the Formica countertops, and mysterious brews bubbled angrily on the stovetop. A pile of spinach lettuce littered the floor near the fridge, and Els was up to her elbows in a giant lump of dough.

She looked up at me sadly. "I can make a multicompound analgesic, but I can't cook. Look at this pizza dough! Is it supposed to be this gummy? And my chocolate mousse didn't gel at all."

"Don't worry. When you get married, it won't be for your cooking skills," I said. "Here, let me do that. We can have Robert run down to the corner store and get some Ben & Jerry's."

I took the lump of dough from her, washed my hands, and got to work kneading while she resumed her attempts to toss a spinach and feta salad with roasted pine nuts and a tamari–balsamic vinaigrette without feeding the entire mess to the linoleum.

It was then that I noticed a suspicious glint in Els's bright blue eyes. My own gray-blue eyes narrowed.

"So, who's coming tonight?"

"Well, let's see. Robert and George, of course. Teryl and Eric. Katie. Pieter and Anna—do you remember them from the German-American club? Oh, and a first-year student in my program. Colin's his name. I'm his mentor. We met last week at orientation." Els tossed the salad furiously, her lean, tanned arms going in what seemed like every direction at once.

"Hmm. Colin. Now, why haven't I heard of Colin before?"

"He's a great guy. Too short for me, and of course I have Rainer, but really smart, you know? And he's only been in San Francisco a month. I think he said he was from Kansas City. Or maybe it was Oklahoma City. One of those middle places. He really doesn't know anybody yet," she said with satisfaction. Els finished abusing the salad and set it on the dining-room table.

"Ha!" I snorted. "A setup. I knew it! Let me guess, you're seating him between me and Katie."

Katie met Els in Holland while she was attending an exchange program at the university in Leiden. Katie was first-generation Vietnamese-American from Newport Beach, California, and her persona was distinctly New World. The first thing I noticed about her when we met two years ago was that she played down her natural beauty by knotting her waist-length, glossy hair in Bjork-inspired buns and wearing industrial-plastic granny glasses and striped polyester track suits over her slender figure. The second was that she had a mouth that would make a sailor blush. Next to Els and, of course, Robert, Katie is my closest friend in San Francisco, and the three of us women try to spend at least two or three nights together a week.

"Look, he's a nice guy, and why shouldn't you all meet?" Els reprimanded. "Besides, don't be so selfish. The guy doesn't know a soul here, and I think he's lonely."

Great. Now I'm supposed to baby-sit some Midwestern schmo who doesn't know enough to get his rocks off in a town teeming with brilliant, beautiful, sexually deprived straight women.

"Okay, just don't expect anything from me. I had a serious trauma at work this week. And I've given up on men for the time being."

I filled Els in on the trials of life at the Tech Standard and last night's Damon sighting. She made all the proper noises and puffed air through her full lips derisively, which, I have discovered, is the Dutch sign of sisterly compassion.

Els herself maintains a long-distance relationship with a mysterious Austrian artist named Rainer, whom none of her American friends has met and whose tortured appeal is only magnified by the few grainy black-and-white photos we have seen of him lounging in industrial cafés in Europe. Sometimes he writes long-hand letters to Els describing his latest attempts to capture Teutonic angst with his installations made of garbage culled from the streets of Berlin. Having been to Germany on one uninspiring occasion and seen her preternaturally clean avenues, I wondered if the garbage shortage wasn't Rainer's real problem, not inability to commit. But I keep my mouth shut on that one.

Robert and George arrived first. Robert looked luscious in a slate gray shirt and shiny slacks that set off his light eyes. George, Robert's longtime boyfriend, was equally dashing in preppy, assistant-to-the-mayor khakis, his cyclist's body shown off to full advantage.

After everyone hugged and kissed, we opened the bottle of merlot they brought (which made mine taste like pond water) and sat in the living room nibbling crackers and Camembert while the others arrived.

Katie, Pieter, and Anna arrived en masse. Anna was one of those German women who are drawn to San Francisco's women's scene like their fathers are drawn to bratwurst; it was probably love at first sight. Her soft, light-brown hair was buzzed military short, and her creamy, pink-cheeked complexion and feminist fervor gave her face a youthful glow that must have made her a hit at her Berkeley women's studies groups. She had on Birkenstocks, a hand-dyed lavender cotton shirt, and olive green drawstring pants, with a crystal earring in her left ear. Pieter remained an enigma—I'd met him only once—but he seemed tolerant of his wife's escapades. With his classically Germanic looks, he appeared as if he had just jumped off *Das Boot,* replete with snub nose, straight flaxen hair, and the physique of a Gstaad ski instructor gone slightly to seed.

Katie tossed back her shining hair—Els must have told her there was an available male hominid invited tonight—and unbuttoned her red plastic Barbie coat. She had on matching red platform boots and a sexy 50s pinafore and looked like she was going to serve us root beer floats.

We hugged. She drew back and looked at me.

"Hey, Brenner. I heard you got really shit-faced last night," she said.

"How did you hear that?" On countless occasions, I am reminded that Katie's intelligence-gathering network is vast and unparalleled, rivaled only by that of the Mossad.

"I saw Zurik at the artists' collective on Valencia today."

Major oversight! I knew he'd looked familiar. I tried to place him as one of Katie's wanna-be paramours, ex-paramours, or gay husbands. Before she could fill me in, the doorbell pinged and Els called to me from the kitchen to get it.

I opened the door to an attractive, normal-looking guy who was in an obvious state of agitation. He had a bunch of semi-wilted Gerber daisies in one hand and a bottle of wine in the other. He crammed everything under his left arm and shook my hand with his right. I noticed he had a heavy gold ring on—dear God, not a frat boy—and that his handshake was firm and only slightly sweaty.

"Hi, I'm Colin. I'm in Els's program."

"I'm Jen Brenner, Els's friend. Come on in. Those flowers are beautiful. Can I take something from you?"

Colin managed to juggle things around and hand me the wine bottle, retaining his knight-in-shining-armor image by keeping the daisies for himself. He had warm brown eyes, lovely coffee-colored skin, short springy dreadlocks, and an undefined air of gallantry that pegged him as Midwestern even before he opened his mouth.

I deposited him in the kitchen with Els and started transferring bowls of gourmet pizza fixings to the sideboard table. Teryl and Eric, whom I didn't know, arrived next, and we all trooped into the dining room to start assembling our personal pizzas.

I found myself sprinkling smoked trout and capers on my circle of dough next to Colin.

"So, how did you decide to move to San Francisco?" I asked him.

"Well, it's kind of a long story." He had a funny up-and-down sort of accent, like the people in the Coen brothers movie *Fargo*.

"My, uh, mom raised me and my twin brother by herself in Minneapolis. I knew all my relatives on my mother's side. But my dad left us when I was just a kid, and I think he's living somewhere out here. He's a jazz musician. I think he might be living in Oakland or something." Colin gamely picked at the marinated tofu.

Aargh! Why does it seem like I only meet guys who are: (a) on some sort of depressing personal quest driven by their inner child; (b) foreign; (c) foreign and crazy; or (d) foreign, crazy, and on a personal quest driven by their inner child?

Colin stared at me with his large brown cow's eyes, and I now saw that what I had mistaken for the gleam of a male's interest in a female hominid was really the crazed gleam of a neglected boy of color who had been raised by lutefisk-eating gringos and abandoned by his Huey Newton–worshiping African-American father for the siren call of music and loose women in smoky nightclubs.

Feeling suddenly faint, I excused myself, pleading dehydration, and stumbled out of the kitchen and down the hall into Els's bedroom. I pushed the pile of coats and purses aside, kicked off my mules, and burrowed under Els's extra-thick down comforter, inhaling eau de fig or whatever mysterious concoction Rainer had sent her. Why does the pursuit of love have to be so undignified? How did things go so horribly wrong with Damon, the love of my life? Why am I such a freak magnet?

Eventually, the door cracked and Els poked her springy head through the opening. I could hear Katie's big braying laugh from the other room, and Buena Vista Social Club trickled in. When Els saw me quivering under the blankets, she closed the door and came over to the bed.

"Hey, are you all right? What's going on?" She stroked my head, which felt nice, so I whimpered a little and pressed against her long jeans-clad leg.

"I hate parties, I'm never going to meet anyone, and I'm going to be fired for incompetence and drunkenness," I said. "And I think there's a law somewhere that Jewish parents can disinherit their children if they don't provide them with grandchildren by the time they're thirty-five."

Els shushed me and squeezed my shoulder. "Now you're being silly. You're thirty, and a young thirty at that. You're gorgeous, you're bright, and your parents would love you even if you told them you were running away to join the lesbian circus. So stop feeling sorry for yourself and get up and join the party. Everyone's asking where you went. Colin thought he had done something to offend you."

"Did you know that Colin's black father abandoned him and his twin brother, so he grew up in poverty in Minnesota and now he's out here looking for him, probably to make him pay back child support or stalk him or something? I bet you didn't," I said triumphantly. "I bet he isn't even in the program. I bet he's faking it to get cheap housing."

Els looked at me strangely.

"First of all, Colin's father isn't African-American, he's a white music professor who Colin thinks is teaching at Berkeley. And his parents' divorce, from what he was just telling me, was amicable. The family just drifted over the years. And his mother's family are rich southern transplants who own a chain of hardware stores and didn't like their daughter marrying a poor white guy from New York, which doubtless contributed to the distance. He grew up with maids and nannies and trips to Europe in summer, so I don't know what you're talking about."

Shamed by my lack of political correctness and plain old bitchiness, I tried to dig back under the coats, but Els dragged me out of bed and down the hall while I protested feebly.

The party was in full swing. The now harmless-looking Colin was sharing a pesto pizza with Katie, who was laughing at all his jokes and swinging her long fall of hair around. Depressed, I plunked myself down next to Robert and George and swiped a slice of artichoke-olive with marinara. I could eat what I wanted—foreigners liked plump women, and men in search of their inner child were too preoccupied to notice whether I was a size 8, 10, or 22.

I decided to try out the Montana concept on them.

"So, if I moved up to Montana to take that job at Bernie's paper, would you guys visit me?"

George put down his beer and grinned. "Does a bear shit in the woods?"

I punched him. "Seriously. This is a major life decision here."

"I think the best decisions in life are calculated risks," Robert said, looking at George. "I believe in the old chestnut about never knowing if you don't try."

His voice was warm and loving as he met his lover's eyes, and I felt suddenly embarrassed, as if they were talking about something totally different and I was merely a fly on the wall.

Then Pieter was there, asking George about the mayor's decision to extend the subway system to the airport. And Katie and Colin came over to see if we wanted some pesto-olive-caper slices. And then, as conversations will do, that one turned to other things.

CHAPTER 3

the decision

To: Loehmann's insiders
From: Loehmann's
Subject: Summer Sale

You are receiving this newsletter because you have selected this option. If you want to unsubscribe, <click here>. If you want to update your newsletter selections, <click here>.

Dear Jen Brenner,

The Summer Sale is in full swing at Loehmann's! Get up to 50% off on designer suits, slacks, swimsuits, and more in the bargain basement. Plus, get in shape for summer with our new fitness department.

Yours fashionably,
Loehmann's Sales Team

The next few weeks passed in a holding pattern. I struggled with how to act around Nancy and Carl, who, presumably, weren't aware that their betrayal had been discovered. In the meantime, I hung out with Robert and George, went to the movies with Els, and spent one wrenching nuclear-familial afternoon with Jem and her husband, Micah, watching their adorable baby, Milo, systematically destroy their living room and wondering about my own dwindling procreative prospects.

As always, Jem's view of my situation was illuminating.

"Why don't you just take that job in Montana with that friend of Robert's?"

We were sitting in the sunroom of her Noe Valley Craftsman-style home. Organic vegetables, crayons, and *New Yorker*s were scattered across the pine table, and for once it was quiet except for the wind chimes tinkling on the sunny backyard deck. Milo's nanny had put him down for his nap, and we were alone with Jem's old red Lab, Bonnie, who sat snugly on my right foot.

"Montana? Jem, are you kidding? I live here, I have a *life* here. I can't just go off half-cocked to the boondocks for the first half-baked offer I get." I stroked Bonnie's auburn back.

Jem put her latte down and looked at me. Her thick, honey-colored hair was pulled into a messy bun and skewered with a chopstick, and her kind eyes had the kind of crinkly, soft lines around them that only made them look bluer.

"How do you think I ended up in San Francisco, Jennifer? Do you think the Abbotts and the Pierces grow up thinking of the West Coast as a civilized place with cities and culture and decent marital prospects? Hell, no," she snorted. "I know it may seem like nothing to you, but when I decided to come out here alone after grad school, my family took it as a slap in the face. To leave without succeeding on their terms . . . well, it's a kind of failure, and one I wouldn't have risked if I hadn't been in the deepest, most dangerous rut of my life back in Boston. Sure, I could have stayed and married somebody suitable, had kids right away, given up all my ambitions as a writer. You think arranged marriage is a Third World concept, try hanging out with some of these *Social Register* families for a while. I'll tell you, my leaving may have seemed like a lark to others, but to me it was the first spontaneous, unpremeditated act of my life. If I hadn't left, I never would have met Micah, had Milo, or even had the courage to get a job from someone who wasn't a friend of my family's.

"I'm not saying Montana is the panacea for everything you feel is wrong with your life, but you need to look at what is really keeping you here. You came out because of Damon, and I wonder if you're still here because of him. If I were your age, I'd definitely consider it. You're like me. We like everything scripted and deliberate and guaranteed. And that's fine, but it would be a shame for you to miss out on some really interesting opportunities just because you still hold out hope that Damon—who has his own baggage, mind you—will realize what he gave up and come back to you."

I doodled periwinkle happy faces on the corner of *The New York Times* crossword. I knew she was right. I had rationalized my solitude over the past two years as a kind of break between relationships—or at least a break from Damon—and a day didn't go by that I didn't bemoan my lack of a partner to experience life with. It was interfering with . . . oh, just living, and I knew it.

"I suppose it wouldn't hurt to send him my résumé," I said slowly.

Jem gave me her serene, patrician smile.

"I've always wanted to see Glacier National Park." My voice quickened. "I could sublet my apartment, maybe even take a leave of absence from the Tech Standard. It's not like it has to be a permanent thing—more like a vacation, really. A chance to do some beat reporting, see the country, get away from here for a while. If I don't like it, I can come home anytime."

Now I was getting excited. I could reinvent myself in the great outdoors, the Wild West, home of the free and survivalistic. A vision of me slinging a battered four-wheel-drive truck into a snowy parking lot crystallized. I would live in a cabin à la the Unabomber and order all my clothes from L.L. Bean. I would get to know people who gutted fish, shot moose, and maintained stern silences when confronted with the sissified behavior of city folk. I would eat steak for breakfast. I would be automagically skinny, a fortunate side effect of extreme cold and daily tussles with bears. If I didn't rope steer and barrel-race horses myself, I would at least drink beer with those who did.

I was going to Montana.

CHAPTER 4

semper fi, baby

To: Jen Brenner
From: Alaska Airlines
Subject: Ticket confirmation K3280L

Dear Jen Brenner,

Congratulations! Your ticket order has been processed. Please refer to the following confirmation number. Your will receive an itinerary confirmation in the mail within 10 days.

Yours truly,
Alaska Airlines Staff

I was awakened by the tinkling sounds of children's laughter and small feet pattering by my tent. The delicious aroma of coffee wafted through the cutout window, and I rolled over on my Therm-a-Rest air mattress and wiggled out of my spanking-new sleeping bag.

The sun was just rising over the low hills in the distance, blanketing the lake in warm golden light. The Grearsons, who were spending their summer vacation driving around the northwestern United States in their massive RV, were up and about, and Mrs. Grearson waved at me as she slapped bacon on a sizzling skillet.

I stretched and regarded my new home with amusement and delight. Two weeks ago I was struggling to find a parking spot in San Francisco; now I was living in a park. I had ensconced myself at a family campground on Seeley Lake north of Missoula on my way to my new digs.

My friends' and family's reactions to my announcement had been predictably excessive, the Tech Standard's position as expected—indifference with a touch of smugness. But they gave me my leave of absence without complaint, and I felt grateful when I walked to my car after my semi-good-bye party with my departure box.

When I finally tracked down my mother, she was at an ashram in Oregon. She sounded a little breathless after her Iyengar yoga class.

"Jennie, why don't you take a few days and join me up here? It's really quite wonderful. I mean, some of the treatments are sort of extreme, but you don't have to do those."

Trying to quell the image of my middle-aged mother, Victoria Brenner, settling in for a high colonic, I got straight to the matter at hand.

"Mother, I called because I have something to tell you."

Expectant silence at the other end.

"I am taking a leave of absence from my job and moving to Meredith, Montana, to work at a small local paper up there."

Nothing.

"Mother, are you there?" I said.

"Yes, of course I'm here. I'm just, I don't know, surprised. This is terribly unexpected, don't you think?"

As if I should have known that I would receive confirmation that my job, personal life, and prospects for childbearing were all headed straight for the toilet in a single week.

"I know it might seem that way to you, but this is something I really want to do."

"What about Damon?"

My mother's modus operandi vis-à-vis my love life is to act as if Damon and I are just taking a break from each other before we plunge headfirst into holy matrimony.

What I wanted to say: *Mom, I'm so sorry to break this to you, but Damon has passed. He slept with too many blondes with double-D implants and they just couldn't reconstruct his chest. His heart was only an inch in diameter when they went in.*

What I really said: "Mom, Damon and I are not together. He's seeing Kristina now. You know that. I really don't think he should be part of this decision."

"Have you talked to your father about this?"

"Yes, and Dad thinks I should do whatever I feel like doing."

"Yes, he would say that. He's something of a free spirit, your father. Did you know he was in the Peace Corps in Niger for two years? Asked me to marry him, then took off for darkest Africa. I was sort of a girl Friday to an editor at *Gourmet* at the time. You can imagine how I felt, trying to convince my friends that he was a real person."

Characterizing my civic-minded father as some sort of frivolous hippie was like calling Mother Teresa a jet-setter.

"Yes, Mom. I know Dad was in the Peace Corps. They needed doctors, for chrissake. Maybe you could say I'm performing my civic duty in bringing a little multiculturalism to Montana."

It got no better after that.

My conversations with friends were equally unsatisfactory.

I told Katie, Robert, George, and Els one balmy Sunday afternoon. We were barbecuing on Robert and George's pillbox-size deck in their Castro-district Victorian.

"Are you mad? They probably hunt Jews and Asians up there. *Let's git us some dark meat for Thanksgiving dinner,*" Katie twanged.

"That is ridiculous. Meredith's like any other small town in America. You're the ones who are discriminating—against the rednecks!" I cried, prompting an explosion of laughter.

"You're going to have to stop calling them rednecks if you're to live happily amongst them," Robert said.

"I've heard they prefer 'crackers' to 'rednecks,'" said George.

"Yes, but only if the circumference of their skull is more than eighty-two centimeters," Robert cracked.

Everyone laughed, including me.

"Tell us what you're going to be doing again," Els said.

"Well, Bernie says they need a city reporter. I'll be covering local events, politics, business, even sports sometimes. He says I can stay as long as I want, but whenever I want to leave, that's cool too. They also have an intern program through the state university system, and I'll be working with their fall intern." I sipped my beer.

"I'm going to find a room to rent. You can't believe the rents there, they're so low. Els's friend Colin is going to sublet my place here. And that's it. The Tech Standard is giving me a six-month leave of absence. They can't promise me my old job back, but they relocate you to another department if they have to."

"Like the custodial one?" Katie asked.

"Yeah, basically. Who cares? A lot can happen in six months."

I relived that day spent hundreds of miles and a couple of mountain ranges away as I heated my coffee on my camp stove and prepared instant apple-cinnamon oatmeal. The Grearsons' dog, Sledge, poked around my picnic table, nabbing stray bits of sloppy joe from the cookout the night before.

Already I felt different. Lighter, less internalized, and ready to tackle my next challenge, finding a place to live. Colin had overcome his pique pretty quickly when I extended the offer to sublet my one-bedroom apartment in the Mission district. Presumably, he was all moved in now, caretaking my closet full of city clothes, leopard Naugahyde sofa, and vintage 80s record collection.

"Miss Brenner?"

I turned from the stove and faced a man I hadn't met before. Tall and thin, with sinewy muscles bulging from his snug, short-sleeved ranger shirt, he was a babe by anyone's definition. Short, sandy hair flopped over his broad, tanned forehead, and his hazel eyes focused on mine. His name tag said *Ranger John Anderson* under the national-parks logo.

"Yes?"

"You got a message down at the park office. You're to call"—he looked down at the paper in his hand—"a Mr. Bernie Zweben as soon as you can. Do you need his number?" He stood there looking at me, smiling openly.

Not used to such undivided male attention, I stuttered a bit.

"Yes. I mean no, I already have the number. I can't believe you came all the way out here just to give me that message. I really appreciate it," I fumbled.

"Well, Rick Mahon, the other ranger, said there was a pretty girl staying by herself in number 34, and I just wanted to see for myself if you needed anything."

At that, the pretty girl blushed hotly and hiked up her baggy sweatpants, which threatened to expose the pretty girl's flowered cotton briefs.

"Well, I'm fine, thanks."

Unaccustomed to such prolonged eye contact, I stared dumbly, unable to tear my gaze away from his steady hazel one. Wait a minute, was that a wink? Did he wink at me?

"Miss Brenner, I'm leading a nature walk this afternoon if you're interested. We'll be covering all variety of native flora and fauna around the lake."

Including male hominid fauna? I wondered. Already imagining telling my girlfriends back home about what was turning out to be the mother lode of available hunks, I happily accepted and arranged to meet his group at the camp office at two P.M.

With a friendly, perfect ranger wave, John Anderson strode off, tight butt rotating nicely under his regulation chocolate-colored slacks. I imagined him bushwhacking trails and slapping tickets on wayward jet-skiers, and was filled with pure, childish glee.

I spent the next hour picking up around camp and strategizing my outfit for the nature walk. I finally settled on J. Crew khaki tab-front shorts, a tight tank top, sans bra—the kind Els's roommate Richard calls a wife-beater—and my new hiking boots.

Then I strolled down to the camp office to call Bernie from the pay phone there.

He picked up on the first ring.

"Zweben," he answered in his gravelly voice.

"Hi, Bernie. This is Jen. I got a message that you had called."

"Hi, there. Good to hear from you! How was the trip up?"

"It was great. I took my time. Stopped to visit friends in Portland."

"Good. Well, the reason I'm calling is, I'm wondering if you can stop and do an interview on your way into town this week. Apparently, some fish—the chub, I think—are turning up dead in droves up around Arlee, and the local environmental folks think it may have something to do with the big mill, Sutter & McEvoy. I need somebody to go up there and poke around a bit, talk to the mill's press guy. Dave Lefebvre is busy covering the fires, and Margaret isn't coming back from Seattle until Tuesday." Dave was the paper's other city reporter, and Margaret Bloom usually focused on lifestyles—cooking, gardening, home stuff.

"Sure, I'd be happy to."

I took down the information he gave me and promised to call him after I'd talked to Glen Whitehead, the mill's PR guy, in a couple of days.

Later, I went on the nature walk, which was all I had hoped it would be. By the end, I knew all there was to know about the plant, bird, and love life around Seeley Lake.

Apparently Ranger John had just broken up with his common-law wife of eight years—"Woman threw my stuff out of the trailer while I was at a training in Yellowstone and shacked up with a state police officer"—and was ready to make a change. He asked for my number while we pretended to examine a fuzzy yellow flower that looked like the weeds that spring up between the cracks on city sidewalks. My first impulse was to knock him to the ground and yell, *My tent or yours?*, but I suppressed my baser instincts and told him to call me at the paper if he was ever in Meredith and we could go out for a beer. Mustn't squander newfound superpowers on first male hominid encountered. Must ration powers for future hotties, I told myself as we picked our way carefully through the sweet-smelling but scratchy underbrush, plump bees buzzing around our heads.

The next day, I packed up camp, waved good-bye to the Grearsons, jumped in my new used Subaru, and hit the highway.

One misconception about Montana on the part of city folk like myself is that it is a lawless land—no speed limits, no rules against cracking open a brew in the car, and few encroachments on personal liberties. I was finding that the reality was a little different. There were rules, all right, but they emanated more from the trial-and-error method of individuals with different agendas bumping up against one another than a government bureaucrat sitting down and documenting what he thought the people needed to be protected from. A waitress I had talked to at a pit stop in the Bitterroot told me that, until recently, Montana drivers carried five-dollar bills in their wallets on long trips. If pulled over by a cop, they just handed over the money and sped off.

The waitress's tone had been easy to read: I may know my way around Miami and San Francisco, but when it came to Montana, I had a lot to learn.

I pondered this as I cruised down the two-lane road. The craggy peaks of the Swan range, still capped with snow, loomed on my left, and miles of lowlands dotted with lakes blanketed the other side. Once in a while, a settlement would whiz by, and I would catch a glimpse of a road sign in front of a few tired buildings: GET GAS HERE, BIKERS WELCOME, CHEAP FURNTURE.

Lunch was a delicious burger and a mound of fries at a road-

side diner, topped off by a splendid huckleberry shake. I mowed
through every crumb. Although I was eating like there was no tomorrow, two weeks of the outdoors life had redressed my city pal-
lor and softness: My thighs felt achy and muscular from all the
hiking, and my normally pale olive skin had a rosy glow from af-
ternoons spent reading in my folding chair on the shores of the
lake. My hair, uncut, sprang from my head in a tumble of dark
curls, lacking style but clipped back with blue plastic barrettes on
either side.

After lunch, I asked the cashier, a skinny boy in Wranglers, if
there was a phone. He pointed toward the bathrooms, and I went
to call Glen Whitehead at the mill.

"Sutter & McEvoy," said a nondescript female voice.

"Hi. This is Jennifer Brenner with the *Meredith Gazette*.
Could I speak to Glen Whitehead, please?"

"Please hold." I waited for several minutes while they tortured me with a Muzak version of "You Light Up My Life."

"Glen Whitehead." Deep voice.

"Hi, Mr. Whitehead. This is Jennifer Brenner. I'm a reporter
for the *Meredith Gazette*. As you know, there've been reports that
the chub are dying in record numbers downriver from the mill,
and some environmentalists are attributing the deaths to the mill.
I'd like to hear your side."

"No problem," he said smoothly. "Are you free tomorrow
morning? I have an hour at ten A.M."

"That's perfect."

He gave me directions, then said he looked forward to meeting me tomorrow and hung up. All very cooperative and forth-
coming. So much for Rocky Mountain intrigue.

I got back in my car, and the last hour or so to Meredith
passed uneventfully. My plan was to spend the rest of the day
checking out rentals in town. I'd set up appointments with three
landlords and was looking forward to seeing the possibilities.

My first appointment was with a Harold Marvin, who had
posted an ad on a local Web site's message board saying he had a

room for rent. I followed the simple grid of streets on the map and parked in front of an immaculate box of a house with a carefully manicured hedge of roses in the front, à la Edward Scissorhands.

I threw on my fleece vest—a breeze had picked up—and strode toward the house in defiance of a wave of homesickness, suddenly feeling more than a little nostalgia for my own cramped one-bedroom in San Francisco. I rang the bell and waited. And waited. I heard rustling within and was about to flee back to the car when an old man opened the door.

Ancient. This was the word that popped into my head when I gazed at Harold Marvin's frail, twisted little body. He had heavy jowls, and his wrinkled skin was marked with age spots. A tattoo that probably once said *Semper Fi* and now read something like *Smpf* sagged off his bony forearm, and he leaned heavily on a knotted cane. He wore a white wife-beater tank that was three sizes too big and gaped under his sticklike arms.

"You Jennifer Broomer?" he rasped.

"Yes. Brenner, actually. Are you Mr. Marvin?"

"What do you think?"

He waved me in, and I reluctantly followed him into a dark hallway. An American flag large enough to swaddle King Kong hung on the wall.

"Thank you for seeing me on such short notice, Mr. Marvin. I saw your ad on the Internet."

"Oh, yeah. My grandson put it there for me. I don't have no computer, but he's pretty smart on 'em. Has his own Web site. Aryan brotherhood and all that. Don't approve myself, but it's a free country, and I fought for it, Miss Broomer."

Remembering Katie's observation about Montanans eating swarthier folk for dinner, my mouth suddenly felt like it was stuffed with cotton, and I looked frantically around for the nearest escape route. Did white supremacists, like animals, have the ability to sniff us out?

Harold Marvin continued down the hall to the back of the

tiny house and opened a door. I followed slowly. The room was clean, with decent hardwood floors and double-paned windows, according to Mr. Marvin. A spit-shined double-barreled shotgun hung over the bed next to a pair of dusty antlers. A magazine was curled up in the trash, boasting this headline, HEAD SIZE AND IN-TELLIGENCE: THE NEW SCIENCE OF RACIAL DIFFERENTIATION.

I thanked Mr. Marvin, promised to call him, and almost knocked the old fart on his ass as I blew out of there.

Praying he wasn't representative of the average Meredith resident, I moved on to the next place, which did not—surprise, surprise—have any Aryan brotherhood paraphernalia in evidence. It was a studio attached to a ranch house on the edge of town, and lacked light.

My last appointment was with a longtime friend of the Zwebens, who rented an in-law unit out of her house from time to time. Gladys Pepper lived in a well-kept, buttercream-colored bungalow on a shady, tree-lined street in town.

The door was cracked open when I arrived, and I stuck my head in tentatively.

"Ms. Pepper? It's Jen Brenner. Hello?"

"Come on back. I'm in the yard."

I followed the voice through the house to the back. A polished oak staircase gleamed in the hallway, and the smell of cookies wafted from the pale turquoise 1940s-style kitchen.

The yard was dominated by a lush weeping willow tree. Gladys Pepper was ensconced in an Adirondack chair, drinking from a yellow mug. A well-tended garden with tomatoes, lettuces, and giant sunflowers occupied the space behind her, and a stone Buddha grinned at us from beneath a canopy of azaleas.

Gladys leaned forward and took my hand. "Hello, my dear. Bernard said you'd come all the way from San Francisco. Would you like some tea? It's a favorite of mine—Evening in Missoula. I get it when I go down to visit friends at the university."

"I would love some tea. Thank you."

She poured me a cup, and we sat down together, sipping, as light and shadows played over us.

Gladys Pepper had the most erect posture I'd ever seen and reminded me a little of the actress Bea Arthur. Her strong-featured, weathered face was capped by thick silvery-white hair and dominated by large, dark eyes. She was wearing Wranglers and a multicolored poncho. A cheesecloth with various herbs I didn't recognize was spread across the tiled garden table at her side.

"How do you and Bernie know each other?" I asked, sipping the tea, which was fragrant and delicious.

"We grew up together, here in Meredith. Lived kitty-corner from each other for about twelve years. Of course, there was a long period when we were out of touch—when he was in the army and then living in New York and raising a family with Elaine." She paused to sip her tea.

"I remember the day they moved in. My mother made apple brown betty and made me and my sister, Maudie, put on dresses and come with her to welcome the Zwebens to the neighborhood. Mrs. Zweben answered the door, and I thought she was the most glamorous creature I'd ever seen. Red lipstick and heels—during the day, mind you—and this tiny boy peeking out from behind her dress. I guess Bernard was about seven, and I was about twelve, and I stuck out my tongue at him, and he stuck his out right back, and we were both sent to our respective rooms without any dessert, and for some reason we were friends ever since."

Gladys leaned back her head and released a peal of laughter. Her good humor was contagious, and for the first time all day, the blanket of homesickness that had been weighing on me lifted a little.

"Here, let me show you the room." Gladys gathered teacups and paraphernalia briskly and led us toward the house. A fat, lazy tabby dozed on the back porch, eyeing me.

"That's Nefertiti, Neffy for short. She's waiting for her cookie, aren't you, you little devil?" Gladys stroked Neffy's tangerine back and the cat arched her spine, purring.

"My father added this room on after the war as his office. He was a country doctor," she added as she opened a door off the kitchen.

The room was a perfect square with windows on two sides and a door that presumably led to the side of the house. It was warm and sunny and had its own bathroom. Gladys opened the south-facing windows, which looked out onto a flowered hedge.

"You have your own entrance, but we share a kitchen. I don't always rent the room. Just to one of Bernard's interns, or sometimes a student. One year I had a nice smoke-jumper boy, but he was out fighting fires most of the time.

"You'll have your privacy, of course, and I mine, but I usually make dinner for my guests a couple times a week. It's always worked out just fine."

I sat down on the high four-poster bed and contemplated. I was a thousand miles from my second home and three thousand from my first. I had a job as a reporter at a paper with a circulation of 25,000. I knew exactly three people in Meredith, and one of them was an ex-Marine with connections to the Aryan brotherhood. Things were looking up.

"I'll take it," I told her.

CHAPTER 5

something fishy

To: Robert O`Hanlon
From: Jen Brenner
Subject: Hello from Montana

So, I'm here, and it's *amazing.* In my first week in Montana I have seen two mountain ranges, three lakes, gotten one ranger's phone number, and consumed four huckleberry shakes.

I miss you guys. Give George and Petey big hugs for me. And write, dammit!

Love,
Jen

Sutter & McEvoy had been pressing wood pulp into paper since before the turn of the century. The first employees at the mill were paid thirty cents an hour for their labors, and it wasn't uncommon for twelve-year-olds to go home after fourteen-hour days with grain-stained hands and aching backs.

As one of the primary employers in an otherwise economically depressed area, Sutter & McEvoy enjoyed kid-gloves treatment from all levels of government. But in recent years, environmentalists had started to turn a more critical eye on its practices.

The mill was located on the highest of a group of greenish gold, rolling knolls about eight miles from the town center, next to a brightly gurgling creek. It was an impressive structure. The plaque outside told me it had been renovated in 1964 but retained much of the original brickwork on the facade.

Unsure about what qualified as business casual in Montana, I had settled on charcoal slacks and a gray shell, with my newly shined black oxfords. My wild tumble of curls was held back with a tortoiseshell plastic headband, and I held my reporter's notebook and tape recorder in my worn leather bookbag.

My plan was to talk to Glen Whitehead, then drop by the offices of the Montana Environmental Alliance in Missoula, the group that was leading the campaign to subject the mill to an environmental audit.

The interior of the mill was cool and slightly damp. I was shown into a fashionably loftlike waiting room by a snub-nosed blonde with the type of sausage-roll curls junior-high girls spent hours perfecting in 1983. Grainy black-and-white photographs of the mill and its workers going back to its inception adorned the walls, and I studied them while I waited for Glen Whitehead.

"Ms. Brenner? I'm Glen Whitehead. Welcome to Sutter & McEvoy. C'mon down to my office."

In one of those funny twists of fate, Glen Whitehead *was*, his flaxen hair just brushing the collar of his plaid work shirt. He led me down the hall, entered a doorway on our left, sat me in a plush chair opposite his large, cherry-wood desk, and got me a cup of coffee himself.

"I don't recall seeing your byline before. Are you new to town?" he asked. He mixed sugar and creamer delicately with his big hands.

"Yes. I just moved here from San Francisco. This is my first story for the *Gazette,*" I confessed.

"Well, I'm sure you'll find our town politics rather more

quaint than what you're used to. If there's one thing that charac-
terizes the Montana point of view, it's countrified parochialism."

Was I imagining it, or was there a trace of patronizing smugness underneath Whitehead's smooth words?

"Well, as I'm sure you know, I'm here to ask you about accusations that effluents from the mill have contaminated the river,
causing fish to die and possibly infecting the water table. Do you
mind if I tape this?" He shook his head. "Great. Let's get started,
then." I placed my Japanese microrecorder on the desk and got
out my notepad.

"First of all, if there's nothing going on, why are the fish dying?" I asked.

He sipped his coffee. "Well, nobody—including the MEA—
really knows for sure. The thing is, it's not unusual for fish
to die of unexplained causes every once in a while. The last
recorded incident of something like this was on the American
River in California five years ago. The environmental groups' first
instinct is to blame manufacturing interests, but then, as now,
they were unable to find proof linking the damage to industrial
outputs."

Whitehead leaned back in his fancy wire-sprung chair.

"Sutter & McEvoy has as much of an interest as anybody in
protecting the local environment. Most of the mill's management
lives here, like everybody else. Our kids drink the water, and we
fish the river and enjoy the benefits of living in one of the country's few remaining unspoiled wilderness areas. Last year, the mill
donated half a million dollars to local environmental projects.
Our track record is as good as it gets."

We were interrupted by a staccato rapping on the heavy oak
door. The blonde, whose face now had a petulant cast, stuck her
head in and motioned Whitehead over to the door. They exchanged words in low tones for a minute, glancing at me once. I
caught the words *park* and *MEA*. Then she left, shutting the door
a little too hard. Whitehead stifled a look of irritation and smiled
at me.

"Looks like something's come up I need to deal with. I'm terribly sorry to cut this short. Perhaps we can meet another time?"

Knowing a brush-off when I saw it, I told him that would be fine and gathered my belongings. He escorted me to the lobby.

"Petra will see you out. Let's plan on picking this up where we left off, okay? Sutter & McEvoy definitely wants to be on good terms with the *Gazette*'s newest—and may I say also the prettiest—reporter." He shook my hand and strode back down the hallway, already raising his cell phone to his blond head.

What is it with men in this state? It's like they think a few flattering remarks about your smile are going to win them instant access to your Victoria's secrets.

Chuckling at my own (sad) joke, I got into the Subaru and popped in a Macy Gray CD. I watched as, about one hundred yards away, Glen Whitehead hustled into a bulbous machine that looked like the pseudotanks you see at monster-truck rallies and sent gravel flying as he peeled out of the parking lot.

Curious, I started up and followed him. Well, I didn't really mean to follow him, but since there's only one road back to town, the opportunity just presented itself.

We toodled along at about eighty-five miles per hour. When he got to the outskirts of Meredith, Whitehead hung an aggressive left and followed the river toward a park area I had noticed the day before with picnic tables and a kid's carousel. He slung his truck into the lot and stalked toward a group of people who were gathered in a gazebo that stood at the river's edge, stopping at the edge of the crowd with his arms folded tightly over his chest.

I grabbed my notepad and sidled over to the footpath on the river, hoping to mix in with the joggers and cyclists who occasionally sped by.

A middle-aged woman with long straight hair wearing a purple-and-gold dashiki held a sign that read, *First our fish, then our children. Stop Sutter & McEvoy.* The crowd was pretty mixed, an amalgam of granola-eating, Birkenstock-wearing types, PTA-ish soccer moms, college students, and ranch and factory workers. Two young people in sweatshirts that read *Montana Environmental Alliance* on the back unfurled a banner across the gazebo's latticework.

A dark-haired, intense-looking man in his late twenties approached the mike that was set up at the gazebo's entrance. He took the mike off its stand and brought it to his mouth, striding back and forth across the stage like a rock star.

"Thank you for coming today, folks. I think you all know why we're here, but I'll go over it for newcomers and our members of the press." Did that mean me? I glanced around for other reporters but didn't see any obvious candidates.

"I'm Steve Wald, and I run the Missoula chapter of the Montana Environmental Alliance. I'm here to talk to you today about an environmental travesty that's being committed right in our own backyard."

He paused for dramatic effect, staring at the crowd.

"Sutter & McEvoy, like many old-style paper mills, uses sodium hypochlorite, a chlorine derivative, for bleaching reprocessed paper into paper pulp. Sodium hypochlorite has been shown to release dioxins and furans, as well as large amounts of chloroform and hundreds of other bioaccumulative and toxic organochlorines. What does this mean in plain English, folks? These are highly toxic substances that have been shown to kill and sicken any living thing they come in contact with over time." His silken voice was just youthfully enthusiastic enough to sound sincere and trembled slightly with indignation.

"The EPA started setting pollution limits for pulp and paper production in 1998, but these rules, ladies and gentlemen, apply only to bleached-kraft pulp mills. Sutter & McEvoy's primary business is as a secondary fiber mill, and, as such, this mill—the mill that sits on the banks of your local river and looms over your drinking water and your fishing—is exempt from the environmental regulations that seek to control these toxic by-products."

Wald gazed earnestly at the crowd. "Last week, hundreds of

chub turned up dead downriver from the mill's landfill. We believe this is just the beginning, and we seek an immediate moratorium on production until the federal and state governments can conduct an environmental audit of Sutter & McEvoy's dumping practices."

"Hey, Wald," a man's voice shouted from the crowd, "you going to put dinner on my family's table?" A rumble rose up in the crowd, some voices adding to the dissent, others arguing against it. I scanned the crowd to find the source of the voice, and my gaze fell on a stocky man in Wranglers and a fleece jacket as he laid his hand lightly on an irate-looking man's shoulder. Stocky Guy glanced away from the stage, and, for a moment, his dark eyes flashed against mine. Feeling suddenly faint, I leaned against the railing and reached into my bag to get some cranberry juice. Low blood sugar, I guess.

Wald raised one knee and placed a mud-encrusted work boot on a folding metal chair. "I know some of you work at the mill. Believe me, I understand your concerns. This isn't a witch hunt, and it's not intended to put anybody out of work. But what good is dinner on the table if your kids are too sick to eat it?" This set off a wave of murmurs and grumblings. I scanned the crowd for Glen Whitehead and saw him standing apart from everyone, listening intently to a man decked out in what I've taken to calling "rancher chic"—snakeskin boots, crisp white shirt, bolo tie, and the ubiquitous Wranglers.

Wald was wrapping up his speech and taking questions from the crowd as I pushed my way into the throng. My friends weren't going to believe my first few weeks in Montana. Between getting cruised by smooth-talking park rangers, attending environmental rallies led by activists who looked like they'd sprung from the pages of L.L. Bean, and escaping from marauding white supremacists, I was getting more excitement than I did in a year in San Francisco. Emboldened by my newfound persona—overworked, celibate city girl turned Montana man-eater supersleuth—I raised my hand. Wald pointed at me from the lectern.

I took a deep breath so my voice wouldn't shake.

"Jen Brenner from the *Gazette*. Mr. Wald, if the landfill has been contaminating the ground and river water for some time, why hasn't it turned up evidence of environmental damage before?"

Wald repeated my question into the mike. Some crowd members nodded in affirmation. Up close, Wald's eyes were a startling blue, his teeth very white and straight as he smiled confidently— or condescendingly?—at me.

"Ms. Brenner, it's not unusual for it to take years to measure and quantify environmental damage caused by effluents leaking into water. All we're asking is for the government to proceed conservatively here, by taking the time to ascertain whether there is, in fact, a problem. We think the alternative—allowing the mill to continue its current level of outputs while we test—is unacceptably risky."

I scratched out his answers in shorthand while he responded to other questions. After about fifteen minutes, people started drifting back to their cars. Since it was pushing one o'clock, I decided to head over to Main Street for a huckleberry shake and whatever meat product was unlucky enough to cross my path today.

"Ms. Brenner!" I turned away from the Subaru and saw Steve Wald walking toward me. He had jogged across the park, but the only signs of breathlessness were mine. Really, up close the man's looks and charisma were striking: near-black, uncropped wavy hair; physique a little on the short side but a body that could give Mark "I can't keep my shirt on" Wahlberg's a run for its money; a direct, rather stern gaze; and those amazing blue eyes. Yummy.

"I just wanted to formally welcome you to Montana. John Anderson is a friend, and he said to look out for you," he said. John Anderson? Oh, yeah, chocolate slacks. Flora and fauna. The ranger without a manger to call his own.

"Well, thanks. My first few days have been pretty interesting."

He nodded sagely, as if there were all manner of secrets

waiting to be discovered by enterprising reporters in western Montana, human population 50, bear population 568.

"I was wondering if you'd join me for a bite to eat tonight at the lodge. There's always live music there on Thursday nights. Don't worry, I won't try to recruit you—yet." He grinned. Ha! Recruitment was the least of my worries.

I accepted, and we arranged to meet at the lodge at eight o'clock. Then he trotted off and I got in my car and headed for the *Gazette* offices, which turned out to be on the first and second floor of a cute bungalow at the intersection of Cedar and Defoe Streets.

Introductions were friendly but low-key. Bernie gave me an enthusiastic handshake, then introduced me to Dave Lefebvre, a slender man in his late forties with basset-hound eyes, and Madeleine Blankner, a tiny older lady in a straw hat and orange lipstick who daintily grasped my hand in her white gloved one. Jessie Kerrigan, the receptionist, offered me coffee, and then everyone drifted back to work while I unpacked the few items I'd brought with me and placed them on my metal desk: my carpal-tunnel squeezie ball, a chipped green MacWorld mug, and a framed photo of Robert, George, Els, Katie, and me hiking on Mt. Tam in Marin County.

I logged on to Hotmail and checked messages. There were two from Robert, one from Els, one from Colin, seven from Katie (five forwards with bad joke written all over them), one from my parents' home account, and another from my brother, Ben. Apparently, Robert and George were going on vacation to Korea in two weeks. Rainer was talking about coming out to San Francisco for Christmas, and Katie and Colin had discovered a mutual passion for kung fu movies—and possibly more—since I'd been gone. Also, the toilet had flooded in my apartment, ruining my red shag bath mat. Oh, well.

Everything else was business as usual. Mom and Dad had run into Damon's parents at the movies in Miami, and Ramona had indicated that all was not *bueno* with Damon and Kristina.

Gee, should I send a sympathy card? And Ben wanted to know if he could come out for Labor Day weekend and visit. My shy, sweet-tempered, thirty-four-year-old brother had recently split with Julie, his girlfriend of six years, back in Miami, and he needed every pick-me-up he could get. Excited, I sent him promises of fly fishing, rafting, and other adventures if he'd get his skinny butt on the next plane out.

I spent the next two hours hammering out the piece on the dead chub, including Glen Whitehead's brief taped interview from earlier in the day and the MEA rally. Bernie and I spent a half hour discussing local environmental politics, and it was a pretty twisted little history. Apparently, Meredith fell under the jurisdiction of the Pacific Northwest office of the EPA, and the local agent was a guy named Bruce Mortensen who was based in Helena but worked part-time out of a satellite office in Meredith.

"Mortensen has a solid reputation around here. He's a local boy, grew up in Whitefish, a resort town up north. You ought to contact him for a quote," Bernie told me.

I agreed to do so, then zipped home to get ready for my date with Steve Wald.

CHAPTER 6

first date

To: mkim@koreanadoptions.com
From: George Pitt
Subject: travel confirmation

Dear Mr. Kim,

This confirms our arrival on August 25, 2000 at the Downtown Hilton in Seoul. Robert O'Hanlon and I will be at your offices the next morning at 11 a.m.

Regards,
George Pitt, Esquire

Gladys was home when I arrived, so we retired to the back porch with Evening in Missoula tea and her favorite snickerdoodle cookies. She told me her life story: She had attended college at Bowman, earned her teaching credential, and taught high-school history and composition for more than forty years. She had never married. I told her about my family, my work, that I didn't know where my roots were these days, that things just hadn't been right since Damon and I broke up two years ago. Then we sat in companionable silence for a while, listening to the birds rustling in the hedge and watching Neffy do a passable imitation of a fur rug.

Finally, Gladys pulled herself out of the Adirondack chair and went inside. It was the final night of a play she was stage-directing at the community center, and she wanted to get there early to prepare for the wrap party.

I went to my room, stripped my clothes off, and took a long, hot shower. I had that humming feeling in my belly I associated with exams, flights, and dates. The problem with sporadic dating is the fear that you have forgotten how to do it: the awkward con-versation, the tense discovery, the expectations, and, sometimes, if you're lucky, that first searching kiss—all lost because of some blunder.

I rifled through my army-surplus duffel—I hadn't unpacked yet—and found a sea green knee-length skirt with swirling sparkles, black platforms, and a form-fitting black tank. Kind of cityish, but that's what I am, right? I topped it with a girlish black cashmere sweater and tiny flower earrings, and put my wallet and favorite lipstick, BeneFit's Liars Lips, in my purse. My hair was still wild, so I spritzed on toxic air gels and sprays and hoped for the best.

Yelling good-byes to Gladys, I exited through my side door and drove to the Meredith Valley Lodge, an imposing structure with a grand entrance and a sign that said, *Home of Marlboro Williams and his Red Hot Jammers: Thursdays at 9 P.M.* Glancing at my watch, I saw that I was still a bit early—it was 7:45—so I headed to the bar, which, by the way, didn't look *at all* like DK or any other bar I had been to.

Big moose heads stared out from the wood-paneled walls, glassy eyes stuck in fierce repose. At one end of the bar, some kind of large cat loomed over a dwarfish deer, fangs bared over its prey's neck. I shuddered and ordered a Moose Drool ale.

Waiting for Steve, I checked out the lodge's Thursday-night crowd. Townfolk and rancher types seemed happy to be out on the town after what was presumably a hard day's work. Everybody appeared to know one another, and there was a lot of backslapping and handshaking going on.

My eyes settled on an attractive couple eating dinner in the corner of the dining room. The back of the man's head looked strangely familiar; he had coarse dark brown hair flecked with gray and a thick, manly neck. The woman across from him faced me, and I could see that she was stunning. Her hair was long, large, dark red, and flowed in waves over her slender shoulders in the style favored by *Entertainment Tonight* anchorettes. She had luminous pale skin set off by an emerald green off-the-shoulder top that was excessively formal for the lodge, yet exactly right for the redhead. Their food sat untouched in front of them, and the redhead was gesticulating angrily with her elegant hands. The man sat very still, nodding once in a while.

Suddenly, I felt a hand on my arm and turned around.

"Jen? Hi. Sorry I'm late."

Steve Wald was wearing the same outfit he'd had on this afternoon—Levi's, a sporty jacket, and the muddy boots—but he had shaved and smelled minty and, yes, edible.

"That's okay, I was just enjoying Montana's version of *When Animals Attack*," I said gamely, nodding toward the savage tableau above the bar.

Steve laughed and took my arm as we walked over to the hostess, who leaned over her guestbook as she checked off our reservation, showing us a wide valley of freckled cleavage. Steve seemed oblivious. *Hel-lo, this is one guy who's too busy saving the rivers to ford the valleys.* Life was good: I was in Montana, had written my first story for the paper, and was on my first date— second if you count the nature walk with Ranger Anderson—and it was only my third week here.

The Hostess with the Mostest showed us to a quiet table in the corner. Steve pulled out my chair for me, and I took off my sweater and hung it over the raw-wood chair.

"You look great," he said, gazing at me in that intense way he had.

"Thanks. You smell minty." Oh, God, why did I say that? But he laughed again as he picked up the menu.

The menu featured all manner of dead things with parents and faces—venison, mooseburgers, fish—and we had just ordered when a commotion in the corner caught my eye. The redhead was striding angrily toward us, heels clacking on the floorboards. She swished by, followed by her dinner partner, who—surprise!—turned out to be Stocky Guy from the rally. More surprising, Stocky Guy caught Steve's eye and stopped at our table, where I got a close-up look at him for the first time.

Though not conventionally handsome, the man had that indefinable quality that would draw attention in any milieu. My initial impression of heaviness had, I saw, been erroneous—the man was definitely muscular but had the hard, stocky body of someone accustomed to physical labor, as opposed to the self-consciously crafted body of a weight lifter or trained athlete. He looked to be in his early forties, and his springy hair showed a generous sprinkling of salt in the pepper at the temples. Right now his large, dark eyes were shadowed, and he rubbed a scar on his chin with a callused hand.

"Wald. How are you?" he asked politely. "Nice crowd today."

"Yeah, well, folks are interested in what's going on on their land and in their rivers," Steve replied, sticking to the party line.

I felt the man's eyes on me, and Steve jumped in.

"Bruce, this is Jen Brenner, the new reporter at the *Gazette*. Jen just moved up here from San Francisco. Jen, Bruce Mortensen is our local Environmental Protection Agency rep out of Helena."

Bruce Mortensen and I shook hands, and a frisson of something deep and disturbingly provocative passed through me. My hand seemed unbelievably small in his. After a fraction too long,

Bruce let go of my hand, said his good-byes, and followed the red-head out of the restaurant.

"What was that all about?" I asked.

"The redhead? That's Bruce's wife, Melina. I guess she might be his ex-wife now. She's supposed to be a hellion, Melina. I've only met her a time or two, but she struck me as the kind of woman who's gotten her way her whole life. Not so much be-cause of her looks, though they would definitely be a factor, but the whole package, I guess. Her father is Mike Curran. He's a big real-estate developer in the state, and he also holds a majority in-terest in the mill."

The waitress set a basket of bread and two iceberg-lettuce salads on the table.

"They've been separated for a while now. The daughter is staying with Melina at her parents' ranch. I'm sure that's what got Bruce so hot. He loves that girl, and he can't be happy about them living under Mike Curran's roof."

Still curious about Bruce Mortensen, I let Steve shift the conversation to the MEA's goals for the mill protest. We spent a pleasant if somewhat tepid evening, and by the time we finished the last bites of our huckleberry-rhubarb pie, I knew that Steve was originally from upstate New York, had, like my father, served in the Peace Corps (Ecuador), had an older brother who was an orthodox rabbi, and liked high-maintenance, neurotic Jewish women who were stuck on their Cuban ex-boyfriends (this one I deduced without asking).

Pleading exhaustion and an early deadline, I had Steve escort me to my car.

"I had a great time tonight, Jen. Can we do this again?"

In the moonlight, his dark hair shone almost blue, and his sharp cheekbones curved downward around his sweet-shaped mouth. His eyes were earnest and very, very blue.

Without thinking, I let him put his hands on my nape and pull me toward him. He trailed kisses around my mouth, and his tongue probed gently between my lips. It felt good, and after about ten minutes of good, hard kissing I tucked my head down out of sheer exhaustion and sighed into his flannel chest.

We stayed that way for a few minutes, then I pulled away and tucked myself into the Subaru. A final kiss, a promise to talk soon, and I left him standing in the lot waving, looking like every city girl's dream date.

CHAPTER 7

burning down the house

To: jen.brenner@meredithgazette.com
From: Walgreen's Pharmacy
Subject: Prescription #214296 has been filled

Dear Ms. Brenner:

Your Ortho Tri-Cyclen prescription is ready to be picked up at
Walgreen's Pharmacy.

Thank you for shopping at Walgreen's.

At 5:45 A.M., I was yanked out of a delicious dream in which I
was being awarded the Pulitzer prize for journalism by the U.S.
men's Olympic swim team. It was the clanging of Gladys's old-
fashioned phone. Groggily, I snatched it off the nightstand and
pressed it to my ear.

"'Lo?" I croaked.

"Brenner, this is Bernie. There's been a fire at the mill. We
need you down there right away. Do you have your camera?"

I mumbled vague affirmations and hung up. Bernie sounded
like he'd been up for hours. At that moment, I was sure he was

the devil incarnate, but I'd probably downgrade him to mischievous imp after I'd had my coffee.

I crawled out from under the patchwork quilt and splashed cold water on my face at the sink, moaning. I threw on my jeans, sneakers, and a sweatshirt, grabbed my bag and 35-mm Nikon, and crept from the house.

The morning had that thick, glassy stillness you find only in the wee hours before dawn. Montana smelled damp and grassy this late-summer morning. Starting up the car, I tried to remember the feeling of San Francisco's temperate dawns and Miami's subtropical ones and found, to my surprise, that I couldn't recall their nuances. Driving through Meredith's silent streets, only the occasional barking dog and softly glowing kitchen light reminded me that I wasn't all alone under the Big Sky.

The scene at the mill was chaotic. Fire trucks lay across the entrance gate like barges, and various grim-faced emergency personnel ran around, shouting orders and lugging hoses and sprayers.

I hopped out and started documenting the scene, snapping photos of the activity and looking for someone to talk to. The police were cordoning off the mill's main entrance, and I exchanged a few words with a young state-police officer with a crew cut and a pale face.

Apparently, the fire had started in the production area and the cause was unknown. It had raged into full bloom sometime during the night but wasn't discovered until the first shift of workers arrived a few hours ago. Nobody knew why the mill's fire-alarm system hadn't gone off. It was mostly contained now, and, no, it didn't appear that anyone was hurt.

Scratching the patrolman's comments and badge number on my pad, I thanked him and walked around the perimeter of the charred building.

The air was acrid with the smell of burnt wood, brick, and timber, and a thin gray ash blanketed the manicured lawn around the building. Coughing, I rummaged in my bag for my handker-

chief and tied it around my face. Whitish smoke was still billow-
ing out of one part of the structure as the sky's eastern horizon
was pierced by flamingo-colored rays.

Shift workers with metal lunch boxes who had shown up for
work were clustered around the mill's gate, mouths drawn tightly
shut. Presumably, if the mill didn't operate, they didn't get paid,
so they couldn't be happy with this turn of events.

I spotted the mill's spokesperson, Glen Whitehead, in a
group of men standing with what looked to be the police chief
and a couple of senior firefighters. The man in the bolo tie who
Whitehead had spoken with the day before at the MEA rally was
also there, and he was clearly unhappy with the situation—red-
faced, he had his index finger right up in the police chief's face
and was shaking it as if he were castigating a small child. Whitehead tried to calm him down, then gathered himself together and
came to speak to the reporters who were clustered like feeding
chickens near the police line.

Whitehead raised his arms up, calling for silence, and the
buzzing simmered down as my five or six comrades, some from
television and local radio stations, thrust microphones forward
with hands that weren't gripping steaming cups of coffee.

"As you can see, we've had a fire in the production unit of the
mill," Whitehead said gravely. "At the present time, the police
and fire departments don't know what caused the fire but will be
investigating."

"Do you believe the fire was set deliberately?" a TV guy asked
from the crowd.

"Signs of arson are always considered as part of an investigation. We aren't ruling anything out," Whitehead replied.

Lynn Verchenko from KXGY raised her hand. "Has anyone
claimed responsibility, like the MEA?"

Whitehead was silent for a moment.

"As of this time, I am not aware of anybody contacting Sutter
& McEvoy or the police with information about the fire. But, rest
assured, if we have reason to believe that this fire was started

purposefully and illegally as part of a campaign to cripple the mill, Sutter & McEvoy will make sure the perpetrators are prosecuted for their crimes."

Fighting words said, Whitehead excused himself and strode off with a group of important-looking men. The sky was pinkening as I gathered my belongings and trudged back to the Subaru.

Recalling Steve Wald's earnest face and zealous lips from the night before, I tried to imagine him conspiring to burn down the mill and decided it was an unlikely MO for someone who liked the soapbox so much. But apparently that feeling wasn't shared by local officials. I guessed that he would be routed from bed this morning, much as I had been, and brought down to the police station for questioning.

If not Steve's group, then who? Assuming the fire wasn't accidental—a safe assumption, in my view, since the fire-alarm system hadn't gone off—someone with a vested interest in shutting down or threatening to shut down production had to have committed the crime.

Feeling a little like Kinsey Millhone, I decided to spend the morning on the Web researching the MEA and the mill's finances. I would need background on the state of environmental politics in Montana. Hey!—I'd contact Bruce Mortensen, the EPA guy. He works for the federal government, so he should be impartial, after all. Thoughts of Mortensen's hard face and powerful hands sent a shiver up my back, which I attributed to exhaustion and hunger. Shaking my head, I started up and left the scene.

After a brief stop at home for a quick shower and clothes change, I went to the office. When I opened the door, the heavenly aroma of bacon and eggs drew me toward the kitchen, where Bernie, decked out in a frilly white apron and Seattle Seahawks baseball cap, was whipping chunks of cheddar and pinches of fresh herbs into a fluffy omelet. Coffee percolated in the machine, and New York bagels from Bernie's semisecret stash were browning in the toaster oven.

"Good morning, Brenner. All my hardworking reporters get breakfast after a rough night," he said, expertly flipping the cheesy mass.

Immeasurably cheered, I sat down at the table and relayed the latest developments while we devoured a generous pile of buttery eggs. The mill stories were officially mine, and Bernie told me to follow the trail wherever it led. I explained my plan to get a quote from Mortensen, and he grinned.

"Have you met the fellow yet?" he asked, mouth full.

"Yes. Last night, as a matter of fact." Thoughts of Steve pulling me toward him in the parking lot and Mortensen gripping my hand skittered across my mind, and I felt my cheeks redden.

"He's a bit gruff, our Bruce, but a more honorable man you never will meet," Bernie said. "I can't imagine it's easy to be stuck between the causes he relates to, Uncle Sam, and the big manufacturing interests, including those his father-in-law is involved in. But he navigates it all pretty well." He scraped his plate clean of eggs with a well-done crust of bacon.

Fascinated, I begged him to continue.

"Well, I think I told you Bruce grew up here in Montana, right? His family didn't have a pot to piss in, from what I understand. Just a dirt-poor mill family in a small town near Whitefish. But young Bruce, who started working at the mill himself when he was sixteen or seventeen, caught the eye of our very own Melina Curran, daughter of the mill's owner. Now, Mike Curran came down on them like the proverbial ton of shit. But her daddy didn't raise Melina to be a girl who is denied things, and she raised holy hell until Curran caved in and took the boy under his wing. Paid for his college education at Bowman—master's in environmental science, I think. Personally, I think Bruce would have liked to go the nonprofit or private route, save-the-forest stuff or environmental lawyer or something, but I guess working for the feds seemed like the least contentious route."

We pondered the story in silence as we drained the remainder of our coffees. Then Bernie shooed me away when I tried to do the dishes, so I wandered over to my desk to check e-mail and start the MEA research.

Ben had booked a flight for Labor Day weekend and was looking forward to the visit. I sensed a visceral pain behind his words that he couldn't hide. Maybe the women of Montana would be as much a cure for his fractured heart as the men had been for me. Rainer wasn't coming out to see Els for Christmas after all; he had a show in a gallery in Berlin. Colin bought me a new bath mat—sunflower yellow. Mom wrote from Martha's Vineyard, where she had run into Ahnuld and Maria while doing a story on blue-blood holiday towns that don't discriminate against the nouveau riche. Maria, apparently, was quite lovely in person, and her hair wasn't as big as it looked on TV.

There was one more e-mail left, from someone called secret_friend@hotmail.com. I clicked on the message and read this:

To: jen.brenner@meredithgazette.com
From: secret_friend@hotmail.com
Subject: don't believe the lies

The fire at the mill was not an accident. Somebody wants the mill shut down, you better believe it.

;-0

Apprehension settled in my belly, and I had an urge to peer out the window, as if the message's author would be planted across the street in an overcoat and dark glasses. What was this nonsense? Was there real danger here, or just some small-town bozo looking for a little excitement?

I debated whether to show anybody the message and decided to sit on it for a while.

I sometimes think, if I had told anyone about the warning then, everything would have turned out differently.

baggage claim

To: Els_Janssen@ucsf.edu
From: rainer.yes@dalta.co.de
Subject:

dearest elsie. you know how much i love you, and how much pain it gives me to tell you this, but i cannot be with you anymore, not in the way you need. why, you ask, can rainer not be with you—well, it is always the art, you see, i cannot produce art when i am tied down to one womens and it does hurt me to say that you have given me so much i know that. Remember the time we went to san sebastien and made love all night in the courtyard of the pensione? well, i used to remember that too, but now not so much. also, i met someone. her name is marina she is a hungarian and does the most amazing sculpture out of the bones of dead animals on the . . . how you say? . . . autobahn. beautiful. but that has nothing to do with us, dear els, i just need a little time to discover who rainer really is, you know, who i can be if i do not have the love of a good womens weighing on me from above. yours always, rainer.

Ben flew in on the Friday before Labor Day weekend, and I picked him up at Meredith's tiny airport, where moose heads festooned the walls and high-school girls in shiny tube dresses and white shoes clustered, waiting for prom dates from other towns.

I spotted him immediately in the mass of Wranglers and cowboy hats. His dark-blond wavy hair stuck up from his head like a bird's wing, and his white button-down shirt was wrinkled from the long flight from Miami.

Excitement flooded me, and I ran toward my big brother. We enfolded each other in a big bear hug, and, to my embarrassment, errant tears sprang into my eyes. He was just so familiar and dear, his warm hazel eyes turned down at the corners and wide, mobile mouth ready to laugh or deliver an unexpected joke.

"Hey, Jennie. Let me look at you." He held me at arm's length. "You look amazing," he said, squeezing my upper arms like they were cantaloupes at the farmer's market.

"Yeah, well, you could use a little work," I said lightly, trying to mask my concern. Ben's usually tan face was pale and drawn, and his already thin frame had lost a few pounds where it didn't need to.

"My God, just what I need, another mother. You'll fatten me up on mooseburgers and steaks, okay? I came here to get away from the griping," he warned, and I realized then that our parents had been more worried about him than they let on since the breakup with Julie.

Suspicious, I glared at him, but he just swung his carry-on over his shoulder and strode off toward the baggage claim. I did the little-sister thing and scooted after him.

Glad to be together again, we wrapped our arms around each other while we waited and chatted about people from home. Like our father, Ben was a doctor, and he had a pediatric practice in the economically depressed part of Miami. He and his partner, Dr. Lucy Garza, administered medical care to the children of newer immigrants and brought to the work a missionary zeal you didn't often find these days in the young, privileged, and highly educated. When Ben was in high school, Karen, our older sister, started calling him "Brother Teresa" because he adopted so many causes. He met his ex-girlfriend, Julie, when the Spanish-language radio station she was marketing director for sponsored a Christmas meal for the underprivileged. Ben was a volunteer. Sometimes his enthusiasm could be annoying, but you couldn't help but admire his commitment.

Ben's tattered Samsonite bag appeared on the conveyor belt, and I grabbed it off and swung it to the floor, accidentally hitting the khaki-clad knees of the man standing next to me. I glanced up to apologize and found myself face-to-face with Bruce Mortensen.

"You're dangerous with that thing," he said, smiling.

I stared at him, mute. For one thing, he looked totally different than the first few times I'd seen him. Instead of the government-agent poker face he'd kept on during the rally and the ill-fated dinner with his wife, a wide grin showed his white teeth, and his eyes crinkled at the corners toward the speckled gray patches at his temples. In a red T-shirt, khakis, and well-worn cowboy boots, he was absolutely gorgeous. How could I not have noticed that before? Disturbed, I reminded myself that the man was at least ten years older than me, still married (albeit by a thread), and I was already seeing someone halfway decent for the first time in two years.

"Ms. Brenner, this is my daughter, Emily. Em, Ms. Brenner is the new reporter at the *Gazette,* so you'd better be nice to her," he said, smiling again as my heart skittered around like a windup toy.

Except for the dark, heavily fringed eyes she had inherited from her father, Bruce's daughter was a near replica of her striking mother, Melina. She looked about eleven or twelve, and her long auburn hair was slicked back into a ponytail. She was wearing baggy jeans and a leotard top and had a Britney Spears backpack on.

We shook hands like grown-ups, and I told her to call me Jen, then introduced them to my brother, Ben, who had just returned from the bathroom. Like the good kids' doctor he is, Ben crouched down next to Emily and started a friendly argument about the relative merits of Christina Aguilera and Emily's apparent heroine, Britney Spears.

Bruce and I stood there awkwardly.

"Would you have some time to meet with me this week?" I burst out. "I'm doing a story on the chub and the mill fire and I'd like a quote from the EPA." Ben glanced up at me strangely, and I thought, oh, God, was I babbling?

But Bruce just stood there with his arm around Emily, who was now clinging to his waist like a barnacle, and said, sure, he had time this afternoon if I wanted to swing by his office. We exchanged cards, and everyone waved good-bye as Ben and I left the terminal.

CHAPTER 9

big guns

To: jen.brenner@meredithgazette.com
From: Katie Nguyen
Subject: els is a mess

Hey Jen. How goes? Robert said you met some guy up there. Whaddup wit that? Need dirt. We took bets: Were his first words to you, "squeal like a pig"? I guess I should tell you that your bathroom didn't really flood. Colin just said that because he was too embarrassed to tell you that we ruined your bath mat, um, doing the nasty. Yes, it's true. You take off for parts unknown and your own friends violate you in ways you can't imagine, yeah yeah. I don't know if it's true love or anything, but it's cool right now. He's really a sweet guy. But the reason I'm writing is that I'm worried about Els. That kraut bastard finally broke it off with her and I think she's a wreck. She hides it really well, as you would expect, but I think she's really depressed. Do you think you could invite her up to bear country for a little R&R? Her fall trimester doesn't start till the last week of September. Anyway, just thought you should know.

Hold your freak horse, baybee! Giddyap!
KN

After lunch at the Big Dip—where Ben downed two and a half huckleberry shakes, large fries, and a double cheeseburger with extra onions—I dropped him off at home to relax and checked messages. There were three. Steve had called, inviting us to join him at Meredith's annual Picnic in the Park tomorrow night. Bernie left a message saying he liked my mill piece and it would run in tomorrow's paper. And Robert was uncharacteristically cryptic, saying only that he had something really important to tell me and could I please call him as soon as possible.

Gladys took to Ben immediately, and I left them in the back-yard with herbal tea and her family's photo albums. They were deep into a conversation about what it's like to practice medicine in a small town versus the big city.

The EPA's Meredith sub-office was a one-room storefront on Main Street. The main office, which was itself puny, operated out of the capital, Helena. I wondered if Bruce had wangled a dispensation to telecommute because of Melina and Emily.

When I arrived, Bruce was on the phone. He waved me in and I eased through the cluttered doorway and plunked myself in a battered government-issue chair. The walls were bare except for a few topographical maps of the northwestern United States and a framed picture of Jeanette Rankin, the first woman—and a Montanan to boot—to serve in the U.S. Congress.

I pretended to go over my notes while I covertly studied Bruce's profile, hoping he couldn't see me staring. His wavy dark hair was a little scruffy in back, a sure sign that there was no woman taking care of him properly, and his shoulders were broad and muscular under the leather holster that—yikes!—held a big-ass gun. Dreamily, I indulged in a quickie fantasy of him chasing perps with his firearm drawn, jeans-clad legs pumping as he leapt through the window into ... my bedroom?

"Jen?"

Horrified, my eyes snapped open as Bruce leaned over my chair.

"Can I get you a cup of coffee? Looks like you need it," he

said, as he manipulated an orange-topped Mr. Coffee machine circa 1973.

I nodded mutely and tried to salvage my dignity by setting my notebook and recorder on the table. Little Miss Reporter. He poured himself a generous cup, eased his big body into a comfortable position, and nodded that he was ready to begin.

"So, here's my understanding of the situation," I began, yawning discreetly behind my palm. "We've got a bunch of dead fish and no satisfactory explanation for it. We've got environmental groups pointing the finger at the local paper mill, which, because of loopholes in environmental legislation, uses production methods that have been shown to compromise rivers and water tables. And we've got the mill, Sutter & McEvoy, standing by its practices and claiming a halt in production will cause undue damage to the local economy, a position that is also held by a number of citizens of the area. What is the government's position on this, and what steps are going to be taken to protect the people from a potentially toxic event?"

Bruce nodded at my brilliant summary of the situation and took a sip of his brew, which tasted, to my San Francisco–indoctrinated taste buds, like a cross between cigarette breath and river mud.

"Contrary to what you might think, the government's position, or the position of individuals in the EPA, which has jurisdiction here, doesn't matter that much," he replied.

"EPA's mandate in cases like these—and I'm not saying there is even something to call a case yet—is to look at the situation in terms of legal compliance. Establishing cause and effect through science could take years, and we just don't have the resources for that."

I nodded in what I hoped was a sage, attentive manner. How did his forearms get like that, all strong and sinewy? Was it from roping steer or something? In addition to the thick, keloid scar on his chin that he thumbed when he was nervous, he had a pale, jagged streak that ran along the top of his left arm. Probably the result of a childhood accident, I thought. Doing something naughty, no doubt. Wait. Could it be work-related? Possibly the result of some heroic act that saved the lives of thousands of little fish, bear, and human children?

"...and that's generally the process for investigating these cases," Bruce finished.

Shit! What was wrong with me? Oh, well, at least the tape got it all, I thought. I scribbled a few notes to myself, appalled that he'd caught me daydreaming not once, but twice. When I raised my eyes, he was gazing at me levelly, his look warm and interested.

"So, how did you end up here?" he asked.

Embarrassed at being on the other end of the interrogation table, I fiddled with my pen cap. You know how it's often necessary to develop a simple story out of what is, in reality, a complex and even inexplicable set of motivating factors and events? The story you tell people to avoid telling the real story? I wasn't going to tell anybody—especially this insanely butch *man* person—about Damon's sad green eyes, or my callow ambitions to be managing editor at the Tech Standard, or how I hadn't had sex in twenty-two months and—dear God—seventeen days.

"I really wanted to do some beat reporting again," I said lightly. "It's kind of one of those funny stories of people with matching needs bumping into each other. I needed to get away for a while, and Bernie needed a reporter. So it worked out."

He asked me about San Francisco and Miami, and we talked about regional attitudes and differences. I explained how, as kids in Miami, my girlfriends and I would troll the private beaches, looking for sandals to swipe that their wealthy owners presumably wouldn't miss. He laughed and pointed to the scar on his arm. Turns out it came from a youthful escapade in which he and four friends broke into a dairy farm drunkenly intending to steal a cow. They were nearly caught, and Bruce tore his arm scrambling over the barbed-wire fence during their escape. I confessed my fear of heights, and he said the first time he shot a high-powered rifle at the government's training facility, FLETC, he fell over and knocked down the instructor out of sheer anxiety, even though he'd been hunting all his life.

Before we knew it, it was four P.M.

"Oh! I've got to meet Ben," I exclaimed, reluctant to leave. Bad sister.

"Yep." Bruce extracted himself from his chair and busied himself gathering coffee cups.

I picked up my few items and moved toward the exit. Ever the gentleman, he reached across me to open the door and brushed my right arm with his hand, sending a delicious shiver through me. We stood inches from each other in the crowded doorway, and it seemed to me that our breath was coming in little gusts. His aftershave smelled faintly briny, like salt water. I imagined licking it off his neck above his shirt collar and felt my eyelids fall to half mast.

"You know about Picnic in the Park this weekend, right?" His voice was rough.

"Uh-huh." I nodded, thinking that attending with Steve Wald would inform the whole town that we were officially an item.

"You might find it kind of quaint, but it's really a lot of fun. I'm taking Em and her friends. She somehow roped me into sitting in the dunking booth for their school," he said, and we both smiled.

"Well, I'll see you there, then."

"Sure thing."

I squeezed by him and nearly fainted from the proximity of our bodies.

I turned around.

"I may need to follow up with you to check some facts," I said, trying not to sound too eager.

"No problem. My card has all my numbers on it."

Waving, I climbed into the car and crept down the street,

hands trembling. I didn't pull over and rest my forehead on the steering wheel until I had rounded three corners and was sure that Bruce Mortensen, with his tender, observant gaze and his framed desktop photo of his beautiful wife and daughter, was sufficiently far away that the danger of discovery was nil.

oh, baby

To: KarenMendelsohn@vita.co.il
From: benjamin.brenner@yahoo.com
Subject: hi from the wilds

Kar, Hi. I'm writing this on Jennie's computer. I'm up in Montana if you can believe it. It is incredibly beautiful here, like nothing I've ever seen. Gigantic open spaces, prairie almost, but mountains always nearby, very majestic and dramatic and overlooking everything going on down below. How are things, sis? Did the kibbutz ever get that tractor you were looking for? I bought coonskin caps for Tomer and Tali, which should be a novelty. Tell them raccoons only live in North America, and two had to die for their hats (just kidding). Give them a big kiss from their uncle Ben, okay? Gotta go—Jennie and I are going to some sort of hippie festival tomorrow and I need some shut-eye.

Love, Ben

When I got home, Gladys was puttering around the kitchen listening to big-band tunes on her ancient turntable, occasionally sliding sideways, arms akimbo in a solitary waltz step. Ben snored softly in her living-room recliner, *Into Thin Air,* the controversial Everest misadventure by Jon Krakauer, open on his lap.

I said hello to Gladys and went to my room to return calls. Clothes were strewn around the bed, and crumpled printouts from the earlier stories I'd filed topped the pile like dirty snowballs. Disgusted, I resolved to put things in order and proceeded to do so as I dialed Steve's number.

His machine picked up, playing some sort of enviro-hippie tune about forests or some such in the background. I told him Ben and I would be happy to join him at tomorrow's picnic and thanked him for dinner the other night. Trying to push Bruce Mortensen's rugged—married!—visage out of my mind, I concentrated on Steve's intense eyes and wicked grin, and smiled to myself even as I sighed and hung up. Being single in a town with men who actually wanted to interact with women wasn't so bad.

Next up: Els. Her voice mail picked up immediately, which probably meant she was on-line. Choosing my words carefully, I said I was concerned about her and that she was more than welcome to come up here anytime and stay with me. I hoped that she was doing all right and that things would look better soon. Believe me, I'd been there.

Feeling clumsy and ineffectual, I dialed Robert's number last. George picked up after a couple of rings, sounding breathless.

"Hello?"

"George, it's Jen!"

"Jen, hey. How are you?" He jiggled the phone around, and I heard sounds I couldn't identify in the background. Was that something whining, maybe their dog, Petey?

"I'm good. Robert left a message for me to call him. I've been busy working a story and haven't had time to get back to him. Is he around?"

"Yeah, let me put him on." Sounds of phone passing hands, George whispering something in Robert's ear, and an affectionate smack.

"Hey, mountain mama." Robert's deep voice.

"Hey, what's going on? Your message got me curious," I said.

"Well, George and I just wanted to share our good news with you." More of those strange whining sounds. Petey must be begging for food or something.

"What's up?" I asked as I flung a still-sweaty Jogbra into the hamper and sniffed at some gym socks.

"You'd better sit down for this one, Jennifer." Stymied, I sat on the edge of the tumbled bed.

"George and I just became the proud fathers of a little girl," he announced, his voice tinged with fatherly pride and none of the out-to-shock mischievousness I'd expect from such a statement.

Stunned silence. Was this a sort of David Crosby–Melissa Etheridge situation? Did Robert and George provide dual shots of fertilizer to a lesbian friend who wanted to play Russian baby roulette?

"Her name is Zoë Pitt O'Hanlon, and she's the most adorable sweetheart you'll ever meet in your life. We adopted her in Korea."

I could hear him making chucking noises and tried unsuccessfully to reconcile this image with that of the Robert I knew, who was prone to cluck over a postmodern sectional sofa or a particularly lovely Waterford vase. Now that I knew what was going on over there, canine yelps morphed into the gurgling cries of an infant. Holy shit.

I collapsed back into the tangle of sheets and clothes, clutching the cordless like a lifeline thrown to a Titanic passenger.

"She's eight months—aren't you, sweetheart—and she's got the cutest little cap of shiny black hair, and the most beautiful little button nose, and dark eyes, sort of like George's color." How could a Korean orphan have George's eyes? "And she's into everything she can crawl to, which you'd expect at this age. And she stands up to Petey when he gets naughty." A perfectly timed, resentful-sounding bark seemed to confirm this notion.

George's voice interrupted from the other phone.

"We were considering this for ages, Jen, but we didn't think we should mention it to anyone, partly because our chances of getting a child were fairly slim, and also because we didn't want to hex it by talking about it too much."

I knew I had to say something.

"Well, I'm ... I guess I'm floored, but congratulations, you guys. I know you'll be great dads. It's just hard to imagine. I mean, I have to get used to the idea. She sounds wonderful," I stuttered.

My thoughts skipped ahead. "Have you told your families yet?" Since Robert's father took off around the time Steely Dan released "Hey, Nineteen," and his mother lived in a trailer in the Mojave Desert with a sporadically employed poker dealer and a twelve-pack of Pabst Blue Ribbon, I didn't think that was likely, but they were on good terms with George's parents, who lived about an hour north of San Francisco in Santa Rosa.

Robert confirmed that George's parents had already met Zoë and fallen in love with her. Robert had tried his mother's number but found it was out of service. Go figure.

"What about friends?" I asked, feeling a little out of the loop up in Montanaland.

"We had everybody over last night for a potluck and viewing. Zoë kept trying to suck on Katie's buns," George laughed.

"Where exactly did you get her?" I asked, imagining a sort of warehouse of black-haired babies cocooned in pristine swaddling clothes as far as the eye could see.

"We went through a Korean adoption agency. Zoë's from a small town near Seoul. Her mother was healthy, but young. Really young, like fourteen. Apparently got pregnant by the boy next door and couldn't even consider keeping the baby," Robert said.

"We were over there just long enough to do the paperwork, get her a passport, get her used to us," George added. "It's hard with adoptees, you know, but she's still very young, and has been cared for and not abused, and there's every reason to think things will work out fine. Robert's going to be working at home for a while, and I have access to the city government day-care facility right in my building, so we're covered as far as that goes."

Zoë let out a screech.

Robert again. "Well, I'm so glad we finally got to tell you. It felt weird to have Zoë in our lives without you knowing. Zoë needs to meet her auntie Jen just as soon as she can, right?" More kissy noises. "We'd better get going. It's dinnertime around here."

We said good-bye, and they promised to send jpeg photos of Zoë by e-mail, and I hung up, feeling both exhilarated by and a little bit envious of their good fortune.

Dazed, I wandered into the living room and found Ben reading again.

"Guess what?" I said. "Robert and George adopted a little Korean girl. In Korea," I added stupidly.

Ben looked up, his large hazel eyes thoughtful, and nodded.

"Well, that's great. I always thought they seemed the paternal types," he commented, then went back to his book. I harumphed. My brother, who can only be propelled into action by an asthma attack or a particularly severe ear infection.

"So, what do you want to do tonight?" I asked Ben. I sat down next to him on the faded flowered sofa.

"Well, I thought maybe just dinner and a little bar-hopping. I'm kind of beat from the flight."

"That sounds great," I answered.

The doorbell chimed.

"I'll get that," I called to Gladys. I could see the vague outline of somebody tall and blond behind the door's stained glass.

I swung the door open and there was Els, clutching a suitcase and sobbing like she'd just lost something utterly, irrevocably precious.

dumped

To: Dad
From: Melina Curran
Subject:

Daddy, have you seen the extra key Mattie keeps to the toolshed? It's gone missing and I thought you might have it.

Just so you know—Emmy's going to the fair with Bruce tomorrow. He's picking her up at noon, and I want you two to make nice in front of Emily. Promise?

M

By the time we got Els settled in front of the fire Gladys insisted on setting (it was a balmy 68°F outside), she had calmed down enough to hold her chipped mug of herbal tea without shaking.

"I just couldn't stay in San Francisco a minute longer," she said in a shaky voice. "I felt so terribly alone there. All these years Rainer and I have been apart, yet I always felt he was there, like a lifeline home." Her accent, usually slight, had deepened in grief. She seemed content to sit back with an afghan blanket over her knees, Ben's doctorly hand patting her shoulder.

"I know what all of you think—thought. That Rainer and I had a relationship of convenience, that we were two free spirits off pursuing our own things. But it's not true. Not really. In my mind, I always thought I would go back home to Amsterdam after my degree was finished and we'd get a houseboat or a canal house and I'd be a pharmacologist and Rainer would show his work in the galleries, and, oh . . ."

Her words trailed off into hiccupy keening, and Ben's worried eyes met mine over Els's curly blond head. In despair, after a day's travel and little sleep, her rosy complexion shone against the wild aureole of hair, and her reddened eyes made her normally slate eyes glow like blue embers. It was hard not to be affected by her, though she was one of the most unself-consciously beautiful people I had ever met.

I knelt in front of her, squeezing my legs against her red leather boots.

"Here's what we're going to do," I said, holding Els's hands in mine. "You're here, and that's great. You did the right thing, coming up here. That's what friends are for. There's no harm done. Richard and Evangeline can hold down the fort at home, you don't start your new semester for a couple of weeks, and it's good to be somewhere different and anonymous when you're going through a breakup."

There, I'd said it. I was in full girlfriend-giving-a-sister-the-help-she-needs-to-stop-the-madness-and-denial-and-start-healing-now-so-you-can-get-back-in-the-saddle-as-soon-as-possible mode. It felt good. Els had been there for me through many a post-Damon meltdown, and I was there to return the favor.

"We'll just put you in my room with me, and we'll all go out to dinner and drinks and drown our sorrows a little bit. C'mon."

I hauled her up, Ben hoisting from the other side, and we got her up and into the bedroom. I shut the door when I heard the shower running and collapsed on the sofa. Talk about overstimulation! First picking up Ben at the airport, then entering fucking fantasyland with Bruce Mortensen, Robert's becoming a father, and Els's arrival. Oy.

Gladys, who had been hovering around like a mother hen, leaned over and pursed her lips.

"That girl's going to be just fine. You wait and see. When Bernard left for Korea, I thought the world was going to just literally cave in on me. I thought I would die."

Amazed, I stared at her as, lost in memories of love lost with my crotchety gnome of a boss, Bernie Zweben, she picked up her knitting needles and held them, steady as cupid's crossbow, in her wrinkled fingers.

By the time we arrived at Charlie's, the evening was in full swing. Glad to be young and alive after our respective traumas, Ben, Els, and I had stuffed ourselves with spinach lasagna and garlicky mashed potatoes and tomato-mozzarella salad drizzled with raspberry vinaigrette at the town's only vegetarian restaurant and topped it off with a good many locally brewed amber beers before we staggered over to the bar.

Mindful of the rules of fashion in Meredith, I'd shoved all my flowery, slinky, and diaphanous garments to the back of my closet in favor of a tight black T-shirt and form-fitting black 501s with boots.

Ben and Els appeared to be hitting it off and were veering back and forth between discussions of Julie's and Rainer's various character flaws—all recently discovered and shockingly uncharacteristic, of course—and the efficacy of the new antistaph antibiotics.

I excused myself as the conversation turned to the initial symptoms of the Ebola virus and wandered up to the bar for another drink.

I squeezed in between a bleached blonde in a fringed suede jacket and a rancher type in faded denims and a soft plaid shirt.

"What can I get you?"

The bartender, a huge man with fingers the size of kielbasas and a sloppy gut overhanging his silver belt buckle, swiped at the worn oak counter in front of me with a dishrag.

"Moose Drool, please," I said. The bartender slapped a pint glass under the tap, and amber liquid streamed into it. I felt a tug on my sleeve.

"You the Jennifer Brenner who works at the *Gazette*?"

The man at my side couldn't have been more than five foot three, since I towered over him. He had a dark, wizened face and sagging cheeks peppered with dark moles that bespoke years of sun and cigarettes. He fluttered his fingertips nervously against the countertop.

"Yes. Can I help you?" I answered.

"You're writing the articles about what's going on at the mill, right?"

I nodded.

"Well, somebody's feeding y'all a line of shit, if you'll pardon my French." He glanced toward the doorway, as if the bad guys were going to burst through the swinging doors any minute, guns blazing.

"Why do you say that?"

"That fire, at the mill? Well, the fire alarm was turned off before second shift left for the day. Came down from above—turn off the alarm, they said."

"Who said?" I asked, mentally kicking myself for not bringing a notepad. "Do you mind if I take a few notes?" I asked, swiping a cocktail napkin from the pile next to the olives, cherries, and swizzle sticks, and feeling in my pocket for a stubby pencil.

"Suit yourself. All I'm saying is, the brass knew about the fire. Maybe they even set it." His eyes darted toward the door.

"Will you go on record with your comments, sir?" I asked, scribbling furiously in my personal shorthand.

"No way, José." The sinewy man backed up a few steps, as if I would force him to talk. "Can't afford to lose my job. I just thought you should know what's going on over there. And another thing—last week I saw the office secretaries"—he pronounced them *sek-tries*—"chopping up files when I was in the office to deliver a screwed-up work order to the shift supervisor. They're probably out back in the Dumpster," he finished.

Gulping his drink, he laid a few greasy dollar bills on the counter and skedaddled out the door before I could press him for more details. Or ask him if he was the secret friend who had e-mailed me. He didn't seem like the e-mail type, but you never knew.

Disturbed, I sipped my beer and tried to make sense of the little I knew. The fish turned up dead downriver from the mill last Tuesday. Steve's group accused the mill of bad dumping practices publicly at the rally on Wednesday. Glen Whitehead told me they would look into it the same day. The fire occurred in the early hours of Friday morning. And now this guy's implying it was set deliberately by the mill's owners themselves. Why would they want to do that? To cover up a crime that could cost them even more than the fire damage? But I guess insurance will cover that, I surmised. To distract from the real issue, which is environmental noncompliance?

Feeling foolish and a little out of my depth, I decided I would be remiss not to follow the tip and check out the Dumpsters behind the mill's offices for evidence of malfeasance. It was Friday night, and as far as I knew, everything would be shut down and I'd be alone. I glanced at my watch: 11:34 P.M.

Trotting back to where Ben and Els sat chatting happily about this or that virulent contagion or bleeding orifice, I laid out my plan: tell them I was dropping by the office to pick up some work I'd left there, then jog back to the house—I was already regretting that lasagna—pick up the car, and drive out to the mill. Ben would never let me go by myself, and I didn't want to announce my presence there with a tall, skinny, drunken Miami doctor and an equally tall, drunk, blond pharmacologist in tow.

They accepted my story equably, and I quickly walked the

few blocks to Gladys's. I pulled on a fleece vest and dark baseball cap over my already spy-worthy outfit and stored my camera and Mini Maglite in a small day pack.

The drive to the mill was uneventful. As I sped by, dim lights from closed-up gas stations and truck stops flashed, turning to moonlit rolling fields as I approached the river and, next to it, the mill.

Mindful of the rules of spying, I killed my headlights at the entrance to the mill and rolled into the lot, gravel crunching way too loudly under the Subaru's tires. I turned off the ignition and eased out of the car into the moonlight that dappled the front lawn and highlighted the imposing, partially burned-out structure. The fire's acrid smell still permeated the grounds, cut through with a thready perfume of night jasmine and overlaid with river damp.

I skirted the facility and didn't see any signs of life, so I crept around the back to where, it seemed to me, the back doors of Glen Whitehead's and the other offices would be.

Two dented metal Dumpsters stood next to the back doors. Shuddering, I looked around for rats or other creatures before I approached the first one. I hoped there wasn't any food waste and the Dumpster was used mainly by office types who—surprise, surprise—didn't believe in recycling paper.

Suddenly, viselike hands gripped my mouth and upper arms from behind and swung me against the wall. A shriek tore out of me, but the hand clapped over my mouth quelled it. Heart hammering, I looked into the dark, heavily fringed, and very angry eyes of Bruce Mortensen. We were so close, our fleece-covered chests formed a synthetic sandwich, and heat spiraled up between us. I could feel the outline of his holster against my breasts and rib cage. One of his thighs pressed my legs flat against the mossy wall, and I struggled to free myself.

"Are you out of your goddamn mind?" he hissed.

"Let me go," I said aloud, slapping his hand away from my face.

"*Shut up,*" he whispered harshly, lips against my ear. "There's somebody in there."

His words had a paralytic effect on me, and a cocktail of fear and adrenaline coursed through my veins, making me sag against him. Grasping his useless package in one strong arm, he pushed me into a damp corner behind the Dumpster and assumed a semi-crouch behind the cover of the wall, gun drawn.

"What are you doing here?" he said softly, without turning his gaze away from the back door.

"Some guy came up to me in Charlie's tonight and told me he saw the mill admins shredding paper. He said the fire was set deliberately," I whispered back.

"I got an anonymous call on my voice mail at ten-thirty suggesting I check out the Dumpsters. Cute." He sounded disgusted. "You're just lucky I was here, even if it was a setup. From now on, Miss Investigator, do us a favor and call law enforcement when a stranger reports a possible crime to you, okay?"

Stung, I remained silent and tried to press myself back into the shadows.

After about twenty minutes of waiting, we were rewarded by the sound of footsteps in Glen Whitehead's office. Bruce met my eyes, then brought his finger to his well-shaped lips and motioned me to stay in the corner. Before I knew what was happening, he had disappeared around the side of the building.

Without Bruce's protective presence, the night exploded into fearful noises: cicadas hummed on the riverbanks, charred timbers groaned and snapped in the light breeze, and something rustled around in the loose leaves under the Dumpster.

I strained to hear Bruce's movements from inside but couldn't get past the refrain in my head, which was going, *Why did I ever come to Montana in the first place?* over and over again to the tune of the Clash classic "Should I Stay or Should I Go?" Images of the palm trees lining the Miami street I grew up on and the rolling, restaurant-studded avenues of San Francisco flitted

through my thoughts, and I regretted ever setting foot in this po-
dunk state.

Then a tubular beam of white light bounced off the canopy of
trees along the river. Someone was coming from the building!

Terrified, I debated whether to hide or make a run for it. I
could hear a wet, panting noise getting closer with the light, and
visions of grisly cinematic murder and mayhem filled my mind.
Falling to my knees in the mud, I tried hastily to find religion but
succeeded only in recalling the scene in the first *Halloween*
movie where Jamie Lee Curtis creeps through the darkened hospital in her tattered white nightgown toward the blood-soaked
killer, eliciting screams of dismay from the audience. I didn't
want to be the comely but ill-fated heroine! The wiseass best
friend, the speedily dispatched sex interest—anyone but the object of the crazed murderer's wrath. . . .

The light rounded the corner, and a brownish blur streaked
toward me as I screamed. Wetness ran down my face and I fell
back into the puddle, beating at the god-awful beast.

Then the beast was yanked away, and I lay back in the mud
puddle, prepared to die as my lifeblood seeped slowly from my
lacerated face and limbs.

Someone loomed over me, silhouetted against the moonlight,
and I cringed, expecting the final blow. Curiously, I felt no pain,
but, then, it's always that way at the end, isn't it?

"Jen. Get up. It's just a dog." Bruce's gravelly voice was tinged
with laughter.

I turned my head, and a smallish caramel-colored mutt with
doe eyes started lapping at my face. Too embarrassed to be relieved, I sat up gingerly and surveyed the situation.

I resembled nothing so much as a wayward piglet wallowing
in a mud hole. My sophisticated spy outfit was streaked with
mossy greenish ooze, and dog drool laced my face and hair.

Bruce knelt beside me, restraining the scrappy dog, who
yipped excitedly and strained at her choke chain.

"I guess the noise I heard earlier was just Millie here, my father-in-law's dog," he said, stroking her floppy ears. "She's usually not on the premises without Mike. Somebody must have left her here."

Grasping my hand, he hoisted me out of the puddle, and I managed to find my footing without further mishap. Oh, God. The City Slicker strikes again.

Bruce sat back on his heels while I swiped futilely at my muddy clothes.

"You can wipe that shit-eating grin off your face, Bruce," I said nastily, trying to stuff my hair back under the cap.

Bruce just smiled at me.

"You're cute when you're pissed, Brenner, but I like you even better when you've had a shower," he said.

Appalled, I swatted him in the shoulder, and he grabbed my arm and pulled me in close to him. We were close enough to kiss, and I could see beads of sweat drying on his forehead.

Instead of a kiss, I got a lecture.

"Don't you ever follow a lead without backup again," he remonstrated. "You don't know what was waiting for you out here. That's all the police need, is a silly tourist wandering around private property in the middle of the night. They could have had security posted. You could have been shot."

Not wanting to rise to the bait and defend my reporter's rights to a rednecked federal agent who probably thought a woman's place was somewhere between the kitchen and the bedroom, I simply brushed a few stray leaves off my jeans and strode toward the Dumpster.

"What are you doing?" he called, still holding Millie's leash.

"Searching the Dumpster for shredded papers," I retorted over my shoulder.

"You just don't quit, do you?" he said, coming up beside me. Obviously recognizing a fellow stubborn ass when he saw one, he capitulated and tied Millie's leash to a water pipe and pulled himself up on top of the Dumpster.

"C'mon, I'll lower you in." I gave him the evil eye, and he grinned.

"You don't think I'm going to get my new L.L. Bean vest dirty, do you? You're already a mess. Get up here and let's get started," he said.

He pulled me up by my forearms and, gripping me around the waist, dropped me gently into the near-empty bin. I turned on my flashlight to augment the narrow ray coming from Bruce's government-issue club-size torch and opened the first of the three plastic bags that lay on the goo-encrusted bottom.

The first was stuffed with detritus including lipstick-stained coffee cups and Diet Coke cans, and I thought it might be Glen Whitehead's secretary's trash. Zilch. The second one had a variety of things, but nothing remotely incriminating.

Bag three yielded pay dirt. It contained nothing but shredded papers and what looked to be crumpled reports. Excited, I began rummaging through it, trying to identify anything that looked whole enough to piece together.

Bruce leaned into the bin. "Why don't we bring these back to my office and go through them in the morning? You won't be able to sort anything out here, and it's going on one A.M."

"Okay, but we'll bring them to *my* office, and they'll go in the *Gazette*'s safe."

"Whatever. Get out of there and let's get going," he said. I reached up, and he hauled me out with the trash bag trailing behind me.

Bruce untied Millie, and the two of us walked back to the cars, Millie prancing around Bruce's legs.

"What are you going to do with Millie?" I asked. "If you bring her to your father-in-law's place, he'll know you were here."

"I'll just tell Mike EPA got a call to come out here and I found her. He'll leave it at that. We're barely on speaking terms as it is," he finished, teeth clenched.

Seeing the set of his jaw, I held back the obvious comeback, which was that if Mike Curran was the mill's owner, we certainly didn't want him knowing his employees were rolling over on possible criminal violations committed there.

Bruce walked me to my car and waited while I started it up. I turned the ignition and nothing happened, just a rotary whine as the starter whipped around.

Shit.

Bruce motioned me to pop the hood, and he peered in while I tried to restart the car. Bupkes.

His salt-and-pepper head appeared over the hood. "Your battery's dead. Let me get the—aw, dammit, I left the jumper cables in my other car. C'mon—I'll take you home. You can come back and get the car in the morning."

"What about leaving my car here? What if somebody sees it?" I said.

"Don't worry, there are so many shift workers coming and going, and so many green Subaru Legacies, nobody will give it a second glance." I started to argue, then realized it was true; Subaru seemed to be the unofficial state car of Montana.

He opened the back of his battered Wagoneer, and Millie leaped easily into the storage area. Then we climbed into the cab and Bruce started up and we drove the twelve miles to town in silence. At one point, Bruce switched on the radio, and a sultry country-music tune pierced the late-night stillness.

He asked me where I lived, and I said at Gladys Pepper's place, and he nodded, indicating he knew where that was. He navigated Meredith's tree-lined streets confidently, one arm grasping the steering wheel, the other resting on the window's edge. The night was balmy, and the pungent odor of night-blooming flowers— jasmine again?—wafted into the open window.

We pulled up to the alley next to Gladys's, engine idling. Bruce threw the Wagoneer into park and turned to face me.

"Are you all right?" he asked softly. "That was scary, what happened tonight. For anyone."

I nodded, for once rendered speechless by the tender concern in his eyes. The moon glowed silvery yellow against the pitch sky, sending a web of light and shadows over Bruce's stern, chiseled features and whitening the speckled hair at his temples.

He brought his hand up and touched my mud-streaked cheek, then ran his fingers down toward my lips. Traced them with a callused thumb, never breaking eye contact.

Without thinking, I leaned into the caress, and found myself in his arms. My cap fell off, and his hands plunged into my hair, pulling my head back. His mouth came down hard on my neck, raining a trail of nibbling kisses up the soft skin until our lips met for the first time, and—oh, mother of God—it was incredible. His mouth tasted both sweet and smoky, and many minutes went by while we exchanged the same deep, wet, tongue-sweeping kiss over and over again, loath to switch to anything that didn't deliver the same full-body shiver and thought-erasing wave of pleasure and rightness.

All the time, I was acutely conscious that I was being made love to by a man, not a boy, and the difference sent a shot of liquid heat into my belly that drew a low animal moan from the back of my throat.

Bruce's hands, schooled by a quarter century of backseat gropings, straightforward singles sex, and married love, alternately explored my body in naked desperation and closed into fists in restraint. His tongue tasted and licked where his teeth wanted to bite, and he held me away from the hard juncture of his thighs even while he pulled me closer to his questing mouth.

When I finally tugged myself away, panting, the world came slowly back into focus as if through a blurry telephoto lens: Patsy Cline's gilt-edged voice singing "Crazy" from the car radio, then Bruce's hands moving up and down my back, then my legs straddling his, the steering wheel pressing into my lower back, and, finally, the sound of our breathing like a syncopated backbeat, filling the night.

His eyes, dark and heavy with lust, yet also tender and questioning, met mine. I let myself stand on the precipice, feeling the sway of our bodies toward each other and the distracting thoughts bubbling up in the back of my mind like gnats buzzing around ripe fruit.

"Bruce, how old are you?" It popped out before I could stop myself.

"I'll be forty-four next January. Old enough to know chances like this don't come up very often," he said.

"You're married," I stated.

He turned toward the window, showing me his profile. I reached out to stroke the wing of dark hair above his forehead. For the first time, he seemed unsure of what to say.

"Yes. On paper, I am still married to Melina. She filed for divorce last month. Mike flew her to Mexico in his puddle jumper. She's suing for full custody of Emmy," he finished, suppressed anger coloring his features.

Feeling suddenly extraneous, I shifted off his lap. "I'm sorry," I said softly. "I'd better go in."

"Can I see you again?" he asked softly, big hands locked firmly on the steering wheel. We both seemed to know that if he touched me now, we'd be completely lost. I took a shuddering breath and was grateful to whoever had taught Bruce Mortensen that a parting glance and a whispered entreaty held far more power over a wavering woman than hard hands gripping thighs and tits and ass in the front seat of a truck.

"I don't know." I tried to sort out my feelings and found I couldn't. "Let's just see how it goes, okay?"

He nodded, and I reluctantly gathered up my trash bag and backpack, got out, and backed away from the car, still facing him. Bruce started up the Wagoneer and eased away from the curb, holding my gaze until he'd rounded the corner.

My fingers trembled, and it took several tries before the key slipped into the lock and I was able to enter the house. The only sound besides the creaking floorboards was Els's sigh as I nudged her over to take my side of the warmly welcome bed.

CHAPTER 12

oldies and goodies

To: sanchezd@pw.com
From: Kristina Ledermanns
Subject: house list
Attachment: houselist.doc

D,

Here's the list of houses we're seeing this weekend (attached). Now, I know the Cole Valley one is a little out of our range, but Mary says it's a great investment, and there are 2 rental units (studio/1 bedrm). I'll meet you at Zazie's at 9, ok? How's your knee? I asked my trainer about it and he said you should ice it 20 min on/20 min off for 2 days.

Love, Kristina

In my dream, I was groundskeeper of a Miami golf course. As I was scraping cigarette butts out of sandtrap #8 with a rake, a cart crested the hill, and my dad got out, followed by our longtime neighbor, Mr. Krantz, and old Mr. Gonsalves from the corner store. And Bruce. A geriatric Bruce with age-spotted claws for hands, saggy jowls, and the puffy-seated, lemon-yellow trousers of a Florida retiree. "Where's my nine iron?" he yelled. "You took my nine iron!" he said, finger pointing at me, mouth opening into a gaping maw.

My eye cracked open, and I rolled over to check the time: 10:04 A.M. Els was sleeping peacefully in the cadaver position, on her back with long hands folded neatly over her chest and limbs straight. Golden sunlight streamed in between the cracks in the venetian blinds, dappling the rumpled bed.

It didn't take a psychotherapist to figure my dream out: Bruce was too old for me and had too much baggage. If I was going to break my addiction to Damon, it would have to be with someone I could pursue a real relationship with. Someone near my own stage in life, ready to experience all the tribulations of our thirties together, including marriage, parenting, and cutting up Mom and Dad's gas card for good. Someone like Steve Wald, who had, until last night, seemed the perfect prospect—smart, interested, politically engaged, and not unhappily married to the poofy-haired daughter of the local mill owner.

I got up and tiptoed to the kitchen. Ben was stretched out on the couch, bedding folded neatly next to him, the Krakauer book open, and a steaming mug on the end table.

"Hey, I was worried about you last night. Did you get your work done?" he asked.

I made affirmative noises, trying not to actively lie to my brother, who had an annoying lifetime habit of seeing through my subterfuge.

"Did you and Els have a good time at Charlie's?"

"Hell, yes. After you left, the crowd sang a rousing rendition of 'She Ain't No Lady, She's My Wife.' And there were two bar fights. One was nothing, but the other one drew some blood, so I patched up the guys with electrical tape and a dishrag. Medicine, Montana-style," he laughed.

"Hi."

We turned around and there stood Els, gorgeous despite

twenty-four hours of weeping, drinking, and traveling. Her face was pink and puffy, and her hair spiraled wildly off to one side, but she was smiling and clutching my Montana guidebook and she still looked cute as a goddamn button.

She plopped on the couch next to Ben, and I went over to her and put my arm around her shoulders.

"How are you?" I asked.

"Okay. Realizing some things. Did you know that Rainer hasn't remembered my birthday for four years? I don't know how I rationalized that before." She shook her head sadly.

Ben brought us some mint tea, and we sipped it in silence as we woke up after the night's adventures. I was dying to tell them about the story, the curious e-mail, the guy in Charlie's, and last night's trip to the mill, but I was afraid they would—rightly—attack my judgment, so I kept quiet. Bruce was a different story. It would be damn hard to tell your overprotective big brother that you spent last night making out with a crabby, married government agent who has a kid, is somehow involved in the story you are pursuing, and is, oh, fourteen years older—but who's counting?

Ben and Els wanted to go river rafting, so we arranged to meet for Picnic in the Park at four P.M. at the food tent, where we were scheduled to hook up with Steve Wald. I remembered that I'd left my wheels at the mill. Thankfully, Els had a rental, but I'd have to ask Gladys for a lift to avoid revealing last night's misadventure.

After they left, I got dressed and picked up my car without incident. By day, the mill looked harmless—a sad, partially burned-out structure that had its roots in another time. It was hard to believe that it was just a few hours ago I'd crouched in fear behind a Dumpster. Bruce had been right about the activity level. Apparently, midnight Friday is the mill's lowest ebb. Today, dozens of workers and contractors bustled in and out.

Gladys pointed out the rancher-looking man in his sixties I'd seen several times before. He was examining blueprints of the building with a couple of men in hard hats and radiated a calm authority.

"That's Mike Curran, the mill's owner. I believe his father was self-made, but Mike's the one who really expanded the family's interests all over Montana and Idaho. I've never talked to the man myself, but I hear he's quite formidable in person."

Yeah, well, Mr. Formidable is going to have to answer to whatever's in those shredded documents, I thought, watching Curran direct his hired hands. My plan for today was to go through the papers at the *Gazette*'s offices, file a story including quotes from Bruce, and make contact with an environmental consultant at the university Steve had recommended during our date who could possibly help me interpret the documents' meaning.

The *Gazette* had slowed down to a crawl on this Saturday afternoon. No one was around but Margaret Bloom, who waved to me as she left with a stack of mail and her two little dark-haired boys in tow.

The first thing I did was call Valerie Renard, the environmental scientist Steve had suggested. She picked up after about eight rings, when I was waiting for the voice mail to kick in.

"Renard." She had a slight accent, pronouncing her name *Renarr*. French?

"Hi, Dr. Renard. This is Jen Brenner with the *Meredith Gazette*. Your name was given to me by Steve Wald. I'm following the story on the dead fish that turned up on the south fork of the Swan. There might be a connection to production practices at the Sutter & McEvoy paper mill, and I wanted to consult with an environmental specialist about some mill documents that turned up"—I cleared my throat—"at the site."

"Yes, Steve called me and told me about it. When do you need me?" *Steve* came out as *Steef*.

"Well, I was going to go over them myself now—"

"Fine. I'll be there shortly."

"Great! We're at—"

"I know where you are." She hung up.

Valerie Renard must be a true believer, I thought as I poured myself a cup of coffee, sat down, and spread the contents of the plastic bag across the scarred conference-room table. Either that or she's sleeping with Steve Wald.

Dreamily, I closed my eyes for a second and imagined Bruce and me in the car last night, steaming up the windows like a couple of high-school kids. I worried that I was attracted to him only because he was openly attracted to me—and that wasn't a good enough reason to overlook all the unhealthy drama that came along with him. The fact that he'd been married wasn't so bad— if the marriage had been officially over. His having a daughter wasn't even a big deal; she seemed like a sweet kid. But if it meant becoming a target in what was sure to become a vicious custody battle, I just wasn't up for that. It was probably just a fleeting crush, destined for the relationship garbage disposal. I shook my head and forced myself to think about the task at hand.

Most of the papers were torn beyond recognition, but a few had large chunks attached that were still legible. Whoever had shredded them had been rushed or lazy. Instead of trying to make sense of them, I organized them into piles based on condition— shredded scrap here, partially readable there, relatively whole at the end.

Then I logged on to my e-mail to check messages. There was one from Robert with photos of Zoë, who, strangely, did look like a much cuter version of George, with a tiny nub of a nose, a black spout of silky hair, and deliciously fat arms and legs. One from Nancy Teason at the Tech Standard asking me where the free-lancer contracts were, and a final one from Jem asking how I was doing and detailing Milo's latest accomplishment, which was sticking a Tic Tac so far up his nose it had to be surgically re-moved.

I typed up quick replies to all of them promising news at a later date and was just finishing my daily ritual of reading the six credible versions of my horoscope that are published on the Web when the doorbell chimed. I glanced out the second-floor window and saw a nest of henna-red hair set against a purple velvet scarf. Assuming it was Valerie Renard, I buzzed her in.

Valerie Renard, Ph.D., turned out to be something of a surprise. Medium height and whippet-thin, she had the bad posture of an academic and the parchmentlike complexion of a seasoned smoker. Her brassy burgundy hair showed at least two inches of dark roots, and she was wearing a tattered turn-of-the-century velvet smoking jacket and the kind of lace-up black boots favored by Laura on *Little House on the Prairie*. Turns out I was almost right about her accent. She was French Canadian and had done her graduate work at McGill. Still, the woman had charisma, and I could see why Steve Wald might have found her large, intelligent eyes and commanding manner attractive.

I introduced myself, and Dr. Renard nodded and pulled a cigarillo from her ragged book bag and jammed it in her mouth. Violating *Gazette* rules, I grabbed Bernie's ceramic cereal bowl, made a mental note to buy some industrial-strength Ajax later for cleaning, and plopped it in front of Dr. Renard on the table, where she was already examining the pile of paper.

Ten minutes passed while she sorted through the mess, occasionally grunting or nodding in assent as a curl of ash wormed its way off the end of her miniature cigar. I tried to look reporterlike by scribbling my shopping list on a notepad, but Bruce kept insinuating his way into my thoughts.

Finally, she leaned back with a loud sigh and tapped the cigarillo on the edge of Bernie's cereal bowl, releasing a blanket of ash, a smidgen of which fell in the makeshift ashtray.

"There is no definitive proof of anything here, but these documents are highly suggestive that Sutter & McEvoy are in noncompliance with EPA regulations that control the bleaching of paper pulp. Also, a Mr."—she glanced down at a tattered clump of papers—"Whitehead owes a lot of money to Caleb Walksalong of the Little Big Horn Casino. But that's neither here nor there," she sniffed.

"See here," she continued, pointing to a relatively unmarked document. "This is an internal compliance form. Mills conduct their own compliance reports and turn them in to the government and watchdog groups. Which forms they are required to use is based on their compliance history. This one is an X9940. But I would guess they never turned this one in to the EPA. It says here that more than the acceptable amount of furans and dioxins were released during the bleaching process in 1999."

She took a deep drag off her cigarette and blew smoke out her nostrils.

"The EPA went on record in 1994 saying that even minuscule exposures to organochlorines can cause cancer, loss of reproductive capabilities, learning and behavioral disabilities, birth defects, and compromised immune systems in wildlife and humans," she said, sounding as if two-headed elk babies were as titillating to her as a Benjamin Bratt sighting was to the rest of us.

She gathered her ratty velvet coat around her thin frame and stubbed the cigarillo out in a shiny gold trophy that said, *Meredith Gazette: Best in Montana, 1979.*

"I don't want to know how you got these papers," she said. "But you should pass them on to the appropriate authorities. I'm sure Steve told you that this area is like the powder keg, waiting to explode. There is a lot of tension between environmental activities and academics and manufacturing interests, not to mention workers. You should be very careful whom you show this to. A lot of activists have been threatened. A colleague of mine quit the department last year after he appeared as an expert witness against a textile mill and received anonymous phone calls threatening his family."

She handed me a coffee-stained business card. "My contact information is on here. Bring me in if you make it to court. I'm not afraid of those bastards." *Zos bas-tards.*

I walked her to the door, my mind struggling with the implications of her words. When we got to the stairwell, she turned to me and issued a long, pointed stare.

"Steve said you are a tenacious woman. Yes, I can see that," she said, nodding. "I am glad he has found someone who can match his energy at last."

On that alarming note, she left, leaving a whiff of smoke and patchouli in her wake.

CHAPTER 13

whore of babylon

To: Mom
From: Karen Mendelsohn
Subject:
Attachment: tomer15.jpg, tali24.jpg

Hi, Mom

Thought you might like some pictures of the kids from Tomer's birthday party. If you look in the bottom left-hand corner of the one with Tali, you'll see the Teletubby you gave her for Hanukkah. She doesn't let that thing out of her sight for even a second!

So, what is going on with Ben and Jennie? I feel like the whole family has been body-snatched by aliens or something. I mean, Ben actually sounded better the last time we spoke, but I'm worried about Jennie. Don't you think she's just in denial, going up to that place to avoid Damon? Did she tell you about this Steve guy? Apparently, she met him at some environmental protest, and they've been seeing each other. She never tells me anything, but what's new?

Avi sends his love and the kids say hi to Saba and Savta. Give dad a hug for me.

Karen

The park was festooned with balloons and those lamppost banners boasting concerts and festivals that cities hang to show they're culturally superior. Kids buried their faces in pink swirls of cotton candy, and a country band played enthusiastically before a crowd of dancers decked out in shiny boots and crisp jeans. I followed the aroma of barbecued ribs to the food tent, where I was supposed to meet Steve, Ben, and Els. I was a little early, so I bought a Polish sausage, smothered it in sauerkraut, and plunked myself down on the grass to watch my fellow Montanans go by.

I had quickly typed up a story that focused on the effects of toxic pollutants on wildlife and humans, including quotes from Bruce, Steve, and Valerie Renard. It would run in Monday's paper after Bernie top-edited it. I was in a conundrum about what to do about the papers I'd stolen. In a large city, I wouldn't have thought twice about bringing such a thing to my editor, or the police. But in a town this small, such an act was bound to have fallout and impact a lot of people. Bruce would be especially vulnerable, what with shared custody of Emily at stake.

"You're doing serious damage to that hot dog."

Steve Wald leaned over me as I squinted into the afternoon sun and dropped a light kiss on my bulging cheek. I choked down the sausage and asked him how he was doing. Was it my imagination, or was that couple over by the BBQ staring at us?

"Good. I just got back from the Rocky Mountain Ecosystem Coalition annual meeting in Alberta. I'm beat." He planted himself down next to me and asked me how the last few days had gone. Feeling like a liar, I gave him an abridged version of events, including a highly sanitized version of my meetings with Bruce and the latest round of stories following the fish kill.

"Did Mortensen say he was getting a search warrant to investigate the mill?" he asked.

Before I could answer, Ben and Els popped out from behind the carousel. They were laughing at something, and Ben picked a stray wisp of cotton candy from Els's curly blond hair.

"Oh, there's my brother." I jumped up, feeling suddenly nervous, and introduced everyone. Ben and Steve greeted each other easily, as did Els. But I could feel Els's conspiratorial gaze and deliberately avoided meeting her eyes.

Everyone wanted to stroll, so we walked along the central promenade, people-watching and laughing at the antics of a clown whose shtick was grabbing people's hats off their heads.

Steve told me more about the conference in Alberta, and I filled him in on Els's and Ben's arrivals. He swung his arm around my shoulders, and, in spite of my misgivings, I gave in to the delicious feeling of having a beau who wanted nothing more than to walk around a carnival with me, eating caramel-covered apples.

"Hey, let's try this," said Els. "This" turned out to be the dunking booth, and, too late, I remembered this was Bruce and Emily's station. Ben and Els, giggling like children, had already paid the attendant three small pink tickets, and I reluctantly followed the others as they ducked behind the barricade that said *Andrew Carnegie Middle School*.

Emily manned the counter, where sets of softballs lay trapped in pool-ball triangles. Her long red hair was caught in two sleek ponytails, and false silver eyelashes flapped over her dark eyes. Two of her girlfriends lounged behind the table eating cheeseburgers and fries and shrieking with laughter.

"Step right up! Don't be shy. Come on up and sink the man, folks. It's for a good cause."

Emily had mastered the carnivalesque intonation and was clearly enjoying encouraging her friends and neighbors to plunge her father into the tub. Bruce was sitting on a slat with his legs swinging over the water and had obviously avoided the pool thus far. He wore a baseball cap, T-shirt, and jeans, and was teasing the cluster of boys who were trying to lob the ball into the paddle in a good-natured, fatherly way.

Seeing him jolted me, and last night's misadventures came back in a molten rush. I felt my cheeks redden and fumbled in my bag for my trash-can-lid-size fashion shades.

After the boys turned away in defeat, Ben and Els approached the table. I skulked in the shadows with Steve's arm still hugging me tightly to his side, feeling like the Whore of Babylon, or at least the Tease of Babylon. It's funny—you wallow in celibate misery for months on end, praying for some action, and then when you get it, or at least the prospect looms, all you can think about is who you're betraying and why love is a bad idea.

Ben, whose physician's fine hand–eye coordination has never been matched outside the examining room, sent Emily's cohorts to the deck with his wild throws. Els fared no better, and then it was my turn.

"Hi, Jen!" Emily smiled sweetly at me, and I thought how much she looked like her father, despite the pretty features and auburn hair. We chatted for a minute about the fair, then I had to grab a softball and raise my eyes to Emily's father, whose face was a mask of stillness in the back of the dunking booth as he took in Steve's presence.

When Bruce spoke, I detected a tinge of insolence.

"Well, if it isn't Ms. Jen Brenner, Meredith's reporter extraordinaire. Think you can dunk me, Ms. Brenner? I don't know if a city girl has the arm for it." Bruce smirked.

I spun the ball around in my palm, feeling the familiar network of threads gripping my palm.

Bruce might know that I stole rich ladies' sandals and like being kissed on the neck, but he didn't know that I was named Dade County's all-metro third baseman in 1985. Unfortunately for Bruce, my nickname was "Rocket."

Bruce stretched his arms above his head, a picture of calculated boredom, and flexed his legs out over the water. I focused on the paddle and deliberately threw my first ball wide, allowing my arm to fall without sufficient follow-through. In other words, I threw like a girl.

Bruce laughed and shifted on the seat. "Is that the best you can do, Brenner? C'mon, give it to me. Make me wet." He adjusted his cap on his head and I thought, wet, hmm—if you only knew, Mortensen.

I allowed the second toss to go short, inviting another round of jeers from Bruce and the onlookers. Then I wound up and hurled a beaner directly at the paddle. The flap under Bruce dropped out from under him, and he plunged into the tank, eliciting protracted shrieks of laughter from Emily and her girlfriends.

Bruce waded to the side of the tank and hoisted himself over the side, water sluicing off him like the Loch Ness monster. He joined us just as Emily pressed the prize—a large stuffed Saint Bernard—into my arms.

"Well, Wald, looks like your girlfriend's got an arm like Joe Montana," he said, glaring at me from under sodden brows.

"Oh, Jennie was an all-metro softball player back in Miami. Didn't you set some sort of record for first-base throw-outs?" Ben chimed in.

I grunted an assent and tried to wrap my brain around the current situation: Here I am, miles from home. My brother and closest girlfriend, who live three thousand miles apart and are dealing with painful breakups back in the real world, seem to be careening toward romance, if the silly smiles and flirty embraces they're giving each other are any indication. Everyone thinks I am the main squeeze of the town's very attractive, but possibly nutty, environmental activist, who just happens to possess all the qualities in a mate my mother believes will ensure me a lifetime of love, respect, and Jewish children. Moreover, I'm stuck in a love triangle with the town's equally attractive homegrown EPA agent, who's old enough to have been my teenage father and is going through a messy divorce and custody suit with the daughter of the man who is the focus of my investigation. Oh, I coerced the EPA guy into stealing documentation from his father-in-law's mill. And I also steal cotton candy from little girls and run drugs out of Bogotá.

The group chatted for a few minutes more, though Bruce and I stayed silent. Then Ben, Els, Steve, and I left to ride the Ferris wheel, and I didn't see Bruce again until the night the *Gazette* offices blew up.

supersize it

To: Jen
From: Robert O'Hanlon
Subject: we're booked!

Jen,

Surprise—George managed to get a few days off from that slavedriver you all call the mayor, and, of course, my time is my own these days, so the Pitt–O'Hanlons are coming up to see Zoë's aunt Jen! We've booked a suite at the Flathead Lodge, and we'll be there on Wednesday for a long weekend. Hope that works for you, babe. Can you pick us up at the airport? Can't wait to see you, and introduce you to Zoë. Oh, George and Zoë say hi.

Robert

I grabbed my desk calendar, ran my finger across the relevant dates, and sighed. God knows it would be great to see Robert and George—and Zoë—but I'd been spending more time shepherding friends around Montana than rousting environmental criminals. Something would have to give. Just imagining Robert in his usual black button-down dress shirt, cashmere sweater, and fashionably shiny jeans sipping a Cosmo and holding court at Charlie's was enough to paste a silly grin to my face for the rest of the day: I knew what he would do with Meredith—take to it like a fag to Versace—but what would Meredith do with a couple of gay new dads and their adopted Korean daughter?

Since Els and Ben were both leaving on Thursday, we'd all have some time together. I put in a quick call to the lodge for dinner reservations and was gratified to hear that Marlboro Williams would be serenading the lodge's guests that night on his six-string gee-tar.

Time to get down to business. The piece of the puzzle that had been giving me pause was motive: Why would Sutter & McEvoy maintain the facade for so long? What could they hope to gain? Valerie Renard had provided a little insight during our conversation. She said that new equipment can run to the hundreds of thousands of dollars and that companies will sometimes remain in a state of environmental noncompliance until there is sufficient cash flow to pay for the required machinery— or maybe forever. As that seemed likely here, I jotted a statement to that effect down on my notepad, then listed everything else I knew about the situation. I finished by writing BRUCE MORTENSEN in capital letters half a dozen times and circling the letters with clouds and hearts that looked like they'd been drawn by a seven-year-old. By one-thirty, I had my facts straight and figured the hard-nosed reporter deserved a little lunch. I grabbed my bag, waved to Dave and Margaret, and went out to the parking lot.

It was a gorgeous day. Montana was earning its Big Sky moniker, the wide, crisply blue sky dotted with airy little stratus clouds. The breeze smelled of sage, and I inhaled deeply as I approached my car.

A folded piece of paper was trapped under my wiper. Thinking it was a promotional leaflet—*Dry Cleaning Special! Two Shirts for One!* or *Prenatal Massage with Lindsay!*—I swiped it and threw it in the backseat, which, in a pinch, doubles for the trash can.

I started up the car and eased out of the lot, turning the corner onto the quiet residential street behind the office. First, I'd hit Dairy Queen, then the whole-foods market for some staples. Lard and lentils. Yin and yang. Like my mother says, it's all about balance.

I was fiddling with the radio, feeling cheerful, when a dark shape loomed in the rearview mirror. I did what any city-raised, tough-as-nails crime-beat reporter would do in this situation: I screamed. I screamed loud and long and earsplittingly. Even in my terror, hearing my normally hoarse voice suddenly go falsetto sounded oddly right for the situation.

The Subaru swerved wildly as a rough hand clapped down around my mouth and grabbed at the steering wheel. But I had lost control of the car, and we careened off the road into a shallow rain ditch, where I popped the clutch and the engine sputtered out with a jerk. Frantic, I scrambled for the door, but before I could escape, the intruder's hand grasped my arm and I saw his face for the first time.

It was the whistle-blower from Charlie's.

The wiry little guy seemed about to cry. He begged me in a raspy whisper to stop screaming, which I did. With trembling hands, he unfurled the white leaflet that had been tucked against my windshield and showed it to me:

REMEMBR THE GUY FROM CHARLIES WHO TOLD YOU ABOUT
THE FIRE. THATS ME. I HAVE SOMTHING TO TELL YOU. IM IN
THE BACK SEAT OF YOUR CAR. DONT SCREAM!!!!

So much for the screaming part.

"Mind if I smoke? You scared the living bejeezus out of me."

I shook my head no, and Little Guy took a packet of rolling papers and loose tobacco out of his oily-looking sheepskin vest and started assembling a cigarette.

"Shit!"

Attempts number one and two resulted in piles of tobacco leaves on the Subaru floor. He made it on the third try, and I turned the ignition on and cracked the window. The cloud of smoke morphed into a thin wisp that curled out of my nonsmoking vehicle.

We were still resting crookedly in the flood ditch and got out to survey the situation. Since it was late summer and there hadn't been any rain, the tires were able to get traction. With Little Guy directing me and pushing from the front end, we managed to get the car back on the road. Luckily, we had landed against a thicket of juniper bushes, and, aside from a few dings and scratches, there was no damage.

"Can we go somewhere?" Little Guy asked, eyes darting between the street and the ends of his tobacco-stained fingers.

"Yeah. Where do you want to go?" I asked rather snippily. So much for the smooth sophisticated source who delivers nuggets of information from behind Armani shades in dark bars.

"I dunno. How about the Dairy Queen on Bridge Street? Nobody from the mill goes to that one," he said.

That got a laugh out of me, which Little Guy took to be a positive sign. He gave me a weak grin, made himself comfortable in the passenger seat, and pulled his John Deere cap lower over his face, all the while emitting a thick stream of smoke.

We drove in silence for the ten minutes it took to get to the fast-food restaurant. Feeling silly, I pulled into the drive-through with my mole. The hard-nosed reporter ordered a California chicken sandwich with extra onions and a chocolate shake, and Little Guy got three child-size hamburgers with extra pickles, large onion rings, and a thirty-two-ounce Coke.

We got the food and pulled around the back of the restaurant. The only person around was a teenage boy in an apron, sitting on an empty milk crate and smoking a cigarette.

"So what did you want to tell me?" I said, taking a mammoth bite out of the sandwich. Apparently, finding an intruder in the backseat of my car and driving into a ditch wasn't enough to quell my legendary appetite. So much for the car-jack diet.

Little Guy ate like a mouse, picking at stray bits of burger, bun, and iceberg lettuce that fell onto the bag in his lap.

"I heard something I thought you should know," he mumbled between nibbles. "I was in the stockroom yesterday and two guys I never seen before were talking to Mr. Whitehead. He was telling 'em to make sure there was nothing insinuating over at the EPA office. He wanted to know if they were being investigated by Bruce Mortensen. He said to check Mortensen's house too."

I felt fear for Bruce settle at the base of my neck like an icy droplet. I put my sandwich down and turned to Little Guy.

"What exactly did Whitehead tell these men to do?"

"Well, he said, you know, go on over to Mortensen's and look for anything that shows Sutter & McEvoy in a bad light." Little Guy licked his greasy fingers, and my stomach did a backflip.

"Did anyone mention Mike Curran at all?" I asked.

Little Guy appeared deep in thought. "I don't think so. Nah. Well, maybe. I dunno."

Great witness.

I took a breath. This was all well and good but not eminently publishable. I decided to try the guilt method. I mean, that's what got Little Guy talking to me in the first place, wasn't it?

"I think we are going to have a hard time taking this to the authorities without someone going on record with these accusations," I told him. "I think the person who goes on record will be regarded as a hero in the community and will be protected by the police and the federal government."

Little Guy pulled a classic about-face.

"No way, ma'am! I came to you under conditions of anonemnity," he said, anxiety causing him to mutilate the English language. "If they find out I'm telling you this, I could get killed . . . or worse!"

Wondering what fate was worse than death—no Happy Meals for life?—I tried a different tack.

"Look, you've never even told me your name. How do I know what you're saying is even credible? Maybe you have a grudge against the mill. Maybe you just want to stir up trouble. I can't be sure you even work at the mill," I said, trying to sound indignant.

"Now, just wait a minute. I'm telling the truth! I don't have nothin' against the mill. They always done right by me before. I just don't think it's right to hide the truth from the town, that's all. Plus, if someone's doin' bad things, they ought not to get away with it just because they're rich."

Silent, I tried to focus on what my next steps should be. Little Guy was right: They oughtn't to get away with murder—even if it was of the piscatory variety. But how could I warn Bruce without sounding completely ridiculous or giving away my source? Worse, how could I warn him without being close enough to the man to smell his aftershave and see the stubble lining the hard jaw? If he even glanced at me in that way he had, I could not be held responsible for my actions, which, due to my current state of chastity, were bound to be sexually deviant and unbecoming to a journalist of even my (lowly) caliber.

Before I could respond, Little Guy swung the door open.

"Miz Brenner, I gotta go," he said, and darted across the street, disappearing behind a wall of juniper.

Used to his antics, I simply gathered up Little Guy's food wrappers and stuffed them in the empty Coke container.

CHAPTER 15

oh, boys

To: bwald@netcom.com
From: Steven Wald
Subject:

Bri,

Question of the day: When you met Cheryl, did you know immediately that she was "The One"? Or did it kind of sneak up on you?

I met a great girl. Her name's Jen. She's cute as hell, funny, and smart. She just moved here from San Francisco, but is from Miami. I'm going to ask her up to Whitefish for the weekend, to that lodge we all went to when you came out for Thanksgiving. Hey, do me a favor: Ask Cheryl what she thinks about a weekend. We've already gone out twice.

Do your little bro a favor—whatever you do, don't tell Mom. Don't want to hex it.

Steve

It's a good thing the airport is so close to town, since I'm spending all my time there. You know that flight from San Jose to Austin they call the Nerd Bird? Maybe they could call this one the Jen Junket.

I pulled into the small outdoor lot at about four-thirty on Wednesday afternoon. Robert, George, and the baby were connecting from Salt Lake City and should have been on the ground by now. I prayed that the rest of Meredith had been watching *Will & Grace* with as much enthusiasm as I had. I was pretty sure the Pitt–O'Hanlons' arrival in western Montana was as history-making as integrating Mississippi elementary schools.

I trotted into the small, institutional-looking building and waved at my friend the stuffed grizzly bear guarding the door. He reminded me of Bruce a little: all big and gruff and hairy, but basically pretty harmless until he opened that mouth of his and showed his teeth.

The plane was one of those Coke-can-size varieties favored by small regional airlines, where they ply you with fancy microbrews throughout the hour-long junket in the hope that you'll forget you're hurtling through space in a projectile that's smaller than a Jeep Cherokee.

Robert and Zoë were the first ones off; George followed, weighed down by what looked to be the entire inventory of Baby Gap.

"Hey!"

I surged toward them, halting when confronted with the tiny black-haired creature papoosed on Robert's chest, asleep.

"Omigod, she's the sweetest thing, you guys."

And she was. Her eyelids were small half-moons, lashes lying like caterpillars against apple cheeks. A quiff of black hair sprouted from her perfectly round head, Fu Manchu–style. The boys had resisted the urge to poodle-ize her with a bow, opting instead for a discreet pastel yellow headband and matching onesie.

Dear God, I knew what a onesie was. Somebody shoot me.

We all hugged, careful to avoid crushing the little pupa. Robert looked nothing short of magnificent, his dark hair grown out into a strategically tousled halo and his handsome face ruddy with new-mom pride. George was his usual put-together self. Both had just the right ratio of sporty REI pieces—fleece vests and low-top hikers—mixed with worn-in jeans and shirts. I wanted to check to see if they were from Ralph Lauren Polo's Americana line, but decided asking them to remove their shirts at the baggage carousel was a little too Castro for midday, midweek Meredith.

We made it to the car before the inquisition started.

"So, who's this mountain man we've been hearing so much about?" Robert asked, expertly implanting the baby seat into the Subaru's midsection.

"I thought we'd agreed to let Jen tell us about her love life when she was ready, hon," George admonished.

Robert snorted. "If we waited till she was ready, we'd be dropping ZoZo off at UC Berkeley for her freshman year."

He turned to me. "Soooo—who's the oaf with the nine-grain loaf, sweetheart? Katie dropped some wee hints last weekend at brunch. And I can tell there are some serious, um, loaves around here." He scanned the lot in a lecherous, only partially contrived manner.

At that precise moment, a gaggle of ranch hands in Stetsons and poured-on Wranglers sidled by, oblivious, and we all exploded into laughter. I hustled Robert and George into the car before the cowboys heard us and gave us some Western justice.

"I've had a few dates," I said primly as we hit the highway.

"A few dates? C'mon, tell."

So I told them about Ranger Anderson of the chocolate slacks, and Steve Wald of the tree huggers' brigade. I got to the part about Steve showing up at the carnival just as I was scarfing down a kielbasa, and we were all in stitches. For some reason, I kept Bruce to myself. I'd always told Robert everything, but that was back when my paramours were under thirty-five and unencumbered by wives, kids, or the desire to telephone women they'd gone down on the night before.

Within fifteen minutes, we pulled up at the Flathead Lodge,

a rustic but charming inn just outside of town I'd passed from time to time since I'd come to Meredith. George and Robert unpacked Baby Gap, and I got to hold Zoë for the first time. She was awake now and making little cooing noises that threatened to erupt into wails. George handed me a bottle of formula, and I managed to stick it in the right end quickly enough to avoid serious hearing damage.

When we got inside, George and Robert went to check in. I stalked the lobby, bouncing Zoë against my chest the way I'd seen done in such instant classics as *Baby Boom* and *Three Men and a Baby*. Apparently, even Steve Guttenberg had more maternal instincts than I did, because Zoë started screaming almost immediately in the manner of someone getting a root canal without Novocaine.

"Well, somebody's got a set of lungs, don't you, little one?"

I turned around, feeling my eyes literally snap with irritation—and fear that Zoë was going to break into pieces, her body was so rigid.

"Do you want to hand her to me for a minute? I have a daughter, so I know how it is."

Speechless, I handed Zoë to Melina Mortensen, arms outstretched like a robot. If Melina had, at that moment, ordered me to leap off Mt. McKinley or describe her husband's kissing style in graphic detail, I would have done it, I was so surprised.

Melina tucked the baby expertly against her body and clucked at her. Zoë grabbed a chunk of the woman's burnished hair and wrapped it in her tiny fist. Her wails downgraded into choked gasps. The old lady knitting in front of the fire nodded approvingly. Game, set, and match to Mrs. Mortensen!

I was livid.

"I'm Melina Curran," she said, extending a lean, French-manicured hand. Apparently, nobody'd told her she was still married to Mr. Mortensen. Go figure.

"Hi, I'm Jen Brenner."

"Oh, I've heard all about you," she said.

Oh, Melina, you are too good. Refusing to snatch the bait, I pretended to inspect the Persian rug, which actually did have a suspicious stain off to the side.

"Glen, have you met Jennifer yet? She's our new reporter over at Bernie's little paper. And so young too!" She managed to rock Zoë, wave at a frightened-looking Glen Whitehead, drop a few heavy names, and upgrade me to Jennifer, a name I've always found cumbersome and excessively girlish, all at the same time.

Whitehead slunk over, looking like a teenage boy caught with *Playboy* under his mattress. At least someone in this sordid circus had the grace to be embarrassed.

"Ms. Brenner and I met a couple of weeks ago at the mill. Nice to see you again," he lied. He shook my hand, and I had to resist the urge to wipe it on my pants.

Just then, Robert and George came over. My dual gay husbands on white steeds, as it were.

"Hi, I'm Robert O'Hanlon, and this is my partner, George Pitt. We're friends of Jen's from San Francisco. I see you've met our daughter, Zoë." Robert held out his arms and Zoë lunged sweetly into them. Melina couldn't have looked more shocked if he'd bitch-slapped her or emerged from the front desk wearing leather chaps and nipple rings.

She recovered quickly and welcomed them to town. In another life—or without my stony, blatant disapproval—they might have liked this woman. After all, she was beautiful, sleek, well-preserved, bitchy, and looked a little like Judy Garland from the side. But, alas, it was not to be.

A little part of me—my conscience, perhaps?—poked its finger into my side and whispered, Hey, you made out with this woman's husband, who are you to get on your high horse? But I promptly quelled such distracting thoughts. How long, I wondered, watching Melina Curran Mortensen and Glen Whitehead leave the inn and slide into separate cars, have they been seeing each other? And, more important, why doesn't Melina care if they get caught?

and then it went *boom!*

To: jen.brenner@meredithgazette.com
From: vbrenner@earthlink.net
Subject: hiya sweetie

Jennie,

How are you holding up, sweetheart? Are you taking care of
your hands? I hear it's very dry up there. Aloe vera and a few drops
of essential oil should do for that. Daddy and I just got back from
Boca. Marvelous new spa there. We'll have to take you when you
come home for the holidays—you are coming, right? I keep telling
your father to wear sunscreen, but he just keeps roasting himself.
The man looks like an old saddle if you ask me! Will you try talking
to him? He won't listen to a thing I say. We heard through the
grapevine that Damon moved in with that blonde which I'm sure
you already know. (You know, right?) Perhaps you're better off
without him, honey. Now, I really liked Damon, but people just
outgrow each other. You'll meet someone who shares your love
of food and . . . all the things you love. Don't worry. You're
beautiful! Gotta run—having dinner at the Herschorns. Hope

they don't serve red meat like last time. Who eats red meat anymore?

Love,
Mom

"So, what do we really have?"

Bernie stood at the front of the *Gazette*'s undistinguished conference room, holding a chipped coffee mug and looking like a bantamweight pugilist. Very Harvey Keitel. Very *Bad Lieutenant*. Margaret Bloom glanced at me sympathetically as I rustled through my notes, hoping for a divine intervention.

"Well, we've got Valerie Renard. We've got some incriminating paperwork that they attempted to shred. And we've got my source." An image of Little Guy crammed into a suit on the witness stand with his ever-present roll-your-owns popped into my mind. Believable to a jury? Not bloody likely.

"He's not willing to go on record right now, but I'm pretty sure I can get him on board," I finished lamely.

Bernie stalked the perimeter as if expecting us to throw him raw meat.

Dave Lefebvre cleared his throat. "I've got friends over at the mill, Bernie. No offense to you, Jen. You do great work. But this might be one of those cases where a local will get more cooperation."

To my embarrassment, my face reddened immediately. Dave was one of those guys who seemed to be with the program, but had his own ax to grind. Late forties, mournful-looking, and resentful as hell to be stuck reporting on new municipal parking structures and bingo parlors. He wanted out—maybe Seattle or Portland, or San Francisco for that matter—and a story like this could be his ticket.

As Wayne and Garth said so eloquently—dream weaver, baby. I was on this one like a supermodel on Ex-Lax.

"Bernie, I'm this close to breaking through to this guy," I said hotly. "I've got a good relationship with Bruce Mortensen, who's open to looking into this further"—further, indeed—"and I've got an appointment with Steve Wald to go visit the res and talk to some of the old guys who fish subsistence out near the kill. What more could anyone else do?" I glared at Dave as I said this. He studied his fingernails.

Bernie seemed to ponder this for a minute. Or maybe he was just licking his fangs.

"Okay, Brenner. You've got two weeks to make something happen, or we drop this story and move on to something else. Anybody has an issue with that, you can—well, just don't have an issue with that."

Great. Now I just had to figure out how to get Steve Wald to accompany me to the reservation.

I doubted such a diverse group had ever graced the smoky interior of the Meredith Valley Lodge.

Two doctors (well, Els was technically a pharmacologist, but since she routinely sticks needles in live rats, I counted her). Two gay dads. One Korean orphan (I suppose adoptee would be more accurate). One senior citizen with a penchant for gin martinis. One babelicious environmental activist. One lovesick—or sex-starved, depending on how you looked at it—reporter. One pair of Prada pants (Robert, natch).

All rocking to the tuneless melodies of Marboro Williams and his Red Hot Jammers—with the exception of Zoë, who was snoring softly in her carrying case. (Okay, my baby knowledge stopped at onesies and Baby Björns.) Adorable lavender muffs smothered her tiny ears, saving her from death by Marlboro.

I was wedged into a booth between Steve Wald, whom I'd invited at the last minute in a balls-out attempt to exorcise Bruce from my tortured psyche, and my darling landlady Gladys Pepper. Darling Gladys was three sheets to the wind, having tucked away three martinis and a "medicinal" sherry—before dinner.

"So, did you support that?" George asked Steve.

"That" was the actor from *Cheers* suspending himself from the Golden Gate Bridge to protest, oh, some environmental thing, a couple of years ago. Woody, right? Nice abs, I recalled.

I leaned over to hear Steve's reply. Our thighs were pressed together. His felt warm and solid and healthy, like my mother's tofu loaf.

"Well, yeah, I did. I mean, when these celebrities come out and make a grand gesture like that it always gets a lot of attention, and that's never a bad thing. We're always working on several different tracks at once. Some are policy-oriented, some are fund-raising, some are straight PR. If it doesn't hurt anyone, I suppose it's gotta be good, right?" Steve said.

I studied him in the dim light: His profile was sweet and terribly earnest, his nose aquiline above his wide mouth. My hand went to my own lips, trying to remember our kiss in the parking lot. Maybe I could give it another chance. Maybe I was just being crazy, pining for Bruce. Maybe I was one of those people who was congenitally cursed into wanting things she couldn't have. Maybe I could sell my plasma if I got fired from the paper. . . .

I stared across the table at Ben and Els, Robert and George. My brother and my closest girlfriend looked like the kind of lovers for whom the word *fated* was invented—deliriously happy, yet totally aware of their good fortune and only mildly smug about it. I didn't know if they'd actually slept together yet—some instinct told me not—but they were clearly headed for some sort of carnal encounter or long-distance romance. More power to them, I thought, watching Ben whisper something in Els's ear, his still-gaunt cheeks creasing in a giddy grin when she giggled at his witticism.

Robert and George, having been hitched longer than Luke and Laura's tête-à-tête on *General Hospital,* had the easy companionability of an old married couple. Why did some couples do long-term so well, and some—Damon and I, for instance—take to it like flies to an electric bug zapper? Robert, I knew, had had his share of relationship blowouts before George came along, but even I could see he'd learned from his mistakes. Even Katie Nguyen, notorious for her ruthless dismemberment of men's hearts after they'd dared to feast at the table of her affections, had tumbled into a bona fide boyfriend–girlfriend arrangement with Colin and was going home to meet his mom and siblings for Christmas. For God's sake, they'd bought a bath mat together! Okay, so it was my bath mat, but still. Everyone knew: Once you'd survived a trip to Target together, you might as well register for china.

And here I was, copping an occasional feel from, well, a cop, for goodness' sake. And stonewalling a perfectly decent guy who would someday teach our children to chain themselves to trees, sing "Where Have All the Flowers Gone?", and fashion a mean bridge sling.

Meshuggenah, as my eighty-eight-year-old, occasionally nudist grandma would say. (If the nudism part doesn't convince you my family is quite mad, I don't know what would.)

I was trying to eject the image of my topless, tan-line-free, Raisinet-skinned grandmother from my head when the lodge was rocked by a rather grand blast.

Like good San Franciscans, Els, George, Robert, and I dived under the solid pine table, leaving Ben, Steve, and Gladys staring at a profusion of potato skins, empty beer steins, and baby-back-rib carcasses.

"What the hell was that?" Ben said, articulating the thought we all shared.

The shaking had stopped almost immediately. About five minutes passed while people righted themselves and their tables and the buzz of conversation kicked in.

Suddenly, the hostess ran into the lodge's main dining area. Her eyes were filled with tears and her freckled cleavage quivered like tapioca pudding.

"The *Gazette* offices blew up," she choked. "And they're saying Bernie, Bernie Zweben, may have been inside!"

I learned a lot about Meredith—and about real love—that night.

After dropping Robert, George, and Zoë off at the inn, the rest of us drove over to Cedar and Defoe to see if we could help. Ben grabbed his physician's bag from the car and strode over to the cops to check what was being done in the way of medical care. The rest of us hung back, scared of what we might find.

Gladys had sobered up in a flash, ever the doctor's daughter. It was easy to imagine a young Gladys answering the door for one or another of her neighbors in the middle of the night, pulling her robe closed against the cold, showing them to the living room while her father splashed water on his face to wake up.

Right now, her lined face was rigid, gazing up at the building with horror held in check. It wasn't that bad, as explosions go, but a corner had caved in, and firemen were still hosing down charred corners. Quite a crowd had gathered outside, and people were openly crying and hugging their neighbors. Someone had brought a thermos of hot coffee and foam cups and was distributing it to rescue workers and observers alike.

Tears suddenly welled up in my eyes. What if this had happened because of me? Because of my stubborn refusal to accept that my story was dead and stop covering the fish kill and the mill? I didn't think I could bear it if anything happened to crusty old Bernie, who was rapidly annexing the part of my heart that had heretofore been reserved for craggy, crotchety maestros like Walter Matthau and the inestimable Abe Vigoda.

Had this been an attempt to obliterate the shredded papers Valerie Renard had analyzed, as well as my notes? Ironically, both were safe, the notes contained on my laptop, which was lying on my desk at home, and the papers sheathed in an accordion folder in my trunk, slated for delivery to Bruce Mortensen's office, per our agreement.

Perhaps sensing my dismay, Steve put his arm around me,

and I pressed against his chest, resisting the urge to mew like a milkless cat.

He rocked me quietly, and a sliver of comfort wended its way into my heart. Was this the beginning of something? Was my body telling me something my mind wouldn't—or couldn't?

At that moment, the crowd parted as if for Moses, and Bruce emerged, his brow furrowed and his shoulders leaning forward, as solid and unwavering as a bull—or a gum tree. His gaze collided with mine. Meowwww!

I leapt away from Steve's embrace as if burned, but not before Bruce's eyes flashed a veritable mayday message: Whore of Babylon, Mother of Harlots and Abominations of the Earth—or whatever the Bible has to say about women who cut their losses and fornicate with men fifteen years younger than the guy they snogged last week.

Maybe I was projecting just a little bit, hmm?

Bruce walked over reluctantly and we all shook hands, which was kind of goofy under the circumstances. I figured Bruce had the edge on the rest of us, being law enforcement, so Ms. Reporter kicked into action and began doing what she does best—*besides* kvetching: the interview.

"Do the police know yet if this is deliberate or not?" I asked, my voice all quavery.

He raised one black brow, as if to suggest that my aspirations of getting information out of him were terrifically amusing. I felt like waggling my brows à la Groucho Marx: *Ve haf vays of making you talk. . . .*

"I'm sure they have their own opinions," Bruce said.

"Do you have an opinion?"

The brow jumped.

"No, I don't have an opinion," he said, his gaze boring into mine like a half-inch power drill.

Steve interrupted the party.

"Jennie, I'm going to take Gladys to that bench over there for a rest, okay? If you need me, I'll be there," he said.

I nodded and squeezed Gladys's hand before they walked away. Did I imagine it, or was Steve glancing pointedly at Bruce?

Inner voice #1: *Now, don't fight over li'l ole me, boys.*

Inner voice #2: *Ah, there's a new one: Jen Brenner as Scarlett O'Hara! Don't miss this once-in-a-lifetime performance!*

Inner voice #3: *Literally once. In a lifetime, that is. So for God's sake, woman, don't squander it!*

"There seem to be a lot of buildings burning down in Meredith these days," I said inanely, instead of the clever rejoinders careening around my mind.

"Yeah."

This was like pulling teeth.

"I have those papers for you. They're in my car," I said.

"I shouldn't have let you talk me into taking them."

When he said that, he looked a bit sad, as if he worried that his personal problems—cheating wife, impending divorce, custody battle—were taking a toll on his job performance. Bad family life, bad agent.

"Well, you fell to a pro, Bruce," I answered, feeling his name roll off my tongue like a chocolate kiss. "I have talked a lot of people into a lot of things in my time."

He smiled, and his face did that transformation thing where it goes from stern to radiant in two seconds.

"I don't doubt that, Brenner," he said, and I wanted to crawl into his lumberjack flannel shirt and set up camp there.

I kicked at the loose dirt next to the sidewalk's edge.

"If anything happened to Bernie, I will make it my life's mission to hunt down the person or group who did this and see they get exposed and prosecuted—and possibly drawn and quartered," I vowed.

Western Justice, Brenner-style. Boy, I've learned a lot in Montana 101.

Bruce grinned again, indulgently now.

"Do Meredith a favor, Brenner, and this time leave the law enforcement to the badges." He smirked. "Things have a way of exploding and burning down after you've reported on them. I'm sure your new boyfriend wouldn't want you taking any risks, in any case."

He's not my boyfriend, I wanted to scream—yes, whoever said you learn everything you need to know in kindergarten was absolutely right—but I bit back what would have been a sharp, pathetically transparent response and played the cool card.

"Steve and I are just friends. And I'm done with amateur hour. I just want Bernie to be all right," I said.

Bruce nodded.

Just then, shouts erupted from the rubble area. It was hard to see from behind the cordoned-off zone, but the crowd surged forward in anticipation. Cold terror settled at the pit of my stomach: Would they be bringing bodies out, or survivors?

Gladys and Steve came back. My landlady had aged about twenty years in the last hour. I realized for the first time that Gladys Pepper was old, in years if not in spirit. I reached out and took her bony hand in mine. Her skin felt as soft and weathered as an old suede shirt.

We heard men yelling orders and the sharp yips of rescue dogs brought in to search for people.

Finally, a group of paramedics and firemen rounded the corner of the crumbled structure with a stretcher.

Bernie was on it.

I could see his bristly gray aureole of hair from here. It was obvious almost immediately that he was arguing with his rescuers, trying to get down off the platform.

Joy!

They got to the edge of the crime-scene zone, where the ambulance was waiting. Elaine, Bernie's wife, who had been sandwiched between two formidable-looking middle-aged women—one tall, thin, and stoic, the other short, plump, and stoic (stoicism not being in short supply in Montana, I'd noticed)—exploded into sobs at the sight of him and rushed forward.

I felt a pain in my hand and realized that Gladys was squeezing it, the half-moons of her nails digging into my flesh. Her eyes were not on Bernie but on Elaine, and I could feel her whole body quivering, torn between the desire to run to Bernie's side and the knowledge that she was consigned to the sidelines, to remain with the other onlookers, Bernie's friends, acquaintances, associates.

Suddenly, random details crystallized into a cogent picture: the shy young boy who had just moved to town from the city peeking out from behind his mother's skirts at the slightly older local girl who lived across the street and was tugging impatiently at her too-tight Peter Pan dress collar. Both young people bookish and spirited, plagued by the knowledge that social wizardry escaped them but heartened by the kernel of independence that burned, deep inside, that told them acceptance was not the main ingredient in their lives' recipes. Both with the sense that their lives would take them beyond the confines of this small town. As teens, exchanging notes in the library, making fun of the football player Gladys was tutoring because he was flunking composition. Hugging awkwardly on the eve of Officer Bernard Zweben's departure for Fort Harrison to join his U.S. Cavalry unit. Gladys making arrangements to go to teacher's college in Idaho when Bernie returned from the war with his budding, ebony-haired bride, Elaine Landau from New York City.

Gladys was still in love with Bernie.

How could I not have seen this before? I'd been so absorbed in my own melodramas, I'd failed to register the beautiful yet ineffably tragic romance that had bloomed between my landlady and my boss, unconsummated for more than fifty years. Unrequited—or unrealized—love was only romantic in the movies, I thought. In life it must hurt like the proverbial knife cut, perhaps dulling over the years to a persistent ache. But never far from the surface. Never fully locked away so that time could age the memories into yellowed love letters, mementos tied neatly with a string, stored in a tidy keepsake box, far from heart and mind. Oh, the pain of it—to contemplate the overtures not returned, the commitments not made, the paths not taken, all because of the intoxicating, delusional power of your fondest wish.

This knowledge, and Gladys Pepper's stoic, tearful profile, extracted from me a fervent promise in the cool Montana night: The next time love visited, I would swing the door wide and greet it with the effusive embrace of a long-lost friend. I would tell it it's been too long. And as the stars are my witness, I would tell it to take off its coat and stay awhile.

big dogs and rose petals

To: Alexandra Whitehead
From: Elise Feldman, Attorney at Law
Subject: Your call

Alex,

At the risk of scaring you even more, yes, this is a problem. As your attorney, I strongly advise you to stop with the Secret Friend stuff and start working on the paperwork we talked about last week. Focus, Alex! Believe me, I know how you're feeling right now, and if it's any consolation, with the case we're building, Glen will be lucky to end up with a trailer in Great Falls. Please forward me ALL of these Secret Friend emails and I'll take a look at them.

<<What were you thinking, girl?>>

Elise Feldman, Attorney at Law
Feldman, Feldman, and Brown

This email message is confidential, intended only for the named recipient(s) and may contain information that is privileged attorney-client communications, attorney work product, or exempt from disclosure under applicable law. If you are not the intended recipient(s), you are notified that the dissemination, distribution or copying of this message is strictly prohibited.

Several weeks had passed since Labor Day, and Montana was in the throes of a perfect Indian summer. I stuck my head out the window and let the wind whip my hair against my cheek. It felt good to hit the road. The air smelled of baked wildflowers, and we had Ani DiFranco in the CD player. Ani was belting out "Going Down," which foretold an end either dismal or sublime, the irony of which could be taken either way.

Steve laughed and playfully grabbed my back belt loop, his other hand gripping the steering wheel so we wouldn't hurtle off the two-lane highway into a ditch.

"Get in here. You're going to fall out."

I slid back down in my seat and grinned. Steve mussed my hair. I batted my lashes. Ah, shucks. The little woman's flirting again.

But, seriously. It felt good to be wanted. It really did. I was both excited and apprehensive about the upcoming weekend. Two paramount questions loomed: (1) Would there be sex? and (2) Would there be good water pressure in the shower? (I would have added *Would there be a shower?* as number three, but it seemed kind of redundant, what with number two.)

Then there was meeting Steve's fellas, who just happened to be a couple of erudite Indian gentlemen with truckloads of academic and Native cred. I envisioned them as stoic men with long gray braids and names like Stands-with-a-Master's-Degree-in-Civil-Engineering and Dances-with-Sun-Valley-Movie-Stars. The prospect of discussing Native rights with people of this caliber was no walk in the park.

I'd done a little research this week on Native American subsistence fishing and land rights so I wouldn't completely shame myself in front of the elders. It was pretty much as you'd suspect: Time and time again, white folks had cheated the original locals out of the natural bounties that were their birthright. Water, land, intellectual property, you name it—the Euro-Americans had found a way to appropriate it, either by war of attrition or just plain war. Water was a particularly contentious issue in Montana and the rest of the American West, where the climate is mostly arid. In one landmark case in the early twentieth century, white settlers near the Fort Belknap Indian Reservation in north central Montana diverted water from the Milk River, away from Indian settlements. I think the Indians won that one, which would make it the exception that proved the rule.

Lately, it's gotten even more complicated, as traditionally friendly groups have ended up on opposite sides of the fence vis-à-vis Indian water rights and the U.S. Endangered Species Act. And that's not even counting the frenzy of dam-building that went on throughout the twentieth century. When you actually start reading about vibrant salmon- and steelhead-clogged rivers like those in the Columbia–Snake River Basin being bisected by engineers to make dams and mutated into listless pools, it makes you wonder if that $8.95 electric bill is really worth it.

But I digress.

The thing is, in the end I just called Steve Wald up and asked him to take me to see his friends at the Flathead Reservation. I figured they could tell me something about fish kills that could help me, or recruit me, or just plain bore me to tears, but it seemed well worth the trip.

And I'd made a decision—I was going to have a relationship with Steve Wald. Okay, perhaps I use the word *relationship* loosely—would a co-shower at Motel 6 qualify?—but the important thing was to get back in the saddle, to ride this opportunity like an unbroken filly, to dig my spurs into the flanks of life. (Somebody please stop me, lest I take the equestrian metaphor to its inevitable, lascivious conclusion.)

Some might call me callous, or frivolous, or accuse me of using Steve for my own selfish ends (um, just the lower end, please), and they may be right. But I refused to wallow in guilt about it. I was a grown woman. Between an arsenal of sex toys that rivaled Mattel's more innocent inventory and a stack of bodice-rippers, I had needs that were simply not being met. I wanted true love, and I was ready for it, but if it wasn't going to waltz into my life just yet, I was going to keep ye auld parts nice and oiled until Mr. Right came along.

At least, that was the mantra I kept chanting to myself every twenty minutes.

Truth be told, I was scared witless.

One thing about living alone and sexlessly: For all we denigrate the lifestyle, you do achieve a kind of equilibrium after a while. Sure, there are nights when you crave the feel of warm male flesh beside you as you plug in your Pocket Rocket, when self-love and your fantasies just aren't enough. But, for the most part, you simply get used to it. All those psychovangelists and New Ageists and hippy-dippy types try to teach us that change is good, when it is patently obvious to anyone with a brain cell and a television that change is bad. Staff changes on *ER*, elections in the Middle East, Felicity's haircut—change is good? *Hello?!*

To have sex, to relate, meant change. And, boy, did that present a problem for me.

A couple of weeks ago, before he'd left, I'd asked my brother, Ben, if he thought resistance to change was congenital, like male-pattern baldness or blue eyes.

"Absolutely not," he said, while we waited for his flight to be called in the Jen Brenner Terminal. Els's flight had just left, and she'd vacated the state as tearfully as she'd entered it but infinitely happier.

"But look at Mom and Dad. Mom's been complaining about Miami's cultural deficiencies for years, but they've never budged, and Dad always talks about going part-time, but he'll never do it. I'm pretty sure I inherited it from them," I said.

"You *learned* it from them. Completely different."

"I guess."

These thoughts swirled around in my head as Steve's truck

ate up miles of scrubby flatlands. Finally, we turned onto a narrow road.

"Marty Devereaux lives in a trailer a few miles down," Steve said.

Surprised, I realized we were already on the reservation. Aside from a discreet sign on the main highway, it was indistinguishable from nonreservation lands. There may have been a few more traditional-looking folks getting out of cars at roadside businesses, and, once, we passed a car that said *Tribal Police,* but other than that there was no demarcation. After having read about Indian activists like Leonard Peltier and seen *Incident at Oglala* and such, I'd always imagined at the very least an imposing gate: WHITE MAN, KEEP OUT.

We pulled up to a rather ratty-looking trailer, one of three clustered together on an expanse of prairie, like loose stones that had rolled to a stop in the most arbitrary of locations.

It's funny how normative our concepts of poverty are. I mean, aside from the obviously universal unfortunate conditions of hunger, cold, and inadequate shelter, what constitutes poorness is a pretty subjective thing. What we all think of as insufficient living conditions is largely determined by how we ourselves grew up, and where. I imagine that Tori Spelling, stepping out of a car in front of my parents' home in suburban Miami, would wrinkle her bobbed nose in horror at the pink stucco and plastic flamingoes in the yard. *Quel pauvres!* she'd exclaim, running a manicured hand experimentally along my mother's 1981 Volvo wagon as if it were part of a museum exhibit on poverty in the Sunbelt.

I was fighting to quell those feelings now. Even the word *trailer* is enough to conjure up images of scrawny, swell-bellied children playing in raw sewage while terminally angry dogs and feral cats snapped at picked-over chicken bones in parched yards.

I left my stuff in the truck and followed Steve up to the door. He turned to face me when we got there.

"Marty's cool," he said. "You look nervous."

"I just have to pee."

He stared at me for a moment. Then surprised me by leaning over and kissing me once on the mouth, hard.

The door opened.

"Why you making out on my doorstep, man?"

The first thing I noticed about the guy in the doorway was his hair: braids, sleek and long on either side of his face, a pure blue-black cut through with wiry filaments of gray. Also, he had glasses on, incongruously feminine-looking wire-rimmed grannies, which lent his face a learned, fussy air. He was average-size, with a red-and-white checked shirt that had seen many washings and the ubiquitous Wranglers again. (Had the white man come bearing Wranglers? I wondered. Hey, you wear Wranglers and we wear Wranglers—can't we all just get along?)

He extended his hand to me, peering out above the glasses.

"I'm Martin Devereaux. It's a pleasure."

"Jen Brenner. Thank you for seeing us on such short notice."

"Oh, this guy's all right. Kinda hyper, which I guess you've figured out if you're kissing already. I figure you're with him, you're all right."

His voice had the up-and-down cadence I'd heard from time to time at the supermarket and around town. But underneath, there was a fine, cultivated layer that spoke of a formal education in good schools. That, and the twinkle in the pitch eyes when he said "kissing" made my shoulders come down a little.

Marty ushered us inside, and I mentally slapped myself for my preconceptions.

Pure magic, was Marty Devereaux's trailer.

Books, undulating, crazy piles of books, rose up on every available surface. The inside walls had been paneled in 1960s teakwood and hung with Native art, which gave the smallish space the feel of a cozy cave. But the coup de grâce was the collection of bottles lining windowsills, shelves, and cabinets. Everything from ancient soda bottles to milk jugs to antiquated medicine containers, all filtering incoming sunlight through the amber, blue, green, and milky prisms. It lent the small room a beach-house air, a thousand miles away from the Washington coast. A speckled dog with a red bandanna around its neck and mismatched eyes nudged against my leg and pressed his wet nose into my palm.

"That's Otsikheta. It's Kanienkehaka for sugar, or candy, I guess. My ex-girlfriend named him. She's Mohawk. She left, but Sugar stayed. Liked me better, I guess," he said.

Otsikheta/Sugar eyed me hopefully, and I wondered if he lived up to his name and was fishing for something tasty. I shrugged my shoulders and he seemed to accept my lack of an offering, opting to curl up at the foot of Marty's brown leather recliner.

"Can I get you something to drink? Coke, beer?" Marty asked.

Steve asked for a beer and I said water would be fine.

Marty rustled around in the kitchen while we sat on the funky Naugahyde couch. It wouldn't have looked out of place in a San Francisco loft, but I suspected Marty hadn't chosen it for its retro charm.

I sipped my water gratefully, glad to wash the grit from my mouth, and listened to Steve and Marty catch up. Finally, we got down to business.

"So, Steve tells me you're writing about the mill," Marty said.

"Yeah, I'm trying to put together enough evidence of toxic dumping to get EPA involved."

Marty nodded, his gaze bisected by the gold rims of his granny glasses.

"I thought you might know some people who fish the river on a regular basis who could help us figure out what happened," I added.

"Yeah, I can think of a few."

Marty stopped there, and I wondered if it was an Indian thing, the ability to say only what was necessary and not a word more. Then I thought of how angry Katie had been when we'd seen the fourth *Star Wars* film together and she'd exclaimed over

Lucas's depictions of the bad guys, whom she viewed as thinly veiled stereotypes of "inscrutable Asians."

"Caucasians think our faces don't show emotion like theirs do," Katie had fumed. "That's part of thinking we all look alike, I guess. Look at these guys! The world's burning down around them, and they're like, 'We're so bloodless, the total carnage doesn't even bother us.' Totally racist," she'd muttered as we left the theater. With her rage and, at the time, hot pink hair swirling around her, she'd cut an imposing figure, and a group of small boys had edged away from us, eager to wallow in starstruck escapism for a few minutes longer.

I just raised my eyebrow at Marty Devereaux. It's a favorite technique of transparent Jewish women. It works on most men, with the exception of the profoundly visually impaired.

Marty's glasses may have been weird, but they obviously worked.

"Uh, so why don't we go over to Arlee and talk to Sam Lockyer. He fishes just about every day. He'll be able to help you out."

Sugar raised his head as we left for town, stared at us balefully with one blue eye, then tucked himself into a doughnut and fell fast asleep, to dream of rabbits and dog treats, perhaps.

Arlee was a settlement about thirty miles north of Missoula, near the Swan River. It looked like you'd expect a town of five hundred on a Montana reservation to look: scattershot, with the prefabricated feel of a place whose municipal buildings were assembled elsewhere and driven in on flatbed trucks, plunked down, and left to weather.

As we bounced along, Marty explained that the town's name came from the English phonetic spelling of the Indian word *Alee,* which meant *red night.* Alee was a Native leader from the mid–nineteenth century. A few years ago, scientists had found coliform and nitrates in the town water, causing a half-hearted mutiny, but otherwise Arlee's inhabitants had traversed their town's ups and downs much like those from other sparsely populated places—with a wry sense of humor and a fair amount of alcohol.

I enjoyed his stories immensely, and told him so. Turned out Marty was an English instructor at Salish Kootenai Tribal College, which would explain his profusion of books. His special focus was coyote stories, legends and fables that used the mythic symbolic figure of the coyote to deliver a variety of morality tales. He taught a couple of classes a week at the college and supplemented his income with an occasional speaking engagement at a mainstream university or New Age retreat.

We pulled up at a sort of general-store-bar-café-library-type establishment. That's one thing I'd noticed right away about Montana: Unlike cities, whose denizens rely on specialization as an indicator of commercial competence, small towns, for obvious reasons, agglomerate all their services under one roof. This often results in unintentionally humorous combinations of services, such that it's not unusual to buy dental floss, check out library books, pick up mail, and even arrange a funeral from the same proprietor. This didn't seem to call into question the skill set of the entrepreneur. The maxim about doing a lot of things, and none very well, simply didn't apply in places like Arlee.

The store was dark and our feet thudded on the hardwood floor. A few Native men and women and white folks drank at the bar, played pool, and shopped for staples in the crowded aisles.

Across the room, a man raised his hand to Marty and Steve and got up to join us.

"That's Sam," Marty said. "He's an environmental and land-rights lawyer. Does some work for the Wild Rivers group and the local tribes."

When he loomed over us at the table, I felt my mouth go dry. Sam Lockyer may have been the most beautiful man I had ever seen. If I were ever charged with producing a wall calendar based on the concept American Lawyers in Speedos, he would definitely be Mr. January.

His hair was black, thick, butt-skimming, and glossy as a wet seal. Instead of looking feminine, it gave him the air of someone primal and macho, whose idea of applying hair product was smearing moose blubber from one of his kills on his brow in homage to some ancient animal totem. With his sinewy body, gleaming incisors, and inscrutable—sorry, Katie—visage, Lock-yer was straight out of central casting for *Dances with Wolves*. Had he approached the table on a buckskin pony flicking his loincloth, I could not have been more charmed.

I wish.

Sam shook hands all around and ordered a lemonade from the hugely pregnant bartender. When he leaned back in his chair, his faded T-shirt rode up, exposing a flat expanse of brown belly.

Apparently, my "relationship" with Steve did not extend to a moratorium on impure thoughts concerning other men. Silently, I chided myself: Focus, Jen—dear God, is that a tattoo of a hawk on his stomach?—and get down to business.

I cleared my throat and gulped at my Coors Light. I have noticed an inexplicable phenomenon that causes otherwise inferior beer to taste good when consumed in the immediate presence of teetotalers. This phenomenon is even more pronounced if you are also horny enough to booty-call the most repulsive of your ex-boyfriends and are in the presence of two eminently screwable male hominids.

"I can bring you down to the river tomorrow morning to talk to some of the people. There's a woman, Cora Slow Elk, who has been fishing that river for almost fifty years. If there's anyone can tell you when the dead fish started turning up, it's Cora," Sam said.

"Thanks, Sam. I really appreciate it," I said. Now, how about that calendar?

We spent the next few hours talking. By seven P.M., the sun had slipped over the lip of the horizon and was casting its long, orange rays into the store. A few dozen people had shown up for evening victuals, and there was even music playing—a blue-grassy, twangy number that had me itching to dance. Marty and Sam were good company once they warmed up, and clearly all three men had the kind of respect for one another that let them poke fun at their sillier shortcomings. Sam told a funny story about Steve's first powwow, down at the Crow Reservation south of Billings, when Steve had stepped on an elder's foot during the Round Dance, the part of the ceremony where visitors are invited to join in, prompting the old lady to christen him "Boy Who Smashes Foot." That got a round of laughs from the table.

Throughout the afternoon, I had been conscious of Steve's eyes on me, and, after consuming three or four beers, I was returning his glances with matching heat. I still didn't know where we were spending the night, but I was drunk enough to bed down with the pregnant bartender on a tumbleweed.

Finally, Marty and Sam got up from the table.

"I got to get home and feed Otsikheta," Marty said.

"Yeah, Louisa is going to take a switch to me I come home late again," Sam laughed.

Damn. Lucky Louisa. You can spend the night at my house if that mean woman kicks you out, I wanted to say. As long as you leave all those nasty clothes at home. . . .

Grinning like a lottery winner, I obediently followed Steve and Marty out to the truck. Apparently, we were going to pitch a tent in the rock-strewn corral that doubled as Marty's garden and use his facilities. I thanked the alcohol gods for giving me the forbearance to face a first encounter with a man sans body wash.

By the time we got to Marty's place, the colors in the western sky had conflagrated into a psychedelic rainbow of oranges and reds. The breeze carried with it a dusty sweetness, as if the earth itself were layered in overripe fruit. Sugar stood in the doorway like a canine duenna, watching us with his strange mismatched eyes.

"This old-timer's going to hit it. But you kids make yourselves comfortable. I've got Cokes in the fridge, some food, and plenty of books. Steve knows where the bathroom is," Marty said, pointing to the—egads—wooden shack with a moon carved into the door, about thirty yards away behind the trailer.

"It's been real nice to meet you, Jen. I'm sure you'll be a good influence on Stevie here."

Then Marty surprised me by leaning over and pecking me gently on the cheek. His kiss felt soft and smelled of warm, manly things, like tobacco and Old Spice.

We watched his checkered back go down the hall. All this talk of "good" and "influence" scared me. When I moved here, my mission had been to be as anonymously bad as possible, without actually exacting pain from others, of course. No tethers attached. Now, wise old Indian men were telling me I was a good influence on the new man in my life. What the hell was that supposed to mean?

Steve put his arms around me and rocked me gently in his embrace.

"How about if I set up the tent while you get ready for bed?" he said.

Bed?

"Okay," I whispered.

I pulled out my overnight case and snapped open my compact. My cheeks were flushed, either from beer or the impending end of the Age of Celibacy, or both. I tore off a paper towel from the holder over the sink, splashed my face with cold water, and rubbed hard. In the living room, with Sugar watching, I slipped out of my jeans and into something more comfortable—a pair of men's boxers and a wife-beater tank. I did a little shimmy for Sugar's benefit—and to psych myself up—and repacked my belongings tightly in my day pack.

It had been long enough since I'd had sex that I had pre-exam jitters, and even a touch of melancholy, which I attributed to my incipient failure to break the world record for substituting chocolate for intimacy. For a split second, my inebriated mind produced an image of Bruce Mortensen's face that night at Gladys's as I'd clambered off his lap and out of his car—and, in a way, out of his life. My traitorous mind etched the deep creases on either side of the sensual mouth, the crisp hair I'd laced through my fingers, the body that made me feel oh so small—

"Jen? You almost ready?"

Steve's hand rested between my shoulder blades. A shiver ran down my body, and, misinterpreting, he smiled lazily and ran his index finger down my spine. After a while, it started to feel damn good.

Banishing thoughts of Bruce from my mind, I followed Steve out to the tent, which was glowing in the dusky night. We kicked off our shoes and crawled through the flap. Inside, Steve had piled our sleeping bags on top of an air mattress. Rose petals the color of old blood were scattered over everything, releasing a pungent perfume that carried me all the way back to summers in Miami. A single candle burned inside a lantern, throwing undulating shadows on the walls of our makeshift domicile.

"Oh, Steve, this is amazing. I can't believe you did this," I said.

"You're amazing," he said. In the darkness, his blue eyes were nearly black.

Then we kissed, and things got very hot indeed after that.

CHAPTER 18

the kernel of hope

To: bmortensen@mail.epa.gov
From: emilym@yahoo.com
Subject: hey dad

Dad—I'm at school and I just thought I'd e-mail you but I'll also call
you later. Are we still going fishing tomorrow? You said you'd take
me and Toni to the Creek. You don't have to work do you? Anyway,
e-mail me back. I love getting messages.

Em

p.s. Mom is acting totally crazy. I wish you were here.

Panting woke me up.

Startled, my eyes fluttered open and I went rigid. Where was
I? I could feel a warm lump beside me, and something heavy was
lying on my leg. The air was crisp and cold.

I turned my head and saw Steve Wald sleeping next to me.
His arm was flung over his head, and a narrow rivulet of drool
laced his bottom lip.

Oh, God.

The screened tent window was to my right. In it was Sugar, red bandanna askew, sitting patiently with his wide pink tongue hanging down like a moist banner.

Trying to be quiet, I unfurled myself from the tangle of sleeping bags and limbs, unzipped the flap, and crept out of the tent. My watch was in the house, but I guessed it was before six A.M. Sam Lockyer was coming to pick me up at six-thirty. Steve—the fair-weather activist—had decided that was too early for him and was staying to help Marty rototill the yard. Sam and I would drive up to the Swan River and meet Ms. Slow Elk and talk fish.

I stumbled over rocks and the thick weeds choking the non-path to the toilet, accompanied by my furry friend. It was another beautiful early fall Montana morning, the eastern sky flaming with color and wispy, textured clouds. I managed to relieve myself by clamping my nose shut, pissing like a racehorse, and flinging myself outside to pull up my shorts.

Over the past two celibate years, I'd imagined this moment countless times: the long-awaited night of good healthy sex, followed by the morning stretch. The dawning "oh, yes" realization. The early-morning fondle. The post-show shag. The eventual phone calls to Robert, Els, and Katie, in which pertinent details like orgasm frequency (or at least yes or no), kissing style, and appendage circumference were traded like baseball cards. The feeling of hard satisfaction that came from the knowledge that I'd had a need and gone out and sated it. Like a grown-up (or an addict, depending on how you wanted to look at it). The slight edge of regret that was tempered by the harsh good humor of my stalwart friends, who would quickly and accurately assess my post-coital state of mind and level just the right ratio of kudos to insults. Best of all, the kernel of hope that, if the guy was suitable, the encounter would morph into A Long-Term Relationship, complete with dual-household toothbrushes, weekend jaunts to extortionate vacation rentals, and cheese-laden Sunday brunches.

Right now, I felt only some of those things.

The relief, yes. The compulsion to call Robert, yes. The orgasm count, yes (two). The desire to take a hot shower, most definitely, yes. The kernel of hope, no.

Where was my kernel of hope?

Seeking the emotional wisdom that emanates only from large dogs, very old people, and tortured Southern writers, I grabbed Sugar's broad head and scratched his ears. He stared back blankly. Nothing. Nada.

I did a quick self-assessment and was troubled to discover that, although my body and mind registered a certain rightness, a physiological imbalance that had been redressed, the desire to spin a few moments in time with a lovely man into wild fantasies of future couplings, smug cohabitation, and games of What Would You Name the Kids (Montana? Shmulie? Steve, Jr.?) was curiously absent.

It was truly puzzling.

For now I decided to focus on the more immediate puzzle—how to get through a morning with Sam Lockyer without tackling the man forcibly to the ground and demanding to see his etchings.

The human adult woman really is an insatiable creature, isn't she?

Sam arrived promptly at six-thirty in a big-ass Ford truck with primer spatters on the rear bumper. I hoisted myself in, and we took off for a morning of adventure and pent-up lust. (His expectations I couldn't tell you.)

He had very kindly brought a thermos of coffee. I would have liked to set up an IV with the stuff but thought Sam might be put off by needles in the morning, so I refrained.

If anything, Sam presented even better in the morning, when the otherwise cruel light of day illuminated the symmetrical perfection of his strong features and taut physique. Next to his knee-buckling beauty, I felt puffy and plain, and I resolved to never again find myself within one hundred yards of someone who has been—or might be—photographed for money.

"You ever fly-fish, Jen?" Sam asked.

"Not really. But I did see *A River Runs Through It* one and a half times."

He smiled inscrutably.

"Well, then, you should do just fine."

Yet another puzzle: If all we were doing was going to talk to Ms. Slow Elk, why did I have to know how to fish? As far as I was concerned, a fish's place was on my plate—preferably raw and topped with wasabi. Certainly not gallivanting around in wild rivers rubbing its scaly fins against my legs and nibbling my toes.

These Montanas have a way of being extra humorous on cold mornings, I'd noticed.

The drive was brief, and before I knew it, we'd pulled up to a trailhead. Sam leapt out of the car like a deer, and I resolved to tell my friends, in the inevitable retelling, his name was Young Deer or something equally evocative. What's a harmless white lie that'll make people happy, when there is so much misery in the world?

"I brought you Louisa's stuff. You're about the same size," Sam said.

I couldn't help being gratified that he'd noticed my size. Now, there's a first.

"Stuff?" I replied.

"Well, you think Cora Slow Elk's gonna be on the shore, missy? The lady's a first-class fly-fisherwoman. She'll be out in that river catching cutthroat trout big enough to water-ski on, I imagine."

Sam shook his head sadly, as if my aquatic reluctance was a freakish disease, like Munchausen's by proxy or elephantiasis of the testicles.

So I stood gamely while Sam tossed me two plastic tubes (these turned out to be something called waders you actually *stand* in), a pole, and various equipment. Most of it looked harmless, but then, all truly evil things did. (Thank you, Hannah Arendt.)

We tromped down to the river. I had intended to bring my notebook computer, but now that I realized the interview was to take place in the middle of a churning flood, I left it in the car with the rest of my cherished belongings.

"That's Cora," Sam said, gesturing vaguely toward a figure in the water. "She doesn't know we're coming, because there's no way to reach her. No phone. But that's okay. Let me just go out there and tell her who you are, then you come on out, okay?"

Before I could answer, he stepped into his waders, stripped off his shirt—I swear, that part is true!—plaited his horsey black tresses into a shining braid, and set off for the short, round blob in the center of the flowing stream. There were a few people here and there, but I couldn't make out individual features, as they were out in the middle of a body of water that looked to be at least the distance from Alcatraz to San Francisco's Fisherman's Wharf. Maximum-security distance, if you will.

I tried to pretend I wasn't going to enter the frigid water at seven A.M. by inspecting the wildflowers on the shoreline and going over the important questions in my head. Unfortunately, Sam started waving at me almost immediately. I considered ignoring him and hightailing it for the main road, then decided that was the kind of chickenshit maneuver that would bar me from ever being considered as a potential sex partner by Sam "Young Deer" Lockyer—should Louisa ever abandon him for Brad Pitt or embrace polyamory or something.

In the waders, I felt as clumsy as I did the year Ben, Karen, and I dressed up like Budweiser beer cans for Halloween. (Trussed up in chicken wire like human sausages, it never crossed our minds we might want to *sit down*.) Louisa may be my size, but her feet were big enough to sail down the Mississippi. Almost immediately, I could sense the three inches of extra space at the toe snagging on rocks and waving in the current. Damn. I picked my way through the marsh grasses and stepped between boulders, working my way toward the river center. I figured I'd be there by nightfall. Thank God for Daylight Savings.

Suddenly, I felt something slam me in the knees, beneath my center of gravity. Before I could stabilize myself, I was in the river. The cold was like a slap in the face, and I literally felt my breath being ripped from my body. Terrified, I struggled to raise my head but only succeeded in spinning around so my skull was facing downriver instead of my legs. I had gone white-water rafting once, and in between long pulls off her bong, the guide—a sun-ravaged blonde with boccie-ball biceps and an eyebrow ring—told us if we fell in to always place our feet downriver so they'd be the first to hit boulders, tree trunks, and any other lurking dangers that can cleave a human head better than a double-edged ax.

Easier said than done.

Try as I might, I couldn't seem to get a firm footing. It felt like I'd been in the water for hours, and I was vaguely aware of swallowing great mouthfuls of river. My heart still hammered, but I was also tired. Sometimes I'd pop to the surface, sputtering, staring straight up at the sky. The clouds looked incredibly fluffy against the celadon-blue backdrop, like stage scenery you'd find in the closet of a repertory theater.

My last thought before I passed out was, I wonder if Steve will try that rose petal thing with his next girlfriend.

Then it was just cold.

The water was still icy when it gushed out of me.

You would have thought that my body heat would have at least warmed it up a little, but no: I heaved up a Niagara Falls of river, and it was just as uninviting as when it went in.

I had been out for only a few seconds when someone plucked me from the river and, clasping my sodden 138.8 pounds to his chest, made his way back to shore. I was too out of it to identify my savior, trying instead to concentrate on sparing the Good Samaritan the worst of my upchucked breakfast.

I was dumped unceremoniously on a sandy spit, where I lay,

gasping like the proverbial trout, until I could trust my voice enough to speak.

Water streamed into my eyes, obscuring my vision. I pushed my soggy hair off my forehead and pulled myself to a sitting position.

Bruce Mortensen crouched in front of me, thick forearms crossed over his chest. His expression wasn't hard to read: *What the fuck do you think you're doing, you crazy bitch?*

And then the funniest thing happened.

I started to laugh.

Tears ran down my cheeks, mingling with river water. Soon, giggles exploded into full-blown guffaws, then graduated into wet-your-pants level hysteria. I was conscious of the concerned faces surrounding me—Bruce, Emily, Sam (still shirt-challenged, I noted), Cora Slow Elk—but I was powerless to stop. Then, to my horror, the laughter congealed in my throat and great sobs burst out of me. I keened like a small child who'd left her favorite doll at the playground. Too maniacal to be embarrassed, I allowed the wails to ring forth with gusto. Snot ran down my face, but I didn't care.

Then Bruce's arms came around me, snugger than a straitjacket. My lungs contracted like a punctured bellows, and I knew I was hyperventilating. I flailed futilely against the iron grip, which felt, at that moment, incarcerating. *Smack*—Bruce's rough palm cracked against my face and it seemed to dislodge something foreign and willfully defiant inside me. After a minute, the band loosened and the hands became emotive once again, demanding that I relax into the warm valley of his chest.

"You hit me," I said, pleased. I wanted to tell everyone else, even shirtless Sam and underage Emily—*especially* underage Emily—to bugger off and leave us alone.

"Well, you were hysterical. Sometimes that helps."

"Umm."

"I can't leave you alone for two minutes, Brenner," he said.

But his voice was tinged with affection, and I knew implicitly that the show of exasperation was for the people surrounding us.

"You know what they say about saving someone's life." I spoke softly, so only he could hear.

He leaned in and whispered in my ear, "You're responsible for them forever."

Surreptitiously, Bruce held my hand while he wrapped the blanket Sam had brought from his car around me. His touch was rough and warm and banished thoughts of Steve Wald and Sam Lockyer and anyone else in my life unlucky enough to not be Bruce Mortensen. My denial, held in check for weeks, found release like a gaggle of butterflies rising up en masse from a secret garden. At that moment, the kernel of hope that had lain dormant for so long burst to life, its tender, curly shoots wrapping themselves around my heart. Frightened and exhilarated at the same time, I allowed my senses to be taken hostage by this person, this man, who had alternately enraged and delighted me from the moment we'd met.

"I missed you," he said, louder this time.

CHAPTER 19

savor

To: Carl Hanson
From: Nancy Teason
Subject: HR issue

Looks like we're going back to HR to fill the managing editor spot.
McCabe is just not working out. Do you know where Jen Brenner
ended up? Wyoming, wasn't it? I just might give her a call.

p.s. Last night was terrific.

Nance

Whoever said "love stinks" was more right than they knew.

By the time I got home Saturday night, after two days in
which I had guzzled cheap beer, fornicated like a rabbit, slept in a
musty tent, nearly drowned in a muddy river, and stewed in an
overheated car, I was ripe as a Georgia peach.

The first thing I did was strip off my rank clothes. The second
was open my notebook computer and transcribe Cora Slow Elk's
commentary. I was naked and bruised and reeked to high heaven,
but in possession of a few more facts than I'd had before. I was
one step closer to nailing Mike Curran's wide ass to the wall.

Yes, she got the interview, folks.

It is a well-known fact that I, Jen Brenner, lack the gene for creeping away from embarrassing situations in shame, never to return. When confronted with such a circumstance—the time I ran into Damon and Kristina at Nikki's and insisted on getting the name of her cosmetic dentist is a fine example—I am compelled to trudge forward with my mission in the face of despair. Goat-like, I place one cloven hoof before the other and slowly ascend through the clouds of grimness until I emerge at the summit, clutching my breast in triumph. I guess I am one of those people who thrive on adversity. Perhaps it is the Russian-Jewish pedigree (double dose of dour stubbornness if you ask me), or maybe the fact that my first formative film experience was a made-for-TV movie about a flight attendant who survives a plane crash in the Amazon jungle, only to have insects plant larvae in her back, which are plucked out with primitive scoops by unsmiling natives as she continues her trek down the snake-infested river that ultimately leads her to freedom. I don't really know.

What I do know is that Cora Slow Elk observed some curious things that week at the river. Things that pointed to the cover-up I'd suspected since the beginning.

And I was going to get to the bottom of it. But first, I was going to indulge in a full-tilt, no-holds-barred fantasy about the man I was in love with. Then I was going to strategize how to break up with my lover.

But before all that, I was going to take a shower.

Bernie's ass was white, droopy, and hairier than Tony Danza's head.

I tried to calculate how much ten years of therapy to treat post-traumatic stress disorder would cost me. I figured I'd be at least forty before I'd be able to handle car backfires without jumping under a bush, maybe fifty before I could move to a halfway house and get a job bussing tables at Burger King. The most I could really hope for out of life at this point was a gradual reintroduction to daily excursions under the watchful eye of qualified medical professionals. Nobody wants to see her boss's naked derriere, least of all if your boss is Bernie Zweben, and even less if you are off the clock.

I cleared my throat discreetly, and Bernie leaned back in his hospital bed.

Thankfully, he did not turn the other cheek.

"Brenner, good to see you! Did you bring what I asked for? I'm so hungry I'm about to chew my arm off. The nurses here are goddamn mean. Nasty bitches all. Won't give a man enough nutrients to feed a goddamn baby," he grumbled.

Bernie's the only guy I know who can utter "goddamn" and "baby" in one sentence with impunity.

I unpacked the backpack I'd stuffed with Harmony's barbecued baby back ribs, slaw, corn on the cob, and gravy-dunked rolls. Bernie's eyes lit up like a drag queen's in a stiletto shop. The boss man let me tie a bib around his neck before he tore into the spread.

Watching him feed, I thought I might need a few more years tacked on to that treatment plan. . . .

"So, what you got, Brenner? Anything new for your beat-up old boss?"

"I filed stories on the game against Billings High and the proposed development in the Bitterroot."

The game was a preseason football match against Meredith's high-school rival. Billings had obliterated the cocky Meredith team. I had spent the entire afternoon in a daze, lost in an elaborate fantasy that involved me, Bruce, and a jar of Nutella. This dream was punctuated by nightmares of me telling Steve I didn't think we were going to work out. When the whistle blew, I had to ask someone what the score was.

"What about the mill investigation?" he asked, gnawing on the corn.

I told him a hugely edited version of my meeting with Cora

Slow Elk. The way it sounded, I'd gotten up early, gone for a brisk morning run to clear my head, made it to the river by seven A.M., interviewed Slow Elk in a civilized location over coffee and crumpets, and driven home to organize my notes before taking an early bedtime.

As Val Kilmer's Ice Man put it so blithely to Tom Cruise's Maverick in that paean to military homoeroticism *Top Gun: Bull. Shit.*

But very believable bullshit.

"So, she actually saw someone come out to test the water?" he asked.

I nodded. "She went up to him and asked what was wrong, but he wouldn't give his name. Cora had the presence of mind to follow the guy out to the trailhead. The jerk was driving a mill-issue truck. Now, that in itself doesn't mean much, but the timing was highly probative. She said the first dead fish started earlier that week and just kept coming. Then the mill sends someone out to check pollutant levels. Then the fire at the corporate office. Then that e-mail and the warnings from my mole. It's loose, but weird, you know?" I finished.

"That shows some sort of premeditation, I suppose. You think they knew they were violating the standards?"

"Absolutely. I'm not sure exactly how it all works, or who's in on it"—an image of Melina Curran and Glen Whitehead in the hotel lobby popped into my head—"but I think there's not only noncompliance but some kind of cover-up going on. I mean, Bernie, have the cops given you any idea why the office was bombed? Have they?"

He shook his head slowly. Bernie had gotten off lucky if not scot-free, but a fractured arm and deep bruising couldn't be pleasant at any age, let alone his.

Bernie looked thoughtful. "Here's what I want you to do: Get in touch with Bruce Mortensen and find out how EPA is treating the case. Of course, he won't tell you everything, or maybe anything, but at least make sure you have that angle covered. Then get back in touch with that French scientist and see if she'll go on record with her expert opinion. I'll check with the lawyers, so they can vet the story for libelous claims. Can you have something by Wednesday?"

"Yep." And hopefully it won't be a social disease, I thought.

"Good job, Brenner. Tell you the truth, I wasn't sure you'd make it up here, city gal like yourself. But you're doing a fine job." Bernie stopped talking to grab another rib. "Gladys was in here yesterday. Brought me a book to pass the time. My two little career gals, living under one roof!" he rasped.

I decided I'd better clear out before I broke his other arm. To love Bernie is to want to hurt Bernie, you know?

The drive home from the hospital gave me time for considerable self-reflection.

You might be wondering why, if I was so in love with Bruce M., I had yet to do anything about it.

Good question, my doves.

The answer would be this: I was in savor mode. That's *savor* as in yum yum, not *saver* as in cheap. Now, I'm not the most patient person in the world, but even I am wont to understand that there's something about the calm before the connubial storm that is so perfect, so blissful, so on par with one's expectations—in a way that reality almost never is—that one should simply prolong it as long as possible. This is one of the primary differences between women in their twenties and women of a certain age, like me: In your youth, you are more inclined to run headlong into the wall of love, clutching a rose in your teeth, than to itemize the baggage each party is bringing to the table. Or revel in the *prospect* of a great love affair. But the period of revelation has a purpose beyond just fantasizing yourself into a state of mad lust or idealizing your first encounter with your man on the white steed. In your thirties, taking inventory is easy—it's deciding to wreak major damage on the precarious inner peace you have established that's so difficult. You've been around the block a few times, and you don't actually believe you're going to walk off into the sunset together without some major work. And I mean *work* the way Deepak Chopra means work, you know?

I know what my mom and my friends and anyone else with a proprietary interest in my business would say: Why is she kvetching about love when she's just found it? And what was that whole speech on opening the door to love all about? Why take all the spontaneity out of it before it's even begun? My answer: Because that's how you exorcise love demons, baby. You face up to your fears and hope that by doing so you'll earn the right to be happy. (I ain't my mother's daughter for nothing.) Mess with Texas, but for God's sake don't mess with karma.

So, in the interest of karma-building, I decided to take psychological inventory of our prospects. Here's what Bruce and I would be facing, if we gave it a go:

- Impending nasty divorce.

- Bitchy ex-wife.

- Gorgeous ex-wife (same, but I definitely get credit for two strikes here).

- Traumatized daughter who, when the bombs start dropping, is going to revert back to childlike behaviors in an understandable ploy to get her father's attention.

- Custody battle.

- Resentful ex-boyfriend with access to an army of non-shaving, tree-hugging maniacs.

- Career conflict of interest.

- Incompatible lifestyles (he likes crossbow hunting; I like cross boy hunting).

- That pesky fourteen-year age difference.

To be fair, a list of pros was also in order:

- Impending divorce.

- Bitchy ex-wife (all the better to lend new girlfriend the Halo of Sweetness*).

- No one over eighteen ever got arrested for sleeping with someone their uncle's age. Derided and ridiculed, yes; arrested, no.

- Animal attraction that threatened to leave both of us awash in a Sea of Lust** (stole that from one of my bodice-rippers).

- My mother wasn't around to say, "Over my dead body..."

Still lost in self-reflection—okay, self-absorption—I pulled the Subie up to the curb and hopped out. Gladys was in the yard tending her garden, which was almost frighteningly lush and green for autumn. Her well-loved plants tended to have a man-eating aspect that was either cartoonish or scary, depending on how you looked at it.

---

*The Halo of Sweetness is a phenomenon encountered only during the earliest days of a romance, in which the new love interest is imbued with all the fine qualities perceived to be lacking in the former love interest, who is demonized in direct proportion to the idealization of the new love interest. Get it?

**The Sea of Lust is a physical state characterized by an unexplained desire to listen to Christopher Cross songs, mild hearing impairment, "mentionitis"†, and a continually goofy grin. On rare occasions, the Sea of Lust can be fatal, resulting in the purchase and repeated playing of the twelve-inch single "I Will Always Love You" by Whitney Houston. Treatment consists of consummating the relationship between the patient and the object of lust and continued exposure to the object, whereby the patient develops immunity to the object's charms.

†The authors are indebted to the groundbreaking work done by Helen Fielding in this area. Dr. Fielding was the first to prove mentionitis's connection to the Sea of Lust.

"Jen, you had a couple of calls," she said, smearing dirt on her gardener's apron. "Steve Wald and Bruce Mortensen. Bruce asked that you call him right away. He said it was work-related."

I studied Gladys's face for a suspicious twinkle but didn't spot anything. Apparently, the idea of me, irresponsible, accident-prone, thirty-year-old Jen Brenner, getting it on with forty-four-year-old, paternal Bruce was too far-fetched for most people. Good. Very good.

I thanked her and went inside to get settled, grateful for the warm, clean home that always smelled like rosemary bread and potpourri. I spent the next half hour killing time by channel surfing through reality-television shows and laundering bras. (Ever notice how disgusting a bra can get under the arms?)

When I figured enough time had passed between Bruce's phone call and my (casual) reply, I picked up the phone, cracked open my PalmPilot, and dialed the number. Gone were the days when I'd hesitate on the last digit and end up redialing ten or twenty times before I had the courage to call. I guess turning thirty just sort of galvanized me, eh?

"Hello?"

"Hi, it's Jen. Brenner," I added at the last second, feeling foolish. Surely there's only one Jen in his life now? Or, at least, one Jen who falls conveniently in rivers so he can save her.

"Hi. Hang on a sec. I've got to go in another room."

In the background, I could hear television voices and possibly a dog.

"Okay, I'm back."

"Bruce, tell me you aren't watching *Love Doctors*. I'll have to hang up right now. . . ."

"No, no. I've got Em tonight, and she's kind of addicted to it."

"Yeah, right."

"Listen, Brenner, you're making me sorry I marched into that river to save your butt. That water was damn cold. I'm not thirty anymore, you know."

Did he have to remind me?

"Okay, okay. So, you called because . . . ?"

"I want to invite you to dinner. Em and I are having a barbecue tomorrow night, and I thought you might . . . maybe want to join us." He sounded unsure. Somehow, the absence of the delectable bravado he had displayed the other day was even more delectable.

"I'd love to come over for dinner," I said, relishing the words. "Bruce, I usually don't mix work and play, but I have to interview you about the case. Is that something we can do?"

He sighed.

"Why don't you meet me at my office tomorrow afternoon and we'll talk shop. Then I'll drive us back to my place. I can swing you home afterward."

If I made it home, we were no doubt both thinking. Could I hide a change of clothes in my purse? A catsuit, perhaps?

"Sounds good."

"Okay, I'll see you tomorrow, then?"

"Yep. See you tomorrow."

I hung up. There, done. I had a date with Bruce Mortensen. There was only one question now: What in God's name does a woman wear when you want whatever it is to be summarily ripped off your body?

bent halo

To: Els_Janssen@ucsf.edu
From: Benjamin Brenner
Subject:

Els, I can't stop thinking about you. It's been 135 hours since we got on our separate planes, and every one has been hell. Well, maybe not hell, but some pale approximation of it. I know I'm not supposed to say things like that, but, well, fuck it. I'm 34 years old and that's how I feel. I have one, no, two questions for you: When are you coming to Miami? and How do you feel about a fourth doctor in the house for a weekend?

Ben

Tuesday morning dawned grim and overcast.

I wanted to call it "tornado weather" or some other exotic descriptor, but that would have been inaccurate: It was simply gray and dull, like an old overcoat with a raw spot in the seat.

I thought it was beautiful.

My plan was to go to the office for a few hours, file a story on the Meredith Children's Theater stage production of *Willy*

Wonka and the Chocolate Factory, grab a quick lunch, and beautify for my meeting with Bruce.

Also, it would be nice to have sex again. In this century.

A thought: with which one?

Another thought: oh, God, am slattern.

Still: I. Had. Sex.

So: why do I feel so confused?

All I know is, my blood feels like it's humming in my veins at sail-snapping speed, and everything—sky, clouds, Gladys's barrel-bellied neighbor pruning the hedge—is glowing like a string of Christmas tree bulbs dipped in plutonium. The grin that's been tugging at my mouth since my eyes fluttered open this morning wouldn't depart my face if I was just told I had three days to live—locked up in a veal pen with Rush Limbaugh. While brushing my teeth, I even caught myself clicking my heels together à la Fred Astaire. (Okay, Fred Astaire wearing lead shoes and a balconette bra.)

In the midst of all this blissful glee—yes, I think that's the most accurate description—are two more familiar emotions jockeying for position: fear and guilt. Fear because there's a little voice in my head telling me not to mess this up. And guilt because I feel so good, I almost don't care what happens next.

Here's what the inside of my brain looks like at the moment: Steve and Bruce. Bruce and Steve. Jen and Steve. Jen and Bruce. Bruce. Ben & Jerry's. Bruce. Bruce shirtless with a pint of Ben & Jerry's. Bruce. Jen and Steve and Bruce. Jen and Steve and Bruce shipwrecked on a black-sand beach in Moorea with an extra-large bottle of baby oil and a year's supply of Ben & Jerry's and no shirts (such is the irrepressibly optimistic nature of female sexuality).

In between bouts of giddiness, I'm paralyzed with—naturally—indecision and self-doubt.

You see, fantasy life to the contrary, I'm really a one-man girl at heart. Polyamory, I've found, is all well and good in theory, but the whole remember-where-you-left-your-panties-while-you-ask-your-girlfriend-to-lie-about-your-whereabouts-for-you thing leaves me a bit depleted. Plus, I suck at it. Plus, it just doesn't jibe with my (admittedly idealistic) view of love. I'd like to believe there *is* something fated and magical about love, that we are drawn by pheromonal force to certain others who possess the exact chemical composition that will neutralize our own petty antagonisms, our unique brand of self-loathing, our hidden addiction to Harlequin romances featuring heroes with small brains and big estates. I'm not really a fatalist, but sometimes, nestled under the down comforter in the dark of night, I allow myself to dream of a world where predetermined meaning rules the day. Where sleeping with the wrong man at the right time is nothing more than a moral misdemeanor, a necessary detour on the path to true love. Where the warm, wet embrace of strong arms bearing you out of a raging river and the steady thrum of a heartbeat against your own is all you really need to know. Where deciding between the Steves and Bruces of the world is as easy as ordering à la mode on your apple pie.

A consultation with my Celtic rabbi was clearly needed.

I punched in Robert's number in San Francisco.

"Hello?"

"Hi, Ma Kettle."

"Auntie Jen!"

"Are you busy?" I asked, expecting Zoë's wrenching screams to hurtle down the line and skewer my eardrums at any moment.

"No, I've just put ZoZo down for a nap. And George is at work, so it's just me and you and Oprah, kid. What's up?"

I gave him the unabridged version of my weekend: the drive, the swim, the, uh, ride.

"Jorge," Robert shrieked, elongating it into "Whorrrre-haaayy," our code for ladies and men of a certain ill repute. Ladies like me.

"Total Jorge," I agreed. "But now I'm trying to avert disaster by bowing at the altar of your superior wisdom."

"Smart move, my child. I'm going to ask you a series of questions that will reveal the one true path."

"Oh, good." I fluffed up my mound of pillows and assumed

the requisite 45-degree therapy position. "Should I tell you about the sex now?"

"Forget the sex. That's just an oil change. What about the kissing?"

"What do you mean?"

"I mean, how do you feel when Steve kisses you?"

I revisited the tent. "Um . . . good?"

"Fireworks exploding while you down a glass of Veuve Cliquot Gold Label with Brad Pitt on his 150-foot yacht in the Bahamas good, or scratching a mosquito bite good?"

"Scratching a mosquito bite," I said quickly. "Is that bad?"

"Patience, my child. Now, what is kissing Bruce like?"

I closed my eyes. Instead of remembering Bruce's lips on mine, I conjured the moment his palm cracked against my cheek, the tender apology in his fingertips afterward as they stroked my burning face, and the almost nauseous happiness that flooded me anytime I was in proximity of him.

"Oh my God," I managed to croak.

"I thought so." Robert sounded smug.

"What?"

"You're in love with Grandpa Wrangler."

"I'll admit there's a small physical attraction," I stammered.

He snorted. "You've got it bad."

"I'm sure it's just the, you know, circumstances. I mean, you could put anyone in jeans and boots and give him a big gun and a sexy job and he'd be—"

"Jen, please shut up."

"Steve's such a great guy! We have great conversations! I mean, when he's not talking about the mating habits of the spotted owl or fecal compost, then they're great—"

"Jen—"

"Did I tell you his brother's a rabbi?" I continued, my voice rising. "And he wants kids. And he has blue eyes. And apparently his cousin went to Harvard Law at the same time as Ben's college roommate Rohan—"

"Whoa! Time out. Just hush for a minute and listen to me, okay? You don't have to sell me—or, more importantly, yourself—on Mr. Green Machine. There's nothing wrong with Steve Wald. Except one thing. You're not falling in love with him. You're falling in love with Bruce Mortensen."

"In love . . ." I repeated.

"You know, that state where everything seems just a little brighter than normal, where the angels sing and pigs fly and you can't stop grinning like an idiot and you suddenly find yourself whirling around like Ginger Rogers."

"Fred, actually," I said faintly.

Robert harrumphed.

"You know what has to be done, right?" he said.

I grunted.

"You must inform the Spotted Owl Avenger of your feelings as soon as possible," Robert said rather primly.

"But it's not like we even discussed anything! For all I know he's wishing it hadn't even happened."

Disapproving silence.

"So, I guess I need to talk to him, huh?"

"Hmm."

"But what do I say? I don't want to slay him. This is a small town. I'm not saying we'll be able to be friends, but I certainly don't want to be watching out for him everywhere I go," I said.

"Tell him the truth. That after a night of passion, you have decided to seek satisfaction elsewhere, and if he wants to find you, you'll be at the geriatric ward administering mouth-to-mouth."

"Robert! Come on . . . I know—I'll tell him I've developed a rose allergy!" I snorted.

"Say you hate nature . . ."

"No, that he's not Jewish enough . . ."

"Too Jewish . . ."

"Too much like my father . . ."

"Not enough like your father . . ."

Our conversations always degenerate this way. It is such a

comfort to have someone with whom I can face life's challenges head-on, with potty-mouth humor and sophomoric behavior.

"So, what you're saying is I have to have the Breakup Conversation," I said.

"I'm afraid so."

"But I don't break up. That just isn't what I do," I said plaintively to Robert.

"Yeah, I know. You like to wait until the governor's been called out to declare your relationship a disaster area that deserves federal funding. But this time's different. What can I tell you?"

"Any tips from the maestro?" I asked.

"Don't grovel. Don't backpedal. Don't explain. Don't apologize. And whatever you do, don't sleep with him."

Duh.

"Robert?"

"Yeah?"

"What if I'm ... you know ... wrong?"

"About you and Bruce?"

"Uh-huh."

"Then you'll spend the rest of your days knitting purple and orange afghans in your cat-infested studio and wishing a variety of hideous illnesses upon my person."

Terrific. Now, why do I feel like I'm about to fuck up my life? Again.

When I got to the office, the first person I saw was Dave Lefebvre.

He'd had the grace to be embarrassed by his attempt to wrest my story from me, and I was gracious in the face of his defeat. Actually, I knew it wasn't personal, and I kind of liked the guy, but I figured a little hard time was in order before absolution was handed down.

Yeah, Jen, and you're the Queen of England.

Dave smiled at me tentatively over his monitor, and I extended the olive branch.

"How's that story on the foster homes going?" I asked. Dave was doing some nice long-term coverage of an alternative foster care system to the state system that had been founded in Missoula. They were having success where the state had had none, and the neglected kids of Montana were the better for it.

"Oh, good. Thanks for asking. How about that mill thing?"

I rolled my eyes. "It's like you said—hell trying to prove anything." I paused. "Actually, if you want to get involved, there is something you can do for me. Only if you want to, I mean."

"Sure thing. What's up?"

"I haven't had time, but I thought I'd follow up with this e-mail address with the Internet Service Provider"—I showed him a Post-it with the "secret friend's" handle—"and see if I can swindle them into telling me who it is."

He took the sticky paper and nodded.

"Sure, I'll be glad to."

"Thanks."

I turned to walk away, but he called me back.

"Hey, Jen?"

"Yeah?"

"Sorry about the other day. I was just hot for the story, you know?"

"Sure." I can *do* magnanimous.

Pleased, I sat down at my desk and booted up my computer.

My in-box had a few messages. Mom telling me she had gone ahead and booked a ticket for me to come home for Christmas (aargh), Karen with the news that my nephew, Tomer, had won a spot on the soccer team, and Katie delivering two nuggets: she'd cut her hair in a modified shaghawk, whatever that was, and she'd seen Damon and Kristina having a fight—ooh, this was good— outside of Bimbo's. I scanned for succulent details: Apparently, they'd come outside already arguing, and Damon said something to Ye Skinny Blond One that prompted her to bitch-slap him with her Coach purse. Damn! I shook my head in disgust. City people.

Work occupied me for the next few hours. I took a break to call Steve and arrange the dreaded lunch.

He sounded painfully chipper.

"Hi! Where were you last night? I called," he said.

I palpitated my heart to see if this information produced the desirable reaction: pleased flutteriness.

Nothing.

"Oh, out and about," I said. "Steve, are you free for lunch today?"

"Yeah, sure. How about noon at the park? We can picnic."

I tried to factor in the children at the playground if the conversation got ugly, and decided it was a good risk. Hell, they'll hear worse from their parents. Better to prepare them for the harsh realities of love now, while they're still malleable and covered under their parents' mental health insurance plans.

We arranged the meeting, and I felt a slight jolt of depression mar my otherwise pristine state of suspended animation.

Work went on uninterrupted for a couple of hours. At 11:14 A.M., I got another e-mail from the secret friend.

"Dave, check this out," I called.

He came over and we read together:

To: jen.brenner@meredithgazette.com
From: secret_friend@hotmail.com
Subject: what are you waiting for?

While you're out entertaining your city friends, they're getting away with it! You seem smart, so figure it out: who's sneaking around town with something to hide?

;-0

I felt my face redden. It's one thing to have your work performance criticized by, oh, a real person, like your boss. It's another thing entirely to find yourself lambasted by some freak who could potentially—if I'm reading this right—be a bona fide stalker. And that little emoticon at the end—*so* 90s.

"What do you think?" I asked Dave.

"I think it's going to be hard to make Microsoft cough up a user's identity—if it's even a real one. They own Hotmail, don't they?"

"Yeah." I pondered the messenger's advice for a moment. "Dave, if you wanted to find out who's sneaking around, who would you ask?"

He grinned. "Oh, that's easy. The McIntyres, Penelope and Princeton. Penny's been the source to go to for gossip for going on thirty-five years. And her brother, Prince, is no slouch either. Fussy guy. Kind of, you know, fey. They live in that Victorian over on the square. They inherited, so neither one's had to work really, and they make it their business to know what's going on. Kind of eccentric people, but good-hearted. Want me to set it up for you?"

"Yes," I said enthusiastically. I had visions of a latter-day Addams Family, with Morticia and Uncle Fester canoodling creepily around the house. Not to be missed.

I told him I could meet with them tomorrow afternoon, and he went off to arrange it. Nice guy, that Dave.

Then I left for my next appointment: the Breakup Conversation.

By the time I got to Bruce's office, I felt like the world's biggest heel (three-inch platform, not spike—more surface area with which to crush innocent victims).

The Breakup Conversation had not gone exactly as I had hoped.

First of all, Steve brought a friend with him to the park. I could have killed him, but since I was there to let him down gently that seemed a bit counterproductive.

Second, he introduced me to the friend as "his girlfriend." Now, where I come from, one would never use the G—or corresponding B—word without serious discussion. It's presumptuous as hell, and dangerous besides. One premature utterance in that vein and you might destroy a perfectly good relationship. First, the subject must be broached by one party after a great deal of plotting and careful consideration of timing. Nine times out of ten, the bomb is dropped after sex. Why not? You're naked, they're naked, and presumably everyone is happy and open to challenging new concepts, like having a boyfriend with a capital *B,* ordering pizza with anchovies, or trying out that two-pronged dildo somebody gave you as a gag gift. This usually involves the braver—or more invested—party letting it slip out in a jokey, fake-casual tone while punching his or her beloved lightly in the arm, as in, "So does that mean I'm your *girlfriend?*" If the overture is not met with outright horror—characterized by dilated pupils, an immediate stiffening of the limbs akin to rigor mortis, and the rapid donning of discarded garments within reach of the bed— then the process can move forward to step two. In step two, you define your terms, outline liabilities, and slip in force majeure clauses (those trusty bits of boilerplate legalese that promise no responsibility whatsoever on the part of the service provider in the event of everyday disasters like earthquakes, monsoons, pandemics, and bad haircuts).

Third, and, believe me, I'm deeply ashamed of this, I sort of told him the truth.

I know, it's disgusting. Telling the truth is an absolutely incomprehensible breach of relationship etiquette and accepted social norms. There are some who would have you believe that truthsaying is next to godliness, that you can't go wrong ethically by just telling it like it is in matters of the heart. These are the same nitwits who have their VCRs programmed to record *Touched by an Angel.* In reality, truth is a luxury we can't always afford. I mean, telling Steve that I really liked him but I had to curtail our dalliance because I had a hard-on for a not-yet-divorced EPA agent fourteen years my senior was not going to win me any friends. Having committed this heinous act, I am officially a freak, consigned, like Roman Polanski and Marv Albert before me, to the bitter reaches of the sociomoral stratosphere.

Fourth, I almost reneged on the whole thing when Steve ran his finger along the nape of my neck. Say it with me, kids: S-L-A-T-T-E-R-N.

When I got to the park, I spotted Steve at a picnic table over by the swing set. Kids of all ages and Ritalin dosages zigzagged across the freshly cut grass like meteors, colliding with one another and the occasional steaming pile of dog poop.

Sitting with Steve was a woman I would have pegged as his type in a heartbeat. She had long, blondish dreadlocks, a dozen silver spoon rings, and the tan, fatless body of an unemployed vegan. Beneath her purple Guatemalan skirt, dirty bare toes peeked out.

If I wasn't trying to curry favor with the love gods and earn some divine guidance for the next thirty minutes, I would have loathed her on sight.

"Hi, I'm Luna," she said, smiling hugely, revealing one charmingly crooked front tooth. "I was just telling Steve how cool it is that you're from San Francisco. I'm from Santa Cruz!" she chirped, as if being from a plot of land that contained almost seven million souls inspired intimacy.

Steve pecked me on the cheek. I tried to send him warning messages with my eyes, but if he picked up the signals, he didn't say.

He unrolled our spread, which consisted of organic water (!), gluten-free bread, lentil stew, and some cookies the texture of wooden planks. We chowed down while Luna entertained us with stories of her trip to Tibet ("supercool") and the latest in clothes-free hiking ("great, but only go when it's warm").

Finally, when I thought that the pressure inside me was nearing explosive proportions, Luna announced an impending Capoeira class, hugged us both to her bony bosom, and disappeared.

"She's nice," I said, trying not to grimace.

Steve raised his eyebrows. "Oh, come on. You were making faces at everything she said."

"Well, you like her, and that's what's important."

We munched in silence. I tried to figure out how to segue into the Breakup Conversation. What had Robert advised? Something about not apologizing and not having sex with Steve? Finally, I just put down my cookie and jumped in.

Looking back on my approach now, it seems incredibly ham-fisted. But, then, I would hardly call myself a breakup expert. What transpired went something like this:

Me: "Hi." (Smile.)

Him: "Hi." (Smile. Lean over. Kiss. Scratching mosquito bite feeling.)

Me: "So."

Him: (Tuck a lock of my hair behind my ear. Stroke my neck. Smile.)

Me: "Steve?" (Instant snapshot of us getting married in Temple Bat Something-or-other with parents looking on, eight sets of eyes glistening in proud wonder as my ivory duchess satin gown floats around my waspish(!) waist. Begin choking on lump of lentils . . .)

Him: "Yeah?"

Me: "I really like you." (Watery junior-high cheerleader smile to go with vapid dialogue. Swallow lentils.)

Him: (Smile.)

Me: "But I don't think I'm ready to get involved in a long-term relationship."

Him: (Frown. Kind of sexy, in fact. Oh, shit . . .)

Me: "I know this sounds trite—God knows I've had it said to me enough times—but it really has more to do with me than anything you did or didn't do." (Tentative smile.)

Him: "Look, Jen, I really like you too, and I would never push you into something you didn't want." (Smile. Aaah! Why does he have to be so reasonable? Snapshot of our two beautiful corkscrew-haired children, both eminently reasonable like their father...)

Me: "So, you're okay with this?"

Him: "Well, I'm disappointed, sure. But it's not like you're dumping me for some shmo. I figure we'll work it out eventually." (Smile. Fleck of black bean skin on lateral incisor reduces sexiness factor a notch.)

Me: "Well, actually..."

Him: (Frown. Not sexy. Mad?)

Me: "Okay! So I'm in love with Bruce Mortensen! Sue me! I was in friggin' denial about it when I slept with you last weekend, but now I know, and, yes, I can't wait to go over to his house tonight and screw him till the cows come home. In fact, I've already reserved us adjoining beds at the hospital because I anticipate us needing medical care after I get through with him... and, yes, I know I'm a complete imbecile who wouldn't know good boyfriend material if it crawled into bed with me, and we would have looked fantastic under the *huppah* at Temple Bat Something-or-other so don't bother to remind me!"

Actually, that last bit is a gross exaggeration, but does capture the tenor of my ineptitude. He *did* gaze at me with the sort of pity generally reserved for deluded serial monogamists and the institutionalized, and I *did* confess to the reduced crime of wanting to "see" other men. Eventually, I ceased my babbling, Steve stood up, and, with great dignity, told me to get out of his life, get some therapy, and a few other things I won't repeat here. Then he stomped off across the grass, leaving the remains of our lunch crumpled on the table. (He must have been really upset if he'd willfully litter.) I sat there for fifteen minutes, trembling with self-reproach, relief, doubt, and, yes, a skein of anticipation at seeing Bruce again.

Now, at Bruce's office, I just felt exhausted.

He was on the phone when I arrived, but he motioned me to come in, so I sat down and checked out the office. Still the same institutional ambience, but the family photo had been replaced

with one of Emily kneeling beside a soccer ball. I noticed a teetering pile of packing boxes in the corner and wondered if they
were evidence that Bruce had moved out of the family digs.

"Sorry about that."

Bruce stood in front of me, a smile creasing his face. It had
been only a few days since I'd last seen him, but, oh, what a difference a day makes, especially when the object of your affection's parting words were "I missed you." Barely a second had
gone by without his visage interrupting my thoughts. To see him
in the flesh, with the tension between us acknowledged but, as of
yet, unconsummated, was as exciting as the prospect of jumping
out of an airplane at ten thousand feet after having been told a
treasure awaited you at the bottom.

Today Bruce had on worn, well-fitting jeans, boots, and a
simple slate-colored shirt that brought out his black, slashing
brows and speckled sideburns. The bridge of his nose and his
cheeks were bronzed, as if he had spent an hour too long in
the sun.

"Did you have lunch?" he asked.

"Yes, but I could use a drink."

"Iced tea? Coffee?"

"Tea would be great," I said, wishing for a double gin and
tonic. Even discussing banalities, my insides fluttered.

He brought me a mint tea with a slice of lemon in it, and we
sat down at the coffee/conference table. Something poked me in
the ass, and I shifted uncomfortably.

"Sorry about the seats. Your tax dollars at work," Bruce said.

"For all I know, you guys have one of those golden toilets in
back," I answered, and Bruce laughed.

"So, where do we stand with the investigation of Sutter &
McEvoy?" I continued, launching into it. Might as well get it over
with; dinner was waiting.

Bruce filled me in on the details that were available to the
public, which were few. A case had been filed, which I already
knew. But it would be a few weeks before all the evidence was in.

Subpoenas had been issued and served and document access provided, though judging by the state of the shredded papers we'd found after the fire, who's to say whether they'd given up any incriminating information.

"Are you in trouble for letting me and Dr. Renard see the shredded papers?" I asked. It was something that had been bothering me. It felt almost as if I'd taken advantage of him in a moment of weakness—give it up or I'll straddle you to death. Ha, ha.

He shrugged. "Probably. I haven't hidden anything. And that was a fuck-up. I wasn't thinking straight, you know. I'd just moved out of the house, Emmy was crying herself to sleep every night, and Melina had filed for sole custody, so I was looking at a divorce and a lawsuit and God knows what else. The fact that I am investigating a company in which my former father-in-law is a partner should have forced my removal from the case by now, and would have if there was anyone even remotely qualified available to replace me. My mind certainly wasn't on work, it's true. Plus, I was distracted by a certain curly-haired reporter who was driving me nuts." He smiled and stretched, folding his arms behind his head, which thrust his muscular arms into bold relief.

Ay, caramba.

"So, what are your next steps?" I asked, pretending curiosity while I studied the curve of his full lower lip.

"We'll determine cause and build a case, charge those responsible—at least those we can make a case against."

"Do you feel there's a motive?"

"You mean beyond just avoiding expensive equipment upgrades?" he said.

I thought about the secret friend's admonition to look at who was sneaking around, and my informant's obvious fear. "Yeah, I guess I'm thinking, what if the motivator was funneling the funds earmarked for upgrades to something else? How hard is it to trace where it may have gone? Like, who at the mill is living above his means, or something."

He looked pensive. "We always follow the money, if that's

what you're asking. It's the surest way in law enforcement to prove motive. I can only speak generally about that, you realize. I can't tell you more than that."

"Understood." I couldn't help thinking of Melina Curran and Glen Whitehead, and wondering if Bruce knew about their affair and how long it had been going on.

"Bruce, is Melina involved in her father's business?" I asked tentatively.

"Absolutely not," he scoffed. "She always said the mill was what kept the Currans yoked to this cow town. She was happy enough spending Daddy's money, of course, but actually contributing? Forget it."

"Well, that's all I have," I said.

"Let me just wrap up a few things and we'll get out of here. Em should already be at the house. Melina was going to drop her off around four P.M."

He glanced at his watch. "Is there any way you can run by the store and get some wine? Something red? We're having steaks."

I said sure and grabbed my purse to head for the door.

"Hey," he called softly. "Come here."

I felt myself moving slowly toward Bruce as if he were reeling me in on a fishing line. The top of my head came up to the little crevice between his collarbones.

He put his hands on my shoulders and stroked me lightly. Electric sparks shot from my heels to my belly and up to my neck.

"It's really, really good to see you, Jen," he said.

His kiss, when it came, was warm and tasted of caramel and coffee.

Emily hated me.

That was obvious as soon as Bruce and I arrived at his house, which was a gorgeous tree-houselike structure tucked into the woods west of town.

She'd been sweet when I was introduced to her as the new

reporter in town; now that I was invited to the house as a "friend" of Dad's, I was public enemy number one, and she wasn't about to let me forget it.

"Hi, Dad!" she cried when she opened the door. She threw her twiggy arms around his neck and nearly launched herself into his arms. I was left standing on the deck feeling like an idiot, with a bottle of merlot and Cougar the mangy tomcat as my companions.

"Hey, kiddo, take it easy on your old dad," Bruce said, easing her down gently. "You remember Jen, right?"

Perhaps sensing my reluctance, Bruce placed his hand on my back and pushed. I stumbled into the entryway with less grace than a newborn colt. Emily narrowed her doe eyes and extended her hand coldly.

"Sure, I remember you," she said, with the enthusiasm of a dental patient in for a root canal.

"Daddy, Mom said I could have a puppy at her house. Did I tell you that?" she said excitedly as we entered the kitchen.

"No, you didn't, hon. But what's Bugle going to say to that?" Bugle was Bruce's bluetick hound.

"Bugle won't mind. As long as I scratch him under the ears three times a week."

She was actually kind of cute, in a *Lord of the Rings,* hobbity creature kind of way.

Bruce glanced at me, and what I saw there warmed me to the core: *Thank you. I know you're being put through the wringer,* the look said.

He knelt beside Emily, whose red waves were tucked into a sweeping ponytail, and placed his big hands on her shoulders.

"Em, can you do me a big favor and set the table out on the deck? And turn the outside heat lamp on, will you? I'd ask Jen, but you know how to do it better," he said.

God, was he good.

Emily's little mind was obviously working overtime, calculating the pros and cons of cooperation. In the end, she decided to draw more flies with honey, and she kissed Bruce on the nose and ran outside to fulfill the instructions.

"God, is this going to be rough." Bruce sounded weary.

Tentatively, I came up behind him and inched my arms around his waist. My face fit comfortably against his shoulder blades. Bruce swiveled in my arms and held my upturned face in his hands.

"You're beautiful. You have the most amazing mouth," he said, apropos of nothing—and everything.

Good. No need for Botox yet.

I stroked his face. It felt so . . . exotic. To be able to touch him without freaking out or wondering what was going to happen next.

"It's bound to be brutal for her now. She's already lost something that can't be replaced in her family home, and she's understandably frightened of losing more," I said sagely. And I did feel empathy for the little minx—when I didn't want to smack her.

He leaned in to kiss me, his dark eyes resonating with a cocktail of affection and lust.

Suddenly, we heard a tapping.

Emily stood there, holding a stack of plates.

"Do you want the regular ones or the special ones?" she said, eyeing me like I was the devil incarnate.

"Oh, I think regular," Bruce answered lightly.

Emily whirled around and disappeared outside. We glanced at each other.

"They say it's better for the kids in the long run to not see their parents fighting," I offered, feeling helpless. "So many of my friends' parents divorced, and they all say things were actually better after the separation. It just takes time."

"Yeah, I know. It just feels incomprehensible that the exact thing I need to recover and get back to living again is the thing that's going to hurt her the most right now. It's like our interests are diametrically opposed, and that's never happened before."

Bruce uncorked the merlot and poured us each a glass, plus a third for Emily filled with grape juice.

"Grab that, hon, and I'll give you a tour of the house. We're just having steaks and potatoes and I made the salad earlier, so I just have to start up the grill."

On the way to the stairs, Bruce stopped to put some jazz on the CD player, and Nina Simone's throaty timbre filled the room. The redwood home had an airy yet solid feel to it, all exposed beams and vast, rectangular south-facing windows.

"Did you and Melina live here together?" I asked. It was hard to imagine them here; the place was so essentially Bruce. Besides, I didn't relish the idea of sleeping with him in what was essentially their honeymoon suite.

"Actually, no. This was my bachelor pad before we got married, and I hung on to it. We rented it out most of the time. Sometimes it stayed empty, which suited me fine."

I followed him up the staircase, and the unreality of the situation sunk in: Here I was insinuating my way into the life of a recently separated man with a traumatized daughter and probably other problems I knew nothing about. I had just slept with somebody else for the first time in two years, and broken up with him to boot. On the other hand, I firmly believed the maxim that the body doesn't lie. And my body had been telling me—nay, *ordering* me—to go to Bruce Mortensen since the day we met. I was tired of thinking with my head. Let the ovaries rule the day!

"This is my favorite room," Bruce said.

He led me into an attic so open and artfully constructed that it could have been a bird's nest. The bilevel space fanned out around a wood-burning stove, and windows encircled the center almost 360 degrees around. Hardwood floors were warmed by thick furry rugs, and wind chimes tinkled in the breeze. We were high enough to look out directly into the tree branches.

"I can see why. It's wonderful. If I lived here, I'd never be able to leave."

We stood quietly for a moment, drinking in the piney autumn perfume and taking occasional sips of wine. Bruce's right arm lay loosely on my shoulders, his fingers burrowing in the tangled curls at my nape. Later, I thought, please let him kiss me right where he's touching now.

"We'd better get dinner on. And make sure Emmy hasn't burned the house down," he said.

"Or stuck pins in a voodoo doll that looks like me," I said cattily.

He just laughed.

"I could say something inane about how she'll love you when she gets to know you. But since I barely know you myself, that would be kind of specious, wouldn't it?" he said, stroking my hair back from my face to soften the words. "She's awfully stubborn, is my Em. Kind of like you, actually. And like my ex-wife. I seem to have a habit of falling for women who are going to drive me nuts. What did the therapist call it? Self-sabotaging, I think it was."

"What therapist?" I asked quickly, before I could stop myself.

Bruce smiled. "The one I've been seeing for homicidal urges and my unhealthy attraction to long-haired goats, Jen. C'mon," he chided, seeing the expression on my face. "No therapist right now. But Melina and I gave it a shot until we knew it wasn't going to work for us. That was about a year ago."

I couldn't decide whether to be pleased or disappointed. Where I come from, therapy's like mother's milk: wholesome and natural and absolutely necessary for survival.

When we got downstairs, we found Emily lying in front of the PlayStation jockeying Mortal Kombat, Bugle snuggled by her side. I wanted to connect with her but knew that trying too hard would be the kiss of death. Bruce went off to start the barbecue, and I perched on the couch and took a nice long pull of merlot.

"What are you studying in school right now, Emily?" I asked.

"Oh, stuff," she answered without turning her head.

"Interesting stuff or boring stuff?" I tried again.

"Boring stuff."

Ouch.

"Where I grew up, in Florida, they had a special program where kids could go out to the Keys—those are a string of islands that run along the coast there—and study the marine life. It was pretty cool. I thought I might be a marine biologist someday, but I became a reporter instead."

Emily leaned into the joystick and blew the head off some creature. Something purple oozed out of his neck.

"It seems like you're interested in animals. Maybe you'll be a vet someday," I said.

She stopped playing and turned around. Her expressive eyes brimmed with rage and tears.

"You don't have to be nice to me. It doesn't matter. He'll like you anyway. My mom says you're just Jell-O bait anyway, so why don't you just leave me and Bugle alone!"

She got up and flung herself out of the room, yanking the PlayStation cord out of the machine on her way out.

Bugle stretched obliviously on the sisal rug.

If this performance was a sign of my maternal proclivities, I'd better not miss a pill.

Dinner would have been an awkward affair, if it weren't for Bruce's impressive ability to maintain two totally separate conversations at the same time. Somehow he managed to get food on the table, indulge Emily—who emerged from her room sniffling but otherwise under control—by milking her for details about her school day, and throw me an occasional bone. I'd seen capable Bruce, and stern Bruce, and even silly, funny Bruce, but this was a new side—smooth, effervescent Bruce, who was able to deliver perfectly tender medium-rare steaks and leap tall silences in a single bound.

Finally, we finished eating. I figured he'd want to drive me home soon, and was surprised when a car pulled up outside and he told Emily to go upstairs and get her bag.

"Where's she going?" I asked, all innocence.

"She's spending the night at her friend Toni's. Prearranged with Melina. That's Fran Reilly outside now."

Outside, I could see a tall woman with frizzy blond hair swatting at animals and children in the backseat of her SUV. She held a cell phone to her ear like it was a lifesaver. Bruce waved at her and motioned toward the upstairs, where Emily was getting ready, and Mrs. Reilly nodded and waved back. I felt she may have been craning her neck to get a look at me, but couldn't be sure. I was sure she'd get an earful later from Emily via Toni and that I'd be lucky to come out an ounce under three hundred pounds, with bad skin, messy hair, and warts on my nose.

Emily came down a few minutes later. She pointedly ignored me and stood in front of Bruce, who enfolded her in a gigantic bear hug.

"Who's my muffin?" he said, touching his nose to hers in what was obviously a much-loved ritual between them.

"I am."

"What are you?"

"Your muffin." Her voice was muffled in his tan neck.

He kissed her cheek.

"I love you, sweetheart."

"I love you, Daddy," she said.

Me too, I wanted to say.

"Bye," she called.

"Aren't you forgetting something?" Bruce asked.

"Oh, yeah. Bye, Bugle!"

"Something else."

Emily examined me, much as one would a particularly gruesome insect in a petri dish.

"Bye," she said grudgingly. I hoped Bruce wouldn't demand more. I thought if he tried to make her hug me she'd sink her teeth into my jugular or something. Thankfully, he didn't, just swatted her in the fanny as she ran out the door.

"Have fun at school tomorrow," he shouted, but she was already in the car.

Bruce closed the door. The house seemed suddenly smaller and warmer.

He turned to me and faux-collapsed in my arms, knocking me against a telephone stand.

"God, why can't you just send them somewhere until they're twenty-one and college-educated?"

"You can. It's called military school. I've got the number in my purse," I said.

He rolled his eyes and took my hand, sweeping me into a waltz stance. I considered pointing out that waltzing wasn't part of Generation X's social education, but then Nina kicked into something bluesy and deep, a black river of a song with a torturous longing running through it like a swift current. I closed my eyes and let Bruce fold me into his arms. We rocked slowly, getting comfortable with the feel of each other's body, the taste and smell of the other's breath. We fit very neatly together, every bent knee and elbow finding a corresponding valley in the other in which to nestle.

We swayed this way for five or so minutes as the sun sank beyond the western mountains. The song ended on a long, shuddering sigh. Bruce held me tightly against his length and gazed intently into my face.

"Why does this feel crazy sometimes and just right other times?" he said.

"Because your dementia is sporadic?"

Oops, relying on defensive humor again.

He put on a stern face.

"Ah, the little joker. You're going to have to be punished for that, Brenner. What punishment fits the crime? Perhaps a feather run lightly against the underside of your foot, hmm? No, maybe I'll tie you up and lay an ice cube on your stomach. Oh, I know—tickles. You are going to have to be tickled, my friend. Agonizing tickles in all your good spots, which I will ruthlessly learn . . . now!"

I let him get the jump on me, having been distracted by his decidedly kinky ideas. Bondage, ice cubes, and feathers? There was clearly more to this man than met the harness.

Bruce leapt on me like a cat and wrestled me to the ground,

which wasn't hard because I was tipsy with lust and, yes, fear. Lust that licked at my insides like a wildfire. Fear that I wouldn't remember every luminous moment of this night when, later, reality intruded and the magic inevitably hardened into banality, rejection, or a combination of the two.

Our mouths met roughly, teeth gnashed, sloppy and even a bit brutal. It was nothing like last time, when each kiss had dissolved into the next as Patsy Cline urged us toward a sweet conclusion. I yelped as Bruce bit into my bottom lip. I could feel him rise under his jeans, and a small burst of panic coursed through me. Bruce sat up on his knees and in one motion stripped off his shirt. His torso was thick and muscular, furred with a medium-thick thatch of hair. I nearly died when he popped the top buttons of his pants, exposing the silken arrow that ran between his belly button and his crotch. He leaned over me and rubbed his knuckles against my cheek.

"Are you okay with this? You seem, I don't know, reluctant."

I tried to think. One of the huge benefits of growing up in the postfeminist age was that men and women of a certain ilk actually considered this a legitimate question. I certainly felt entitled to the right of refusal.

"I'm not. It's just, I've been imagining this for weeks now. It's—" I struggled for the words. "It's hard to do something that you've thought about so much. I guess I don't want to disappoint you. Or myself."

Bruce looked at me from under thick lashes. Then he stretched out beside me, his thigh flung across my legs where, three days ago, Steve Wald's had been. Up close, his stubble was sooty against his tan neck. Fine lines fanned out from his eyes, which only highlighted their depth and liquid golden-brown color. I had the sudden urge to run my tongue along the deep curve of his upper lip.

"It would be impossible for you to disappoint me," he said, running his fingers along my breast and down my belly. I shivered.

His hand moved to my thigh.

"You provoke me somehow, and I like it. It's very chemical, our attraction. I like that too. It...it feels like something I can trust. I'm not sure I've ever felt it so strongly with anyone else before. I think it's the feeling of inevitability that turns me on so much. As if one or both of us could refuse, and it really wouldn't matter that much—we'd eventually find ourselves back in the same place. Different time maybe, but the same place."

Then I understood that what I was really resisting was letting go of a way of life. The way that told me I had to conceive contingency plans for failure even before I had finished charting the waters of my mission. I wanted to be done with that. I wanted to start something without planning its demise. Sensing my capitulation, Bruce scooped me up in his arms and carried me—divinely, as you would expect—up to the nestlike room he'd shown me earlier.

He laid me gently on a pile of sheepskin rugs and threw a few logs and kindling in the stove. In a few seconds, flames crackled to life, and the logs groaned and popped. In the firelight, Bruce's naked flesh glowed amber. His muscles rippled (true).

What followed was the most exquisite sensual experience I've had the pleasure to know. Better than the scene in *Out of Sight* when J. Lo shackles George Clooney to the banister, leveling her devastated yet stoic gaze upon him as she leaves him to his fate. Better than an It's-It ice cream bar on the first night of your period. Even better than the bubbly high you get from drinking beer at a baseball game on a toasty afternoon.

Better.

He came back and, with excruciating languidness, removed my shirt, bra, jeans, and underwear. I'm always conscious at moments like these how far true life strays from the silken transitions captured in the movies. Like how clothes just seem to fall off the beautiful people like abandoned snakeskin, instead of catching on boot heels and bunching around necks.

This was like the movies.

When we were both naked, Bruce rolled on top of me and nudged my legs apart with his knee. His ass was round and narrow and solid. I cupped it and was gratified to hear him groan out loud.

"I want to fuck you, Brenner," he murmured.

And then he did.

CHAPTER 21

in flagrante delicto

To: jen.brenner@meredithgazette.com
From: Nancy Teason
Subject: Hi!

Jen,

I hope this gets to you. I got your new address from HR. I'm sure
you're having such fun up in Missouri! That postcard you sent of the
Lewis & Clark memorial was great. I actually have a specific reason for
writing. I hope you'll hear me out. I'm afraid the person we hired to
replace Jemima Pierce didn't work out, and without launching into a
huge explanation that nobody has time for, I'd like to invite you back
to fill Jem's role. Of course, we'd have to do an interview to make it
official, but we've decided you're really the best person for the job.
And you should know that the Tech Standard supports its employees'
outside interests. I guess what I'm saying is, if you want to keep free-
lancing for that little newspaper you're writing for, we'll by all means
let you do that. So, Jen, call me as soon as possible and let me know
your thoughts.

Nancy E. Teason

I woke up to the sound of wind chimes.

Unsure where I was exactly, I nevertheless felt snug and satisfied. It must, I inferred, be somewhere good. Thick, white fluffy rugs blanketed me, and warmth still emanated from the wood-burning stove at my head. Light filtering from the trees outside the windows dappled the room.

Then it all came rushing back: dinner, dancing, hot sex, hot sex again, shower, hot sex. Bruce.

He slept beside me, his arm around me and his knee curled up against himself like a child. In sleep, like most people, he looked younger than his years, the thin grooves under his high cheekbones mere lines, his thick hair sticking up in unruly tufts.

Experimentally, I licked his ear. He stirred, so I moved to his neck, which was slightly sticky. I burrowed under the covers and trailed kisses down his hard abs, following the furred arrow to his crotch. His cock rose to attention, bobbing. I wrapped my hand around the hard column. Suddenly, muscular thighs closed around me and I found myself on my back.

Bruce gripped my wrists, holding my arms over my head. His heavy-lidded gaze wandered to my breasts and I felt my nipples peak.

"Are you trying to wake me up?" he said.

"Yes."

He imprisoned my wrists in one hand and used the other to rub the pink tips. I purred before I could stop myself.

"Well, I'm up," he said, unnecessarily. His cock was pressed insistently against my leg and felt as stiff and unyielding as a day-old baguette.

Before I could fling back a response, he flipped me over to my stomach, holding me up on all fours with his hand under my belly like a waist cincher.

Now, I've always had a thing for doing it doggie style. I'm serious—get me on my knees with my ass in the air and I'm yours for the taking.

Bruce seemed to sense my excitement, and he plunged two

fingers inside me, holding me tightly with his other hand. Within seconds, his ministrations had slickened me to the consistency of Prince William Sound after the *Valdez* struck. Panting sounds came from my throat, threatening to upgrade into animal moans.

He withdrew, and I felt him slip a condom on from the pile we'd left on the floor. Then he loomed behind me and positioned himself behind my hips. Reflected in the window about ten feet away, I could see his face, tight with urgency, almost pornographic.

Bruce slid into me swiftly and went deep, thrusting as far as he could go. He used one hand to grip my hips; the other buried itself in the hair at my nape and clung like a cowboy riding an unbroken mare.

We only lasted a few minutes.

My orgasm, when it came, was explosive. When I began bucking against him, Bruce let go with a long, shuddering moan, pounding into me until I thought I would split in two.

"Jennie, Jennie," he cried into my ear, then poured himself into me.

We collapsed partially on the rug. My face scraped against the wooden planks of the floor, already raw where his beard growth had rubbed during last night's escapades. Bruce's welcome weight crushed the air out of me, and I could smell the sweet tangling of sweat and sex between our bodies.

Then the doorbell rang.

My first thought was, some neighbor will just have to get her pat of butter elsewhere this morning. Then I remembered that Bruce really didn't have any neighbors; if someone was out here now—I glanced at the VCR clock, which said 7:45—then they were definitely here to see Bruce.

Bruce rolled off me and glared at the ceiling, as if wishing for God to strike whoever had interrupted our postcoital bliss. Then he leaned over and kissed me soundly, stroking my cheek with his fingertips.

"I'd better get that. Don't go anywhere," he quipped, as if I could possibly move without a tow truck or a crane.

He pulled on his jeans, skipping the underwear, and I heard him trot down the long, circular staircase to the front door. The doorbell rang again, insistent, and a sliver of apprehension wormed its way into my mind.

I decided I'd better get dressed. I didn't know what Bruce had planned for today, but I needed to get some work done before I visited the McIntyres this afternoon, anyway. On the other hand, maybe we'd both play hooky and practice everything we'd learned last night. I smiled to myself as I crept downstairs, Bruce's shirt wrapped around me.

I felt her presence before I actually saw her.

When the hallway came into view, and I heard voices shouting, my kidneys suddenly seized, as if I had just witnessed a car accident and seen the people inside crushed and battered.

Melina Curran screamed at Bruce, her loose auburn hair whirling around her head like a Medusa.

"I told you, she wasn't there when Fran and Toni got up this morning!" she shrieked at him. "She's gone, gone. Where the fuck is she, Bruce? Where is she?"

While I watched, he grabbed her arms and pushed her against the wall. Firmly. Her head struck the plaster hard enough to bring tears to *my* eyes. Melina's were already streaming, her mascara in runnels down her flushed cheeks.

"Have you called the cops yet?" he asked.

She shook her head, hiccupping.

"Are you sure she wouldn't have gone somewhere? I can see her going somewhere on her own. She's not exactly happy about us splitting, Mel. She could have gone to school early or be in one of her favorite places. The bridge, or the park or something."

"I checked everything. What do you think I've been doing for the last hour?" she said icily, having regained some modicum of control when her skull cracked against the wall.

Then, like a beacon, her gaze was drawn to me on the stairs, where I stood frozen, a deer in the headlights. I saw something fragile and tenuous literally snap in her eyes before she let loose a stream of invective.

"Oh, God. You're asking me why Em's gone when you've got this...this *whore* here with you? This slut half your age who couldn't wait till our papers were signed before she'd moved in on you. That is just rich, you...you *fucker*..." she screamed, flailing at him with small fists.

Then she seemed to collapse in on herself, crumpling to a pile on the floor. She looked up at him, her eyes startlingly green, iridescent with tears.

"She was here last night, wasn't she? Emmy was here with you and this *jailbait,* and now she's run away and it's your fault, because you couldn't control yourself. You just have to be the guy who can fix everything, don't you? You'll be, like, the only guy in the western world whose kid's going to *like* his slut...." she sneered.

Melina started sobbing convulsively. My legs shook.

When Bruce turned to me, his eyes were dead. There was no sign whatsoever of the man who had run his tongue over every inch of my body, who had made love to me in the bath with soap in his eye, who, near midnight, had told me he loved me.

"You'd better leave. My keys are on the table. Take the car and I'll pick it up later at your office."

I ran upstairs, finished dressing, and slammed the door to the car before the tears came.

Fool. Fool. Fool.

I snapped on the radio, sure that an appropriate accompaniment to my misery would ring out. Something about foolish hearts and don't leave me now and crushed hearts.

Instead, I heard Bob Edwards's alto announcing NPR's "Morning Edition."

As I drove, I tried deep breathing to calm myself, though my mind was racing. On the one hand, my innate paranoia whispered, Melina Curran was just the type to interrupt an ex-husband's first night of passion with a new lover, the type to cry wolf with stories of disappearances and malicious intrigue, suspecting, if not knowing full well, that Emily was in the school library or Starbucks with her science book cracked. On the other hand, my rational voice suggested, it didn't matter what the reason; if anything could have happened to Emily, it had to be Bruce's first and truest instinct to do whatever it took to find her. His first responsibility was to his daughter, not his jailbait. (Frankly, I preferred Emily's unintentionally kinder *Jell-O* bait, even with its cellulitic implications.) That sense of responsibility, which ran from deep familial love to civic pride, was one of the things that first attracted me to Bruce, and I had to keep that in mind, I chided myself. You can't have it both ways: passionate father and devastating lover 24/7. (Well, you can, actually, but only for one night. Very bodice-ripper. Very country music.)

Then there was the guilt: If Emily Mortensen had run away and harm befell the girl before she could be found, I would never forgive myself. More important, Bruce would never forgive me. Our "inevitable" coupling would be over before it started. We'd go down in romantic history as one of the world's most ill-fated unions, along with Julia Roberts/Lyle Lovett and Dennis Rodman/Carmen Electra.

I categorically analyzed each of our (mine and Emily's) miserable encounters over the past twenty-four hours and determined that the likelihood of her running away to get back at Bruce was either: (a) high; (b) pretty high; (c) assured. My first instinct was to drive around town looking for her, but the thought of her running for Bruce's car only to find me, the trollop, behind the wheel was too much to bear.

When I got to town, I decided to stop by my house and wash the night's passions away as best I could. As my dad the doctor always said, there was little a hot shower and a good night's sleep wouldn't resolve. (Obviously, dear Dad had never been merci-lessly ravished with an eight-incher in six official Kama Sutra po-sitions.) Then I would get ready in time to make my meeting with Princeton and Penn, or Harvard, or whatever that silly woman's name was.

After a good cry and a shampoo with some of that herbal stuff that purports to give you cranial orgasms, I emerged from the shower whole, if not transformed, and ready to take on the world. I dressed for the occasion in an outfit from my not-so-distant ur-ban past: DKNY City navy suit with slightly flared legs and a navy stretch tank. My eyes were too irritated from crying to wear con-tacts, so I substituted my skinny, square-ish, tortoiseshell glasses. My hair, uncut now for almost two months, was almost bob-length, a mass of brunette tangles, and needed trimming more than an uncircumcised Lubavitcher.

I yelled good-bye to Gladys, who was deep into Ursula Hegi's *Stones from the River*. She waved distractedly as she sipped her tea.

Main Street was sparsely populated and bleak, as if people had stayed home out of deference to Emily Mortensen's disap-pearance. (Either that or embarrassment at the screams of plea-sure coming from Bruce's mountain aerie last night.) I parked the car on Cedar Street in the *Gazette* lot, which was open again after having been cordoned off while the police gathered evi-dence from the bombing. Whatever the perpetrator's intent, it hadn't stopped the newspaper from running: two days after the incident, the structural engineer had pronounced the building's first floor safe for reentry, and we'd moved down there while cleanup took place in the small portion of the second floor that was destroyed.

I slipped Bruce's keys on top of the front left wheel, slammed the door a little harder than was necessary. Then I went in and drowned myself in work—or pretended to—for several hours.

At noon, I trotted off toward the McIntyres' landmark Victo-rian in the town center. As I walked, I issued a silent prayer for

Emily's safety and Bruce's sanity. My future with Bruce, which a few short hours ago had been coalescing into something tangible and real, had disintegrated like a supernova, hurling matter through space and time even faster than the warning sounds that had preceded it.

As I traversed the cobbled walkway toward the McIntyres' monstrous, ornately carved door, I fancied I saw a parlor curtain move slightly. Probably just my imagination running away with me. Either that, or clan Addams was up to its old tricks.

Before I could ring the bell, the barn-size door swung open, and I faced the most diminutive woman I'd ever seen. Her arm straining for the doorknob gave the scene an almost *Alice in Wonderland* aspect, and I found myself smiling for the first time since Bruce turned to me with those cold, dead eyes.

"Are you Miss Brenner from the paper?" the tiny woman asked. Her voice sounded as if it were being played at 75 rpm.

"Yes, I am. You must be Ms. McIntyre?"

"Yes, Penelope McIntyre. How rude of me—come in, come in. I'll get Terence to bring us some sandwiches and tea." She hustled me into the cavernous entryway, which resembled the tourist entrance to St. Peter's Basilica in both size and ratio of gold leaf to red carpet.

"Now, you just take off that jacket and make yourself comfortable while I call Princeton. He's working on his novel, you know, but he said he'd come out for you."

She held out her pudgy little arms for my jacket, which I gave her. Fascinated, I watched her toss it over a coatrack twice her height, then press a button hidden in a wall alcove. Within seconds, a sullen-looking teenage boy appeared.

"Terence, I would like some of those lovely watercress and cream cheese sandwiches brought to the parlor, and also those Pepperidge Farm cookies." She turned to me. "I hope you don't mind store-bought, but those mint Milanos they make are just scrumptious, don't you think?" She went on before I could answer, in that chipmunk voice. "Terence, please knock on Mr.

McIntyre's door, if you would. Now, remember what he told you about knocking—it's three light taps, not that loud banging that can upset his heart."

Judging by Terence's scowl, a good tap in the head was just what he'd like to give his fussy employers.

Penny beckoned me down a hallway plastered with paintings of stern-faced men and minuscule women. In one, the seated subject's tiny feet dangled above the floor. When we entered the parlor, I had to stifle a laugh: If Liberace ran a brothel out of Victoria's Secret, the decor would have been tamer.

Frescoes swirled overhead, distracting the eye from the heavy purple drapes and gold moldings. Every available surface was piled with tchotchkes, from gaggles of glass unicorns to silk roses tied with gilt braid to Persian-inspired atomizers.

I sat on a velvet chaise; Penny chose a red damask Louis XIV chair. A cross-eyed Siamese immediately jumped into her plump lap and purred, waving its narrow ass in her face.

Soon, scowling Terence came along with lunch. The china tray looked absurdly delicate in his ham-shaped hands, which shook as he laid it down, spilling sugar out of the silver-trimmed bowl at its center.

Miss Penny pursed her lips but said nothing until he was gone.

"I just don't know why I put up with that boy," she squeaked. "But I suppose it's for the betterment of society, at least that's what Prince says. It's part of the furlough program with the jail. Instead of halfway houses, they place them in jobs with upstanding citizens like us, to help them transition to normal life and contribute," she parroted.

Penny leaned in closer. "I don't feel entirely comfortable with Terence Marvin in this house, really, but with his grandfather being a known white supreme and all, the social-services lady thought a live-in arrangement was the best option."

A distant alarm bell clanged in my mind, along with an image of Harold Marvin, my would-be Aryan Nation landlord, saying his grandson had posted the ad on the Internet for him. Poor Penny. Poor Terence. Poor Harold. I wondered if anybody had called Harold a "white supreme" to his face and lived to tell the tale. What would Diana Ross think of such a concept?

"Penny, aren't you going to introduce me to our guest?"

Princeton McIntyre was about sixty-five. His hefty body was encased in a bona fide smoking jacket and cravat—his literary costume, I presumed—and the Grecian Formula he used liberally, along with the Dali-esque mustache, lent him the benign charm of an aging flamenco dancer.

I tried to shake hands, but he foiled me by sweeping my hand to his lips and air-kissing it. Oh, my. It's the Rockies' own Julio Iglesias.

Penny giggled.

"So, I'm not sure how much Dave explained on the phone," I began, wanting to avoid another groping, "but we're investigating environmental practices at the mill, and we have reason to believe that some of the players may be involved in some, ahem, unsavory activities. Dave said you are both very well informed on what's going on in town and might be able to give me some background we can use to shape our investigation."

Penny McIntyre nodded gravely, as if awed by the weightiness of her observations.

"What she means, Pen, is that we're fat old gossips and everyone knows it," Prince cackled.

"I'm sure Miss Brenner didn't mean that, Princeton McIntyre," she shot back, glancing at me for affirmation.

"Sometimes reporters just need to get a feel for the people they're dealing with," I said with a straight face, as if we were conducting a debriefing in the CIA's white room.

"Well, Pen and I have lived here all our lives and spent the better part of them documenting the foibles of our friends and neighbors. Who is it you're interested in?"

"Oh, anyone connected with the mill. Management, partners, backers, that sort of person. Anyone who'd have an interest in the mill's financial standing, for sure," I said.

Penny and Prince McIntyre glanced at each other, lips pursed in twin moues.

Penny began. "Well, I don't like to spread rumors, but Cyrus Tuttle over at the casino on the reservation told me that Glen Whitehead, who I believe is the Vice President of Marketing and Public Relations since Ivan Jeter retired, has been spending a lot of time at the place. In fact, I think Cyrus said Mr. Whitehead owes them some considerable amount of money."

Score one for the people of Meredith!

"Considerable? Pen, the man said Whitehead is in to the tune of $150,000. Now, I'm sure he makes a good salary, but that's not small potatoes to anybody. Certainly not the casino people. What I think Ms. Brenner really needs to know is who Mr. Whitehead's been consorting with in the minimal amount of spare time he has left after losing his shirt to the casino."

"Oh, Prince, are you sure? I mean, what if it gets back to, you know . . ."

"Ms. Brenner is a professional. I'm sure she can keep work and play separate," he said, glancing at me slyly.

Yeah, they're about as differentiated right now as my right and left ventricle.

"Well, I suppose we can tell you, Miss Brenner. You seem like a very nice girl." She took a deep breath. "It's common knowledge that Melina Mortensen and Glen Whitehead have been having an affair. I heard Alexandra Whitehead already got herself a lawyer out of Helena. I think it started about a year ago, after the mill had its annual costume ball at the Rotary club. Melina went as a French maid, I recall, which seemed a bit risqué for a married woman and a mother—"

"Penny! Get on with it," Prince said.

"Yes, well, it's a shame, really. Melina is as much a part of this town as anyone. I mean, her father, Michael Curran, must be apoplectic. Of course, he didn't truck with Bruce Mortensen when he first came along, because no one was good enough for his little girl, but—what's that saying about cutting the wheat from the chaff?—anyway, Bruce earned Mike's trust and respect. So, it must kill him to know that everyone knows it was Melina's fault that the marriage went south. Bruce stuck with it long after he should have, if you ask me. For the little girl, of course."

"What Penny's trying to say, Ms. Brenner, is that if White-head's in debt, and he's been diddling Melina Mortensen for some time, and her father owns a controlling interest in the mill, *and* the mill's being investigated for violating environmental law and there's money missing, well, it's just a little too incestuous, you see?"

I certainly did. And, as far as incestuous went, these two must be experts, so I listened carefully.

"You know what they say, don't you? Follow the money. If it wasn't being spent on upgrading equipment, where did it go? That mill's been in the black for one hundred years. All I know for sure is that Mike Curran would do anything, and I mean *any-thing,* to protect his little girl. There's your angle, missy. That, and Glen Whitehead's gambling habit."

Looking smug, Princeton snaked a crustless sandwich from the coffee table and popped it in his red-lipped mouth whole.

Now it was Penny's turn. "So, is it true that you're seeing Bruce, dear? We were so sure it was going to be Steve Wald. They're both darling boys, but Bruce has so much going on right now, what with the divorce and the custody battle over Emily." She looked me over with an appraising eye. "Why, you can't be a day over thirty-five. How old is Bruce now, forty-one, forty-two?"

Damn munchkin. Thirty-five, my stretch-marked ass.

I think he's pushing fifty, actually. We were going to go get him some Depends undergarments this afternoon, but his daughter ran away instead, I imagined saying.

Actually, I said, "Oh, my mother always says age is a state of mind," or some other tired aphorism.

When Penny smiled, her cheeks squished her small eyes shut.

I stood with my briefcase. Terry Marvin was back to remove the dishes, and I didn't want to witness him clocking her with a jade vase or a croquet mallet.

"I can't thank you enough for taking the time to talk to me. You've been incredibly helpful," I told them.

They walked me to the door, back down the hallway I had privately christened The Vagina.

Princeton helped me put on my jacket.

"I sure hope they find that little girl soon," Penny McIntyre chirped as I left. "All kinds of bad things can happen to little girls out by their lonesome."

I passed the office but didn't see Bruce's truck. He must have picked it up while I was at the McIntyres's. I decided I'd drop in, check e-mail, and mope, not necessarily in that order.

While the news that everyone knew about Glen Whitehead and Melina's affair had not been stunning, it lent my involvement with Bruce a certain sordid aspect that did not help elevate my mood. On the other hand, the as-of-yet-unsubstantiated rumor of Whitehead's gambling debt set the wheels of conspiracy theories turning: Could Whitehead be behind the misdirection of funds? Could he actually have stolen money earmarked for upgrades to pay off his personal debts? And, if so, why would Curran protect him? It didn't seem like protecting his daughter's lover's reputation would be enough to make him endanger his business. And the fire: Had it been set to destroy evidence, or to distract from the corruption going on? It was clear that a thread of logic was starting to emerge, but where it led back to was still a mystery.

"Hey, Margaret," I greeted the lifestyles editor. "Any news on Emily Mortensen?"

"Didn't you hear? They got a ransom letter this morning. It

was sent to Melina Mortensen's e-mail. Nobody knows yet if it's real or a hoax."

Oh, Bruce, I thought, feeling my blood run cold, how can you stand it? I fought the urge to drop everything and run screaming down the street, offering myself in place of poor Emily. I unfurled my clenched fists mechanically and tried to sound calm.

"What were the terms?"

"I think they asked her for $150,000, which her grandfather can pay in a heartbeat. Poor Bruce and Melina. Emily's in the same class as Kendall." Margaret's son, Kendall, shared his mother's cap of dark hair, sweet disposition, and striking hazel eyes.

I tried to wrap my brain around this. Glen Whitehead owed the casino $150,000, at least according to Morticia and Uncle Fester. Now the granddaughter of the richest man in town, who just happens to be Whitehead's employer *and* his lover's father, is held ransom for the same amount.

Too much coincidence for yours truly.

I thanked Margaret and went to my own desk to work a little. Feeling faint from lack of sleep, I laid my head down on my arms and tried to wallow in the ferocity of last night's lovemaking.

At one point, with his cock still inside me and my legs wrapped around his waist, Bruce had picked me up and set me on the arm of the couch. I'd arched backward and he'd rubbed my crotch with his hand, still pumping, until I came. Then he'd climbed on top of me, pushed my legs over his shoulders and finished in four or five hard thrusts, his face reflecting the lust we'd been hoarding all these weeks.

In all the years I'd been with Damon, he'd never flung my legs wide open and buried his face between them like a man lost in the desert who'd found an oasis, or soaped and combed my tangles out with baby shampoo in the bath, or confessed that he'd once followed me home from a bar without my knowledge to make sure I didn't have an accident.

I'd spent seven years with a guy who knew me nearly half my life but didn't know I preferred rear entry to missionary.

Now, maybe that was my fault too. Maybe I'd changed. Maybe my former self would have tolerated or even encouraged that lack of awareness and intimacy. Since I was giving prayers out like candy today, I fervently hoped wherever Damon was, and whomever he was with, that he was happy. As happy as I'd been last night. . . .

I wasn't aware I had fallen asleep until I awoke to Margaret shaking my arm.

"Jen, wake up!" she said. My eyes snapped open. Standing around me were Bruce, a white-faced Melina, and a horde of cops.

"What's going on?" I asked, panic rising in my breast. My eyes locked on to Bruce's, and I thought I saw a flicker of pain there before the shutters came down and his face was stony again.

The senior-looking cop in plainclothes answered.

"Ms. Brenner, we received a ransom note for Emily Mortensen at 9:35 A.M. today. In it, the kidnappers requested $150,000 in un-marked bills to be delivered at 6:00 P.M. today at a location to be named later. Their other requirement was that it be delivered by a nonfamily member. The person they asked for was you."

difficult delivery

To: info@buenosaireshyatt.com
From: Michael Curran
Subject: Rate info and availability

Please send me rate information for a suite with Internet access starting in mid-October. I'm not sure how long I'll be staying.

Michael Curran

Partner, Sutter & McEvoy

I was trying to impress upon Lieutenant Filarski the significance of the $150,000. He wasn't having it.

"Detective, I realize at this point nothing's been proven, but doesn't it seem highly suspicious? Isn't it at least worth some investigation?" I pressed.

Lieutenant Wendell Filarski made *NYPD Blue*'s Sipowicz look like a willowy supermodel. Filarski was in his late forties or early fifties and rotund to the point of comedy, with a pock-marked, ruined complexion and surprisingly friendly blue eyes.

At the moment, his thick fingers were strapping a bulletproof vest on me, which looked quite good with the navy suit. Very *Law & Order: SVU*.

"Miz Brenner, I've already told you we've sent a man to follow up on that lead. What more do you want from me?" He sounded tired, as if losing a child on his watch would not only ruin his day but also end his career.

"I just want to be sure this is being taken seriously, that's all," I said querulously.

"It is."

I shut up after that.

In the past hour, a lot had happened. First, I'd gone with the posse surrounding me to police headquarters, a trim box-shaped building on Second Street. Then I'd listened while the police, Bruce, Melina, Mike and Kathy Curran, and the janitor screamed at one another about what the best response to the kidnappers was.

At some point, Bruce's mother, Diane Mortensen, showed up from Whitefish, her face tear-streaked. She hugged Bruce, Melina, and the Currans in turn. Being the interloper and quite possibly the designated savior—not to mention the hussy—in all this, all I got from Mom was a glance that could have chilled magma.

Bruce must take after his father, who had died ten years ago. Diane Mortensen was a lean and deceptively delicate-looking graying blonde with the kind of fragile skin that doesn't age well. In her case, homemade unguents had saved her skin, and she didn't appear to truck with makeup, jewelry, or anything as frivolous as a coat on this blustery day.

After the screaming match that Bruce seemed to win, the police discussed the pros and cons of allowing a civilian—me—to deliver the money. Just like in the movies—my life has become quite cinematic lately—the cash was stacked neatly in a briefcase, each pile crisscrossed in two rubber bands. Mike Curran had thrown it on the floor forty-five minutes ago after rushing back from his bank.

The option of disguising a female police officer as me was raised and summarily dismissed. This town was so small, it was likely the kidnappers would know immediately that they'd been duped, and someone could get hurt.

My eyes never leaving Bruce's, I told them I wanted to deliver the money. I wasn't really conscious of the danger to myself, only the pressing compulsion to redeem myself in his eyes, to do whatever it took to get back to the place we were at a mere eight hours ago.

After that, I signed some papers denying the Meredith Police Department's responsibility if I was maimed, killed, or forced to shop at Wal-mart. By this time, a haze had settled over the day. Whether it was exhaustion, trepidation, overstimulation, or some combination of the three, I did not know. Melina and her parents treated me like I was simply invisible, another mildly disruptive servant there to do their bidding. Melina's rage had petered out around midday, and she alternately sat zombielike in her seat with her parents fluttering around her or wept softly into her hands. Somehow, her maternal despair heightened her naturally vampish allure, and I could see cops staring hungrily at the woman throughout the afternoon.

At one point, Bruce called me into the hallway, where we had a very unsatisfactory exchange.

"You don't have to do this," he said.

I stared at him. "Of course I have to do this. For God's sake, it's Emily's best chance to get home okay."

The muscles along his jaw twitched. "Just do exactly what they tell you to do. No cowboy shit, no Brenner smart-ass behavior. Are you hearing me?"

Yes, I'm hearing you! I wanted to scream. It was so unfair. How could he even think I'd do anything to endanger his child?

"Yes," I answered dully.

Then he whipped around and strode back into the command center. The hair at his nape was too long and had whorled into a little tail. I wanted to bite it. Hard.

For the next thirty minutes, Lieutenant Filarski and his team drilled me on the different contingencies. I'd like to say I stored every bit of data in that crack photographic brain of mine, but it was sort of like the one time I was talked into skydiving: in one ear and out the other. Needless to say, when it came time to pull the rip cord that day, I'd flailed, and the beefy South Carolinan instructor strapped to my back had to reach over and yank the cord himself so we wouldn't hurtle ten thousand feet to earth.

I considered calling my family and friends to tell them I loved them and might not see them again but decided hearing my mother's resulting screech would only make me want to cry. Hopefully, it would all go as planned, and I'd have an amusing anecdote to tell our kids—mine and Bruce's—someday. Denial: Over thirty billion doses served—and counting.

Finally, as dusk settled over the town, we moved en masse to the drop-off point. My instructions were simple: Leave the brief-case at the base of the fountain in the square. Walk away. Surely even a stubborn mule like me could do that much?

Filarski checked my vest to make sure it was tight.

"You ready?" he asked. I wanted him to hug me since my dad wasn't here but thought that might be pushing it, so I refrained.

I nodded and squared my shoulders. Of the family members, only Bruce had been allowed at the drop-off, a courtesy because he was law enforcement.

"Jen."

At the sound of Bruce's strangled voice, something hard and cold inside me melted a little, and I swiveled to see him standing there, his face racked with pain.

Then we were in each other's arms, wrapped so tightly the breath rushed out of me and I gasped. Bruce brought his head down and knocked me in the forehead.

"Ouch," I said.

But then I realized he was crying, silent manly tears that slipped from the corners of his beautiful dark-honey eyes. He made no attempt to hide them, simply bent his head and let them fall. He made no sound.

Heedless of the onlookers, I reached up and grasped his face in my hands.

"She's going to be all right, Bruce. I know it. I'm going to do exactly what I'm supposed to, and she'll be home by dinner," I said sternly, with more confidence than I felt.

Then, while a crowd of cops and negotiators watched, I kissed Bruce Mortensen full on the lips, with all the force I could muster.

"Let's go," I said to the lieutenant.

The evening was coolish, and I was glad I had my bulletproof vest on.

Ha, ha.

I craned my neck, one of several unappealing rituals I engage in when I am stomach-churningly, eye-blinkingly nervous. (I was saving the hair twirling and eyebrow rubbing for later.)

The briefcase was heavy. If I wasn't so terrified, I might have entertained thoughts of running straight to the Jen Brenner Terminal and jetting off to somewhere exotic and lacking an extradition treaty. But I figured I'd have to go to the bathroom or something and Meredith's crack police force would catch me before I could make my grand escape.

The fountain was about one hundred yards away. Someone had turned it off for the occasion, and it had taken on an abandoned aspect, crumbly and unused. I walked up tentatively and placed the bag next to the fountain.

Suddenly, a figure materialized out of the dusk.

I froze.

Then, to my everlasting embarrassment, I actually puffed my chest out toward the intruder, as if his first act would be to aim a bullet at my heart. I prayed for deflection and wondered if Bruce would visit me in the hospital when I got treated for my broken ribs. I prayed for God to spare my face (especially the expensive porcelain veneer Kristina's dentist had installed). In retrospect, to the officers waiting at the edge of the square I must have looked like some sort of demented bird issuing a mating call or a pre-emptive challenge.

The figure materialized: hair brown and scraggly, sinewy body, twitchy hands. Little Guy?

I nearly fell in the fountain, I was so shocked.

"What are you doing here?" I shouted.

"Hey, shh, stop yelling. Aw, come on," he begged, as my eyes darted to the officers' line.

"Are you involved in this?" I couldn't believe it. My mole, a traitor.

"There was somepin I didn't tell you, those other times." Little Guy hung his head. He looked genuinely ashamed, and I wished I hadn't forked out my own money for those hamburgers.

"I'm working for Whitehead," he said.

"You're working for Whitehead?" I repeated dumbly.

"He's got somepin on me, ya see? I didn't want to do any of it, but he knew about me stealing and said he'd turn me in if I didn't do what he said. And I ain't never going back to prison. No way, no how." He wagged his puny head from side to side as if to illustrate the profundity of his commitment.

A picture was starting to emerge. Our other conversations, littered with half-truths, were an attempt to assuage Little Guy's guilt, the only recourse he felt he had under the circumstances. Glen Whitehead owned his ass and had manipulated us every step of the way, it seemed. Little Guy had never been my bitch, but he had been Whitehead's.

"Little Guy," I started—what else was I going to call him?—"this has gone beyond fires and false trails and hiding evidence and even a bombing. There's a little girl missing, for God's sake. An innocent little girl whose parents and grandparents are crying their eyes out over there. Is she safe? Is Whitehead going to return her?"

He recited as if from a script.

"Here's what you have to do now. She's being dropped off at the soccer field behind the high school. You're supposed to let me take this away unimped—unimpedified," he fumbled. His squinty eyes were pleading.

Oh, God.

"Is that it?" I asked him.

"Yeah." He scuffed the dirt. "Thanks for buying me Dairy Queen that time. Sorry I ran away. That was rude."

I issued a silent prayer that I would show forbearance and not slap his mole-spotted face.

"What's your name?" I said in the no-nonsense tone my sister, Karen, uses with my nephew and niece.

"Marion Casey Gerbill." He hung his head further.

That name would explain a lot. Maybe the judge would go easy on him.

He picked up the briefcase and I ran all the way back to the command station.

They were waiting. Nobody asked me if I was all right. Bruce gripped my shoulder so hard I almost sank to my knees. No more manly tears.

"He said Emily's being dropped off at the soccer field," I gasped. "And that she's fine. It's Whitehead! It's been Glen Whitehead this whole time! And that guy"—I pointed to Little Guy's receding back—"is Marion Casey Gerbill. He works at the mill. Whitehead blackmailed him to do all this."

At the mention of Whitehead's name, I saw Bruce's expression harden into an approximation of granite. His eyes were cold and his jaw clenched, and I could almost see him plotting Whitehead's painful demise.

He cursed. A blue streak. Clearly, Whitehead was dead meat, and Melina didn't come out smelling like a rose either.

"Mortensen. Mortensen. *Bruce!*" Filarski shouted, gripping Bruce's arm in his meaty paw. "Calm down or I'll have Paul drag your ass back to the station so fast your head will spin. I will not have you compromise this operation."

Somehow, I did not believe that even the physically imposing Paul could restrain Bruce Mortensen at this moment. In his fiery rage, Bruce was, quite simply, magnificent.

Then everyone whirled into action. Filarski rounded up the troops, got on the radio, and called a unit to go to the soccer field. Bruce stalked off with Filarski and sped off in the unmarked car. A female police officer with a bumpy nose and a shy smile helped me remove the vest.

She led me to her patrol car, and we followed the motorcade to Jonas Salk High School.

The school was already a hive of activity. Lights flashed everywhere, and an ambulance stood by. I imagined that cops had already been dispatched to Whitehead's house and that Melina would take her own turn in the interrogation room after Emily was safely returned. Somebody had brought them to the recovery scene, and I watched Mike Curran's face, trying to figure out how much he knew.

"We got her!"

The crowd surged like a sea of plankton toward the voice. Two uniforms sandwiched Emily between them. The girl's face was ghostly white and wet with tears, but she smiled bravely as she was enfolded by the knot of officers.

"Daddy!" Emily's voice sirened through the night.

Bruce shouldered his way through the thicket of people so hard he nearly collided with her saviors.

"Daddy, Daddy . . ."

Emily swung like a rag doll in Bruce's arms. He squeezed her so tightly I feared she'd need the treatment I'd imagined for broken ribs. One of her pink tennis shoes popped off and fell on the damp grass.

I couldn't tear my eyes away from the tableau. Bruce was

crying openly now, and he didn't bother to wipe away the tracks streaking his cheeks. Occasionally, he'd pull his head back as if to confirm that the Emily in his arms was real and whole and to kiss the apples of her cheeks and her silky head over and over again.

"Mommy!"

Melina stumbled toward them and fell into their tight circle. Bruce seemed to hesitate for a split second, then enfolded her into their group embrace. Melina's and Emily's red hair mingled into a jumble of waves, the color striking against Bruce's dark head. There was something so perfect and complete about them, I wanted to gnash my teeth together. My relief at Emily's apparent safety was palpable, but just looking at them all together drove a knife of pain into my heart. They seemed so permanent, so inviolate.

"Ms. Brenner?"

Mike Curran stood there stiffly, his hand extended toward me. I shook it. He looked older than on the other occasions I'd seen him, his face puffy and gray.

"Thank you for helping us," he said simply.

"I'm just glad there was something I could do."

We stood in silence for a moment. I wondered if he was figuring out how much he'd have to pay the lawyers to buy Melina's freedom—or his own.

"I put Bruce through college," he said, seemingly out of the blue.

I nodded, curious as to where he was going.

"One weekend, he came home to be with Mel, and we were sitting out on the deck. The women were inside cooking. And Bruce, who was about nineteen or twenty at the time, said he appreciated my help but that he would have married my daughter anyway and to please butt out of their lives, his career, everything, or I'd never see the grandchildren they hoped to have someday. All this from a mill rat who would have spent the next thirty years squeezing paper pulp if I hadn't bailed him out."

He shook his head and looked straight into my eyes.

"Bruce Mortensen is as tough as they get, Ms. Brenner. But I've never known someone to love his family more. My daughter is a damn fool," he said.

As I watched, stunned, Mike Curran hitched up his Wranglers, straightened his bolo tie, and delivered himself into Lieutenant Filarski's waiting arms.

CHAPTER 23

the crash and the spark

To: Ramona1944@aol.com
From: Gilberto Sanchez
Subject: The Big One

Dear Beauty,

What is big and white and red all over, *querida?* Here, I'll make it easy
for you: The answer is Qantas Airlines. That's where we're going for
our anniversary, my sweet. Down Under! See our itinerary below?
This year, we'll experience Christmas in summer!

Te adoro. Happy anniversary.

Gil

"You're a hero, Miz Brenner. By tomorrow, everyone's gonna know
what you did."

Officer Ryan, the young cop whom Filarski had grabbed to
give me a lift home, was young, enthusiastic, and in danger of
having his nuts ripped off by a crazed female. Me.

All I wanted was to get home, crawl into bed, and sleep. Or
cry. Or curse the wicked gods of love. Or call someone who cared.

I couldn't decide, and it didn't matter—Emily was safe, the case, if not cracked, was at least fractured, but Bruce was as gone from me as if he had boarded a space shuttle to the moon.

When we pulled up in front of Gladys's, I mumbled good-bye to Ryan and shuffled to the side door. I adored Gladys, but I didn't want to run into her tonight. I simply didn't have the energy to deflect her questions, her penetrating looks, or her sympathy.

See, I'd lived in California long enough to be indoctrinated with a little bit of New Age-y, quasi-feminist psychofluff I like to call Preemptive Speed-Healing when You Suspect that the Man in Your Life Is About to Wrongly Jettison Your Ass. Preemptive Speed-Healing is the recovery method of choice for SRCSs (Self-Respecting Contemporary Sluts). Part of being a strong, self-sufficient SRCS is knowing when to accept that it's over—here's the kicker—*even if it hasn't yet begun.* Bitterness? That's for first wives with bad prenups. Tears? Unacceptable if you're out of cheerleading togs. Heartbreak? Totally 90s, an unenlightened state endorsed by such cultural has-beens as Sally Jessy Raphael and Celine Dion.

When such counterproductive emotions as regret, sadness, loss or—most regressive and therefore reprehensible—*bitterness* raise their ugly heads, Preemptive Speed-Healing standard operating procedure mandates that they be buried under a deluge of Optimistic Self-Affirming Behaviors. I mean, who can pine for lost love when they're shattering crash dummies' noses in Krav Maga class or reveling in the timeless beauty of henna hand-painting? If you're feeling blue, well, maybe you should take advantage of those fifteen therapy sessions with a licensed social worker covered by your HMO. Whatever, just *get over it,* preferably before next week's Must See TV.

With all this helpful interventionism, Life After Breakup had the tendency to take on the frenetic quality of a large-scale military campaign. Whoever said women can't be soldiers has never witnessed an SRCS Recovery Recon. Recovery Recons have all the ingredients of a carefully orchestrated military engagement, such as:

- Matériel: Self-help books, yoga paraphernalia, aromatherapy candles, pocket-size Zen tracts.

- Heavy artillery: Ben & Jerry's Chocolate Chip Cookie Dough or Chunky Monkey ice cream.

- Gun-toting female mercenaries: *Thelma & Louise, Bonnie & Clyde,* and, in a pinch, *Heathers*.

- Joint chiefs: Your best girlfriends.

- Tactical planning: "On Monday we'll go to the movies, Tuesday to the hot springs, Wednesday to dinner . . ."

- Special ops: "Ma'am, put down the Cuervo Gold and step AWAY from the telephone!"

- The infantry: Jungian therapist (if Jewish). Priest (if Catholic or Greek/Russian Orthodox). Broker (if WASP).

- D-Day: The day you inevitably collapse as a result of too many consecutive hip-hop classes and Hugh Grant matinees.

I'll let you in on a little secret: I'm not entirely happy with the state of the modern breakup. There. I said it. Call me old-fashioned, but sometimes I just want to throw plates at walls and stick pins in jointless, man-shaped little dolls. Maybe it's the ghetto Jewess in me, or something I picked up from the hot-under-the-plunge-neck Cuban women I grew up with in Miami, but a bit of tearful melodrama seems like just the ticket when the possible love of your life decamps with your heart (not to mention your bank-breaking La Perla thong underwear).

Feeling both bitter and weepy, I fell into bed and slept four-teen hours straight.

For the next few weeks, I operated on autopilot. I shopped for nutrients (frozen pizza, beef jerky, green tea, and Ben & Jerry's Super Fudge Chunk). I filed an incisive story on how slipcovers can transform a living room. I went jogging (to the market, where I bought three more pints of Ben & Jerry's). I answered all e-mail from friends with vague confirmations of career, relationship, and domestic bliss. I even started knitting a sweater under Gladys's tutelage, a nappy, tumor-shaped mass that looked like it might crawl off of its own accord. I studiously ignored all developments in the Sutter & McEvoy case, which had blossomed into a sordid web of corruption and sleazy finger-pointing.

When my relationship with Bruce was revealed—not least because of our public kiss at the fountain and my visit with the McIntyres—Bernie removed me from the story and gave it to Dave Lefebvre. When he told me, I reacted to the news with a small, childlike smile and drifted back to my desk, where I played with an extra-wide rubber band for the next three hours. Bernie had looked puzzled and even a bit disappointed, as if he had ex-pected me to raise holy hell and sink my fist into the Teletype ma-chine. I recall feeling genuinely sorry to let him down.

Eventually, I decided I was sick of pretending it was no big deal and indulged in a shitfit that would have made Whitney Houston proud.

It happened like this: I woke up. Saw daylight. Glanced at the phone. Registered the number of consecutive days without attempted communication. Invoked his name aloud: "Bruce, you bastard!" And the sobbing and cursing began. I didn't just sound like one woman keening out her disappointment; the animal shrieks and growls trumpeting from my throat called to mind something on the order of a flock of seals being slaughtered with machetes during the mating season. Finally, when I'd rained curses on Bruce, Bruce's parents, the state of Montana, God, the love of God, my own idiocy, fate, and even Ben & Jerry (okay, I'd really lost it), I collapsed, exhausted, on my bed. My hands made a flimsy attempt to procure snot rags from the mountain of Kleenex, Tums, votive candles, and books on my nightstand, then fluttered weakly to my chest, where they remained as mucus oozed angrily out of my nose and down my slick cheeks.

I think I would have lain there, excreting fluids like a pierced water bed until I simply ran out of stuff to expel and sank, flattened and moist, into the soiled bedsheets, if Gladys had not, after a couple hours of this, knocked sharply on the door of the in-law and asked me if I was going to ruin the second hour of PBS's John F. Kennedy biopic with my caterwauling.

"No," I sniveled.

"Wonderful," she said sweetly, and shut the door.

At 20:44 hours, I scooted to the edge of the bed with the dexterity and energy level of a terminal cancer patient, slid off the mattress, and rose to full stature for the first time that evening, not counting pee runs. (As low as I'd sunk, bedpans were out of the question.)

On the way into the bathroom, I had the misfortune of seeing a reflection of myself in the full-length mirror.

Here's a fashion tip worth remembering: Tank tops look better when they haven't been used as Kleenex substitutes and rent in ritual self-flagellation. Some of the effluvium had had time to dry, and these yellowish spots stuck up like small, peaked tents, making me look as if I had a half dozen lactating nipples. My sweatpants sagged as if I had taken a dump in them. Socks that were cute and fluffy last night had wriggled off my feet into long streamers that extended five inches past the ends of my feet.

Now, on to the bod.

Shoulder hunch. Hivey chest. Arm rash. Killer zit in most painful location next to lower lip. Bloody-looking eyes. Deranged she-wolf expression. White foam at mouth corners the consistency of latte cap. Snarled hair. Stained cheeks. Love handles from too much contact with my dear friends Ben and Jerry.

Needless to say, the monstrous apparition before me had a

galvanizing effect similar to that gleaned from cardio-resuscitation paddles being applied to one's chest.

As the shock of seeing myself in such condition sank in, a tiny ember began to burn inside me. Not a flame, or even a wisp of smoke; just a lively little spark like that emitted by a charcoal briquette lying at the outer reaches of the barbecue, untouched by lighter fluid but warming nonetheless.

The spark—*my* spark—propelled me into the shower and out of the fiercest grip of my lovesick malaise. And, so, on the fourth day, I crashed. And on the fifth day, God created whales. And on the sixth day, Bruce called.

I was in my room counting ceiling spiders.

"Yeah?"

So, no one was going to hire me to be a receptionist, okay?

"Jen? This is Bruce. We need to talk."

Silence.

"Are you there?" he said.

No, I'm in Acapulco dancing topless on the beach with a guy named Umberto, I wanted to scream.

"Yes," I whispered.

"Do you agree that we need to talk?"

"Yes."

He exhaled. "Are you all right? I know it's been very hard. Not seeing each other. Everything that's happening . . . things are crazy right now—"

"I'm fine," I snapped.

If I can't have Bruce, I may as well have my dignity, I thought. Thankfully, no one has ever accused me of being a grown-up in times like these. In fact, I was going to enjoy showing Bruce just how big our age difference really was. Perhaps I'd even give Emily a run for her money in the childish behavior department. Or, better yet, Zoë.

"Why don't you come over tomorrow morning, then?"

"I don't think so, Bruce." It felt good to say his name. Cleansing, somehow. Like lancing a particularly vile cyst.

"I think it's better if we meet on neutral ground, don't you? Are they still letting you eat at the lodge? I mean, that's where you seem to conduct most of your breakups...." I said snottily.

"Jen, for fuck's sake. If you're going to be like this, what's the goddamn point?"

True.

I sighed. "Okay. I'm sorry. It's just..." Feeling a wave of self-disgust wash over me, I cut myself off before I could humiliate myself by telling him how I felt—or begging him to please drop everything, come over, and give me one last searing screw to remember him by.

Then I had one of those revelations that always seem so profound at the time and incredibly trite in the retelling: We're mean when we're hurting because it provokes a mean response from the object of our pain. We do this because even the slightest show of kindness from the other person will set off a cycle of need that will deliver us back to stage one of the Preemptive Speed-Healing process. (I'm sure this has been said in a hundred different ways in all of those recovery tomes, but leave it to me to reinvent the wheel.)

"You know that Italian place off Cedar?" he asked.

"Um, no, but I'm sure I can find it."

I'd been there once and found it vomitous. All congealed Alfredo sauce and flaccid eggplant parmigiana and fried calamari with the consistency of live coral. All the better to end the best one-day love affair of my life with.

"Let's meet there at seven P.M."

"Okay."

He was quiet for a moment.

"Jen?"

"Hmm?"

"I'm sorry."

Those words scared me more than anything.

～～～

Mindful of my tendency to let myself go in times of despair, I dressed carefully for my meeting with Bruce. In my mind, I had started calling it the *Last Tango in Paris,* even though it was in Meredith. (For sheer numbers of sexual overtures, though, I have to say that the City of Drunken Fights has it up on the City of Lights.)

I would try to be civil and dignified. If hysterical pleas or tart rejoinders bubbled up, I would smother them with a lacerating hunk of overfried squid. Whenever tears or anger threatened, I would grasp my wineglass by the stem the way vino snobs do in Napa Valley, raise it to my lips, and take tiny, WASPy sips while I arched my right eyebrow, as if to say, *You thought I wanted a long-term relationship? How utterly common! Absolutely not. I just wanted you to do that crazy thing you do with your tongue between my legs, you know, for the next fifty years. That's all.*

I narrowed it down to two outfits: a crinkly flowered gown that tied in the back with a cashmere sweater and chunky mary janes, or my favorite black jeans, turtleneck, and boots, which I'd been wearing the night we visited the mill Dumpster. I was about to slip on the dress when I flashed back to the Damon breakup two years and three months ago. Us. The apartment. Rain. Broken glass. Flowered dress? Horrors! Same dress! I flung it to the back of the closet as if it were infected with plague and drew my jeans comfortingly up. Of course, jeans were right. They said grrl power, biker bitch, didn't-try-too-hard, and check out that juicy ass, all rolled into one. A girl's best friend, really.

Hair and makeup were a problem. Too much, and he'd know how ruinous the past week had been for me. Too little, and he'd take one look and thank his lucky stars he'd gotten out in time. I ended up applying texturizing gel to the ends, which promised *chunky, wild, thickening, piece-y tresses like you'd get at the beach,* and put on my glasses and plum lip gloss. That's it. Even though my eyes were one of my best features, I felt safer behind my glasses, as if I could see them better than they could see me. Jen, the human ostrich.

Finally, at 6:56 I could no longer justify delaying, and I picked up my purse and left by the side door. Feeling petulant, I drove the five blocks to the restaurant.

My stomach felt like I'd just swallowed a gallon of battery acid.

The maître d' was clearly already expecting me.

Bruce had wisely chosen a table in the back. I glanced around to see if he'd brought backup and was relieved to find he was alone and unarmed.

He stood up as I approached the table.

"Hi," I said, and sat down before he could kiss me on the cheek. I'll accept a lot of things in life, but a romantic down-grade? Forget it.

"I've never seen you with glasses before."

"Yeah, well, that morning at your house I had to drive home blind as a bat. Disposable contacts. Your truck came out okay, didn't it?"

He nodded. It was almost unbearable to look at him. Now that I knew what the crisp dark hair felt like between my fingers, and the texture of the hollow at his throat under my lips, his pres-ence was like a taunt. In the last week, my obsessional thoughts had conjured up the perfect being, but the reality was even better.

"How's Emily?" I asked.

"Pretty good, considering. Whitehead hired two roughnecks to snatch her on her way to school. Apparently, they had a week in which to do it. She left the Reillys' early and they got her as she neared the park. She wasn't hurt, thank God. They caught Whitehead in the Salt Lake City airport," he added, almost as an afterthought.

"Is she—" I hesitated. "Is she coming back to live with you?" There's the rub, I thought—would you forgive Melina her treach-erous and ultimately tragic indiscretion, for the sake of Emily, and try to rebuild your family?

"Yes," he said, looking right at me.

I couldn't help it—my heart sank. I looked around frantically for my wineglass stem to salvage my dignity but realized I had ordered a beer. Great.

"And Melina...?"

"We haven't worked that out yet. The custody suit is dropped, of course. Melina knew about the missing funds. She knew for a long time. And Whitehead's gambling habit. Mike knew too, and he tried to cover it up, but it was too late. They've been cooking the books and they've been in noncompliance at the mill. Melina was part of it. I don't know how much, and I don't really care at this point. I just know Emily needs to be somewhere she feels safe and secure, and that's with me," he said stubbornly.

I could hardly argue with that.

"You said you loved me."

Damn. Just when I was starting to think I'd come out of this one without dropping a piteous bomb, I let go with a clunker.

His dark skin flushed.

"I've been very...It's been very...overwhelming," he said, finally. "Perhaps I said some things I shouldn't have. Things I wouldn't have said if I had been thinking of my responsibilities."

Oh, that is rich.

"I don't think we were really *thinking* at all, were we, Bruce? What ever happened to 'inevitability' and 'never felt this way before' and all that? Was that just my imagination? Tell me! You were there too, rolling around on that beautiful floor of yours, naked as the day you were born." Furious and panicked, I swilled my beer. A single, lonely tear pulsed out and slid under my glasses frame.

"Waiter!" I called. "Another one, please!"

Bruce leaned forward and clapped his hand over mine.

"I didn't mean to hurt you, Jen. You must know that. Everything I said was real, but you cannot ask me to neglect my child. That is the one thing I can't ever do. You know that. And Emily can't handle this right now. I'm not saying she could never handle it, but I can't make any promises. Surely you can see that?"

I was saved from answering by the arrival of the waiter, who dropped my beer on the table like a grenade and skittered away. Smart guy.

"Jen, listen to me. You want to know what I think? I think you are the most incredible woman I've ever met. Bar none, okay? I think you're beautiful, and terrifically funny and brave. You scare the living shit out of me sometimes, but you always make me laugh afterward." He leaned closer and whispered fiercely. "The way you gave yourself to me . . . maybe it's because you're young, and confident and strong, I don't know. . . . I know asking you to wait is wrong, but I don't know what else to do. That's it. I feel like shit about it, and I've been torturing myself all week, trying to figure out another way, but there it is."

If I hadn't been so crushed, I would have been deeply moved by this speech. Really, I would have.

"But why can't we, you know, just have sex, or see each other once in a while? Emily doesn't even have to know about it! We can do it in the car, or at a hotel—or the office," I begged.

He smiled sadly. "Oh, Jen, believe me, I thought all the same things. But in the end I rejected them all. Because we're better than that. And I think if we go that route, we'll end up killing our relationship before it can even start. What, we're supposed to be like Melina, sneaking around, like there's something to be ashamed of? I'm trying to raise my daughter to be honest with me. If I can't lead by example about something so simple, so basic, as who I love, then what's the point?"

Why did Bruce have to be so upstanding? I was perfectly willing to have a sordid, sneaky affair with him. But he had to be Mr. Honesty. My bullshit meter was on and ready to kick into high gear, but I didn't really feel he was manipulating me, just being his usual virtuous self. It was infuriating. A thought wormed its way into my mind: Perhaps virtue *is* manipulating? Perhaps sleazy self-interest is a more honest lifestyle and thus superior? Note to self: Conduct survey amongst friends on this point. Protestations of virtue equal manipulation: Yea or nay?

He picked up my hands. Even his barest touch sent a shock all the way up my arms. Involuntarily, I curled my fingers around his, wanting to feel his flesh rend under my nails.

"Jen, wait for me," he said, his flashing honey eyes never leaving mine.

I was mute.

"Wait for me," he said again.

No promises, I thought. No. Promises.

And, slowly, dry-eyed for once, I shook my head as his eyes darkened to the color of molasses.

"I can't," I said.

homecoming

To: Steve Wald
From: Luna Park
Subject: trippin!

Hi, Steve! How are you? Your girlfriend is really nice. So, I got free tickets to Jewel in Spokane. Do you want to go? It's next weekend. Let me know, 'kay? Darrell and Tiki and Cap are taking the van.

Love, Luna

News flash: There's a reason people leave small towns, and it's not just to find gainful employment.

If you are a city person, I encourage you to try the following exercise: Recall your last breakup—the pain, the avoidance of old haunts, the divvying up of the friends circle, the constant stream of activities to fill the empty, mocking hours. Now, take away ninety-five percent of the city's inhabitants, the same lovely strangers who are providing you with that wonderful cushion of anonymity. Then remove, oh, seventy-five percent of the restaurants, movie theaters, parks, and other social venues. Finally, delete most of your friends.

Now you know what it's like to break up with someone in a small town where your social circle is about as big as the Fundamentalists for Choice.

Yes, it is hell.

In the weeks following my dinner with Bruce I endured the following traumatic encounters:

- Running into Melina at the courthouse, where I was researching mechanics' liens for Bernie. The threat of prosecution and Emily's kidnapping had somehow reinstated her Halo of Sweetness, though she did cut me dead with a flick of her shining locks. I was having a bad hair day.

- Being summoned to the police station by Lieutenant Filarski to debrief on poor Marion Gerbill, who had been rounded up within forty-five minutes of the kidnapping at his usual haunt, the Bent Penny. When I arrived, who should be occupying the other chair in the waiting room but Bruce Mortensen? I was having a bad hair day.

- Shopping at the natural-food store on a rainy Sunday, I rounded the produce aisle only to run headlong into Steve Wald, who had a sack of heirloom tomatoes in his hand. He wrinkled his aquiline nose in what looked to be disgust and left without buying his food. I was having—guess what?—a bad hair day.

- Getting pulled over for speeding—speeding in Montana!—on the way to the buffalo preserve and having the cop say, "Hey, aren't you the girl who was having the fling with that agent whose daughter was kidnapped by his wife's lover?" He let me off. I was having a *horrendous* hair day.

Around the time of the encounter with the traffic cop, a single titillating thought began germinating in my mind: I could go home. Just hit the highway and let the door hit my ass on the way out. I could wash my hands of this place, throw in the towel, sing "I Left My Heart in San Francisco" at the top of my lungs on the way to the Jen Brenner Terminal. By the time I got there, I'd have sanitized my time in Montana for public consumption. *Oh, it wasn't really a move,* I'd say airily. *More like a sabbatical. Or a spa vacation. The Rockies are so energizing at that time of year.*

Instead of winning and losing the love of my life, I'd say I'd *had a few flings.* Yeah, that's it. *It's the mother lode,* I'd whisper conspiratorially to my single friends back in San Francisco, as if the men of Montana were an endangered species and it was wise to keep this knowledge just between ourselves. *First, there was the ranger. Hmm? Oh, national-park system, dear.* Tight *slacks. Don't know* how *they go after those grizzlies in them.* Shrug. *I guess they find a way. They're very well trained. We went on a* nature *walk— you know, alone in the woods.* I'd waggle my eyebrows, implying that we'd engaged in our own version of animal behavior.

Next I'd move on to Steve Wald.

Then I met this divine environmental activist at a rally—of course *they have rallies in Montana, no, not just survivalist meetings. Dark hair, blue eyes, looked a little like Ben Stiller. Really, I was tired out from the ranger, but Steve was* relentless. *Wouldn't take no for an answer. We did it in a tent filled with rose petals on an Indian reservation,* I'd say.

I'd throw in Sam Lockyer for good measure: *So, you want to hear the best part? He used his own* hair *to tie me to the bedposts! I swear! And he had a tattoo of a hawk. On his stomach!* And *he was a lawyer.* Damn. Maybe I *should* have brought Sam home to meet Mom. It could have gone something like this:

Me: *Mom and Dad, I'd like you to meet Young Deer Lockyer.*

Mom: *Young Deer? What a beautiful name. Do you know*

*Stands-While-Fisting, by any chance? He's Paiute from Arizona.
Marvelous notched-stick player.*

Dad: *Where did you say you went to law school?*

Bruce would be harder to reposition. But, perhaps in time, I
could grow to see our "relationship" as the rest of the world probably did: fleeting, ill-fated, and based entirely on the gravitational
pull of his cock to my crotch. After a respectable amount of time
had passed—I'm a firm believer in the rule that says you must al-
locate twice as much time as you were with the person to get over
the person—my revisionist version of Bruce and Jen might play
as follows:

So, promise you won't tell anyone? Nods all around. *Because
this one is kind of, you know, embarrassing.* I'd hesitate, as if pon-
dering how to possibly convey the sexual gravitas of the situation.

My final affair was with a federal agent. A married *federal
agent, I should say. Now, I'm not proud of that, really,* I'd say to their
shocked faces. *But it was hardly like we had a choice in the matter.
It was, you know, one of those relationships where you know immediately that you're going to sleep with the person. When it's kind of
like, inevitable. We barely had a choice!* Knowing nods. *The first
time, we had sex in his car on the way home from a business meeting. I'm serious! He was playing Patsy Cline. You know how I love
Patsy. Get this—he didn't even take his gun off. I think it was a
Glock nine-mm pistol. It was in a holster. See—*I'd show them the
scar I got being thrown from a horse when I was eight—*it rubbed
me completely raw!*

Oohs and aahs would commence.

I tried to recall why I'd come here in the first place. To
the best of my memory, the following reasons applied: get over
Damon, recover from humiliation at Tech Standard, get over
Damon, see the country, did I mention get over Damon? Based
on those criteria, I suppose you could say my time in Meredith
had been a successful exercise (or exorcise, as the case may be).

In a moment of extraordinary consciousness-raising—emanating, no doubt, from the newfound wisdom I'd learned from

the Bruce–Jen debacle—I realized that I *had* gotten over Damon. Where before there had been pain and the vague sense that having my ex leave me for a blond size-six stockbroker with an aerobics habit was humiliating, now there were only memories. Decent memories. Okay, good memories. The bad ones had seemed to mellow, like club soda left out, the carbonated sizzle and bitter taste going flatter and flatter with time. Sure, Damon-ghost had been replaced by a new specter, Bruce-phantom, but at least I could take comfort from the fact that recovery wouldn't take too long.

Ah, fantasies—what would I do without them?

I sat up and removed the cucumber slices from my eyelids. De-swelling had become a daily ritual, along with two-hour calls to Els, Robert, or Katie, self-indulgent journal entries sprinkled liberally with words like *pain, suffering,* and *never again,* and a late-night visit with B&J.

At the moment, I was stretched out on a lawn chair in Gladys's backyard. The afternoon was clear and cold, so I'd thrown on a fisherman's sweater and snuggled in my sleeping bag. I was trying to make myself laugh by rereading David Sedaris's *Naked,* which had so far been mildly successful. If there was someone even more unfit for love and the country lifestyle than I, surely it was Sedaris.

Davey was my friend.

Then the phone rang. I'd been letting Gladys pick up, and she'd been cutting me slack, due to the "accident," of course. This time, however, it rang and rang. Finally, when I thought the sheer volume of the archaic ringer would cause my skull to split in two like an overripe honeydew, I leapt up, shimmied out of my bag, tripped over Neffy, who screeched and bolted under the house, and ran inside to answer.

"Hello," I gasped.

"Jen? This is Nancy Teason at the Tech Standard. Did I catch you at a bad time?"

Aside from crying for two weeks straight, losing the only

multiple-orgasm-inducing lover I am ever likely to have, enduring unprecedented public shame, and forfeiting my only worthwhile story to a 150-pound backstabber, why, everything's peachy, Nance.

"No, this is a great time," I lied.

"Well, the reason I'm calling is . . . did you get my e-mail?"

I *had* received Nancy's message, which, ordinarily, would have been immensely satisfying and worthy of a few hours of gloating. But, in this case, the gloating session had been pre-empted by twelve hours of smashing, mind-emptying sex with Bruce. Later, what with the kidnapping, breakup, and subsequent withdrawal from normal life, I hadn't had time to get back to her.

"I did. Sorry I haven't gotten back to you sooner. I've just been really busy."

"I totally understand. Minnesota is *so* exciting! So, have you given it any thought? We're kind of on a fast track here. Things are piling up. Jemima's been helping out a bit, but with the baby and all she's swamped, and we really need someone full-time in here right away."

The truth was, in the past few weeks I had given the Tech Standard's offer less thought than I'd allotted to the late Cesar Chavez's battle against the grape growers.

"Oh, definitely. A lot of thought. It's so generous," I babbled, as if I was a movie star thanking my celebrity costar at an awards show.

"So . . . ?"

"I'll take it!" I heard myself say. My voice gurgled like it was under water.

"We're very happy to hear that," said Nancy, in a flagrant misuse of the royal *we*.

"We'd like you to come down and go through the formal interview with the executive team," she continued. "As I said before, it's really just a formality. Then we can hit the ground running!"

I was reminded of the game my Tech Standard coworkers and I used to play in Nancy-led meetings. It was called Bullshit Bingo, and it consisted of crossing off squares on a bingo sheet whenever Nancy uttered one of the forbidden phrases: *Are we on the same page?*, *moving forward*, *hit the ground running*, and *co-branding*, to name but a few.

Um, do I sound bitter?

For the next five minutes, Nancy and I hashed out particulars: I'd take the Monday flight to San Francisco by way of Seattle and meet with them Tuesday morning, on their dime. I'd have to move home and start immediately, say in less than two weeks, which would give me time to drive the Subie back to California with all my stuff in it.

When we'd pretty much nailed everything down, I said goodbye to Nancy and hung up. Nefertiti pressed against my leg as I leaned against the Formica kitchen counter, and I reached down to stroke her soft fur. I exhaled deeply, trying to shrug off the mantle of failure I felt encircling me like a velvet cloak.

I was going home.

poor little girl

To: jen.brenner@meredithgazette.com
From: Robert O'Hanlon
Subject: Re >> coming to SF

Of course you can stay here. We've got the guest room (Zoë's still sleeping in a crib in our room). We can't wait to see you. Send me your arrival time and I'll pick you up at SFO.

Robert

>Hey, can you put me up Monday and Tuesday night next week?
>Sorry it's so last-minute.

>Jen

I felt like I imagined Fergie does when she periodically returns to Mother England from her base in New York: dethroned, publicly reduced to shilling for an American diet program, yet also freed from the unyielding conventions and restrictions of her home turf.

I could hardly say I had fulfilled my dream of returning to San Francisco triumphant in love and life, but I did have something to say for myself despite my emotional battering: I had relieved myself of the baggage of involuntary celibacy. Yippee! Welcome to the world of the living, I thought as I deplaned. No longer would I be limited to San Francisco's prescribed selection of love partners, comprised mostly of rock climbers, "biz dev" whizzes with busy PalmPilots, wanna-be artists/rock stars/novelists, and tousle-haired boys in Diesel jeans. Now I knew I had the gumption to seek my carnal fortune in more exotic circles: cowboy bars, the Sierra Club, and the district offices of the Federal Bureau of Investigation, to name but a few.

I hadn't checked any baggage, so I scooted over to the long line of shuttles waiting to transport the hordes of tourists and business travelers to their hotels. Mindful of Robert's new responsibilities as a stay-at-home mom, I had refused his offer of a ride.

Cutting off a family of pink-cheeked, befuddled Germans, I squeezed into line and told the frazzled Nigerian shuttle driver my destination. He nodded, wrote my name on the list, and gestured toward the van: I was in! I tossed my rolling travel suitcase in the back and hopped into the van.

About five minutes later, as we were about to pull out, the check-in clerk halted the van for a last-minute passenger.

A slim woman in body-conscious black jersey stepped in, her fall of silky platinum hair hiding her face. We all moved over for the latecomer, hoping that her stop would fall after ours on the route. I love San Francisco's neighborhoods as much as anybody, but the last thing I want after a day of air travel is a meandering tour.

"Where you going?" the driver asked her in his singsong voice.

"Pacific Heights."

The soft voice sounded familiar, so I pretended to check out the new terminal while I studied the back of her blond head.

She reached up to scratch the back of her flaxen locks with a slender hand, and that's when I was blinded by the shot of forked lightning emanating from the mammoth rock on the fourth finger of her left hand. In the aftermath of the engagement-ring sighting, her identity became crystal clear: Kristina. BMW-driving, aerobicized, Damon-stealing Kristina.

One thing San Franciscans will alternately laud and bemoan is the smallness of our town. Sure, it's a city, with all the attendant challenges and benefits of city life, but it's also a water-locked 46.7-square-mile playground that denies its denizens the God-given right of anonymity on a regular basis. I guess it's the price we pay for the sublime food, the dramatic vistas, and the opportunity to sing the Rice-A-Roni jingle while riding the California Street cable car.

Pained, I hunched in my seat, letting my coat ride up around my neck, turtlelike. The last thing I needed right now was a stilted conversion with the Barbie look-alike for whom my ex had jilted me.

Unfortunately, the gods of airport-shuttle drop-offs were not smiling on Jen Brenner. The two other passengers in my row got off first, prompting Kristina to move to the back row, away from the seat-hogging man in the camel-colored leisure suit who had insisted on keeping his duffel bag beside him until he was delivered to the AAA-approved TraveLodge.

"Jen! I didn't even see you."

Yeah, we brunettes can be hard to spot against the swarthy backdrop of life, Babs.

"I didn't recognize you from the back either. Did you darken your hair?" I said cattily.

She looked shocked, as if each step away from stark blondeness was a travesty on the order of wife beating or ethnic cleansing.

"Uh, no." Hesitation. "So, I heard you were living in, whatsit, Arkansas now? How is that going?" she said. Her hands were folded delicately in her lap, but I wasn't fooled for a second: the rock, whose size rivaled that of the Mir space station, glinted meanly in the dim light.

"Actually, it's Montana. I'm not really living there," I said blithely, testing the party line for the first time. "I just took a sabbatical before I start my new position as managing editor of the Tech Standard."

"Oh. I guess Damon got it wrong, then."

I laughed in what I hoped was a plummy, what-a-silly-man sort of way.

"Well, you know Damon. He gets a little confused sometimes." Like when he left me after almost seven years for a woman whose idea of dinner is a sprig of basil and an Ex-Lax.

She repositioned the rock so that its gamma ray threatened to disintegrate the front windshield.

I didn't bite.

"What are you up to these days, Kristina?" I asked.

"Well, actually, Damon and I are looking for a condo. And I guess the really big news is we got engaged."

She raised her hand slowly and reverently to the circle of light cast by the streetlamp, as if it was all she could do to hoist the three-carat boulder against the gravitational pull of the earth. Her eyes glittered, and I was reminded of the hungry, jackalesque look on the other gymnasts' faces when Russian superstar Svetlana Khorkina fell off the uneven bars in the 2000 Sydney Olympics.

"Wow," I said appreciatively. "That looks just like the ring Star Jones bought for her self-marriage. I guess congratulations are in order."

Note that I did not actually congratulate her.

"Well, thanks. You know," she said, easing closer to me on the bench, "we can talk girl to girl, right? Damon always said you were, you know, upset about the breakup, but I've always wanted to thank you for being like a sister to him and helping him grow up. We wouldn't be engaged right now and looking for a place together if it wasn't for you. I want you to know that."

Would death by biting qualify me for manslaughter or murder one?

I adopted a sisterly expression.

"Well, Damon's happiness has always come first with me," I said. Saint Jen, the patron saintess of murderous ex-girlfriends everywhere.

We pulled to a stop in front of Kristina's candy-colored Victorian flat. The driver got out and helped her unload her three-piece baby-blue luggage set, including a cosmetics case that would probably survive a jet crash.

She leaned into the van.

"Bye, Jen. It was great to see you. I'll tell Damon you said hi," she offered, then skipped into her high-security building with her belongings trailing behind her like leashed show dogs.

Some homecomings just aren't what you'd hoped they'd be.

Bruce stroked my hip and repositioned himself so that we were facing each other, stretched out lengthwise on the rug. The fire flickered, casting golden shadows across our faces. I could feel my naked breasts pressed against his chest and was conscious of the fact that a mere four hours ago, we had never been unclothed together. His body held that drugged fascination for me that can only exist in the extreme infancy of a relationship, when every angle and square of flesh revealed is a sensory marvel. I took in his trim waist, thick shoulders, muscular abs, sexy scars. He rubbed his foot absently against my ankle, and the hair on his shins tickled mine.

Without speaking, Bruce moved his stroking fingers to the small of my back, running them up and down my spine between my shoulder blades and the curve of my butt. Reflexively, our mouths came together and we kissed deeply. His jaw sandpapered my chin, in stark contrast to the soft, wet marriage of our tongues. I felt him harden against my leg and sighed. Surely he couldn't be ready for another round already?

But instead of rolling me over and easing my legs apart, he crouched over me and licked a path of molten heat down my belly until I felt his thick hair under my fingers. Unhinged, I drew memories of him whispering in his father-in-law's ear at the environmental rally, sitting stiffly across from Melina in the restaurant, and in his office that first time, his holster pulled tight against his broad chest as he explained EPA's investigative practices while I mentally traced the curve of his sensual mouth. The knowledge that the same man, a stranger, who had played all those roles was now burying his head between my legs, licking and licking, excited me to no end, and I bucked against his wet face. He held me firmly at the waist with one hand and slid his finger into me with the other, continuing with his syncopated rhythm. I felt the buildup of pleasure peak and crest—

I woke up with my heart hammering and my breath coming in little gusts.

Ugh. Another dream. Regular as clockwork, they'd been plaguing me since, oh, the exact moment at the restaurant when I knew Bruce and I were not to be. I'd be lying if I said they were solely about lost love and the intermingling of souls and deep undying devotion; the dreams, whatever their meaning, played less like *Love Story* than *9½ Weeks*.

The alarm clock glowed green in Robert's guest room: 5:38 A.M. Knowing I wouldn't be able to sleep again, I switched on the lamp, squinting. It was still dark. Outside, downtown San Francisco glittered between the two stems of the Bay like a swath of diamonds. Robert and George's flat clung to the steep southeastern hillside of 17th Street, and if you were huddled on the deck or gazing out the guest-room window, you felt as if the light twinkling off the water and jumble of buildings was beckoning you toward the heavens.

Feeling strangely alienated by a view that had always thrilled me, I slipped into the shower and tried to lose myself in the hot jets buffeting my body. It was going to be a busy day: Before I headed down to the Tech Standard's Peninsula offices, I had to swing by my apartment and meet with Colin, and visit Jem and Milo. Tonight, my friends had organized a dinner party at a popular North Beach trattoria. Ordinarily, such an agenda would fire me up, but today I simply felt drained. Like a persistent flu, my yearning for Bruce and confusion over my life's direction waned and spiked, leaving me alternately hopeful and despondent.

I dressed quickly in black slacks and a gray boat-neck top and slipped out into the cool morning to get breakfast. The Castro was just starting to wake up. Heartened by my first encounter of the day—the sight of a beautiful dark-haired boy with a cocky grin and gold lamé pantaloons doing the A.M. walk of shame—I trotted down to the bagel store and bought a sackful of halitosis-inducing rounds, plus lite lox schmear. Next up was coffee. Just the rich smell of real San Francisco grounds percolating, as opposed to the sewer water I'd been forced to drink in Montana, was enough to launch me into a fit of ecstasy and life-affirming platitudes—see, life *was* good, I said to myself as I inhaled against the lid of my double soy latte grande. I grabbed a *Chronicle* and *The New York Times* and trudged back up the hill.

Inside, it was just like *The Brady Bunch,* sans Alice, Jan, Cindy, Marcia, and Mrs. Brady. I guess what I meant to say was, it was a picture of domestic nuclear-familial bliss, minus the dumb, whiny, blond women.

Robert bustled around the kitchen in jeans and a white T-shirt with a spit-up rag over his shoulder. George was busy feeding some sort of white goo to Zoë, who joyfully lobbed spoonfuls at his suit. Thankfully, he'd had the good sense to don an apron over his work clothes.

"Bagels, cream cheese, coffee, newspapers," I chanted, stopping to press a kiss against Zoë's head, which smelled like a virgin piña colada. I swear.

"Bless you," George and Robert said at the same time. We all laughed, and, like a professional cycling team, we rotated places faultlessly; I took my turn feeding the little monster, George washed his hands, and Robert picked up the paper.

For the next five minutes, I focused on shoveling the mush into Zoë's maw.

"Look at this. Isn't this your story?" Robert said. I glanced at the paper. Sure enough, on page A-22 was the latest on the Sutter & McEvoy debacle. It had been picked up by AP and had Dave Lefebvre's byline. Good for Dave. Maybe they'd graduate him to reporting on cow insemination in Great Falls.

"It says that some guy named Glen Whitehead, a VP, planned the whole thing. He took money earmarked for upgrades and used it to pay his gambling debts *and* paid people to burn down the mill and blow up the newspaper offices. Nice guy," Robert said, shaking his head. "It says, *Whitehead confessed to the crimes after being apprehended by authorities in Salt Lake City, including aggravated kidnapping of his lover's daughter for ransom. The kidnapping, Whitehead claimed, was a last-ditch effort to secure the monies before his creditors called in his debts. Whitehead's lover, Melina Curran Mortensen, is the daughter of Sutter & McEvoy partner Michael Curran. Curran is being charged with conspiracy to violate the Clean Water Act and obstruction of justice. No charges have been filed against Melina Curran Mortensen as of yet. Local environmental officials first became aware of the problem when fish began dying in large numbers on the Swan River,* blah blah blah . . . *The case was complicated by the fact that Melina Curran Mortensen was recently divorced from Bruce Mortensen, the senior special agent in charge of the Environmental Protection Agency office in Helena, Montana. Mortensen could not be reached for comment at the time of publication.*"

"Poor little girl," said George.

"Yeah, but I'll get over it," I said bravely.

Robert rolled his eyes.

"I think he meant Emily," he said.

Oh.

"Her whole world pretty much caved in on her," George continued. "I just hope that father of hers has the sense to get her some therapy."

"I'm sure he will," I said faintly. Why'd Bruce have to go and break it off with me when he did? I could have gone to therapy with them—I was great at therapy, had a veritable black belt in it.

If anyone was qualified to weigh the relative merits of Prozac versus Xanax, it was I.

"Georgette, the father wanted Jen to wait for him, as in *I love you but I can't be with you, won't you please wait for me.*" Robert hooted.

He and George had taken to referring to Bruce as "the father," perhaps in deference to their own newly acquired parental status or maybe just to annoy me by reinforcing Bruce's extreme age and/or primary loyalty to the fruits of his loins. Whenever they said this, I always thought of Richard Chamberlain's Father Ralph de Bricassart in *The Thorn Birds,* which, as anyone with a romantic cell in her body could tell you, is the undisputed paragon of stories of forbidden love. Naturally, I thought it should get a posthumous—or whatever the cinematic equivalent is— Emmy Award.

I got up.

"I've got to go. I'm meeting Colin at my apartment and seeing Jem Pierce before I head down to Lawton City."

"Car keys are on the foyer table. You'll be back for dinner?" Robert said.

"Yep."

Now, back to ye olde homestead.

It felt funny to ring my own doorbell.

Colin buzzed me in and I walked up the rickety staircase. In the months I'd been gone, the pale pink building had taken on an alien, fussy aspect, quite unlike the squat pragmatism of Gladys's bungalow or the sensual, floating quality of Bruce's aerie. Suddenly, I missed the pungent earthy smell of Montana in the fall, replaced, as it had been, with San Francisco's concrete emptiness and the aroma of sizzling lemongrass from the Thai place down the street.

The door was open, so I went in.

"Colin?" I called.

Everything looked the same, though marked by that dank, slightly soiled ambience that says *Straight Man in the House*. The shades were closed against the cheerful light of day. My cool Eames-style coffee table groaned under a subdivision of beer cans, and the whole place smelled faintly of pot, or wet gym socks, or both.

This man was going to be a doctor? For shame.

Colin appeared.

"Sorry about that. My dad called. I was cleaning up, but..." His voice drifted off and he shrugged, his dreadlocks forming a blondish aureole around his head.

"So, welcome back." We hugged awkwardly, probably based on the triple dose of weird we had going: he was sort of my tenant, since I was subletting to him, he had become my friend's boyfriend in my absence, and he'd had sex on my bath mat. But, then, I'm not sure he knew I knew about the last one. Two and a half.

"So, I guess you found your dad," I said, remembering our first encounter and the lecture I'd gotten from Els.

"Yeah, I did. He's teaching at Laney College in Oakland, plays in a band. I got to meet my half sisters and my stepmom. They're cool. I have dinner over there sometimes. Katie came with me a few times." He glanced at me shyly, as if Nguyen's and my friendship might have bestowed on me facts about his life that were otherwise private—like his tendency to talk dirty while hiding the salami. Oops.

"Do you want something to drink?"

"No, thanks. I actually have to get going. I just wanted to come by and talk about me coming back and stuff."

"When do I need to be out by?"

I calculated.

"I'm going to leave Montana early next week. It'll take me a couple of days to get home. But if you need to stay a few extra days, I could always stay with George and Robert," I said.

"Well, actually, Katie said I could start moving my stuff in this weekend." He actually blushed.

"You're moving in together?" I couldn't help it—I think I gasped.

"Yeah, well, it seemed like a good thing. We're both poor, and I don't want to look for another place in the middle of the semester, so . . ."

Someone notify the people that hell hath officially frozen over. I was a little worried for Colin. The last guy who attempted to cohabitate with Katie ended up moving back in with his parents in Ames, Iowa, after she kicked him out on Christmas Eve. I heard he spends his days watching television and serving as Webmaster for his mother's on-line antique-doll trading business. I believe Katie's last words on that fateful occasion were, *Never again*.

"That's great," I said. Being in med school, I supposed he had a pipeline for Prozac, which was fortuitous.

We resolved the bits and pieces, and then I left to visit Jemima Abbott Pierce.

Jem's Noe Valley neighborhood was as pristine and breeder-friendly as ever. One could easily mistake the main thoroughfare, 24th Street, for a minivan used-car lot, and the many hip young parents teeming in the village's coffee shops, bagelterias, and natural- and gourmet-foods stores seemed casually affluent, as if maternity/paternity leave was an inalienable right, not a privilege.

I parked Robert's car and wended my way toward Jem's home through the hordes of procreative yuppies in Patagonia fleece jackets. All of them appeared to be holding leashes with an adorable Jack Russell terrier or interracial child at the end of it. That was one piece of the puzzle Bruce and I hadn't had time to assemble: Would he, nearing forty-four, even have wanted more kids? Feeling maudlin, I envisioned a brood of curly-haired tots with Mom's dimpled thighs and Bruce's honey-colored eyes and thick brows.

I rang Jem's door. Godzilla answered. Actually, it was little Milo standing in front of his mother.

"Jen!" she said.

Jemima scooped up Milo, who looked as if he had been fed a steady diet of bovine growth hormone or something. Truly, he was enormous.

We hugged, and Milo grabbed a chunk of my hair and pulled.

"Ouch!" I yelled.

"Milo, stop it," Jem said, disengaging his monstrous paw. "Come on in, Jen."

I plunked myself down in the midst of controlled chaos. Even Jemima, who had all the help old family money could buy, couldn't keep Godzilla from wreaking destruction, it seemed.

"So, you got the job."

"I got the job," I concurred.

"Took them long enough. Do you care?" she asked.

I shrugged.

"Want some tea?" Jem said.

"Yeah."

While my former boss boiled water, I kept an eye on Milo, who had turned his wide-eyed gaze to my backpack. Back off, buddy, I mouthed. I filled Jemima in on the latest developments, prepared to relish her pearls of wisdom and wallow in a little sisterly commiseration.

"So, why'd you leave?" she asked, setting a mug in front of me.

"What do you mean, why'd I leave?"

"I mean, why didn't you consider staying on in Montana and seeing this through?"

I stared at her, trying to see if she was being facetious, but saw only straightforward curiosity in the kind, cornflower-blue eyes.

"Um, because I was raised to be a strong, independent woman, and sitting on the sidelines while someone else calls the shots is bound to earn me a lifetime of misery and desperation, not to mention help put back the women's movement about fifty years?" I answered.

Jem shook her head. "Bad answer."

"Okay, how about it seemed like the fates talking, given the enormous list of strikes against us working out, and I thought I might just listen for a change," I said.

"Better, but not insurmountable."

"Okay, then, maybe it was out of deference to his daughter, who's the real innocent in all this, and the one we should all be thinking of."

"Yeah, I'll buy that."

We sipped our tea while Milo did his best to disinter the innards of the VCR.

"So, tell me about him. Why him and not that other guy—Steve, was it?"

How to explain my attraction to Bruce? Sure, he was rugged and handsome in a Marlboro Man sort of way, and his chin scar rivaled Harrison Ford's for sheer butchness, and he fucked like a wildebeest on Viagra. But that was the least of it.

The things I thought of first were all his internal contradictions. I liked how Bruce's sarcasm was always tempered by affection, how he was able to articulate his feelings without relying on the cheesy prefabricated confessions of the self-help generation. He had an almost mournful way about him that manifested in tenderness instead of depression. He'd been raised to work in a mill but loved Nina Simone. His daughter came first, and he didn't apologize for it. Also, he thought I was hot. That was a big one.

"He has many reasons to be sad, and yet he's not," I concluded out loud.

Jem frowned. "Explain."

"I don't know. It's not that he is an eternal optimist or anything that repulsive. It's that he has an ease, a comfort level, that is sort of addictive to be around, like it's contagious or something. And it's so inviolate, it's like nothing could ever take it away, no matter how disruptive or traumatic. It can be very sexy, but also very . . . maternal, almost. Remember that feeling that your mom would protect you from anything? It's like that."

"The only thing my mother ever protected me from was running off to Luxembourg at eighteen with a dubious count, and that's only because she thought Prince Charles was still a viable prospect," Jem said.

"Well, use your imagination."

My own mother, who vacillated between heedless indifference and supreme overprotection, depending on her current healing regimen, could be relied upon only to protect me from the vagaries of an ill-timed polarity session or a particularly vile urine therapy, so I understood Jem's position.

"Hey! Stop that. . . ." Milo had removed his pants and diapers and was squatting behind the sectional sofa. Jemima took out the cattle prod and zapped him a good one.

Actually, she picked him up, laughing, and pressed kisses all over his proud face.

I stood up.

"Gotta go. Hef awaits."

During our previous tenure together at the Tech Standard, we'd taken to calling Nancy Teason "Hef," which was short for heifer, which really needed no explanation. That's what I love about Jem: She may be wise and kind and ooze inner peace, but she's not above a lowbrow, unprofessional potshot if it'll contribute to team unity.

We hugged. Milo squirmed in her arms, ready to embark on his next act of terror, no doubt.

"It's so good to see you, Jen. And don't worry about anything. I'm sure you made the right decision for you. There's no one right path, you know."

"Well, see you soon, okay?"

And now, part three: The prodigal daughter returns.

CHAPTER 26

prodigal what?

To: bmortensen@mail.epa.gov
From: aquinn@mail.epa.gov
Subject: confirmation

Mr. Mortensen,

This e-mail confirms your meeting with the board at 4:30 P.M. December 22, 2000. Your ticket is electronic and your itinerary will be mailed to you. Please arrive at the San Francisco office no later than 15 minutes before your scheduled session. Please bring any materials you feel will help your case with the board.

Sincerely,
Antonia Quinn

Executive Assistant to Jonathon Barry
EPA Internal Affairs

The Tech Standard's Lawton City offices sprouted out of an asphalt pasture southeast of the nest of freeways that comprised the 101/92 interchange. Lawton City had been rolled out on reclaimed swampland during that unfortunate period of the 1960s when the words *planned community* were not yet anathema to the tasteful and upwardly mobile. Now, in addition to the thirty thousand or so residents, the preternaturally landscaped grid hosted a sprinkling of dotcoms, juice bars, and Home Depots.

Once, in a fit of boredom, Raquel, a work friend, and I had scoured the city's Web site, which read like a parody of Orwell's *1984*, rambling on about *orderly development* and neighborhoods that *age attractively*, as if a city should be treated with the same youthful revisionism some people bestow on their bodies.

Before Montana—that is, before my eyes were opened to the stark contrast between rural and suburban environments—I thought of Lawton City as a decent if not inspiring place to spend nine hours each day, a sort of mild penance for the inflated salary I earned in the burgeoning Internet field. San Franciscans like myself could derive some benefits from the daily journey, such as lunchtime runs on blissfully horizontal terrain and shopping at uncrowded supermarkets. Now, however, the sparkling man-made lakes and aggressively cheerful strip malls just seemed depressing. I missed Meredith, with its stunning mountain panorama and variegated smells and colors.

I got off the freeway and circled around the cloverleaf exit. The familiar sign that said WELCOME TO THE CITY OF LAWTON CITY greeted me, reinforcing quite splendidly the self-referential absurdity that is permitted to run rampant in America's suburbs these days.

My heart was sinking lower by the minute.

Moving glacially, I traversed the parking lot and entered the building. What was supposed to be a triumphant return was feeling more like a dismal failure, as if I had come crawling back to my former employer rather than the other way around.

"Jen!"

In my stupor, I had nearly walked into my friend Raquel Birney. We hugged. Raquel worked in accounting, was possessed of a gigantic supercomputer of a brain, and was forever on some self-masticating diet or another.

"What are you on? C'mon, tell me!" I insisted.

"Macrobiotics!" she said. "Now, who is it this time?"

It was a little game we played: I acted like a querulous mother who suspected her daughter was "on drugs," and treated her perpetual dieting like an unfortunate addiction, and Raquel teased me about my crushes on unattainable men.

"You don't even want to know," I said ruefully.

"You can tell me about it at lunch," Raquel said. "Sushi at No-Name?" she asked, referring to the generic Japanese eatery we used to frequent.

I agreed and hustled into the lobby to tell HR I was there.

There was a new receptionist I didn't know, which was no surprise, as the Tech Standard's office manager was reputed to be hell on Easy Spirit pumps. I gave her my name and waited to be escorted into the inner sanctum. There was just time for a brief fantasy in which Bruce and I were delivered into holy matrimony in an Aruban destination wedding presided over by *Love Boat*'s Captain Stubing, which lent me about 120 seconds of blushing ecstasy before Dara Wentworth arrived.

There must be something about human resources that attracts the most anal-retentive and falsely jovial among us. I have never met an HR person who would so much as utter the word *shit* in mixed company, yet it often seems as if seething rage and homicidal despair underlie their manic cheer, ready to explode into volcanic-magnitude lunacy at any moment. If you ask me, postal workers have gotten a bad rap, and it's really personnel managers who are likely to suddenly bust out AK-47s and mow us all down while stacks of group health-insurance forms lie, unattended, on their desks.

"Jennifer. You look so *well*," Dara trilled, and the petty editor part of me that loves the difference between *good* and *well* quietly convulsed and died. Now who's anal?

"Thanks. So do you. Are you doing something different with your hair?"

Dara unconsciously stroked her shellacked titian cap, which resembled a strawberry-hued 1920s cloche hat.

"Well, I got it colored last week. Maybe that's it."

"Hmm."

I followed her to her corner office. That's another thing: HR always got office space all out of proportion to their station, ostensibly because needy employees looking for a shoulder to cry on—or getting pseudo-sympathetically reamed out for some manufactured transgression—required privacy. *Hello*—isn't that what the parking lot's for?

"So, we were so excited to hear you wanted to apply for Jemima Pierce's position," Dara said, settling her broad ass in her wire-sprung chair.

Before Montana, that would have annoyed me. Now that I knew I could run away with impunity and have sex with regiments of beautiful men under a canopy of nature, I merely smiled beatifically.

"Er, right. So, we have you first meeting with Nancy Teason, then Carl Hanson." She leaned in closer. "I'm not supposed to say this, of course, but since you're family and all, I'm going to tell you that this is really all a formality. A little bird told me that the position has already been given to you, Jen!"

Yippee! I felt like I had just been told I'd won the Publishers Clearinghouse Sweepstakes—and the contest was worth ten dollars. What was wrong with me? This was exactly what I'd wished for when I left for Montana in a huff—yes, it was a huff by anyone's definition—and now I found myself actually missing Bernie's crazy midnight phone calls, the *Gazette*'s homey staff meetings at which someone inevitably had to leave to breed their cows or drive their kid to rodeo class.

I nodded my way through the rest of Dara's long-winded explanations, then let her lead me to Nancy's office. We stopped to grab mineral waters on the way.

"Jen!" Nancy leapt up from her desk and sort of air-hugged me.

"Nancy!" Ooh, I'm funny.

"Great to see you!"

Once we'd established that (a) it was great to see each other, (b) things weren't the same without me, and (c) I had been living in Montana, *not* Minnesota, everything was peachy. We talked shop for a while, and I even found myself looking forward to picking up with my fussy stable of contributing writers, among other things.

Then something interesting happened, or, at least, something I would have found interesting *before the accident that took my sight, stole my life, and killed my dog.*

"Jen, I'd like you to meet our new features editor, if you have a little more time," Nancy said. She leaned out and called, "Ariel, can you come in here for a minute?"

I sipped fizzy lime water and studied my shoes, which were looking rather in need of a shine. Note to self: Buy new shoes. (What, did you think I was going to shine them when I could shop my way back to emotional health?)

A tall man with wavy blond-streaked hair and a wiry physique stepped through the door. He had squared-off, stylish glasses and a sexy smirk, as if he was used to being the most titillating conversationalist in any room. In his hand was a pair of battered running shoes, which gave him the air of a rueful athlete who runs only to give his giant pulsing brain a needed rest.

I felt nothing. Not even the urge to impress, which meant, as any of my friends could tell you, that I was either felled by a nasty flu bug or quite possibly dead.

Nancy introduced us and we shook hands.

"Jen's just back with us from her sabbatical in . . . Mount St. Helens, was it?"

God help us all.

"Er, actually Meredith," I said.

Ariel brightened.

"Oh, Montana's great. I did Outward Bound there just out of college. In Glacier National Park," he said.

Hmm. Past participation in Outward Bound: a sign of either a masochistic messianic complex or exciting personal dynamism, depending on how you looked at it. Judging by the strategically uncut blond locks and slightly rumpled cassock-ish clothing, I would say self-appointed Jesus. Aargh.

We engaged in the professional mating dance for a few more minutes, whereby I learned that Ariel had attended Cornell, climbed Mt. Kilimanjaro, and observed a strict vegan diet while reporting for *Outside* magazine. Then Nancy excused him and Ariel trotted out.

Nancy's eyes followed his round khaki rear until he'd left, like a lioness stalking a particularly tender-looking gazelle.

Ugh.

"Ariel McNitt is a very talented editor," she gushed. Somehow I doubted she'd read his work.

It was funny—Raquel and I always thought old Nancy preferred blue hairs like Carl Hanson. But there's nothing like firm young manflesh to whet the appetite of a straight female in her prime.

Not that I'll ever know again.

The rest of the meeting passed predictably. Carl Hanson was one of those middle-aged executives who seem wholly focused on work, as if decades of excessive computer and telephone use had leached him of all sophomoric or distractible tendencies and left an Excel spreadsheet of a personality in their place. I have found that the best policy with these people is to make them feel safe by restricting your comments to things like, *That's a very compelling strategy, Carl,* and *Should we go to the Vietnamese place for lunch?*

I spent a pleasant lunch with Raquel over gyoza and maguro sashimi, checked in with a couple of other people, then slipped into the sunny Bay Area afternoon on the day of my prodigal return feeling things were just ever so slightly awry. Not horribly wrong, just inexplicably cryptic, I guess.

Which just goes to show that you don't have to be Dionne Warwick to have psychic revelations.

CHAPTER 27

two brides

To: Ariel McNitt
From: ExaltSalon
Subject: Appointment Confirmation

This email confirms your appointment for Friday morning at 10 a.m. We have you down for highlights and deep conditioning. See you then!

Please note that ExaltSalon requires 24-hour advance cancellation.

Kiki

Here's a role I never thought I would play: straight single heroine who saves the day at impromptu lesbian wedding.

Yes, it is true.

I may not be capable of turning the tide of love in my own direction for more than a few careless hours, but I can damn well ensure that women who love women reign triumphant on their Special Day.

When I got home to Robert's after my exhausting day, a pow-wow was going on in the kitchen.

"Jen! Guess what?" Robert asked. His gorgeous Irish eyes were—you guessed it—smiling.

"Bruce called to say he changed his mind and wants me to have his children?"

I wasn't even joking. That's how scary things had become.

"No, silly," he said, as if the idea of a man wanting to plant his seed in my belly was akin to President Clinton keeping his hands off a pretty new intern.

"We just got invited to a wedding!" he announced. "Such fun. You know Lucy, the woman who answers phones part-time at George's office and deejays at Club Byte? She and her girlfriend, Tyra, decided to get hitched at City Hall in"—he glanced at his watch—"one hour. It was kind of spontaneous."

"We were thinking, wedding first, then your welcome-home dinner on schedule at Café Rigatoni. How does that sound?" George asked.

I quickly weighed the prospective pain of watching two Dockers-wearing lesbians cherry-pick my matrimonial destiny against another solitary evening watching reruns of the Love Doctors giving each other *that* kind of injection, and I decided the lesbians were the better bet. Who knew, maybe I'd find my future mate there, and she might even be a *doctah*.

Clan Pitt-O'Hanlon-Brenner immediately set about readying itself for the evening's festivities. Zoë would not be attending, and her regular baby-sitter would be coming over shortly.

Do same-sex domestic-partnership ceremonies at City Hall possess the same style mandates as traditional nuptials? Who knew—but it didn't matter much, as I would rather don pasties and a fur-lined G-string than wear white shoes or clothes that might compete with the blushing bride. (Something about this fete told me I'd be more likely to show up the brides if I turned up in a back-less handkerchief top with Wiccan runes tattooed on my flesh.)

In the end, I chose a red Chinese silk skirt with contrasting olive green piping, beaded mules with tiny box heels, and a tight black sleeveless turtleneck.

I ran out to the living room.

"Is this okay?" I asked the boys.

"Lose the scarf," George suggested.

"Wear the skirt lower on your hips," said Robert.

Without my gay husbands, what would I be but another tarty straight girl from Florida with big hair and pink lipstick?

After settling Minna, the eighteen-year-old art student who lived down the street, in front of the TV with Robert's and George's cell numbers, Zoë's doctor's name, and the restaurant contact info, we set off.

Immediately, everybody started arguing about which route and parking prospects were best. This is a San Francisco pastime that rivals Giants games and eating for most favored activity, and I have yet to see anyone do it better than denizens of the City by the Bay.

Me: "Definitely take Franklin. There's two-hour nonmetered parking within four blocks."

Robert: "At rush hour? I think Octavia to Fell to Van Ness to the little lot next to the TV station is better."

George: "I was thinking of swinging around to Bush and cutting back on Gough."

Me: "Bad idea. What if there's something at the opera or symphony tonight?"

We were driving exactly two miles.

Finally, we squeezed into a moped-sized spot in front of the housing projects located a few blocks from City Hall. Since the nuptials were scheduled to take place in exactly three minutes, we jog-walked to the facility. Well, they ran and I sort of hopped behind, curling my toes to keep my impractical shoes from flying into the gutter.

We got there with fifteen seconds to spare.

A bunch of friends had gathered in the stately wood-paneled room where a justice of the peace processes weddings and domestic partnerships. Tyra, bride number-one, wore what looked to be a mechanic's jumpsuit and an armory of silver jewelry. As I got closer, I realized it was actually Dickies slacks and a dark gray T-shirt that said, *I believe you, Anita* on the front. Tyra had high, firm tits and arms like Gina Gershon's in *Bound,* a movie I highly recommend if you wish to see the best use of a white tank top ever applied in American film, along with some pretty hot fem-on-fem sex. I regarded my own undistinguished biceps, which seemed to have departed for parts unknown, and sighed.

Tyra looked nervous as she came up to us.

"Have you seen Lucy anywhere? She went to the bathroom to change, but she should have been back by now." When she spoke, her tongue piercing gave her a rather appealing lisp.

"Why don't I go check for you, and you can stay here in case she turns up?" I offered.

"Thanks."

I zigzagged over to the bathroom. I knew the building well, having visited it every week for the better part of a year to go to the county recorder's when I was an editorial assistant at a local paper.

I opened the door and listened. Nothing.

"Hello? Lucy, are you in here?"

"Who are you?" a tight voice answered from the last stall.

"Jen Brenner. I'm a friend of George Pitt's. People were wondering if you were all right."

"God, no. Tell them I'm fucked. We're all fucked," she wailed.

You said it, sistah.

I crept up to the stall. For all I knew, the crazy woman would bust out, slam me in the face with the metal door, and ruin my beautiful orthodontia.

"Lucy, do you want to talk about it? I can get someone—"

The door swung open, revealing a diminutive fairy queen in a white pouf of a dress. Black combat boots peeked out from under the mass of tulle. Her hair was dyed black and slicked back into tufty spikes. A garland of flowers encircled the slim neck; then I realized it was a tattoo of tiny skeleton heads. Her child-size hands covered her eyes, as if she was in pain.

"I don't think I can do this," she moaned.

"Um. Well, if you have reservations, you should trust your instincts," I said unhelpfully. Jen Brenner—your friend in the fight against true love.

"It's not that I don't love Tyra. I totally do! It's that this whole marriage thing is freakin' me out. I guess I always thought, you know, that I would be single forever, and just be with a good woman for a while, then meet someone else, and that would be cool, you know? I didn't think I'd meet someone like Tyra and get swept away and then have her tell me there's nothing she wants more than to be with me always and that she wants to get married!" She hiccuped.

I stared at the elf girl in the doll-like wedding dress. Perhaps we can trade lives? I'll just lend her my Chinese silk skirt, and she can step out of the confectionery straitjacket and disappear into the San Francisco night. Then I've just got to find a man—and how hard can that be?

"I guess what I'm trying to say is . . . I kind of thought that compromising even the smallest of your dreams to build a life with someone was like cutting a piece of yourself off and throwing it away. Like, a self-hating act, you know? And I sort of thought, well, because I'm not into men I'll never have to do that to make it work with another person. What a joke! It's not like Tyra's, like, a repressive person or anything, it's more that *I'm* imposing these things on myself. Like, you know, not going to the bars anymore, and getting up early so I can have breakfast with Tyra before she goes to work and stuff. God, I sound like a really superficial cunt, don't I?" she cried.

"No, not at all," I said. I meant it. She wasn't superficial, and, as for being a cunt, well, certainly not in my book.

She shut up for a minute. All I could hear was the sound of her snuffling and the steady plop of a leaky faucet.

"I'm doing the right thing, aren't I?" she asked, looking deep into my eyes with her reddened ones.

"Do you love her more than you ever thought you could love someone?" I said.

"Yes."

"Are you a better person with her than without her?"

"Uh-huh."

"Do you like the way she smells even after she's just worked out?" During my one night with Bruce, I'd made him laugh by burrowing into his armpit and inhaling; if I could have distilled his essence into an aromatherapy candle and burned it on my nightstand, believe me, I would have.

Lucy looked at me strangely.

"I guess." She shrugged.

"Well, then the other stuff can probably be resolved over time," I concluded, glancing discreetly at my watch: 5:17 P.M.

"Um, do you want me to go back there with you?" I asked.

She paused and smiled at me shyly.

"Would you?"

And that, my friends, is how I came to walk a beautiful, combat-booted bride down the aisle toward her moist-eyed, muscular intended, in the honored space usually reserved for fathers and particularly outstanding couples therapists.

"You wanna da parma or da prosciutto?"

I wanna da parma.

I *loved* the waiters at Café Rigatoni. Visiting the shoe-box-size restaurant in North Beach was like getting a massage, a trip to Italy, and a good meal, all in one. First off, the servers were all swarthy, roving-eyed men whose impenetrable Roman and Neopolitan accents and hiked-up trousers recalled that first trip to Europe, where you lost your Euro-virginity to the bellhop in the *pensióne* your guidebook mysteriously called *charming* and *near* the Piazza San Marco. Second, in addition to the usual waiterly duties like pouring water, taking your order, and reeling off the day's specials, Rigatoni's waiters apparently subscribed to the school that mandated steamy, protracted glances, off-color jokes, and neck massages as part of a complete culinary experience.

And, oh, what a well-disciplined school it was.

When Robert, George, and I arrived at the overheated eatery off Columbus, Els and Katie were already at the table, being summarily fondled by an olive-skinned tag team in white sous-chef coats and bright red neckerchiefs.

"Hey!"

We all hugged and kissed, prompting whistles of appreciation from the kitchen, bar, and, judging by the sheer volume of hand claps and shouts, Naples itself.

I was so glad to see them again—my girls. During a time of personal crisis, phone calls were one thing, but inhaling the sweet perfume of Els's and Katie's sisterly empathy was quite another.

"So, have you exorcised that prick yet?" Katie asked.

Really, Katie needed to toughen that skin of hers, if she expected to survive in this world.

"Workin' on it," I replied, tossing my leather jacket into the waiting arms of a hovering Italian, who "accidentally" stroked my breast as he went to hang it up.

"But enough about me," I said, mentally strategizing a protracted Jen Brenner analysis session later, over many rounds of drinks. I waggled my eyebrows. "What's going on with you and Ben?" I asked Els.

She blushed furiously.

"What's going on is, your brother's coming here for Christmas and they're gonna GIT IT ON," Katie yelled.

"Is that true?" I said.

Els nodded.

"Yes, he's coming. I do not know if we'll 'git it on.'" She mock-glared at Katie.

"Well, that's good news. Now, what else are we getting, and

where's the wine? I just served as father of the bride at an impromptu lesbian wedding, and I'm in need of a little sustenance."

Robert, George, and I filled the girls in on our nuptial adventure.

"So, you read from the Wiccan handbook?" Katie was dubious.

"Yeah, well, the woman who was supposed to do it called and said she was running late because her black cat had the flu"—jeers from the table—"so I guess I had some cred, having walked Lucy down the aisle and all, and I did it. Actually, it was quite moving. There were about fifteen friends there, and when the justice pronounced them 'partnered' there wasn't a dry eye in the house," I said.

We paused while a swarm of waiters descended with bottles of cheap Chianti, a platter of antipasto, and prosciutto-wrapped melon.

I felt a firm hand rub my neck. Bruce's spot. Spurt of something dark and yearning, quickly extinguished.

"You have everything you need, miss?"

My waiter-cum-masseuse was darkly handsome, dentally gifted, and not a day over twenty-two.

"I'm fine."

He nodded doubtfully, as if I wouldn't be fine until I'd been stripped of my garments, laid out on his foot-wide pallet at the YMCA boardinghouse, and plundered like a South African diamond field.

"So, I hear Els isn't the only one with news. What's this about you and Colin moving in together?" Robert said to Katie.

For once, she looked unsure.

"Well, Ms. Montana is moving back, and he didn't have anywhere to go, so I thought, for a few months, why not?" Katie tipped her glass of ice water and gulped madly.

"But isn't that going to, you know, cramp your style?" Robert persisted.

"The only thing that's going to cramp is Colin's neck from having to service you every night," I shrieked.

We all laughed.

"Ha, ha," Katie said. "It may surprise you to know that I have deep feelings for Colin. He's not just another one of my—"

George: "Conquests?"

Els: "Three-month diversions?"

Robert: "Hairdo ideas?"

Me: "Human vibrators?"

Katie flushed.

"I can see I am misunderstood by the people I thought were my closest friends. Maybe I should just go," she huffed, and stood up. Unfortunately, the Chianti bottle was resting on the flowing edge of her shirtsleeve, and red liquid soaked the tablecloth, our dinner, and Katie's pale blue flares.

"Oh, crap!" she cried.

Rigatoni's version of the Italian killer bees swarmed again, and, in the maelstrom, Katie was swept off to the kitchen, where, presumably, she would be cleaned, stripped, ravished, and impregnated. (Not necessarily in that order.)

We all looked at each other.

"I'll go back," I offered. Relieved, Robert, George, and Els dug into their succulent pasta.

The "cleaning" was a sight to behold.

Cooking had apparently halted at the entrance of my attractive Vietnamese-American friend. Pots and pans lay where they'd fallen, Alfredo sauce spilling out onto the grill, basil lying half-chopped in a sad little mound on the butcher block. A roasted chicken protruded from the industrial oven, its skin blackening and curdling slightly around the wings.

In the midst of this chaos, Katie stood, helpless, as the various members of Team Cinzano knelt, rapt, before her crotch. Worshipfully, they applied Pellegrino-soaked rags to her thighs, pressing away the wine stain as reverently as they might wipe pigeon shit from Pope John Paul's robe.

"I see things are taken care of in here," I muttered.

Katie and I stared at each other. I wondered if she was still mad. Then we cracked up. I leaned against the abandoned butcher block, cackling. My hand accidentally plowed into a pile of grated Parmesan cheese, and I shook parchment-colored flakes off onto the tiled floor.

"Are you okay? We didn't mean to hurt your feelings," I said.

Katie hung her head.

"Yeah, I'm fine. I know you didn't. It's just, it gets old some-times, people thinking I'm so . . . so hard, I guess. I know it's partly my fault. I guess I've never wanted people to think I'm just an-other pretty face, so I—"

"—act like the worst frat boy we ever met," I finished. We laughed together.

I watched the dream team apply sponges to Katie's pants, consulting with one another in Italian on the best approach to preserving the integrity of the fabric. If there's anything you can depend on in life, it's death, taxes, and Italian respect for textiles.

Finally, Katie had to extricate.

"*Grazie.* No—no, really, it's fine now. See? No more stain. Hey! Stop that!" She turned to me wearily. "Let's get out of here."

It must be brutal. You know—to be so beautiful that head chefs stop cooking to concoct stain removers for your pants.

We returned to the table, and, lo and behold, it was time for the Jen Brenner psychoanalysis session. Honestly, I would have preferred to wait for the dim, confessional ambience of a seedy dive, the warming sting of sour-apple martinis on the tongue, the intimacy forged on having consumed enough food for twice as many people. I guess I had sort of pictured a delicate, heartfelt probing, during which my dearest friends would tenderly but firmly extract morsels of information from me about Bruce, my yearning for Bruce, my risking my life for Bruce's surly offspring, Bruce's sexual behaviors, Bruce's stone-melting honey eyes—oh, and did I mention Bruce?

But, alas, it was not to be. The interrogation started as soon as we sat down.

"Jen, we're worried about you," Robert began.

"Because we think you aren't being entirely rational about this Bruce character." Katie, who had apparently recovered from her own character assassination, was raring to even the score.

"You don't seem like yourself. On two occasions I have seen you wear a color other than black!" Els (the traitor).

I stared into my *puttanesca* sauce, which seemed to me a wildly appropriate choice. What was this—comforting circle of love, or self-serving intervention? George, I noticed, had the smarts to stay out of this little private hanging. He shoveled penne into his mouth with false enthusiasm, eyes averted toward the ceiling's frescoes, which looked like they'd been finger-painted by a blind kindergartner.

"We're really, really glad you decided to come back to San Francisco, before things got more out of hand up there," Robert said.

I thought he sounded like a sanctimonious prig and told him so.

"What's so appalling about me wanting to be with Bruce?" I cried, loud enough to be heard over the gondolier music. "It's not like he's a bad person. In fact, he's a good person! So what if his work is suffering, and his wife is a bitch and he's getting a divorce, and Emily was kidnapped for ransom by nefarious criminals at his father-in-law's mill," I babbled, feeling defensive as hell. Still, *nefarious criminals*? Was there any other kind?

I took a deep breath and let them have it.

"I can't believe you guys! Since when are you so conventional, so self-righteous? You're just against it because he's so much older than me, just like my parents would be. 'Cause you have neat, preconceived ideas of what you want our little love circle to be like, where we all go out with someone who adds value—yes, I'm that cynical—and makes things oh-so-easy for the rest of us. God forbid Bruce would embarrass you or something. Wear cowboy boots in public, or talk about hunting, or reveal that he has a daughter who's almost a teenager." I sputtered to a stop.

They gaped, mouths open in stupefaction and either derision or respect, I couldn't tell which.

Appalled, I felt tears course down my cheeks.

"Your 'concern' is misplaced, anyway. We're not together, so what difference does it make? We broke up! Are you happy? Do you want to have a party? The Jen and Bruce Breakup Party? Do you want to take bets on how long it'll take me to find someone who passes muster with you?

"I'll tell you what's out of hand," I choked out. "What's out of hand is that my relationship with the man who could have been the love of my life lasted about twelve hours."

Jem's words of kindly admonition came flooding back to me.

"And what's out of hand is that it was my own pathetic need to be the independent, takes-no-prisoners, ass-kicking woman we all admire—who, by the way, is a complete fallacy—that got me here. I could have waited for him, but I was too proud, and now it's too late," I said softly.

"Jen, that is so not true." Robert's eyes were wide and sympathetic.

"Jen, please listen to us! We just want what's best for you," Els cried.

But I was already outside, running down Columbus Avenue toward the fierce steeple of the Transamerica Building, the headlights of passing cars glancing blows across my face.

CHAPTER 28

packing it in

To: (recipient list suppressed)
From: jen.brenner@meredithgazette.com
Subject: new e-mail address

Hi, all. Just a quick note to let you know my e-mail address is changing again. Sabbatical over—back to SF! Try me at jenb@techstan-
dard.com.

Jen

Going back was hard, but leaving for good was harder.

I arrived back in Meredith on Thursday evening with a tight
agenda and a mother of a migraine. All the way back from San
Francisco, I'd brooded: Why was everything such a mess? What
had I done to deserve this? Why were my best friends being so
hard on me? The grandfatherly cattle rancher sitting next to me
on the leg from Seattle to Meredith had attempted friendly conversation, but my monosyllabic responses finally got the best of
him and he eventually returned to *Bull's Balls Digest*, or whatever
exciting literature captured his attention.

Feeling like no one understood my need for a little old-fashioned ego stroking and that the whole world had snuck off into domestic bliss while I was out to lunch, I'd called Ben before I left.

"Benji, it's me."

"Hey. How are you? Is everything all right?"

"I don't know. Aside from having a messed-up and nonexistent love life and having alienated all my friends, yeah, it's okay," I sniffed, fishing for sympathy.

"Have you talked to Els lately?"

"Um, yeah. Why?"

"I'm thinking of coming out for Christmas. Did she tell you?" he said dreamily.

I get it, I wanted to scream. You're in love. Bully for you.

"Ben, do you think I'm crazy?"

"No, but you could use an attitude adjustment."

I hung up.

Now, as I drove toward Gladys's familiar homestead, I rehearsed how I might tell Bernie and Gladys and the handful of other people here who might care if I suddenly came down with terminal broken-heart-induced dermatitis that I was leaving, cutting out, striking out for the wild blue yonder.

I felt like the worst kind of quitter.

For the first time, the chill of winter lay in the air. I'd had to blast the Subie's heater. It lent Montana a whole new aspect for me, visions of snowy weekends at local resorts, shoveling cars out in the morning after a blizzard, short, lean days that cut the wheat from the chaff, that defined what Rocky Mountain living was all about.

I guess I was the chaff.

Gladys's lights were on when I arrived, and a jolt of pure gladness seeped through me. It had always been so important to me to know where "home" was, throughout my migration from the tropical vistas of my childhood in Florida to the undulating, careening angles of San Francisco and, lately, to this bowl-like valley, edged in by verdant hills, and farther out, craggy peaks. I needed to know that wherever I landed it wasn't a total accident of fate, that fate, or destiny, or somebody's cosmic sense of humor, had had a hand in getting me there. Sure, I make fun of my mom, with all her chatter about "personal growth" and "karmic cycling," but, truth be told, Mom's relentless pursuit of self-awareness— and the perfect biofeedback session—had affected me. I wanted to believe that I hadn't come to Meredith for nothing, that I was driven by more than a vague, wandering carnality and chronic escapism, and that, if I had been plunked down in Schenectady or Fargo or Albuquerque, I would *not* have had an affair with the local, *married* sheriff/bank manager/air-traffic controller, a boss with a fuzzy halo of hair and a raspy voice, a proud landlady, and a potboiler-worthy misadventure.

I entered the house. Gladys occupied her rocking chair, Neffy nestled doughnutlike in her lap. The vintage radio crackled and hummed a stream of big-band tunes.

"Jen, it's so good to see you. We missed you." Her softly wrinkled face creased in a smile.

"It's good to see you too, Gladys."

"You must be exhausted. Tea?"

"Thank you, but don't get up—I'll get it."

She waved me off and dumped Neffy unceremoniously on the green velvet love seat.

Relieved, I slid into a chair and stroked Neffy, who purred and rubbed against my legs. Outside, darkness enveloped our neighbors' bungalows in its sleepy shroud.

"There you go." Gladys handed me the tea, which smelled, this time, of lemon verbena and a hint of orange spice.

"How was San Francisco?"

I hesitated. "Not what I expected."

"How so?"

"Well, you always expect this big homecoming, as if things had stopped when you left. So self-absorbed! Then when you get there and find that life goes on without you, that things are pretty much going to happen whether you're there or not, it's kind of disappointing. Kind of makes you wonder what your purpose is in life, I guess."

Gladys nodded wisely, her afghan wrap and fluff of hair giving her a Yoda-like air.

"Are you going home, then?" she asked quietly.

I nodded. "Yes, I guess I am. They offered me my old job back. Actually, a promotion. Guess my little snit did the trick." For some reason, I felt like crying.

"You know, I'm proud of you, Jen. Just like your parents must be. They raised a fine woman in you."

Surprised, a bitter laugh popped out.

"Even though I came here and bumbled nearly everything? If it wasn't for me digging into what was going on at the mill, Bernie wouldn't have been hurt, the *Gazette* offices wouldn't have blown up, Emily might not have been kidnapped, maybe Bruce and Melina might have worked it out, even poor Marion Gerbill would still be in his favorite chair at the Bent Penny instead of moldering in county jail...."

She waved her hand dismissively.

"Nonsense," she said. "Some things have an inevitability about them. Bruce and Melina were cursed from day one, and Bernard's as tough as an old shoe. And Emily's going to be fine, she's got her daddy to take care of her. No, I'd say you were just what this town needed. We were all getting pretty complacent before you came along and shook things up."

There's that *inevitable* word again.

"But what about Steve? I didn't do him any favors, that's for sure," I argued.

She sipped her tea.

"Oh, that one. Well, don't lose any sleep over that boy. While you were gone—when did you leave, Monday?—I think he managed to overcome his pique. I saw him at the cinema on Tuesday night with that little hippie girl in the blond braids. *Funny Face* with Audrey Hepburn was the film. They looked pretty chummy, that's for sure." She smiled wickedly. "I guess we're not quite the

262 ~~~ KIM GREEN

personification of evil we thought we were, hmm? That might relieve you to know."

Damn. I closed my eyes and remembered Steve Wald and his
rose-petal-strewn tent, the way our bodies had glowed deep red
in the light of the lantern, and smiled. Good for Steve.

The phone rang. This time, I insisted Gladys sit.

"I'll get it."

I trotted into the kitchen and answered.

"Hello?"

"Hello. Is Miz Brenner there, please?"

"Speaking."

"This is Lieutenant Filarski with the Meredith Police. How
are you, Miz Brenner?" His gruff voice sounded lukewarm, which,
I imagined, was as close as tough-as-railroad-spikes Wendell
Filarski ever got to such mamby-pambiness.

"I'm good. Thanks for asking. What's up?"

"Well, I was wondering if you could come down to the station
tomorrow. We got your statement, of course, but we need you to
talk to the DA directly about a few things. Would ten A.M. work
for you?"

I wanted to ask him if Bruce Mortensen would be there, but
that seemed a little much under the circumstances, so I merely
said yes, sure thing, and hung up.

And that, I think, was the moment when a dignified exit from
town, a quiet departure in the wee hours of the morning, a slick
vanishing, became virtually impossible.

CHAPTER 29

jail break

To: Kristina Ledermanns
From: Walgreens Pharmacy
Subject: order confirmation

Dear Mrs. Ledermanns,

This e-mail has been sent to notify you that the following on-line order has been shipped:

- [2] Maybelline Waterproof mascara (brown)
- [10] Cheetos (24 oz.)
- [25] Ex-Lax (8 oz.)
- [30] Snickers (1 oz.)

Thank you for shopping at Walgreens!

There exists a phenomenon I like to call the Rule of Crossed Paths. Now, before you infer from this name something Zen, or literary, or profound, consider this: I conceived it while crouched behind a dusty potted plant.

The Rule holds that, the more you wish to avoid crossing paths with a particular person, the more likely it is that you will, in fact, find yourself sharing the same square foot of space. Conversely, yearning feverishly for a mere glimpse of your beloved will ensure a heartbreaking paucity of contact. It is almost like an emotional algorithm: move further away from neutral on the scale in either direction, and the pranksters of the universe will ensure that the exact opposite of your desired plan occurs.

Potted plants aside, there is nothing like the aggrieved woman's imagination to generate visions of fantastic horror or exultation in advance of a potential encounter (depending, I suppose, on whether she has been spurned or pursued prior, and on her particular set of neuroses).

On the day I first isolated and defined this phenomenon, I had arranged to meet Robert for lunch in The City. Initially, I was heedless as I strolled the overdesigned hallways of Kleiner Price, concerned only with my impending culinary choice: Caesar or mixed greens? Then, like a cow struck by lightning on its way to the feed trough, I was jolted by a sickening sight: Andy, the mailroom clerk, rounding the corner of a nest of cubes with his ever-present cart jutting out obscenely, a giant postal phallus. Horrors! My previous contact with the man had consisted of a single tortured exchange at Robert's company picnic—being a progressive firm, domestic partners *and* straight wives were welcome—which had apparently prompted Andy to query Robert as to my romantic availability. The exchange in question had taken place on the sidelines of a vicious Ultimate Frisbee match and had gone something like this:

Andy: "Hey."

Me: "Uh, hello."

Andy: "You like Frisbee?"

Me: "Sure. It's good exercise, I guess."

Andy: "Wanna go out with me?"

Me: "I think I see my husband over there beating up that biker gang. Excuse me."

Did I mention that poor Andy had a rapid-blinking problem and a front tooth that had gone the way of Members Only jackets?

Anyway, the day after I got back from San Francisco and drove to City Hall to meet with Lieutenant Filarski, the fates saw fit to invoke the Rule in the harshest manner possible: old flame, old flame's felonious quasi-wife-unit, old flame's damaged-but-feisty daughter, and me, all crammed into that most torturous of torture chambers—the modern elevator.

I raced in as the doors were closing, something I'll never do again, even if the departing vehicle is the last to leave a burning building, or is in some way analogous to the last flight out of Saigon.

"Thanks," I panted to the room at large as I squeezed past an armoire-size cop in the front.

I saw Emily first. My gaze ran over her red ponytail, which, quite appallingly, was being stroked by a slender white hand that, most horrifyingly, led to Melina Curran Mortensen's shoulder, which leaned in a truly sickening fashion against Bruce's familiar plaid work shirt.

Bruce.

"Oh, my God!" I screamed, then slipped the cyanide pill I had prepared for such occasions under my tongue and fell to the floor in what I hoped was a graceful yet tragic swoon.

Actually, I didn't do any of that.

"Hi," I said brightly, focusing my eyes on the policeman's left shoulder blade, which was as big as an anvil. I prayed for him to fall on me. Just. Fall. On. Me.

Melina just nodded, but I could feel Bruce's eyes burning, and, like the solar eclipses they forbid you to stare at as a child lest you sear your retinas beyond repair, I was unable to turn away.

"Hi," he said simply.

I wanted to say that Bruce had aged twenty years since he sent me packing, but that would have been a lie. Sure, there was a little tightness around the amber eyes, and shadows like violet scimitars beneath them, and a weary hunch to the shoulders I had never seen before. But he still looked good enough to topple onto the floor and lap like sweetened milk.

I hated myself for being so transparent.

I willed myself away from his gaze and turned to Emily.

"How are you, Emily?"

"Fine."

"Anything, um, new?"

She stared at me levelly. "Dad says I can have a horse. He's going to live at Grandpa's."

With whom, I thought nastily, the maid or the family parole officer?

Then we hit the fifth floor, and I pushed my way out first.

"Hey, you dropped something."

Bruce's arm extended toward me as if in slow motion, my—oh, God, unmeasurable horrors!—*hundred-year-old condom* in his hand. Okay, perhaps it wasn't truly one hundred, but it had been moldering in its sarcophaguslike packet, tucked into the random pocket of the bag I *never, ever use,* for at least three years. Before it vanished into accessory oblivion, the ancient rubber had prompted no end of jesting from my so-called friends, who claimed I could always sell it to the Smithsonian Institution for one of their time capsules, or use it as a coffee-table coaster.

My eyes snapped to Bruce's as the doors slid shut, and, I swear, I thought I saw him wink before his smirking face disappeared. Or maybe it was a trick of light?

Fuck me.

Bernie nearly popped a gasket when I turned in my notice that afternoon. For a minute, all that was holy hung in the balance, and I thought he might remove his pants again, just to spite me.

Then his red face cleared, and he plunked himself down in his creaky chair and sighed, long and hard.

"Well, you did good, Brenner. You did good."

I did?

"Yep. Good stories, good writing, good for morale, even if I have this to show for it." He raised his arm, which was still encased in plaster.

"Well, thanks, Bernie. That means a lot to me. It's just time, I think. For me to go back. Before anything else burns down around here," I joked.

Bernie cackled. "You ever want to come back, there'll always be a job for you at the *Gazette*. Can't promise you a story like the mill every day, of course, but I hear the football team's going to be good next year."

Having received the devil's dispensation, I went out and told the rest of the team. Dave Lefebvre, to his credit, gave me an awkward hug, and Margaret Bloom and the designer and the paginators and other folks were genuinely sorry to see me go, and told me so. It was actually quite moving. We celebrated with a big, boozy lunch at Charlie's, which had mysteriously started serving food—or a meat-and-potato-ish approximation of it—in my brief absence.

As with all occasions on which I make a firm decision, I immediately regretted it. If I chose chocolate, I invariably craved strawberry as soon as I had my first lick. Same with the big stuff. Give me a lovely blond squeeze, and my fickle gaze will drift to the brunette honey in the parking lot before we've even stuck the key in the ignition. And we all know how I am about my career. Case in point: I changed my major three times *before* I even started college, over the summer. If that isn't a sign of diabolical indecisiveness, I don't know what is.

However, being an ancient thirty, I did understand one thing: Melancholy at the prospect of leaving a place, a group of people, meant you'd made your mark, that there was something to leave behind. And that did a little to take the sting out of the defection.

That afternoon I drove aimlessly around Meredith, trying to absorb all the places that had come to mean something to me. The Big Dip, site of so many fine feedings and huckleberry shakes to die for. Charlie's, where watery beer, throat-constricting drinks, and animal heads coexist in a perfect state of balance. Alice's Restaurant, which dared to serve a vegetarian menu at a time when Montanans expected to have to wrestle their meal to the plate—or at least fight it for the baked potato. The *Gazette,* where I'd managed to avoid getting fired for almost three months. The park, which I'd always associate with organic water and that crazy Steve Wald.

I studiously avoided three places: Bruce's office, Bruce's house, and the Currans' mansionette.

Feeling like a low-rider cruising East L.A., I swept by the McIntyres' wacky Victorian and grinned: with delicious predictability, the parlor curtains parted, and diminutive Penny's curly head peeked out.

Which reinforced a truism that managed to be both encouraging and sad: Some things never change.

CHAPTER 30

halls, the deck!

To: Melina Curran
From: cjones@foxrealestate.com
Subject: house list

Melina,

Hi! I just wanted to let you know that the Braseltons can be out of the house Thursday at 1 p.m. Does that work for you? Let me know right away—this place is a keeper, and it's gonna go fast! Oh, did you have your father sign those mortgage papers I sent over? The other two-bedrooms I scheduled for Friday. Talk soon!

Calliope

For years, the Tech Standard has inexplicably held its annual "Christmas" party in early January. Citing overbooked venues, prohibitive pricing, and overcommitted employees as reasons for such a bizarre maneuver, it's managed to deliver a tepid, yawn-inducing event each time. When I was with Damon, we used him as an excuse to sneak home in time for Must See TV—*On to the next commitment, I'm afraid! Can't do a thing with the old ball and chain! Bye, everyone!* Last year, when I was single, I found myself pressed against a red-and-green-wreathed balustrade at 12:35 A.M. on January 7, clutching my Pink Cosmo like a lifeline as Gary the Scary Programmer lectured me on the relative elegance of Perl versus Java code. His breath smelled of shrimp cocktail and bruschetta. I'd had to excuse myself and stagger out to the handrail of the docked yacht we'd rented, thinking I might have cause to vomit a rainbow of pasta, sushi, and Cosmopolitan over the side, sealing my fate forever as "the girl who barfed at the not-Christmas party." Thankfully, everything stayed down at that moment, and I later learned that living-room rugs *can* look brand spanking new when you apply a combination of stain remover, soda water, and douche to the puke stains.

This year was going to be different.

For one, the aggrieved outcries of the Standard staff had finally reached the impaired ears of management, and the party was being held in mid-December, when people actually felt festive and postholiday diets and drinking fasts had yet to rear their ugly heads.

Secondly, Gary the Scary Programmer was no longer a factor, having accepted a $150,000-a-year job as a database administrator for a dotcom that allowed visitors to bid for rhinoplasties and tummy tucks.

Third—and I hated myself for even *thinking* this—there was a new man in town. A hot man. A man worth that extra stroke of glittery eyeshadow, that Nancy Ganz abdominal constrictor guaranteed to push your love handles into your ass and launch your belly flab into your strapless bra, worth the three and one half inches of stiletto that will take off ten pounds and cripple you for a week.

Ladies of the Tech Standard, may I introduce Ariel McNitt, he of the flowing golden locks, stinky gym shoes, and Outward Bound diploma.

In the week preceding the event, speculation as to Mr. McNitt's emotional availability (single status had already been confirmed), womanly preferences, and alcoholic predilections reached a fevered pitch. Knots of editors and designers would gather at the copier or the fridge, and an almost precarnal hum would ensue, cut short only by McNitt's arrival or an executive's innocent desire to grab a Coke. Personally, I thought the blond Adonis sensed and encouraged the furor. One day, while a coterie of lunchers ate at the fountain outside the building, McNitt exited the office in his running clothes and started a series of rather *extreme* stretches in tantalizing proximity to the gallery. Folded in half like a human can opener, he flashed his pale, rock-hard buns at us with apparent innocence while we choked on our salads and mentally removed that last scrap of blue nylon with a sigh.

All of which should have made me dislike him more. But I was as ill with need as the rest of them. Think about *that* the next time you seek a little bang for your buck, ladies: If it's a short-term loan, it'll only leave you wanting more.

Truly, what the Tech Standard experienced was a pure case of crowd lust. Anyone who's ever worked in a publishing environment outside of male-dominated wire services will tell you: Plunk a passably attractive male hominid down in a sea of overworked, single-to-celibate women, and you'll see a feeding frenzy the likes of which hasn't been documented since Quint threw the first bucket of chum off the *Orca* in 1975.

If any work got done at the Tech Standard the week of December 11, I'd eat my carpal-tunnel wrist guard.

Now it was party night at last, and the gallery would be ready to rumba. We're talking control-top pantyhose. Eye paint. Body glitter. Swarovski body crystals. Haircuts. Fresh color. Jimmy Choo sandals. Jersey. Velvet. Satin. Décolletage.

Corsets.

Predictably, I was having a three-alarm clothes crisis and a four-alarm organizational one.

I stared out the window of my apartment, which was still saturated with eau de Colin, a unique blend of high beery overtones and gym-socks notes. A gentle rain tapped against the glass. Fear-ing loneliness upon my return to San Francisco, I'd bought two goldfish to keep me company. They died tragically within the week, but their replacements, Ben II and Jerry II, were still going strong, making endless, soothing circles in their watery world. (The second time around, I'd asked for two that had been bred for longevity or fed goldfish growth hormone or something to help them resist the obviously toxic effects of being in my care.)

I'd been home for nearly a month, but unpacking was something I just couldn't seem to get around to. Between working, daily power yoga, and repairing the tattered remnants of my friendships, there was not a lot of time left for nesting. Plus, unpacking would have lent my return an air of permanency, a state I'd somehow begun to associate with the eternal sealing of my knickers against outside invaders.

Montana seemed like a distant memory now. My time there had developed those clean-cut edges that holidays have, clear starts and finishes and sagging middles where, in the retelling, each day drifted by in a haze of leisure and meaningless moments, punctuated by critical junctures like a particularly compelling day trip or a juicy flirtation. After the sixth or seventh storytelling session, with my regular dental hygienist rapt in front of me, I started to believe my own sanitized version of the tale, and the ball of hurt in my chest began, slowly, to loosen and unwind.

I was getting into discipline in a big way, perhaps for the first time ever. I even approached laziness with discipline, if you want to know the truth. There's nothing like a highly structured weekend bookended by two great meals with friends, stuffed with a trip to the gym, a mani–pedi, a 250-page large-print beach book, eight back-to-back episodes of *Sex and the City* on video, and a strategically late Sunday awakening to make you feel as if you have used your leisure time wisely come Monday morning.

So, despite the fact that my army-issue duffel bag and packing-taped boxes remained in the center of the living room, rifled and censorious, I felt at peace. Sort of. Well, okay, I was clinically nonsuicidal and could just about see contentedness lurking over the emotional horizon.

But I digress.

Tonight I had two choices in the outfit department. One was pure sultry dame. The other was definitely more damned slut. Either could work for me. My goals were simple, and not wholly original: Dress up, look good, resist the cheese table, snare the attentions of Ariel McNitt, and feel good about self for duration of evening and potentially into Sunday morning. If the latest issue of *Marie Claire* was any indication, the perfect ensemble could help me do this.

Ensemble #1 consisted of a sleek, A-line midnight blue dress in thick matte satin with spaghetti straps and chunky, retro platforms. It had the following advantages:

- Displayed firm-to-middling, medium-size, as-of-yet-not-in-need-of-augmentation rack to best advantage.

- Rich blue color brought out my eyes, which, one terribly deep male hominid once told me, over soy Frappuccinos, were "like the windows to my soul." (Our dating cycle ended when he grabbed my admittedly child-bearing hips outside the movie theater and announced that I was "built for love." We took separate taxis home.)

- Nonstretch lining reinforced slenderizing effects of Nancy Ganz strangulator—otherwise known as body slimmer—by channeling flesh away from indented areas and toward intentionally protuberant ones.

- Chunky shoes decreased likelihood of ego-disintegrating, postmidnight fall on stairs, dance floor, or deck.

- It looked expensive. (It *was* expensive, but that did not, in my view, detract from its value-to-benefit ratio in the slightest.)

Ensemble #2 was comprised of a thigh-skimming, high-necked, backless number in clingy black jersey, supplemented by fuck-me pumps and a beaded purse. It had the following advantages:

- It was thigh-skimming. (Note to fashionphobes: This is fashionista for *short*.)

- From the front, it presented as bar mitzvah–appropriate little black dress. From the back, it presented as hooker power suit. Therefore, it delivered upon its wearer the element of surprise inherent in all memorable outfits. Also, it was damn slutty.

- I owned it, as opposed to Ensemble #1, which still taunted me from the window at Neiman Marcus and would have to be purchased in haphazard fashion on the way to the party.

So, you see, I had a dilemma.

Naturally, I called Robert. We were on speaking terms again following my outburst at Café Rigatoni, subsequent heartfelt apology, protracted groveling session, and purchase of Ming vase as conciliatory gift. (Actually, it was a *Minng* vase, but the reproduction was so brilliant, I thought even Robert wouldn't notice the difference.)

"Hello?"

"Hey, it's me."

"What are your options?" he asked, getting straight to the point. He knew, of course, it was par-tay night, having suffered through my pre-event cosmetics-shopping blowout, and had generously marked off time on his calendar for a consulting session.

"Demure blue sheath-y A-line or slutty backless black jersey."

A beat passed.

"Weight?"

I pinched the semipermanent ridge of flesh that tended to cling to my hip-meets-ass area like a cascading *favela*.

"Not bad," I said.

"Mood?"

I exchanged pointed stares with Ben and Jer.

"Decent."

"Slutty black."

"Okay, thanks."

"No problem. Have fun."

"Bye."

One hour later, I was dressed, if not to kill, at least to critically wound.

This year's affair was being held on a sort of landlocked art-deco-ish ship museum near Fisherman's Wharf, perhaps in continuation of last year's pseudo-maritime theme. I got out of the taxi, and before I could enter the building, a gusty wind ripped all thirty-six bobby pins from their painstakingly assembled positions in my hair and deposited them like tranquilizer darts into a thatch of Danish tourists hovering near the museum railing. (Don't ask me how I knew they were Danish; just write it off to pure, refined San Franciscan tourist radar.)

This did not bode well.

Fighting off the first signs of post-fashion-traumatic stress disorder—indicated by a profound compulsion to hail back cabbie and return to *Messieurs* Ben and Jerry II, along with two pints of their culinary namesake—I bravely pierced the party perimeter (i.e., I opened the door and went in).

Thankfully, Raquel was already there, clad in a flattering red sheath with orange and gold wrap.

We hugged.

"You look fantastic," I said.

She spun me around.

"You look naked," she answered.

Could Robert, for once in his life, have been wrong? Surely not, I thought, scanning the room for other signs of fleshly exposure and finding only safe LBDs (Little Black Dresses) and a few conservative glittery tank/black slacks combos.

Oh, no.

Where were all the fashion sluts?

Ever stalwart, Raquel stood behind me, blocking my inde-
cency with her modestly attired self, as we crept toward the bar
in a modified conga line.

"What can I get you?"

The bartender was young, Irish, and craned his neck to get an
eyeful of my back. Did I forget to mention that the dress plunged
almost to my buttcrack? Not my fault! I wanted to yell—surely
you can see how short-waisted I am!

"Chivas Regal," I blurted. The froufrou White Russian I had
planned on now seemed woefully inadequate.

The Irish lad grinned knowingly and began whipping up my
Scotch and Raquel's Sea Breeze.

"Is he here yet?" I whispered to Raquel.

She glanced covertly over her shoulder.

"No, but get a load of that."

"That" turned out to be Nancy Teason and Carl Hanson, who
had somehow ditched their respective spouses and were sharing
personal space under the shadow of an enormous ship anchor.
Carl was obviously the funniest closet comedian alive, judging by
Nancy's head-flung-back trill, which threatened to shatter the
plate-glass windows facing the darkened beach.

At least I wasn't the only one making a fool of myself tonight.

"Here you go, ladies."

We grabbed our drinks, and I slapped a dollar tip on the
counter, hoping the red-haired boy would take the gesture as
the subtle role reversal it was intended to be (i.e., john–slut
switcheroo).

Raquel and I joined a group of graphic designers for a pow-
wow on the deck, which was made tolerably warm by space
heaters. An arctic, wet wind blew off the bay, but the twinkling
lights of Alcatraz and Angel Island were gentle and starlike
against the deep blackness of the water.

"I almost brought a date tonight, but at the last minute, I

McNitted and told him I was a lesbian," said Pava, a drop-dead-beautiful Russian emigrée with a long nose and poreless skin that rivaled Milla Jovovich's.

McNitted had become the office code word for episodes of generalized insanity.

"I've completely lost it," confessed Marti Blum, the Standard's art director. "Three hours ago, I went out and bought this getup"—a purple sequined halter with matching hip-slung flares—"and maxed out my credit card!"

Marti was married with two kids. She had *way* McNitted.

"You know, I was talking about this with a friend of mine, and he said guys like that will just chomp their way through the company's women like a lawn mower! They're just waiting for the right moment, that's all. Like the Christmas party! That's why I've decided to bow out of this whole mess," Tina Espinoza, a talented production artist, said.

She had on scarlet lipstick, a velvet bustier, and smelled like she had fallen in a reservoir of Chanel No. 5. Bow out, my Ganzified ass.

"You guys should hear yourselves," sniffed Casey Loughlin, the photo editor. "For God's sake, people, the man's not a god, or even a superhottie. I mean, God, that hair. It's so 1983. It's practically a mullet! And I don't think he even showers after those long runs of his. He's so sweaty, it's disgusting."

Uh-huh. Disgusting like a three-scoop banana split. Ms. Loughlin would be wise to invoke the Lord's help. The one time I gave Casey a lift to work, she invited me in and, flipping through a magazine on her coffee table, I inadvertently discovered a receipt for $625 worth of sex toys, videotapes, and—I shit you not—a bona fide, fully equipped, male Inflate-a-Mate. If I had been nearing the Guinness Book of World Records' title in consecutive celibate days prior to my boondocks bacchanalia, Casey had surely achieved celibatus emeritus status, sort of like Jackie Chan or Dr. Spock in their respective fields.

"Yeah, I'm with Casey on this one. What are you guys saying?

That all I have to do to get a date around here is prance around with my hairy ass hanging out and stop showering?" This from Rudy Guilfoyle, HTML designer extraordinaire, who happened to be hysterically funny, built like a brick shithouse with arms, and just a hairbreadth over five feet tall.

Life really was unfair, wasn't it?

Before this salivating pack of hyenas that passed as women could challenge poor Rudy to show us his hairy ass, the prodigal prince arrived, if not on a white steed, then with comparable melodrama.

He was alone. Golden. Clean-looking. Tall. Bursting with health. And hot. Quite hot, in fact. The gallery froze, then exploded into action like a supernova, heading to bathrooms to smooth hair, apply lipstick, or engage in deep-breathing exercises.

Feeling suddenly cold—no wonder, since I had forgotten to wear something that qualified as *clothes*—I ran for the bar and ordered a warming tonic. Okay, a White Russian, but everyone knows Russians know how to keep warm, right?

"There you go, my girl. And, may I say, that dress is deadly on you," the Irish barman said.

I scrunched around to see if my control top was hanging out or some other faux pas punishable by a second White Russian.

He laughed. "Deadly means *good*. You look good." He looked around and sighed long and hard. "Jaysus, I'm shagged. Want to have dinner with me?" he said out of the blue. His emerald eyes twinkled, and he couldn't have been a day over thirteen.

I was about to answer when I smelled Ariel McNitt coming.

Lest you think I jest, I point to a small, yet pivotal, event in my childhood as proof of my olfactory brilliance. Once, en route to a family vacation destination in the Florida Keys, we were crossing one of their many bridges when I'd piped up that I smelled Mexican food and could we have enchiladas for lunch. Since we were mid-span on a floating bridge with miles of salt water between us and land, everyone laughed. Ben and Karen also took the opportunity to smother me with a pillow and pinch me till I screamed, respectively.

When we pulled into town on the other side, I was vindicated by the taco hut sandwiched between the gas station and the gift shop on Main Street.

I inhaled and turned slowly, in the style favored by Miss America pageant contestants as they depart the runway in the swimsuit competition.

"Hello."

"Hi. Can I get you something?" I offered, rather foolishly since it was an open bar.

"Sure." He glanced at my frothy concoction as he would a particularly generous helping of Spam and onions. "I'll have a beer please," he told the bartender, who was scowling under his fiery cap of hair.

Feeling drunk on my own feminine power—or, perhaps, just plain drunk—I allowed the scudding clouds and the stars and the dulcet tones of the jazz combo in the ballroom to lift me toward euphoria. Life was good! There was hope! I hadn't even been arrested for indecent exposure yet!

"That's quite a dress you have there," Ariel said.

"Thank you."

"Did you leave part of it at home?"

A finger of disappointment wormed its way into my happy daze. Why did he have to be so predictable?

Then he redeemed himself.

"Want to go out on the deck?" he asked. I nodded enthusiastically. That first outing had left my nipples frozen enough to cut glass, but I figured a true player had to make sacrifices.

We grabbed our drinks and departed for the Lido deck in our finery. I flung an apologetic glance at the Irish lad, and he rolled his eyes. Maybe I should sleep with him. It would bring the average age of my lovers back down to a respectable thirty-nine.

As McNitt and I traversed the crowded ballroom, I fancied people were watching, so I adopted a modest yet pretty Princess Diana-ish chin-tuck, to show how much I appreciated the attention of the Little People.

Raquel slipped by me in a cloud of silk.

"Stop doing that chin thing," she hissed. "You look like a hunchback."

Oh.

Ariel McNitt led me to a corner of the deck overlooking the luminous crescent of beach below, which would have been romantic if my stockings had not chosen that precise moment to split from crotch to heel. The resounding rip cut through the *From Here to Eternity*-ish crashing of incoming waves like the world's biggest zipper being yanked down.

"What was that?" His eyes darted around fearfully.

"Haven't you ever heard the tidal nodes?" I improvised. "It's sort of like the marine version of the Northern Lights. It's quite rare, actually. We're lucky to have heard it tonight," I babbled, seemingly impervious to the bounds of believability.

He looked mollified.

"There's so much I still have to learn about this incredible Bay Area ecosystem!" he exclaimed, as if he were trying to impress the Outward Bound admissions committee.

Yawn.

During the next ten or so minutes, I found myself strangely detached from the proceedings, as we discussed Middle East peace, hot springs in Idaho, and the tribulations of the Internet economy. It was peculiar: Here I was, singled out for attention by the strapping blond Adonis everyone had had their eye on for weeks, and our interaction left me tepid. At the exact moment I should have felt smugly content, I registered only restlessness, hallmarked by a strong compulsion to slip out the caterers' door and go home to my fish, my comforter, and the latest Maeve Binchy.

With my peripheral vision, I registered the envious glares and you-go-girl gestures of my coworkers and friends. Still . . .

"Will you excuse me, pleath? I'm just going to the ladies. I'll thee you later, okay?" I said. Uh-oh—was something wrong with the sound system in here? My voice sounded so weird.

"Save me a dance," he called as I hurried away, something I haven't heard since Johnny Pelz sidled up to me in his Harlequin-patterned satin shirt and brown flares at the spring dance in 1982.

I escaped to the bathroom to inspect my hosiery damage and was immediately surrounded by women.

"God, he latched on to you like a barnacle!" said Pava.

"It's that dress. I *knew* I should have worn my sheer D&G top!" wailed Tina.

"He cleans up pretty good," Casey admitted.

They proceeded to deconstruct McNitt, McNitt's (not necessarily deserved) favoritism toward Jen, McNitt's hair, and McNitt's ass. Impatience bloomed inside me like a flower on speed.

"Shut up!" I roared. "If you want him, he's yours. I don't want him. Tho go out there naked for all I care. I'm going home and eating a thalami thandwich on rye," I announced.

Several hopeful-looking ladies all but ran out of the room.

"But first, I'm taking these fucking things off"—I lurched around trying to peel off my torn hose, threatening to crack my head open on the sink—"and getting a White Ruthan to go from that redhead. Where's Raquel?"

Raquel Birney materialized by my side, as if by magic.

"The madneth is over. We are free. Join me for a departing beverage, my *confrere*, my partner in crime, my comrade in arms!" I blathered.

We linked arms—actually, she held me up—and staggered back to the bar looking a bit worse for the wear, as if we'd been out saving Private Ryan or something.

"They're back! The two most gorgeous birds at the ball," the

Irishman said, placing napkins in front of us. He stared deeply into my eyes. Or maybe he was just figuring out whether to cut me off.

"What can I get you?"

"A White Ruthan to go, like in one of those coffee containers," I said.

"I'll have water." Raquel, the pretty *and* smart one.

"Want to share a cab, thweetie?" I asked.

She winked. "Anytime."

Fifteen minutes later, I waved good-bye to Raquel as the taxi sped onward to her house in Glen Park. The rain had stopped and a green, earthy smell filled the night air. It was cold, and the bite sobered me up a little, though I still floated on a happy buzz. Right now, curling up alone with a good book, *Mad TV*, and some simple food sounded like the best thing in the world.

I dropped my purse on the table and saw the light flashing on the answering machine. Whistling to myself, I pressed the button.

"Baby? It's Mom. Don't worry, everything's going to be fine"—choking noises that sounded suspiciously like crying—*"it's Daddy, sweetheart. Daddy's had a heart attack! Just a mild one, the doctors say. He's okay. Oh, God! What do they know, anyway? They're all such bastards. No, of course they're not all bastards. But he's with Connie Costas, and she's the best. Daddy has a lot of respect for her. And Ben's here, of course. Oy, it's so terrible! Call home, munchkin. We love you."* Her voice cut off abruptly.

I stared at the machine in horror, as if the box itself had generated this heinous pronouncement. Like a dream, the White Russian slipped from my fingers and pooled on the sisal rug. My hands shook.

I called the first person I thought of, the only one in San Francisco who knew my dad like I knew my dad, the one who had chosen the only birthday gift my father had ever really liked—a world band radio from Sky Mall, so Dad could listen to his beloved sports in fifty-seven languages.

I savaged my purse for my PalmPilot and quickly called up the unfamiliar number, which I punched into the phone.

Vaguely, I registered that it was after midnight.

On the eighth ring, someone answered.

"Hello?" said Damon, sleepily.

"I need you," I said.

i heart you

To: Toni Reilly
From: Emily Mortensen
Subject: hi!
Attachment: bookreport.doc

Here it is. I picked the one about Jerry and the chocolates. Send me yours when you're done, okay? Marcus Richards is soooo dumb. He asked me if Mrs. Ware cares if we turn it in on Monday, and I'm like, duh, that's why it's due Friday.

Em

p.s. Did my mom say anything to your mom about Jen?

Who knew that the same person whom I'd once referred to as "That Asshole" would become my savior in a time of crisis?

After I told Damon what happened and he offered to come over, I hung up and sat numbly next to the phone, hoping my mom would call back and tell me it was all a mistake, that Dad just had heartburn or something and those bastard doctors had misdiagnosed. Strangely, I couldn't seem to take the next step and call home without someone there to hold my hand. What if his condition had worsened since Mom left the message? Surely it was better to have someone here with me, I rationalized.

I was watching Ben and Jerry II drift around their bowl when the doorbell rang. I floated to the buzzer, pressed, cracked the door, and lay back down on the couch. Everything felt strange and dead, as if I had been socked very hard in the cheek and was lying in the road after the beating, concussed.

I heard heavy footfalls charging the steps, and then Damon's presence filled the room. Literally filled it. I've never known someone to exude such energy; it was simply a fact of his force of personality, and unintentional, I'd long ago decided.

"Hey, how you doing?"

Damon came over to the couch and laid two fingers on my arm, as if more would cross the line into impropriety. His green eyes brimmed with concern. He had on his Florida Marlins sweatpants and a coat over his flannel pajama shirt. A quiff of dark hair stuck up behind his ear like a feather.

I wanted to cry.

"I'm okay. I don't know what's happening, Dame." My voice sounded like it was far away and being piped into the room.

"You want to call your mom now? I'll sit right here. I'll call her if you want. Okay?"

"Okay. I'll call."

He handed me the phone, and I sat up to call. He was eyeing me strangely, and I realized I looked a fright, with my backless dress gone all crooked, the hem pushed up nearly crotch-high and the tattered control top I'd torn from the stockings peeking out. I looked like I'd either been working 16th and Van Ness or partying with rock stars.

I dialed Ben's cell.

"Ben Brenner," he answered.

"Hey! It's me. I just got the message."

"Hey. Are you okay?"

I glanced at Damon, who had eased himself into a chair across from me.

"I'm fine. How's Dad?"

Ben exhaled. "Dad's pretty good. They're watching him, but he's going to be fine, Jennie. I promise. It was a mild to moderate heart attack. They did blood work and an EKG, and he looks stable right now." Ben spoke firmly, in his physician's voice.

"How's Mom?"

"She's okay. You'd be proud of her, Jen. Hey, Mom, you want to talk to Jennie?"

He passed her the phone.

"Jennie?" Mom's voice sounded querulous.

"Oh, Mom!" There's something about hearing your mother's voice in times of stress that just opens the floodgates.

"It's okay, sweetheart. Daddy's going to be just fine. He just woke up during the night and his chest and arm hurt, so I insisted we go to the hospital. We called Dr. Costas on the way and she met us there. And they're taking great care of him now." She sniffled.

"I'll fly out tomorrow morning."

"No! Absolutely not. We talked about that already and decided that, with Ben here, it would be easier if you and Karen stay where you are."

In the chaos I'd forgotten all about my sister and her family, so far away on an Israeli farm.

"Mom, are you sure? Is Dad definitely okay?"

"Yes," she said firmly. "The important thing now, they said, is that he rest. And that's easier if he's not worried about you seeing him like this. You know how he is."

I closed my eyes and pictured my dear old dad lying in a hospital bed and knew she was right. When I opened them, Damon had a questioning look in his eyes, so I gave him the thumbs-up.

"Okay, if that's what you want." I paused. "When can I talk to him?"

"He's sleeping now, but you can talk to him tomorrow, how's that?"

"Good. Oh, Mom, I just remembered, we're all coming out for Christmas in a week." It was December 16—actually, December 17 now—and Karen and I were due to arrive in Miami, she with family in tow, on December 22.

"Well, I wanted to talk to you about that. With Daddy recovering and all, I just don't think we're up to hosting this year."

I started to protest, but she cut me off.

"Wait a minute! I didn't say we aren't getting together like we always do, we're just not doing it in Miami this year."

What?

"Even though Daddy's heart attack wasn't particularly severe, there's some stuff going on that Dr. Costas is concerned about. She wants him to see a specialist and the specialist is at UCSF," Mom continued.

Damon cracked his knuckles, something that had always driven me nuts. I would have thought Kristina the martinet had broken him of the habit by now, since it probably didn't fit in with her Master Plan for Achieving Domestic Perfection with the Perfect Husband.

"So we're all coming to San Francisco," she finished.

"As in, San Francisco, California?" I asked.

Mom chuckled in spite of herself. "No, as in San Francisco, that tiny town in Argentina with mud huts. Of course, San Francisco, California! Don't worry, we'll get a hotel. We're not all moving into your little place. Karen and Avi and the kids have already exchanged their tickets." She rustled through some papers. "You're picking them up at the airport at...let's see...three o'clock on Friday. We're coming in the next day."

Lest she think I wasn't a team player, I quelled my natural response, which was to emit a protracted scream of horror. My parents, here? In my apartment? With my friends? For a week? I recalled San Francisco's long list of spas, both beauty and health-oriented, and thought I'd better prepare myself to be repeatedly

scrubbed, kneaded, exfoliated, abraded, and plucked, if I was going to be spending any time with my mother. As far as intestinal
flushing and therapeutic yodeling went, she could indulge in
those activities by herself.

"Okay, just e-mail me the info," I said, dazed.

"Bye, sweetie. We love you, and Daddy loves you. We'll talk
tomorrow."

"Love you, Mom."

Ben got back on the phone.

"So, looks like everyone's bearing down on you this year. I
guess I'll be, you know, um, visiting...staying...over at Els's
house." I let him fumble around for a while, enjoying being bratty
little sister for a moment.

"Yeah, I know. C'mon! We all know. Get over it, Benji. I'm
happy for you. I think it's great."

"Yeah, well, we'll see what happens," he said dourly, as if hoping would somehow hex his good fortune.

"So, I guess I'll talk to you guys tomorrow."

"Yep."

"Bye, Benji. I love you," I said suddenly.

"I love you too, sis."

I hung up and returned to my supine position on the couch,
tugging my dress down to Catholic-schoolgirl level with much
difficulty.

"So, it sounds like everything's going to be okay," Damon said.

I nodded. "Dame, I'm sorry I got you up like that, but I want
you to know...it means a lot to me that you came over. It's just
that you know my dad better than my other friends do, and I
needed to be with someone who did—does!—" My throat closed,
and the tears, held at bay by panic, finally came down. I covered
my face with my hands and sobbed.

Then Damon's arms went around me. It was so familiar. It
felt good and right. Like being hugged by Benji or my dad....

Something firm and moist was touching my cheek and neck
and—oh, my God—my lips. Kiss?

"Damon!" I leapt back like I'd run into an electric cattle prod. Now, there's makeup sex. And breakup sex. And booty-call sex. And I-had-a-bad-day-at-work-and-you-had-a-bad-day-at-work-so-why-don't-we-do-it-and-get-some-relief sex. And drunk sex. And sex between friends (ill-advised, in my admittedly limited world-view). But who's ever heard of my-dad-had-a-heart-attack-so-I'd-better-sleep-with-my-engaged-to-be-married-ex-boyfriend sex?

No one, that's who.

Damon slumped forward on the couch, elbows on knees, head in his heads.

"Jen, I am so sorry. I didn't mean to do that. I don't know what the hell is wrong with me."

"Well, it's the middle of the night, and I called you over here, and I'm dressed like a refugee from the Victoria's Secret catalog, and you feel sorry for me, so maybe we're both just a little out of whack," I suggested.

He raised his head and met my eyes. God, they were green.

"I broke up with Kristina," he said.

Oh, no.

"Well, I'm sure you'll work it out," I said brightly, in the tone used by department-store clerks who have sold your layaway outfit to someone else.

He shook his head. "I don't think so. It was...it was just wrong. I think I knew that for a long time, but I couldn't seem to stop it. It was like I was on a train without brakes or something. Things just kept piling up, decisions got made, and before I knew it, I'd bought her that insane ring and we were looking for a condo and picking out china and, Christ, it was totally out of control...."

A vision of the rock on Kristina's slender finger popped into my mind. I wondered if they'd had to hire a U-Haul to cart it back to Tiffany's.

"She moved out last week. You should see the place—I've got like two boxes for chairs and a sleeping bag. Bitch took the bed— my Swedish memory-foam bed! I'm so fucked. All our friends hate me now. Oh, crap. I can't believe I'm dumping on you." He looked miserable.

"Hey, that's okay. I know what things are like when you break up with someone, you know." I laughed. "At least she didn't sign you up for a year's subscription to the *Men Who Love Little Boys* digest, or whatever that filthy rag was." After our last and most vile fight, in a rage, I'd located the most appalling journal I could find and ordered it in his name, praying for the shame-concealing packaging to tear in the mail so his neighbors would see it and report him to the police. Pretty psycho, huh?

He grinned. "Actually, it was Internet mailing lists this time. I've been inundated with e-mail! I now get newsletters from fifteen dotcoms, 24 Hour Fitness gyms, and Macy's Shoes."

That girl is about as imaginative as a turnip. How they stayed together as long as they did, I'll never know.

"You want some coffee or tea?" I asked. When I'd left, Gladys had gifted me with a beautifully wrapped package of Evening in Missoula tea.

"Coffee, if it's not too much trouble."

"Still like milk and two sugars?"

He pulled a face. "Kristina made me drink it black. Put in three sugars, will you?"

Ah, the purge is on.

I started up the drip coffee machine and went to the bedroom to change out of my party clothes. What to wear for a late-night rendezvous with your ex, who's just become somebody else's ex, when you're seeking comfort and he's seeking some post-split nookie? I stripped down and threw on some bootleg yoga pants and a wife-beater tank. Bra—why bother? Ain't nothin' he hasn't seen a million times before. Then I scrubbed my face clean of gunk in the bathroom, took out my contacts, applied face lotion and even a dab of zit cream.

Damon had his coffee and my tea waiting when I returned.

"Don't worry about your dad. He'll get through this. You all will."

I sat on the floor and leaned against the couch. "I hope so. I really hope so." I took a sip of tea. "When are you going home for Christmas?"

"Actually, I'm not. My parents' fortieth anniversary is this year, and they're going to be in Australia."

"Why Australia?"

He shrugged. "Dad wants to see the Great Barrier Reef. I don't know. I guess I'm on my own this year. Probably spend it with friends and removing myself from Kristina's mailing lists."

An idea glimmered in my mind, and I said impulsively, "Do you want to join us? God knows what I'll do with the whole family coming, probably just order out something here."

"Thanks, really, but I wouldn't want to impose, especially with your dad being under the weather and all. . . ."

"It wouldn't be any trouble, Dame. They'd love to see you. Although we'll have to prepare them, because my mom might have a heart attack herself—from shock—if she thinks we're together again or something." I laughed.

Damon's brow furrowed in disapproval.

"You make it sound like torture, us getting back together," he said. He'd always looked cute when he sulked.

"Yes, but just torture lite. More prolonged tickling than bamboo shoots under the fingernails," I said lightly. "You should come. It'll be fun. I think I'll invite Robert and George and their new baby, and Els will come. Katie and Colin—that's her new boyfriend—may still be here before they go to meet his parents, and Ben, Karen, and my folks."

"Are you going to make your mom's stuffing?" he asked.

I clutched my throat. "God, no." My mom's stuffing consisted of glutinous floury blobs laced with wheat germ and soy flakes, layered with a generous wad of persimmon chutney.

"Okay, then I'll come."

We grinned at each other, my ex-boyfriend and I, and a rush of happiness sluiced through me. Maybe, just maybe, it was time to be friends. Again.

scrooge

To: bmortensen@mail.epa.gov
From: Forwarded message from Mail Delivery Subsystem
MAILER-DAEMON (see transcript for details)
Subject: Fw>

This message received permanent fatal errors.

>Hi, Jen. I got your e-mail address from Bernie Zweben. Please don't
>delete this message. I've had a lot of time to think over the past
>month, and I feel I left a lot of things unsaid between us. I'm hoping
>you'll give me a chance to rectify that now. I have to attend a
>meeting with EPA Internal Affairs in San Francisco on Friday,
>December 22. I'd like to come and see you the next day if you are
>there and not with your family in Miami. Of course, I'll be flying
>home that afternoon to be with Emily for Christmas. Please let me
>know if this works for you.

>Bruce

Someone needs to just cancel Christmas. Obliterate it. Expose it
as the scourge it is and wipe it off the face of the earth forever

and ever. If some administrative body were to suddenly announce the end of ritualized family gatherings, piney trees festooned with popcorn chains and misshapen angels, drunken Santas propped up in shopping malls with screaming tots writhing on their laps, and the maniacal cheer foisted on us by the department-store chains and toy retailers, I would join the mutinous masses with own heartfelt hallelujah.

And I don't even really celebrate Christmas.

For the record, my family belongs to that class of half-assed but fervent Jews who, cognizant and enamored of our tribal affiliation yet wholly secularized and spiritually lazy, celebrate a mishmash of yearly religious events, ranging from Passover to Easter egg hunts to Winter Solstice to a sort of Hanukkah–Christmas hybrid my brother, Ben, has irreverently taken to calling "Christmaka." With the exception of my sister, Karen, who followed the spirit of our foremothers Sarah, Rachel, Zipporah, and Ruth to the land of our biblical origins, ostensibly to cultivate the land of milk and honey on a kibbutz—personally, I think she spent more time cultivating the overdeveloped pectoral muscles of my judo-champion brother-in-law, Avi, which resulted in the conception of little Tomer—we were a complacent and spoiled lot, deriving our Jewishness more from such activities as overeating, talking at once, and attending medical school than from studying the Torah or going to *shul*.

None of which helped when I was faced with that most daunting of endeavors: hosting my entire family for a week in the immediate aftermath of a health crisis and managing to evade incarceration in the loony bin.

In the week preceding the family's arrival, I was subsumed in a whirlwind of activity. There were hotel rooms and B&Bs to book, restaurant reservations to make, spas to inspect (Mom e-mailed me a list), friends to conscript, and, oh, did I mention that I had to go to work too? Never a dull moment at the Tech Standard, for the Christmas party had spawned not one but *two* torrid romances, both of which had an incendiary effect on office gossip.

First was Nancy Teason and Carl Hanson. Nancy and Carl's adulterous pairing may have been the worst-kept secret since Pamela Anderson's breast implants. Between the coy glances, synonymous and protracted doctors' appointments, and transparent avoidance of speaking directly to each other in meetings, you'd have to be criminally unobservant not to notice that something funny was going on. Since they both had shadowy spouses lurking in the wings, it was a depressing and furtive venture that did not bode well or bring cheer, even though Nancy's normally pallid face was perpetually flushed with excitement and lust.

Not surprisingly, torrid romance number two concerned Ariel McNitt, who had recovered from the Brenner treatment in time to work his magic on at least one single coworker—the luscious Pava—and was suspected of having secured interludes with two others, though the runners-up were of course too embarrassed to confirm or deny the speculation. Suffice to say, if any work got done the week *after* the Christmas party, I'd eat *both* my carpal-tunnel wrist guards.

On top of all that, I was faced with that annoying dilemma familiar to anyone with the misfortune to abort a love affair right before the holidays: the card—to send or not to send. Now, I'm a sporadic correspondent at the best of times, but I thought long and hard about whether Bruce deserved a note from yours truly. The most compelling reason to send one as far as I could see was that it could be used to convey the lightness of spirit and Christmasy benevolence that are the hallmarks of the well-adjusted jilted everywhere. He need never know that beneath the convivial wishes lurked the malignant thoughts of a mad, spurned woman: *Merry Christmas—May all your holiday wishes be smooched by angels and 24-karat gold bullion shoot out of your ass when you sit on the toilet. Peace on Earth!*

The biggest reason *not* to send a card was that he might not send me one. Thus, the action could be interpreted—quite correctly in this case—as a transparent attempt to show Bruce that I'm just fine, thank you very much, never been better, in fact, I've always wanted to explore the sex lives of nuns, and now, thanks to you, I can! In this vein, I've always thought there was a potential fortune to be had in the idea of a cancellation card: *Please ignore the best wishes sent prior; they were all lies,* or, for the younger set, simply, *Psych!*

In all this chaos, one tiny light shone brightly, warming me inside like a fevered reindeer: my budding friendship with Damon, resurrected on the ashes of the old and strangely, unexpectedly satisfying. He'd started coming around after the weekend scare with my dad, a call here, a visit there, a surprise evening drop-in with a couple of Tsingtaos and Thai takeout. At no time did I consider this development as anything other than a fortunate and benign reconnection of old friends—that is, until Els and Katie came over for dinner the night before Karen et al's arrival and set me straight.

"Come in, come in," I said, taking a bottle of wine from Els and flowers from Katie.

We settled in the kitchen after coats and purses had been tossed on my bed. I'd ordered pizza: extra-large double cheese with garlic, onions, and green olives—our usual. Thank Goddess we'd found one another—if our collective breath was any more toxic after our favorite treat, the feds would declare us a Superfund site.

"So, are you ready to meet the parental units?" I asked Katie, who was flying out to Minnesota with Colin on Christmas Eve.

"Blech! It's so nerve-wracking. Don't laugh, but I bought a dress at"—she hung her head—"Laura Ashley. It has flowers on it. They're big." Katie shuddered involuntarily.

"Are you going to wear this dress every day of the holiday or wear your regular clothes too? Won't that just defeat the purpose?" Els the scientist, ever rational.

Katie groaned. "I don't know! What am I supposed to do, buy a whole new wardrobe? It's bad enough I've got this new piercing I can't take out. I was going to put one of those round Band-Aids on it and say I got a wart burned off."

Attractive.

"Maybe you should just be yourself and hope for the best. I'm sure if Colin's family were super tight-assed, he'd have warned you already," I said.

"I believe his exact words were 'My mom may be black, but she acts like she just got off the goddamn Mayflower.'"

Oh.

"What's this?" I turned toward the doorway. Els held Damon's leather jacket in her hand. Drat! I must have left it hanging on the bathroom doorknob.

"Um, the maid's?"

"Nice try," said Katie. "That's Damon's! I never forget a coat! C'mon, fess up—what was Damon doing here?" Her eyes glittered like a hyena's.

"Well, he had this CD of mine, so . . ."

"Lies!"

"Okay, he was in the neighborhood, so he stopped by to chat."

"Brenner." Warning tone.

"Okay, okay, Damon came over when my dad had the heart attack. He was worried."

"How did he know your dad was sick?" Els asked.

"I called him." Meekly.

"Ha! I knew it! And did he bring Blonda Rwanda with him?" Katie always called Kristina that because (1) my ex's ex was as torturous and divisive as a civil war, and (2) Katie just naturally disliked Nordic blondes who worked it like Kristina did.

"Actually, he didn't. Apparently, they broke up. Post-ring!" I added, trying not to sound like I'd just won the state lottery.

All hell broke loose.

"No!"

"You're kidding!"

"Bold."

"Did he get a restraining order yet?" Katie wanted to know.

"I don't know. We really haven't talked about it much," I said.

They looked dubious.

"What *did* you talk about?" Els asked.

"Oh, you know, politics, my dad, stuff."

"Let me guess, after he comforted you all manly-like in your time of need, he told his sob story, then asked to have sex with you—for comfort or old times' sake," Katie said cynically.

Since she was all too close to the truth, I paused. They jumped on my hesitation like jackals on roadkill.

Katie: "Omigod, you had sex with him!"

Els: *"Lekker!* It was—what do you call it?—booty call!"

Katie: "Was it better than before?"

Els: "Does he still do that thing with his teeth?"

"Stop!" I yelled. "We didn't have sex. Yes, he kissed me, but he didn't mean anything by it. It was just a friendly little kiss, like you'd get from your dad or your uncle Jeff."

I didn't have an uncle Jeff, though I did once have a twenty-five-year-old junior-high teacher named Mr. Jeffreys who was, quite frankly, hot.

"There's no such thing as an innocent kiss between ex-lovers. Someone once told me that. Someone who had just barely gotten over a hideous breakup and all but asked me to shackle her to her bedposts so she wouldn't be tempted to call her ex, beg her ex to have sex with her, or otherwise fuck up her life. A certain friend named—let's see, who was it?—I believe it was Jen Brenner! Fancy that! And, besides, you don't have an uncle Jeff," Katie admonished.

"Well, maybe I was wrong. Maybe I was so bitter I couldn't see the healing power of friendship and now I can," I said, aiming for a beatific tone.

Katie snorted. "Maybe you could see the healing power of big Cuban cock!"

Els looked shocked. "You are so cynical! That is disgusting! If Jen and Damon find their friendship again, now that they're both alone, what's wrong with that?"

Alone? I thought I was *exploring my independence.*

"Thanks, Els," I said out loud. "You can come to our wedding." I turned to Katie. "Nguyen—you're disinvited because of that remark about the groom's cock."

"Stop saying that word!" Els shrieked.

"Cock."

"Cock!"

"Cock-o-doodle-do!"

It got increasingly juvenile and profane from there. I will spare you the prurient details.

Suffice to say my friends made their doubts about my renewed acquaintance with Damon Sanchez as clear as the three-carat diamond in Kristina's engagement ring—oops, former engagement ring.

These matters were on my mind as I wound my way through the throngs at San Francisco International Airport to pick up Karen, Avi, and my niece and nephew, Tali and Tomer. I was exhausted from the planning, but excited too: I hadn't seen them in a year, and I really loved being around my big sister—for the first seventy-two hours at least, before we reverted to the eight- and sixteen-year-olds we used to be.

Impulsively, I stopped at the flower cart and bought a luscious spray of stargazer lilies for them. As I was paying the middle-aged Chinese clerk, a peculiar thing happened: My eyes panned over the concourse, where a swift current of disembarking passengers swept through the turnstiles. Drawn as if by magnets, my gaze plucked out a single dark speckled head from the crowd.

Bruce?!

Dropping a twenty on the counter, I grabbed the lilies and ran for the concourse as if I had spotted the last pair of discounted Manolo Blahniks at Barney's warehouse sale.

"Ouch!"

"Sorry!" I yelled at the sour-faced mom who'd snatched her offspring out of my path as I ran.

I lost sight of him as I was absorbed by the crowd. Frantic, I jumped on a bench and scanned the room. Where was he? Why was he here? Was it even him? I had to find out. Surely the fates placing him here at the same time as me was a sign—a sign that maybe, after all, Bruce and I were meant to be together.

"Ma'am. I'm sorry, but you're going to have to come down from there." The airport policeman's eyes were wary, and his hand hovered near his gun, as if I was going to suddenly spray the crowd with automatic gunfire or remove my pants.

I clambered down and sat down dejectedly on the bench. The lilies had taken the brunt of my run, and one alabaster head had snapped off and was hanging, forlorn, against my hand. Breathless and angry, I plucked it off and tossed it in a trash can. Reality settled in like a nasty chest cold: If I was going to chase down every salt-and-pepper middle-aged dude with broad shoulders and a preference for soft lumberjack shirts, life was going to be very difficult indeed. Bruce wasn't in San Francisco, period. He was at home with Emily, and quite possibly Melina, probably hanging silvery tinsel on their massive Christmas tree, which he would have felled himself, out in the yard, and placed in the airy, high-ceilinged living room. The tableau laid itself out in Rockwell-esque detail: Bruce, looking ridiculously strong and fit in faded jeans and those cute little slippers he'd worn around the house; Melina, clad in a matching emerald green negligee and robe, her sweep of red hair drawn into an artfully loose chignon; Emily, comfy in sock-footed PJs, her skinny arms wrapped around Bugle's neck.

A family.

Meanwhile, a thousand miles southwest, Jen was propping up a gangly Hanukkah bush in the already cluttered living room and sweeping tumbleweed-size dust bunnies under the rug. Spinsterly habits you'd expect from a terminally single trouser-chaser hosting her neurotic family for a thrown-together holiday. The counterpoint didn't bear thinking about.

I got up and trudged over to the gate. Since my sister's family had connected through New York, they'd already gone through customs. Finally, I spotted Karen's curly head and Avi's bristly crew cut behind a preternaturally pale Hasidic family.

"Karen!" I called, waving the floppy flowers.

She smiled and pointed at me. Tali, at seven, was still innocent enough to run into her aunt Jen's arms. Tomer, nine, was slightly more circumspect. Both had on the coonskin caps Uncle Ben had given them.

"Shalom," I told them, hugging them both, and they laughed at my atrocious accent. Tali and Tomer were skinny and brown-skinned and smelled like milk and hard candy. I could have kissed them all day long.

"Jennie, thank God." My sister Karen, at thirty-eight, is a shorter, rounder version of me. Her thick curls were pulled back in an unfashionable clip, and smile lines bracketed her full mouth. She looked tired, but happy.

"Hi, Avi," I said, and hugged my brother-in-law. Karen and Avi had met one summer when she was working and learning Hebrew on his kibbutz. She was burning schnitzels in the kitchen the first time she saw him, home for weekend leave from the army and wearing a tank top and obscenely short cutoffs to show off his judo physique; her American boyfriend didn't stand a chance.

"You look good. We need to bring her to Israel and find her a husband," he said to no one in particular, as if I was a thoroughbred mare who had been haltered and brought back to my stall to be injected with fertility drugs.

Thankfully, the kids took after their mother in the brains department.

I shepherded them out to the car. Every ten seconds Tali would tug on my sleeve and ask me a far-out question. "How do planes stay up?" and "Where are your kids?" were two of the best ones.

They were exhausted, so I dropped them off at their hotel, which was near Fisherman's Wharf, then drove back across town to my place. My parents were coming in tomorrow, so I had taken today off. It was funny what thinking I had seen Bruce had done to me. Lately I'd managed to put him out of my mind for relatively long periods of time; editing stories, hanging with friends, doing yoga and everything else helped a lot. But just imagining seeing him sent a frisson of anticipation through me. What would it be like to spend five minutes—one minute—in his arms again? To nibble the little whorl of dark hair at the nape of his neck? To roll around shamelessly on his bearskin rug? Would he still rock my world, or would the magical sexual rapport be gone, replaced by ho-hum fornication or, worse, embarrassment?

The phone was ringing when I got to my front door. I jammed my key in the lock and ran, banging my knee against the coffee table.

"Shit!" I yelled.

"Well, that's nice. What if I was your boss? Or your parents?" said Damon.

"Then I would have attributed my outburst to a sudden attack of Tourette's syndrome."

"What are you doing?"

"Um, taking off all my clothes," I answered, which was quite true. I'd decided to be occasionally coy with Damon, as I was not likely to have another man to flirt with for some time.

"Oh, good. Can I come over?"

"Sure. Bring that donkey-size vibrator Kristina left there, will you? Oh, and wash it first," I said.

"Funny."

Not really.

"I just finished picking up Karen and haven't eaten, so if you're coming over, you'd better bring me sustenance. The cupboard is bare, 'cause I'm shopping for Christmas tomorrow."

"Chinese?" he suggested.

"Um, sushi?"

"Two sake nigiri, one unagi, one maguro and dynamite?"

It's so great when someone knows *exactly* what kind of raw fish you like. Damon may not have been able to retain my top three favorite sexual positions of all time, but eating holds its own in the pantheon of fun activities.

I surveyed the room, decided cleaning up for Damon was unnecessary, finished stripping down, and turned on the bath spigot. Naked, I prowled around the apartment with just my socks and glasses on, something I like to do when I am overwhelmed by details and trying to feel the basic elements of life on my skin: air, earth, water, three-hundred-count cotton sheets.

Just another thing Bruce didn't get to know about me.

I stepped into the bath I'd drawn and sighed. Heaven. Thoughts of Bruce threatened to make me glum, so I tipped my friends—excepting Ben and Jerry II—into the tub. Rubber Ducky and Mr. Fishy bobbed up and down in the water, which I'd laced with a newfangled scent comprised of guava nectar and essence of angel farts or some such thing. I leaned my head back against the bath pillow and closed my eyes. . . .

Next thing I knew, something lovely and soft stroked my forehead. I made little animal-like moans of pleasure and sank into the water, which, strangely, felt tepid.

I opened my eyes to Damon leaning over me.

"What are you doing here?" I shrieked, trying in vain to sink deeper into the water. To my everlasting embarrassment, the two mounds of foamy bubbles that had heretofore covered my breasts floated away from my body like an uninhabited island chain. Tentative reinitiation of friendship was one thing; actual nudity after more than two years of gravitational pull had taken their toll was quite another.

"Mr. Yee let me in. He recognized me, after all this time."

Mr. Yee was my landlord. Next time he saw me, his life would pass before his eyes.

"I'm taking that old ninny to the rent board!" I cried.

"C'mon. It's nothing I haven't seen before, like, a million times," Damon said, as if he were a doctor trying to convince a reluctant patient to drop trou. Then, hopefully, "Did your boobs get bigger?"

Furious, I splashed him, soaking his dark blue khakis and retro bowling shirt.

"Hey! That's cold!"

"You asked for it, buddy!"

"Yeah, but you're going to get it!"

Damon reached into the bath, soaking his shirt to the shoulders, scooped me up, and tossed me on the bed. I was conscious of nippy air rushing to fill my nether regions. Wah! Fleetingly I thought, he *must* have been working out, because when we were going out he couldn't lift a finger to do the dishes, let alone hoist my ice-cream-padded ass from bath to bed.

Before I could even yelp in protest, Damon leapt on me and shamelessly began tickling all my private places, which, let me tell you, were not keen on this treatment and wanted oh so fervently to get dressed.

"Damon, stop it!" I gasped. "For God's sake, let me up. . . ."

"Never!" he said, like a knight refusing to give up on a fair maiden who had shacked up with the evil king.

"My bed's getting soggy . . . and I'm freezing. And the sushi's getting cold." Silly, even for me.

Suddenly, everything stopped, a freeze frame cut off midstream. I felt Damon's pants, scratchy against my bare legs, the weight of him pressing down against the V of my crotch, his face mere inches from my lips. As I stared into his eyes, trying to figure out how to extricate myself from this absurd and potentially dangerous situation, he laid the pads of his fingers gently against my cheek.

"Jennie . . ." he began.

Then a familiar voice cut through the spell.

"What is going on in here? Good Lord, she's naked, Fred."

There in the doorway, faces white with shock against the beaded mermaid curtain, stood my parents, Fred and Victoria Brenner, burgundy American Tourister luggage in hand. Even from my angle, crushed beneath Damon's deadweight, legs splayed on either side of him, I could see the tableau was unfortunate at best.

I would like to say I fainted dead away then, or suffered a well-timed pulmonary embolism, but that would be entirely too wishful.

"Did you take Super Shuttle?" I said inanely, instead.

CHAPTER 33

surprise, surprise

December 15, 2000

Dear Bruce,
Merry Christmas and Happy New Year.
Yours, Jen

Chalk it up to the season, but I just seemed to give and give and give.

With little recourse left to me but to suck it up and plod through the holiday as if everything was normal and my parents' first sight of me hadn't been a beaver shot, I assumed the stiffly noble demeanor of a Joan of Arc or a high-ranking prisoner of war. It was the only way I'd make it through the week without gobbling a bucket of Prozac or driving an ice pick through my heart in a perverse reversal of a fundamentalist honor killing.

After the initial shock of seeing their naked daughter spread-eagle under the body of her supposedly engaged-to-be-married ex-boyfriend had worn off—a pot of tea and several Valiums from Mom's toiletries kit had done the trick—my folks regained their usual sunny ebullience and demanded to know when I could take them to see Karen and the grandkids.

"Well, they're expecting you tomorrow, so maybe you should just let them sleep," I pointed out.

Mom pouted. "But we came all this way!"

A day early, Mom.

"Vic, Jen's right. They're probably all jet-lagged, and I'm tired too, so why don't we have Jen drive us over to the B&B and get settled." Dad, the voice of reason. Thank goodness he'd ignored the doctors' advice and pounded a Scotch, straight up.

"Why don't I take them on my way home," said Damon.

Dad fixed him with a you're-lucky-I-don't-have-my-shotgun-but-next-time-I'll-blow-your-balls-off look, highly inconsistent with the Hippocratic oath he had sworn to uphold.

"That is, unless you've got other plans," Damon said hurriedly.

Mom relented. "No, that's best. We really shouldn't have barged in like this, but we thought we'd just surprise you, taking that earlier flight. That nice Mr. Yee let us in when Daddy told him we were your parents."

Do the Chinese do open caskets? That might preclude extensive scarring.

I helped them out to Damon's Passat and waved at them from the window as they disappeared around the corner, headed for the B&B whose brochure had promised firm beds, en suite bathrooms, and a hearty breakfast of tofu "facon" and organic egg whites.

Then, finally, blessedly, I sank into bed.

Saturday, December 23, dawned cold and bright. White winter light refracted off damp sidewalks, streets, and leaves, lending everything an incandescent glow (insofar as you can achieve an incandescent glow in snow-challenged coastal California). If Santa himself had come barreling over the Transamerica Building in full North Pole regalia, reindeer tugging at their bridles, I wouldn't have been surprised; the day had that kind of magical expectancy about it.

The first thing I did when I got up at 8:15 A.M. was a series of Ashtanga yoga poses. Sun salutations, downward-facing dog, upward-facing dog, and a couple of warrior moves made me feel I'd qualify for anyone's definition of young independent urban female facing life with inner calm and Zenlike appreciation of my surroundings.

Then I pounded a triple espresso from the drug distillery— i.e., coffee cart—on the corner.

By the time the family started arriving for the de rigueur Christmas Eve *Eve* festivities, I was as wired as a teenage girl's mouth after a trip to the orthodontist. Frankly, it was the only way I would survive the endless rounds of drink pouring, food preparing, children's-accomplishment kudoing, brother-in-law ignoring, Ben teasing, Mom and Dad interrogating, and Damon insinuating that I had to look forward to.

At nine A.M., I'd nipped out to the store for coffee, tea, beer, wine, cheese, deli salads, lunch meats, roast chicken, bread, toilet paper, fashion magazines, and other staples. What had started out as a casual, last-minute family gathering had turned into a genuine party, with clan Brenner expected at ten A.M.; Ben flying in at eleven A.M. and picking up Els; Katie and Colin, George, Robert, and Zoë, Jem, Micah, and Milo, and Damon all arriving within a few hours.

My one-bedroom was bursting at the seams. Forecasting imminent destruction at the hands of Tali, Tomer, Zoë, and Milo, I'd conducted a frantic purge of all breakable items, stuffing them in boxes and stowing them in the far reaches of closets and drawers. At 9:40, I panicked and deemed the place insufficiently festive, so I grabbed my wallet and jetted out again for eleventh-hour decorations. Mr. Yee was out pruning his bushes when I left.

"Herro, Jen." He smiled sweetly, showing gap teeth.

"Prepare to die for your sins, old man," I shouted, and clocked him in the head with a ceramic nativity scene.

Just kidding.

"Good morning, Mr. Yee. I'm having a little party today, so if you and Mrs. Yee want to come over, you're more than welcome," I said.

"What time?"

"All day."

"Who cook?" he asked. We had a little joke about my lack of domestic skills.

"Safeway," I answered.

He laughed. "We come, then."

I ran to the market and scooped up random piles of tinsel, stuffed things, and fifty-percent-off Hanukkah tchotchkes—indicating, perhaps, that the Jewish holiday had already passed?—and made my way back to checkout. Francine, the heavily made-up Latina with a name tag stating her years of service to Safeway as twenty-three, greeted me with her usual aplomb.

"Family in town?" she asked, flipping items over the electronic bar-code reader without marring her two-inch acrylic nails, which were decorated with tiny Christmas trees.

"Yep."

"Don't worry, they'll leave soon."

"Yep. You're a doll, Francine. I hope they treat you like the goddess you are," I said impulsively.

"Ha! It's a job. Keeps me in these," she said, waggling her long-fingered hands, which literally dripped with 14-karat gold and diamond baubles.

I huffed up to the door at 9:58, just in time to see my parental units disembark from a taxi.

"Jennie! Come help us with the food," Mom called.

Food?

We proceeded to unload the trunk, which looked like a supply depot for an International Red Cross mission.

"Mom, I said I was handling food," I whined.

Vic and Fred glanced at each other.

"What?" I demanded.

"Well, honey, it's just that the last time you handled the food, we ended up ordering pizza," Mom said.

"Forgiveness is next to godliness," I intoned, not sure if I'd gotten the saying quite right. In addition to having elephantine appetites, the Brenner family is known for its memories of the same ilk. In 1990, at the tender age of twenty, I'd insisted on hosting our holiday dinner in my communal dormitory kitchen. Between the carcinogenic turkey and recalcitrant biscuits, the sodden soufflé and the uninspired salad, my family had vowed never to subject their taste buds to my ministrations again.

Foolishly, I thought a mere decade might have prompted a reconsideration.

So, I ended up unloading a supermarket aisle worth of gourmet tidbits—kalamata olives, truffles, pâté, cheese, crackers, pesto pasta—and carting it into the house to add to the already substantial spread. Truly, it was enough food for a military regiment or an NFL team.

Robert, George, and Zoë arrived next. Naturally, the baby sent my mom into a nearly orgasmic state of grandmotherly bliss.

"We come bearing gifts," George said. He handed me a perfectly baked shrimp frittata and one of those Christmas plants with floppy red leaves whose name always escapes me.

"Thank you, guys. I love you," I said.

Then we did a group hug and I inhaled George and Robert's scent, which was a mix of minty shower gel and a divine cologne. Truly, it seemed unfair: Every other new mom I knew spent the better part of the first year smelling like a supermarket dairy counter, and these guys were never anything less than fragrant. I guess it had something to do with the lack of milk glands.

"Zoë is adorable," my mom announced, expertly bouncing the plump baby on her knee. Zoë chose that precise moment to act like a human depilatory and rip a chunk of Vic's chestnut-gray curls out.

"Ouch!" Mom yelled.

"Here, I'll take her," Robert said. This action took the sting out of the subtext to Mom's offspring-induced pleasure: that my two gay male friends were better at procreating than I, a fertile young woman bursting with estrogenic potential.

"Jen, come with me for a sec?" Robert said, gesturing toward the bedroom.

I followed him into my room, leaving poor George to entertain Fred and Vic.

"I just wanted a minute alone with you. I didn't think we'd get it later," Robert said.

I sighed. "Is it too late to check myself into Shady Acres until January?"

Robert smiled and laid Zoë down on the bed. She giggled and wrapped her tiny fist around his finger.

"George and I were talking about what to get you for Christmas. We wanted to give you something special, because you're our best friend, and you're Zoë's aunt–mom, and even though you're totally crazy, we love you very, very much," he said.

Aside from the totally crazy part, I was touched. Well, maybe *because* of it.

"We thought about all the usual stuff: perfume, massage certificate, Ricky Martin tickets"—a guilty pleasure we three shared and obfuscated as if it were a shameful addiction, akin to watching bestiality videos or sucking toes—"and rejected them because they didn't do justice to the new Jen, the Jen who moves to Montana where she doesn't know a soul and breaks the biggest story of her career and carries on with wild cowboys and rangers..."

Robert threw in a few more superlatives here related to national parks and the men who man them. My acquaintanceship with Ranger Anderson, however brief, seemed to hold a special spot in my Montana anthology for Robert and George, perhaps because of those painted-on slacks.

"...then we thought, what means more to Jen than anything, what's closest to her heart and her dreams and will someday make her terribly rich and famous? And what we came up with was your writing. So we got you this"—he dug a slender envelope out of his back pocket—"and we hope you like it."

He handed me the envelope, and I slid my finger under the flap and tore it open. I unfolded the two sheets of paper and read:

Dear Ms. Brenner,

Congratulations on your acceptance to the Advanced Investigative Reporting Workshop. As you know, the Workshop, held annually since 1985, gathers together 23 of our most promising young journalists for three weeks of intensive instruction in investigative techniques, including high-tech records research, court records searching, factual accuracy, lawsuit investigation, and other areas of focus. Each participant will have one story published in a local New York paper upon completion of the course.

Again, we congratulate you on your acceptance and look forward to welcoming you to the program. Please return the attached acceptance form by January 15, 2001.

Dane Willitsky

Associate Dean, Columbia University Graduate School of Journalism

"We sent them some of your clips, including your series on the mill investigation, and you got accepted out of more than three hundred applicants!"

My ever-ready tear ducts were working overtime. "What would you have done if I hadn't gotten accepted?"

"Ricky in Vegas."

"Oh, Robert," I said, and hugged him hard, Zoë lolling between us on the bed. We could have been a magazine ad for Hamburger Helper or an HMO, we were so damn cute.

"This is so amazing. I can't believe you did this! What about work and stuff?" I babbled.

Robert waved his hand. "We worked that out before we sent

in your application. They're fine. You're only going to miss three weeks anyway. Makes them look good, I think, to have one of their editors win a fellowship. After this, you'll be Teflon over there—no one can touch you. Of course, Dane told me most of their workshop participants go on to have illustrious careers in journalism at the best publications, but you can do what you want," he sniffed.

"Sounds like you and this Dane Willitsky got chummy."

"Oh, Dane and I go way back. Summer of 1990 in that Chelsea flat I shared with Charles and Ahmed. Actually, we met on Fire Island. But that's not why you were accepted," he added quickly.

I didn't care if Robert had promised the guy unlimited oral sex for a year; it had always been my dream to go to Columbia, and three weeks in a special workshop was like winning backstage passes to Ricky Martin *plus* having a genie grant you perpetually firm thighs.

I ran out to the living room and embraced George as if he'd just told us he was reporting for military duty in Belfast.

"Georgette, you are one beautiful person," I murmured.

He held me at arm's length and smiled. "You too, Jen Bear. I'm so happy for you."

In the midst of this mutual lovefest, which my parental units regarded with tolerant good humor, Ben and Els arrived.

Ben was tall, loose-limbed, and had gained at least twenty needed pounds. Els had on slim jeans that made her legs look a mile long, a Guatemalan blouse, and a grin that explained why they were half an hour late.

She kissed everyone on the cheek three times, Dutch style. Her first meeting with our parents was classic, and went something like this:

Els: Mr. and Mrs. Brenner? I am Els. I am so happy to meet you!

Mom: Call me Vic, dear.

[Break while Els kisses Fred and Vic again repeatedly on cheeks.]

Dad: If all the Dutch girls kiss old fogies like me, I'm moving to Holland!

Ben: Els is half Dutch and half German, Dad.

Mom: As in German German?

Els: What is German German?

And so it went.

By the time Karen, Avi, and the kids poured out of their rental car into the foyer, I was hiding in the pantry with a bottle of zinfandel, Ben and Jerry II, and a plate of deviled eggs. They hadn't been here five seconds before I heard a resounding crash and my sister's answering scream. I hunkered deeper into the canned tuna fish, praying for rescue.

Suddenly, the door opened and a sliver of light blinded me. I cringed like a political prisoner sentenced to solitary confinement who hadn't seen the sun for five years.

"You're a freak," Jem said, taking in the scene. Then, "Give me one of those deviled eggs."

I handed my former boss a quivering yellow and white blob and we sat down contentedly to munch our fattening feast in peace.

"Who's out there?" I said.

Jem swallowed a marbled hunk of mayonnaise and cholesterol. "Your folks, Ben, Els, Katie and—what's his name, with the dreadlocks, Collier?—your sister and her kids. Oh, and an old Chinese man who's making fun of your cooking. When we got here, Milo pointed at him and said, 'Baby.' I almost died. He thinks everyone who's missing teeth is like him."

"Is he with Micah?" I said, mentally inventorying Damon's absence.

"Yeah, Daddy's on baby patrol today. Mommy gets to celebrate the end of nursing with a stiff drink."

I passed her the wine bottle and she took a swig.

Jem made a face. "It's not as good as I remember it."

"Yeah, well, neither is singlehood," I said.

"Have you heard from that guy?"

"If you mean Bruce, then, um, no. If you mean Brad Pitt, then also no."

Jem shrugged and kicked back another mouthful of vino.

The door swung open again and my mom peeked in.

"Girls, what's going on in here? Looks like the real party's right here!" Mom whooped and hollered as if she were nineteen and had just dropped acid at Woodstock. I had to mentally count to three before answering. One drink, and my mother had the self-control of an alley cat.

"We're just looking for"—my eyes darted around—"olives," I said, grabbing a bottle off the shelf.

Reluctantly, I hauled myself up and squeezed out of the pantry. Jem filed out behind me with the bottle in her hand and a grin on her face.

"Auntie Jen, Auntie Jen!" I felt a tug on my shirt. Tali stood there with a handblown glass candelabra I'd picked up in Portugal. "Is this a spaceship?" she asked.

"No," I said wearily. "But it turns whoever's touching it into a gigantic apple."

She froze.

I knelt beside her. "Hey, just kidding. Why don't you and Tomer go play with his Game Boy?"

Tali ran off and I drifted into the living room. Mr. Yee was deep in conversation with Dad, probably discussing wayward daughters or something. Robert, Micah, Ben, and Katie were laughing about something, and everyone else was huddled out on the cramped deck, which I'd laced with twinkly Christmas lights. My spindly Hanukkah bush had been knocked off its base and threatened to fall into the hummus, so I attempted to right it.

The doorbell rang.

"Got it!" yelled Tomer. Karen had told me he was really into

answering the door these days. Perhaps I could use him as an unofficial houseboy-consort.

He came back with Damon, and for a moment, as our eyes
met, time stood stark still. Déjà vu cascaded over me like soft
rain. Christmas Eve, 1991. We'd been going out for only four
months. Long enough to spend the holidays with each other's
families; short enough to sneak off to the toolshed for a quickie
under the gardening shears. After Ben cornered Damon to talk
about saving the blind orphaned children with harelips or some
other of his many noble causes, I'd glanced up from the turkey
platter I was arranging and caught Damon staring at me. What
could only be called love—or at least affectionate lust—shone in
his jade, heavy-lidded eyes. He'd mouthed, *Save me,* and I'd felt
Cupid's arrows pierce my breast and points further south.

About ten minutes later, I discovered the difference between
pruning shears and hedge saws.

Now, as the memory dissolved and I snapped out of my
trancelike state, it seemed prudent to keep things rooted firmly in
the sexless present.

"Hi, Damon," I said, and hugged him. I thought of lying
naked under him yesterday and blushed.

"You look great, Jen."

"You too."

He had on worn jeans and a cornflower-blue shirt that deepened his eyes to the color of pondside moss.

Then he bit the bullet and went to greet my parents.

"Hi, Vic, Fred." He shook their hands solemnly, as if he
hadn't been caught tickling their pantyless daughter's jiggly
thighs twelve hours ago.

Respect for him bloomed in my heart.

"Hey, Damon, good to see you." Ben clasped Damon to him
fleetingly in much the same manner I'd seen him greet Avi. Hey, I
wanted to shout, watch it—he's not your brother-in-law yet, and
probably never will be.

Katie had warmed up enough to shake Damon's hand. Love had effected a near-miraculous transformation in my friend, who, like the Tin Man, was reputed to be lacking a blood pumper, at least by her maltreated exes. Katie was one of those women who saw little use in cultivating friendships with exes. Why bother? That's what girlfriends and gay husbands were for. I guess she always figured whatever you achieved with an ex would be a pale, anemic version of the real thing at best.

The table needed replenishment, so I grabbed a few depleted platters and went to the kitchen. The wine I'd drunk in the pantry had counteracted my coffee blitz, and I'd slipped into a contented daze. My family, no matter how challenged behaviorally, was here. Dad was okay. The kids hadn't broken anything irreplaceable. The professors at Columbia University thought I was a real journalist. Damon and I were on our way to becoming friends. My job was, if not awesome, bearable. My friends had proved I could not drive them away, no matter how absurdly self-absorbed I could be. I could finally do *sirsha-asana* without the yoga instructor's help. Also, the thought of being alone didn't seem so bad sometimes. I thought of all the things I could do the way I wanted—eat ice cream for dinner, turn the heat up to 75°F, do the naked-with-socks-on walk whenever I wanted—and grinned.

Karen interrupted my reverie.

"Hey, kid. Need help?"

"Nah," I said. "You can talk to me, though. Tell me how you and Avi are."

She threw her hands back in the universal gesture of women who have had to flip down one too many toilet seats.

"We're the way we are. Avi's a good guy. We've been working out some stuff. The kids are beautiful, though. Tomer's becoming a little man, not a baby anymore. I worry about him in Israel. Part of me wants to move back to Florida before the army can get him. The other part thinks, well, he'll always feel like he copped out of something if I do that. Motherhood is tough, Jennie. I thought I'd know what I was doing by this time, but it's all relative. Just when you think you have it figured out, something comes along that just floors you. You just push through every day and hope you don't do anything too stupid." She popped a curl of sliced turkey in her mouth.

Surprised, I took in my sister's stubborn mass of curls and steely expression. I'd always thought of Karen as someone who instinctively knew what she—and, at times, everyone else— wanted. That was part of the reason I'd moved to San Francisco in the first place: to throw off the yoke of being the perennial little sister, to whom everyone was entitled to give their two cents and lord over with impunity.

"So, what's this I hear about you and Damon getting back together?" Karen looked eager, and I actually sort of hated to disappoint her.

"Who told you that?"

"Who do you think?" she answered, as Mom, with impeccable timing, released another of her war whoops from the living room.

"Well, we're not. We just happened to develop the ability to be in the same room again without killing each other when I came back from Montana. It's purely coincidental." I scraped baba gannouj into a ceramic bowl.

She looked confused. "Mom said she and Dad found you naked together."

"Don't believe everything you hear," I said darkly.

The baba gannouj spilled over the side, so I wiped the bowl clean with paper towels.

"I mean, think about it, Kar. Would Damon even *be* here if Mom and Dad had seen us doing the nasty? I don't think so."

She laughed. "Yeah, too gross! You'd have to, I don't know, commit suicide or something."

Suicide ain't the half of it, sis.

We trooped back to the main room and plunked everything down. The party shifted into high gear at that point, and several

hours passed in festive fulfillment of St. Nick's Christmas Com-
mandments, which went something like this:

- Thou shalt not rush out to reserve a spot for your
mother at Golden Years Minimum Security Home for
the Wayward Senior just because she pinches your male
friend's ass over the gingerbread cookies.

- Thou shalt embrace one's landlord with all the good
in one's heart, even when he says things like, "Jen nerrer
get married. She cook like one-armed woman!"

- Thou shalt eat everything on one's plate—and one's
couchmate's plate, assuming she was foolish enough to
leave it teetering on the end table like that with a half-
finished pig in a blanket and a bite-free marzipan bar.

- Thou shalt not castigate oneself for consuming food
products whose nutritional content is limited to partially
hydrogenated oils and high-fructose corn syrup.

- Thou shalt not spend inordinate amounts of time fantasizing about Bruce Mortensen's Martha Stewart–ready
Christmas tableau or how delectable he would look in a
red robe with a curly-haired reporter on his lap.

- Thou shalt not flirt with one's ex-boyfriend—who just
happens to have the nicest hands west of the Mississippi—because he is the only single, straight, available
male hominid at the party.

Around 2:30 P.M., Ben climbed up on a straight-backed chair
and tried to get our attention. His voice was drowned out by the
music and chatter, so he finally had to yell, "Hey!" and we all
piped down.

"Hi, everyone. I think I know all of you now. I'm Jen's brother,

Ben. First, I want to thank Jennie for hosting this year's bash. I know it was kind of unexpected"—he smiled at me, and I raised my glass in acknowledgment—"and to thank my parents for coming all this way, especially Dad—hey, somebody take that eggnog away from him! What, you want another heart attack?—Where was I? Oh, yeah. I just wanted to say Merry Christmas and Happy Hanukkah to all of you and that this Christmas wouldn't be the same for me without a certain Els Janssen, whom I have been so privileged to get to know, and whom I care for deeply."

Els's cheeks reddened, but her eyes shone with pride as she watched Ben. I had the sense that the day's magic, hovering in the air around us, coalesced for a moment into something tangible, sprinkling over our motley assemblage like a spray of confectioner's sugar.

"I'm really without words—" Ben continued.

"Then stop talking!" someone yelled rudely.

"Shut up and let him talk!" someone else said.

"—but I just want to say that I love you, Els, and I'd be honored if you accept this. . . ." Ben stepped down from the chair and knelt in front of Els.

In a heartbeat, the mood of the room shifted from rowdiness to breath-holding expectancy. Could it be true? Was Ben going to propose? All the conventional objections fluttered up to my lips—they'd met only a few months ago, Ben had just broken up with Julie, Els had just left Rainer, they lived on different coasts, spoke different languages, and, except in rare cases such as those incurred by untimely pregnancy or green-card procurement, my friends just didn't *get* married—but I kept my mouth firmly closed and watched the scene play itself out. The room was so still you could hear James Stewart asking Donna Reed if she wanted the moon lassoed in *It's a Wonderful Life,* their TV-crackly voices emanating from the apartment next door. Even the children seemed to grasp the import of the occasion and were mercifully quiet.

Then, in front of everybody, Ben pulled out the Little Black Box, prompting gasps and whistles from the crowd, popped it open, and gazed at Els expectantly.

She seemed to register the crowd of onlookers for the first time, and hesitated. I saw my mom grab my dad's hand. Time hung in the balance, and then . . .

"Yes!" Els cried, finally, with gusto.

Trembling, Ben slipped the glinty band on Els's finger and they embraced. The room erupted into cheers. Zoë and Milo issued twin screams of terror. Mr. Yee hugged Mrs. Yee, who had to hold her fake black bun with her hand to keep it from getting knocked off. Robert and George kissed. Katie and Colin held hands and jumped up and down. Micah twirled Jem around in a giddy impromptu dance. Avi and Karen blurted out prayerful *mazel tovs* in Hebrew and English. Tomer ran around the room, dervishlike, and knocked down the CD rack.

I stood there holding a Dixie cup of cabernet and a half-eaten cookie, the very picture of spinsterly woe. Faced with such an outpouring of true love, my pleasure in solitary independence fled like a looter with a car stereo.

Just when I was about to run and hide in the bathroom to conceal my partnerless, hug-free state, the crowd parted, Red Sea–like, and Damon headed toward me, solid as a human trawler. He opened his arms wide and I fell into them as if drugged. Sound replaced video, and instead of absorbing the overbright colors of merriment and movement, I heard the tinkling of glasses, laughter, and voices bubbling up around us. Everything swirled, like the final scene of a chick flick where the hero returns to his heroine and twirls her around and around in his arms as free-range cameras circle the handsome couple, dizzying the audience. We lacked only long overcoats to add to the drama.

Sweet inevitability cloaked us in its embrace. I raised my face to the ceiling, waiting for the soft collision of Damon's familiar mouth against mine. Please, I thought, let just a little bit of the magic be mine today. The doorbell rang, but I barely registered it, subsumed as it was in the cacophony of celebratory noise.

"Jen?"

"Hmm?"

He stroked my face with his index finger. "You know when I came in last night . . ."

"Uh-huh." What was he waiting for?

". . . and saw you in the bath?"

"Yes."

"It's like I was seeing you clearly for the first time."

Frigging soap bubbles.

"I want us to try again. Do you want that?"

That, my friend, is the million-dollar question.

I opened my mouth to reply, still unsure of what my response would be.

What happened next is the subject of some contention.

Els said he burst in like a bull looking for a red jacket to gore.

Katie insisted he was calm and resolute.

Karen called his demeanor "frightening."

Robert swore he had scored a cup of punch and was seen tickling Mrs. Yee.

All I knew was, the room quieted suddenly. There, his shoulders spanning my rickety doorway in manly splendor, was the apparition I'd tried to conjure for so many weeks. Almost unrecognizable in pin-striped, gray-suited, shiny-shoed, tie-knotted professional packaging, was Bruce Mortensen. Heartbreaker. Father. Montana man.

Prick?

I clung to Damon like a limpet.

"Jen."

The single utterance seemed to carry the weight of the world.

"Can we talk?" he said.

CHAPTER 34

# of mice and miniquiches

To: jbrenner@techstandard.com
From: sanchezd@pw.com
Subject: Important Message From Damon Sanchez

Here is the document you asked for . . . don't show anyone else ;-)

There comes a time in every person's life when she has to Face the Music. Like the World of Pain, Facing the Music is not an elective state. Rather, it tends to infiltrate your life like a mildly annoying parasite, worsening and leaching your spirit until you are forced by your ever-deteriorating circumstances to locate all your survival instincts, dust them off, and stand tall and proud with them beside you, staring the Music in the face.

This was one of those times.

Old Jen could have easily talked her way out of this one, using all the skills at her disposal to evade, avoid, and eradicate the threat.

Be gone, you who come to rebreak my heart! she'd command, sword sheathed firmly in scabbard, ready to be drawn into battle. For I will break you as I have broken many men—er, mice.

New Jen, however, had just enough healthy curiosity to want to find out why in Goddess's good name Bruce Mortensen was here, in her San Francisco apartment, resplendent in his butchness—and looking damn good in that suit—yet strangely solemn.

"Bruce," I squeaked.

"Bruce," I tried again, as if invoking his name would break whatever spell had caused him to materialize in the first place.

He was still there.

Shedding poor deluded Damon like snakeskin, I floated across the room and stood in front of the intruder. Stark silence rushed in to fill my path.

Wordlessly, I plucked my coat from the rack and headed for the door. Bruce followed.

Suddenly, I remembered something important.

"Mom, miniquiches are in the oven. Can you get them out at"—watch check—"a quarter till?"

Mom nodded, for once rendered speechless. Coolly, I wondered if she and Dad had taken in Bruce's graying temples and work-worn knuckles, perhaps mistaking him for my elderly plumber consort or auto-mechanic love interest, all dressed up for the holidays.

As I turned to leave, my eyes made contact with Mr. Yee's. Things seemed to move in slow, cinematic motion. Mr. Yee did this weird thing with his head, sort of a shallow nod, as if granting his approval to my quest. It made him look terribly wise and Confucian. I was deeply moved. I wanted to ask him to accompany us, but as it seemed wildly inappropriate to invite my landlord to the Second Closure, I refrained.

As the Master once said in a particularly wise fortune cookie, *The people may be made to follow a path of action, but they may not be made to understand it.*

By the time we left the house, the day had peaked and waned. White light still bounced off the pavement, and the dome over our heads was still an uninterrupted blue, but the air carried the gray bite of approaching dusk. San Franciscans had shuffled off to their hometowns in droves and the streets were nearly empty, save the occasional party-tray-bearing hipster or homeless person.

We walked in silence to the tiny plot of green park and sandbox two blocks away. I led Bruce to a bench with a peace symbol scratched into it and we sat down. A solitary mom pushed her small son back and forth on the swing set.

I found it hard to look directly into Bruce's face. My desire to do so was powerful, but the fear of returning to the devastated yearning place I'd been several weeks ago was even more so. His nearness set off a vibration deep inside me that felt as deeply layered as a plucked guitar string.

We sat in silence for a minute, following the hypnotic path of the swinging child.

"Didn't you get my e-mail?" he finally asked.

"What e-mail?"

"The e-mail saying I had a meeting at the San Francisco district EPA office and wanted to see you this afternoon."

"Oh. No, I didn't."

He nodded ruefully. Unchecked, my gaze fell to his hands, knotted together in his lap. Once an addict, always an addict; it took every ounce of self-control I had not to grab one and rub its callused palm against my cheek.

Bruce unclasped his hands and swung them behind his head, leaning back.

"I just got suspended," he said.

Shocked, I waited.

"For mishandling the Sutter & McEvoy case. My lawyer wants to appeal. The thing is, I did mishandle it." Bruce leaned forward again and rubbed his chin, a gesture whose familiarity sent slivers of apprehensive lust through my belly.

"Was that your family, back at the apartment?" he asked out of the blue.

"I guess people can't tell when we hide our tails and horns," I quipped.

He smiled. Another shot of lust scorched my insides.

"Your mother's the one with the . . ." He lifted his hands to his hair as if to indicate afro-size dimensions.

I nodded. "The family curse."

He threw me a sidelong glance. "You have beautiful hair, Jen. In fact, I noticed that first thing."

What else did you notice? I nearly wheedled.

"That first meeting we had, at the office, when we talked about being kids, getting into trouble, I think I drank five cups of coffee so I wouldn't be tempted to touch it. I had to have something in my hands. I don't think I slept for two days." He laughed, but the sound had a sharp edge to it. The mom with the little boy looked up for a second, then continued pushing the swing.

"So, you're probably wondering what I'm doing here," he said.

"You can't afford a hotel now that you're suspended and need somewhere to stay?" I parried. We were falling back into our old pattern. I felt safer on sarcastic ground.

Bruce waved his hand. "Nah, they paid for the privilege of firing me, suspending me, whatever you want to call it. That's the federal government for you. Anyway, I'm flying back tonight, to be with Emily for Christmas."

A beat passed.

"A lot has come clear to me in the last few months," he said. He turned to face me head-on, and I felt my defenses crumbling like Roman ruins after a 6.8 temblor. "I'm not proud of the way I handled things at the end, Jen. Not proud at all . . ."

"What else could you do!" I said hotly, wondering why I was defending him. "Your daughter had just been kidnapped, for chrissake!"

"Yeah, and I was pretty crazy for a while. Crazy overprotective too. Emily's set me straight a few times since then, which I'm sure you can imagine. It's just, the idea of losing her, it was too much to handle. It affected me on every level and, to some extent, blinded me to what was going on right in front of me. And to the fact that what was good for me *was* good for Em. Maybe not in an obvious way, but down the road some."

Did this mean we could kiss now?

"Um," I said unhelpfully.

Bruce steepled his hands together. "It'd been so long since I'd been with anyone but Melina. I felt like a schoolboy again, making all the mistakes a green boy would make. I wanted to be with you, see if we could have something between us, but at the first sign of trouble I ran like a stray dog and expected you to chase me. Even though we hadn't known each other long, I should have known better than to think you'd do that. Why would you? You're young, from all this"—he swept his hands toward San Francisco's cityscape, spread out beneath the park in panoramic relief—"you have friends—good friends, judging from what I saw back there. I guess what I'm saying is, I didn't think about the sacrifices you'd have to make. And I didn't realize how much losing you would screw things up for me . . . and my family. My family being Emily. And Bugle. And the truck," he added, smiling.

I realized I'd been holding my breath and puffed a cloud of steam into the cold, still air.

"I miss you," he said simply.

Slowly, seemingly of its own volition, my index finger reached out and touched his cheek. It felt warm and rough. Like a sledge inserted into a fissure, the touch served to widen the crack in my already fragile composure. Bruce's hand came up and grasped my smaller one. Warmer still. Hot, in fact.

"I miss you too," I said.

"What are we going to do about it?" he murmured against my ear. I felt his breath heat the sensitive hairs inside. *Mama mia!*

"Get a room?" I suggested. Rather bold, under the circumstances.

He laughed and chucked me under the chin. "Cut the jokes for a minute, Brenner. I mean, what are we going to do about it permanently?"

Permanent as in till football season ends, or permanent as in the shelf life of my cellulite?

I didn't realize I'd spoken out loud until I heard his bark of laughter and saw him shake his head.

"You're crazy, you know that? Clinically, abysmally, irrevocably crazy."

"Hey," I said, suddenly inspired. "You're the one without the job, right? Why don't you sell the house, pack it up, and move down here?"

At that precise moment, a herd of leather daddies rounded the corner, resplendent in black studded jackets, second-skin jeans, and chaps. One of them playfully slapped another's ass as they crested the hill toward the Castro, the gay center of the universe.

Bruce mimed abject fear and pretended to cower. "Well, if you insist . . ."

"I'm kidding! Even with your superagent skill set, you wouldn't last two weeks here. And not because of harmless guys like that. The edible food alone would be too much for your primitive digestive system," I said.

"I'll show you primitive, brat."

In a heartbeat, he had me flat on my back, my ass pressed firmly into the peace symbol. (Try figuring out *that* symbolism.)

For a responsible older man, Bruce was damned heedless when it came to PDAGA (public displays of ass-grabbing affection).

Kissing him again was like eating your favorite food after a forced hiatus, or being sprung from an iron lung following a nasty bout of polio: just plain relieving. We mashed mouths and bit lips and stroked napes and rolled around, trying not to fall off onto the pavement. Under the silky dress shirt, his chest and abs felt thick and solid and as dense as gold bricks. Breathless, I inhaled his unique scent—yummy. He tasted of berries and cinnamon and wood smoke.

Bruce pulled his head back and gazed at me through those unforgettable, liquid-dark honey eyes.

"You taste like a liquor cabinet and stinky cheese."

I punched him.

"Ow!" he said.

"I was driven to drink by despair at your departure," I cried, enjoying the alliteration—enjoying *everything*—far too much. I felt as if Santa's magical-realist reindeer had leapt straight over the Golden Gate Bridge and nipped me in the ass. *Giddy-up!*

"You drank like a fish before we met. Don't blame that on me," he replied.

"Yeah, well, it got considerably worse when you dumped me. I practically had to go to Betty Ford."

"I didn't dump you. *You* dumped *me*."

"Well, your terms were unacceptable."

"The terms whereby I asked you to love me?"

"I don't recall you saying that . . . exact thing."

"How exact do I need to be?"

Ooh, fun.

"Exact."

"Okay. I love you and will do whatever it takes to be with you. How's that?"

I feigned reflection.

Finally: "I've heard better."

Frown: "From who, that pansy-assed greenhorn in there?"

Feint: "Hey, you know how much Robert means to me."

Jab: "I didn't mean Robert."

Dodge: "Then who did you mean?"

Stab: "The guy you were canoodling with when I walked in."

Faint: "Oh, that guy."

"That your ex?" Bruce sat up and brushed off his suit jacket. His shirt was askew and his tie gone, delivered unto the gods of love and San Francisco park benches. A sacrifice, as it were.

"He wanted to get back together with me. Guess it's going around," I said lightly.

"Going around, my ass."

I shook my head. "He just broke up with his girlfriend and

was looking for something familiar, I think. We made each other miserable then, and we'd make each other miserable now. I think we'll be friends, though," I said carefully, watching Bruce for a reaction.

"Good. He can baby-sit Emily when I come down to ravish his ex-girlfriend," Bruce said.

"That's very naughty of you, Mr. Mortensen." I leaned across the bench and pressed my chest into his arm.

"What do you say we go back to your place and you introduce me to everyone?" he said.

"As what?"

"As whatever you want."

Bruce hoisted me up and held my hand as we walked along the park's edge. The view was stunning. It seemed as if I could almost reach out and run my fingers along the water of the bay. I felt blood singing through my veins down to every corner of my body.

"I'm happy," I murmured.

"What?"

"I'm so fucking happy!" I shouted. Okay, so no one ever accused me of hiding my true feelings.

Bruce slipped his arm under my coat and wrapped it tightly around my waist. We stopped, and he nudged my chin upward until we were eye to eye.

"I'm going to be forty-four in three weeks, Brenner. As far as I can tell, I'm out of a job, unless the review board changes their minds, which, in my experience, is about as likely as you going fly-fishing again. My daughter hates your guts, but she's twelve and kids get over these things. I, however, love you, love your guts, love your sense of humor and every untamed hair on your head, and want to spend the unforeseeable future making you the happiest woman alive. Those are my terms."

"I accept those terms, Bruce," I said gravely.

Then he kissed me, gently this time. One, two, three times, on the corners of my mouth. A sort of yummy benediction.

When we got to the house, I felt a wing of apprehension flutter against my chest for the first time. Perhaps sensing my dismay at the idea of hijacking the party with Bruce's presence and our news, Bruce opened the door himself and extended his hand to me.

We crossed the threshold together.

"Everyone, this is Bruce," I said, soaking up the smiling faces of my girls, my parents, my landlords, my gay husbands.

"Bruce, this is . . . everyone."

CHAPTER 35

the pudding

three weeks later

To: Katie Nguyen
From: Jen Brenner
Subject: Re>something mildly disturbing

This, by far, is the best e-mail I have received all day . . . if not all week!
I suggest you put up a note in locker room, in accordance with Bay
Area standards: "Underwear terrorism not to be tolerated. Panty
thieving free zone! God bless America!"
>knguyen@laughingsquid.com
>Someone stole my dirty underwear at the gym today. I only left it
>there for a second! Believe me, I checked my bag, my pantleg,
>everything. No undies and no men in locker room. Dear Goddess,
>perp was a woman. I feel soiled.

When asked to shed light on the vagaries of human nature by a
certain heartbroken, curly-haired reporter, my former—and quite
possibly future—landlord, the estimable Gladys Pepper, had

turned her high-bridged nose toward me and said wisely, "Jennifer, the proof is in the pudding."

My reaction at the time was somewhere along the lines of "Huh?"

You can imagine my surprise when, lying naked on my couch several months later with a throw blanket around my feet and the heat turned up to a bill-busting 78°F, the truth of that statement finally crystallized and coalesced into meaning.

I sat up, causing *Messieurs* Ben *et* Jerry *Deux* to avert their bulging eyes out of sheer marine modesty.

Life may be ninety-nine percent preparation and one percent consummation, but you can't tell how things will turn out until you hit that last one percent—and it tastes damn good.

The proof is *in* the pudding.

The proof. Is in. The pudding.

Of *course* it is.

Sure enough, Gladys's forty or so additional years of life experience had foretold a more accurate outcome than my own piddling thirty.

Although Bruce and I hadn't resolved all the issues surrounding our relationship—yes, we had embarked on a Relationship with a capital R—most of those matters took an emotional backseat to the pledge we'd made to give it a try. Sure, I was intimidated by the prospect of seeing Emily again this weekend for the first real time since the kidnapping. (I'd suggested a light sedative slipped in her milk for the duration of my visit, but Bruce had pooh-poohed the idea, citing child-abuse laws or some such nonsense. We compromised by agreeing to have her declawed for the occasion.) And the prospect of conducting a long-distance love affair was daunting, to say the least. (At the moment, I was still relying on Robert for weekly foot massages and my battery-operated love gun for satisfying more base urges.) But, all in all, I had come to terms with the challenges being with Bruce without Bruce presented. Plus, I was noggin-over-bunions in love with the man.

At our coming-out party three weeks ago, after the initial

shock had worn off and Bruce had caught a cab to the airport, my mom pulled me aside for some good old-fashioned hallway interrogation.

Afraid I was going to be on the receiving end of one of Vic's are-you-sure-this-is-what-you-want speeches, I focused on shiny, happy thoughts, like the prospect of sitting bare-assed on Bruce's lap while ushering in the New Year.

"Jennie," Mom said after we entered my bedroom and shut the door. "I'm so pleased things are turning out as you wanted them to."

Frightened, I scanned the room for Mom's body, since it was obvious she'd been abducted by aliens and replaced by this rational, motherly, right-thinking *decoy*.

Seeing my reaction, she laughed. "What? You think I haven't noticed how down you've been? I'm sure if you're going to be with this Bruce character"—damn, but these alien decoys were *good*— "then you know what you're doing. Your happiness has always been the most important thing to me and your father."

"You don't think he's too old for me? Too ... unsuitable?" I accused in my confusion. Demented I could deal with; supportive was more unnerving.

Mom chuckled and shook her bushy head. "It sounds like you're the one with the hang-ups, Jennie, not us."

Me? Hang-ups?

"Besides, since we're all coming up to Montana for a ski weekend in February, I'm sure we'll have ample opportunity to get to know one another and decide how suitable—or unsuitable— he is then."

Ski weekend?

"And another thing: Don't you worry about that workshop in New York. You just take care of your career, and the other stuff will take care of itself."

"Did Damon say anything before he left?" I asked.

"Well, he didn't look too pleased. But, then, a man like Bruce Mortensen would intimidate most boys, I would think."

Boys?

"Anyway, I just wanted to tell you how happy we are for you," Mom said.

Then she'd left to check the miniquiches.

And I fell over in a dead faint.

Back in the present, I snuggled deeper under the blanket. On the coffee table next to me lay a dictionary Katie, Els, Robert, and I had used to play Scrabble the night before. I closed my eyes, slid my finger into the thick tome's gilt-trimmed pages, and pried it apart.

I opened my eyes, hoping, as always, for a benevolent soothsaying:

Inconclusive

\In'con*clu"sive\, a. Not conclusive; leading to no conclusion; not closing or settling a point in debate, or a doubtful question; as, *evidence is inconclusive when it does not exhibit the truth of a disputed case in such a manner as to satisfy the mind, and put an end to debate or doubt.*

I smiled, my finger poised for another try.

about the author

Kim Green lives in San Francisco with her husband, Gabe. Yes, she has two cats.

Is That a Moose in Your Pocket?

Or is that the next great novel you want to read?
For something fun . . .
Fashionable . . .
And completely fat-free . . .
Here's something completely indulgent:
Two exciting new sneak peek excerpts from two
novels that are on the "must read A-list."

Turn the page to sample
Whitney Gaskell's

and Sue Margolis's

Neurotica

Meet Ellie Winters. She's under a little pressure....

Pushing 30

a novel

Whitney Gaskell

Pushing 30

by WHITNEY GASKELL

On sale October 2003

The one thing you should know about me is this: I'm the consummate Good Girl. I wash my makeup off every night, no matter how tired I am. I mail out my Christmas cards every Thanksgiving weekend without fail, and thank-you notes are written and posted within three days of receipt of any gift. I've only called into work sick once when it wasn't really true, and even then I spent the entire day too racked with guilt to enjoy it. I'm an extremely loyal and dependable friend, and have never cheated on a boyfriend or tried to steal a man away from another woman. And I never, ever say yes when a friend asks me if she looks fat, particularly if in the throes of a heartbreak she's been hitting the Häagen-Dazs pretty hard, because girlfriends should stick together and not make each other feel self-conscious about their weight. But the problem with being a Good Girl is this—I'm terrible at conflict. Absolutely hate it, am terrified of it, will do anything to avoid it. When it comes to the fight-or-flight phenomenon, my fight is nonexistent, as wimpy as Popeye pre-spinach. Luckily, I am a world-class sprinter when it comes to running away from everything having to do with anything that even remotely resembles strife.

Which is why, as I sat in the wood-paneled bar of McCormick & Schmick's on K Street nursing a glass of merlot, I was dreading the arrival of my soon-to-be ex-boyfriend, Eric Leahy. After weeks of dodging his phone calls, I was resolved to finally end the relationship. And unlike every other breakup I had ever muddled with my pathetic timidity, this time I had a plan: I would tell Eric gently, but firmly, that it was over, and at all costs preserve our dignity. I was a career woman, an attorney (a career you might—as my friends do—find amusing for me to have stumbled into, considering my above-mentioned aversion to conflict), and there was no reason why I couldn't end this relationship gracefully. No matter what, there would *not* be a messy emotional scene, nor would I allow myself to be guilted into giving it a second chance or entering into couples counseling. I had let this relationship drag on for far too long, and just like with a Band-Aid, it's better to rip it off all at once. Of course, as I sat there, hunched up on a hard wooden chair that was putting my butt to sleep, while dipping pieces of pita into a pot of lemony hummus, I didn't feel cool or dignified; I felt sick to my stomach.

I'd come to the bar directly from the office, and I had that end-of-the-workday feel—grimy and sweaty, my feet tired from walking the five blocks to the bar from my office in my three-inch stacked loafers, the waistband of my favorite black-pantsuit digging into my skin. I didn't feel elegant and composed; I was sticky and weary, and dreading what was sure to be an unavoidably messy scene.

Eric arrived. I caught sight of his affable, smiling face as he waved at me and cut through the after-work crowd of yuppies gathered in the bar, heading toward the table I'd claimed. He collapsed in the empty chair I'd been fighting to keep for him, and kissed me on the cheek.

"Ellie," he said. "You look beautiful." Considering how grubby I both looked and felt, I knew he was lying. But as far as lies go, it was a sweet one. And Eric was always saying things like that—heaping compliments on me, telling me how wonderful he thought I was. It was a very appealing trait in a man, one that had kept me from breaking up with him before.

It wasn't that Eric was unattractive—he had glossy black hair, ruddy cheeks, and bright blue eyes, and looked sort of like a pudgy J. Crew model. And while he was a little chunky, and dressed in stodgy three-piece suits and shirts with cuff links (both of which looked pretentious on a thirty-two-year-old man), he was gentle and thoughtful. Not funny exactly—well, no, not funny at all. He tried to crack jokes now and again, but they were always the kind that had obvious punch lines, and he usually mangled the telling of the joke so badly you couldn't even laugh at the sheer silliness of it. But he was a good man. A kind man. Exactly the kind of boyfriend the Good Girl aspires to, and nearly identical in appearance and personality to my last four boyfriends. We even had cutsie, matching names—Ellie and Eric, E & E.

But, just like my previous four boyfriends—Alec, Peter, Winston, and Jeremy—Eric bored me to tears. All he wanted to talk about was his job—something having to do with international finance (although I still wasn't exactly sure what, even though he'd explained it to me more times than I cared to recount)—or whatever football/basketball/baseball/foozeball game ESPN had broadcast the night before. I'm not one of those women who pretends to like sports in order to snag a guy; in fact, I'm pretty upfront about how I couldn't care less about grown men cavorting around on fake grass in Lycra pants with a ball tucked under one arm. But despite explaining my lack of interest to Eric pretty much every time he started a conversation with "You wouldn't believe what happened in the game last night," he persisted in boring me to tears with a play-by-play analysis. Spending dinner with him was pleasant as long as I could coax him into talking about something else, and the sex was tolerable, if not predictable. But just the idea of something more permanent, of lying beside him in bed every night and waking up to his face every morning, made me feel like I was being buried alive.

And besides, Eric just didn't smell right. It wasn't that he had b.o., or that funky ripe odor some men get when they're sweaty. He was very clean and deodorized, but there was something about the way he smelled when I wrapped my arms around him and breathed in deeply that was just...off. And his cologne—Polo, just as Winston and Alec had worn (Peter wore Drakkar Noir, and Jeremy, who had spent a semester studying in Paris, wore Hermès)—which he practically showered in, was overpowering and artificial smelling. Surely the man I was meant to spend my life with would smell sexy and good and safe, and not like a cheesy club promoter.

"I'm so glad you called," Eric said.

"I've been wanting to talk to you about something," he said, stirring his drink, and spearing the olive on a toothpick.

Oh, good, I thought, relieved. He's probably sick of the way I've been acting—ducking his phone calls, avoiding sex, snapping at him when he launches into one of his insufferably long diatribes about the yen—and wants to dump *me*. It will make this *so* much easier. He'll try to let me down easy, and I'll try to look a little stricken, but say of course, I understand, I've been so caught up at work (ha ha!) that I haven't devoted enough time to the relationship. A dignified, understanding split, and I'd be mercifully spared from having to do it myself.

"Oh?" I said, and smiled at him encouragingly. "I've been wanting to talk to you, too."

"Okay. What about?"

"No, you go first."

"Well..." Eric said, and then ducked his head shyly, a nervous smile playing on his thin lips. "I want you to move in with me."

What? Move in. With him. As in *not* breaking up. As in living together. I thought I was going to be sick. No, no, no, this can't be happening, I thought. This is the part where he's supposed to say something like "I never meant to hurt you," or "We've been growing apart for a long time."

Eric—obviously misreading my hesitation—said, "I don't mean without other plans. We could get engaged first. Maybe over Labor Day weekend we could take the train to Manhattan, go ring shopping, maybe see *The Lion King*—" and then, seeing my stricken face, "What is it? What's wrong?"

"It's just...um...is the air conditioner working in here?" I asked.

The bar had become so hot and stuffy I could barely breathe, much less think clearly. Eric's words—"engagement," "plans," "move in together"—were jumbling around my brain. A minute ago I thought we were nicely on our way to a collegial breakup, and now all of a sudden he wanted to live together forever, buy a house in the suburbs, and have babies and minivans. What was it with men, anyway? Why is it that when the woman wants a commitment, they panic and flee the jurisdiction, but grow a little distant and suddenly they're out shopping for diamond solitaires and monogrammed guest towels?

"What were you going to say?" he asked.

"God, it's hot in here. Do you think it's hot in here? I'm burning up," I blathered, and chugged a glass of ice water.

"No, it feels fine to me. Are you okay?"

"Oh. Yes, yes. Just hot," I said gaily, shrugging off my jacket, no longer caring about the stain on my top.

Eric had a strange look on his face. "What were you going to say?" he asked again.

"I was going to say...well, I *don't* think we should move in together," I said weakly.

"You don't? Why not?"

Why not indeed. If I had been incapable of a brisk "It's over. Let's be friends," before, now, in the face of his proposal, I had no idea where to start. "Well...I was thinking that maybe we should think about, well, you know...maybe think about taking it a little more slowly."

"Slowly. But I thought this is what you wanted, to get engaged, to move forward. I thought you'd be happy," Eric said.

"Um," I said.

"What do you mean by taking it slower? I mean, you still want to see each other, don't you?" he continued.

"Er," I said.

"You don't want to see other people, do you?" he asked, in an incredulous tone.

This was just the break I was looking for. I nodded eagerly, and said, "Well, yes, we could do that. See other people. That might be a good idea," I said, as though it was his idea, and I was just going along with it. Encouraging his sound judgment.

But I don't think Eric bought it. Instead, he looked startled, with that deer-in-the-headlights expression people always talk about (although since I don't commune with nature, I've never come that close to running over Bambi).

"See other people," he repeated, and as he absorbed my words his face fell like a child who's just been told that there's no such thing as Santa. "You mean, instead of being exclusive. But you don't want to break up, do you? Not entirely? I mean, you still want us to see each other, right?"

Again, typical male reaction—complete and utter shock at the very suggestion that they somehow fall short of your ideal. And it's not just the smart, handsome, successful, rich men—the stupid, ugly losers are equally flabbergasted that a woman could find them anything less than highly desirable. But when a woman gets dumped, she immediately starts moaning about how if only her thighs were thinner or if she had only been more willing to engage in nightly fellatio, if she could only have been more perfect, then he wouldn't have left. This is a universal female reaction, no matter how brilliant and smart and wonderful the woman in question happens to be, nor how much of a reject the boyfriend is.

"Oh, no. No. Well, I mean, we could see each other," I hastened to say, and then, remembering my resolve about Band-Aids, whispered, "as friends."

Eric just sat there, holding his martini, his head bowed forward. He looked . . . sick. I felt sick. This wasn't going well at all. Why did I do this? Why hadn't I gone first, said my piece, and avoided the whole engagement/move-in-together thing? Why? *Why?*

Eric still didn't say anything. He just got all droopy, and sniffly, and for a horrible moment I thought he was going to cry. He looked at me with wide, wet, dog-being-dumped-in-the-country-because-he's-no-longer-a-cute-fluffy-puppy eyes. And I felt dreadful, worse than a dog deserter—more like a monster who'd just finished gleefully decapitating a nest of fuzzy baby bunnies.

I couldn't bear the silence any longer. "I'm so sorry. I had no idea that you thought . . . that you'd been thinking . . . I didn't know," I finished lamely.

"I noticed that you'd been distant. At first I thought it was just your work or something, but then you never wanted to get together, so then I thought that you were getting annoyed that we weren't making plans for the future. I thought that you wanted a commitment. But I guess that wasn't it at all," Eric said, shooting me another reproachful, teary look. "I thought that we were in love."

And just like that, my resolve wavered. He thought that I loved him. It was such a terrible, terrible thing to tell someone who thinks that he is loved that no, sorry, you aren't. I didn't want to be that person, the one who takes what's all warm and cozy—winter afternoon mugs of cocoa, Saturday night video rentals, Sunday morning crossword puzzles over pancakes—and rips it to shreds. And the part of me that didn't want to be the heartbreaker was pulling way ahead of the side of me that wanted to shake Eric out of my life. I couldn't stand his desolate, reproachful gaze. I was willing to do anything—maybe even go ring shopping—to make it end.

"Oh, Eric," I said, my will collapsing. If at that moment he had said one more word about love, or wanting to give it another try, I would have done it. Knowing all the while that five years later when we'd married and had babies, and I was having lustful fantasies about the neighbor's teenage son who cut our grass, we'd be able to trace all of the marital discord right back to this very moment.

But thankfully, it didn't come to that. Eric pulled himself together. He took a deep breath, drew his shoulders up and his chest in, lifted his chin, and moved from lovelorn victim to Gloria Gaynor singing "I Will Survive." He smiled bravely and stood up, thrusting his balled-up fists into the pockets of his wool Brooks Brothers suit pants with a certain resolute dignity, and stood for a minute at the edge of the table.

"Well. Bye. Maybe I'll call you later?" he asked.

I nodded encouragingly and said, "Oh, yes, please do," while my conscience was screaming, *No! Tell him not to call! Like the Band-Aid! Tell him about ripping off the Band-Aid, and how even if it seems worse now it's actually much, much better in the long run.*

After Eric left, I sat in the bar and finished my wine, which felt like battery acid churning around in my stomach. When I was sure that he'd had enough time to get a taxi, so I wouldn't have to bump into him on the street, I dug my cell phone out of my bag and called my best friend, Nina, and asked her if I could come over.

"I need to talk. It's an emergency," I said.

And then, before leaving McCormick & Schmick's, I went to the ladies' room and managed to make it to a stall just before I puked up all of the hummus and pita bread.

It was five months to the day before my thirtieth birthday.

NeuRoTica

If *He* Always Has
a Headache,
Why Should You
Suffer?

AUTHOR OF THE
NATIONAL BESTSELLER
Apocalipstick

SUE
MARGOLIS

NeuroTica

by SUE MARGOLIS

On sale in trade paperback
September 2003

Dan Bloomfield stood in front of the full-length bathroom mirror, dropped his boxers to his ankles, moved his penis to one side to get a better look and stared hard at the sagging, wrinkled flesh which housed his testicles. Whenever Dan examined his testicles—and as a hypochondriac he did this several times a week—he thought of two things: the likelihood of his imminent demise; and the cupboard under the stairs in his mother's house in Finchley.

It was a consequence of the lamentable amount of storage space in her unmodernized fifties kitchenette that Mrs. Bloomfield had always kept hanging in the hall cupboard, alongside the overcoats, macs and umbrellas, one of those long string shopping bags made pendulous by the weight of her overflow Brussels sprouts. From the age of thirteen, Dan referred to this as his mother's scrotal sac.

These days Dan reckoned his own scrotal sac was a dead ringer for his mother's. His bollocks couldn't get any lower. Dan supposed lower was OK at forty; death on the other hand was not.

By bending his knees ever so slightly, shuffling a little closer to the mirror and pulling up on his scrotum he could get a better view of its underside. It looked perfectly normal. In fact the whole apparatus looked perfectly normal. There was nothing he could see, no sinister lumps, bumps or skin puckering which suggested impending uni-bollockdom, or that his wife should start bulk-buying herrings for his funeral. Then, suddenly, as he squeezed his right testicle gently between his thumb and forefinger, it was there again, the excruciating stabbing pain he had felt as he crossed his legs that morning in the editors' daily conference.

Anna Shapiro, Dan's wife, needed to pee right away. She knew because she had just been woken up by one of those dreams in which she had been sitting on the loo about to let go when suddenly something in her brain kicked in to remind her that this would not be a good idea, since she was, in reality, sprawled across the brand-new pocket-sprung divan on which they hadn't even made the first payment. Looking like one of those mad women on the first day of the Debenhams sale, she bolted towards the bathroom. Here she discovered Dan rolling naked on the floor, clutching his testicles in one hand and his penis in the other with a look of agony on his face which she immediately took for sublime pleasure.

As someone who'd been reading "So you think your husband is a sexual deviant"–type advice columns in women's magazines since she was twelve, Anna knew a calm, caring opening would be best.

"Dan, what the fuck are you up to?" she shrieked. "I mean it, if you've turned into some kind of weirdo, I'm putting my hat and coat on now. I'll tell the whole family and you'll never see the children again and I'll take you for every penny. I can't keep up with you. One minute you're off sex and the next minute I find you wanking yourself stupid at three o'clock in the morning on the bathroom floor. How could you do it on the bathroom floor? What if Amy or Josh had decided to come in here for a wee and caught you?"

"Will you just stop ranting for one second, you stupid fat bitch. Look."

Dan directed Anna's eyes towards his penis, which she had failed to notice was completely flaccid.

"I am not wanking. I think I've got bollock cancer. Anna, I'm really scared."

Relieved? You bet I was bloody relieved. God, I mean for a moment there last night, when I found him, I actually thought Dan had turned into one of those nutters the police find dead on the kitchen floor with a plastic bag over their head and a ginger tom halfway up their arse. Of course, it was no use reminding him that testicular cancer doesn't hurt. . . . "What are you going to have?"

As usual, the Harpo was full of crushed-linen, telly-media types talking Channel 4 proposals, sipping mineral water and swooning over the baked polenta and fashionable bits of offal. Anna was deeply suspicious of trendy food. Take polenta, for example: an Italian au pair who had worked for Dan and Anna a few years ago had said she couldn't understand why it had become so fashionable in England. It was, she said, the Italian equivalent of semolina and that the only time an Italian ate it was when he was in school, hospital or a mental institution.

Neither was Anna, who had cellulite and a crinkly post-childbirth tummy flap which spilled over her bikini briefs when she sat down, overly keen on going for lunch with Gucci-ed and Armani-ed spindle-legged journos like Alison O'Farrell, who always ordered a green salad with no dressing and then self-righteously declared she was too full for pudding.

But as a freelance journalist, Anna knew the importance of sharing these frugal lunches with women's-page editors. These days, she was flogging Alison at least two lengthy pieces a month for the *Daily Mercury*'s "Lifestyles" page, which was boosting her earnings considerably. In fact her last dead-baby story, in which a recovering postnatally depressed mum (who also just happened to be a leggy 38 DD) described in full tabloid gruesomeness how she drowned her three-month-old in the bath, had almost paid for the sundeck Anna was having built on the back of her kitchen.

Dan, of course, as the cerebral financial editor of *The Vanguard*, Dan, who was probably more suited to academia than Fleet Street, called her stuff prurient, ghoulish voyeurism and carried on like some lefty sociology student from the seventies about those sorts of stories being the modern opiate of the masses. Anna couldn't be bothered to argue. She knew perfectly well he was right, but, like a lot of lefties who had not so much lapsed as collapsed into the risotto-breathed embrace of New Labour, she had decided that the equal distribution of wealth starting with herself had its merits. She suspected he was just pissed off that her tabloid opiates earned her double what he brought home in a month.

"But what about Dan's cancer?" Alison asked, shoving a huge mouthful of undressed radicchio into her mouth and pretending to enjoy it.

"Alison, I've been married to Dan for twelve years. He's been like this for yonks. Every week it's something different. First it was weakness in his legs and he diagnoses multiple sclerosis, then he feels dizzy and it's a brain tumor. Last week he decided he had some disease which, it turns out, you only get from fondling sheep. Alison, I can't tell you the extent to which no Jewish man fondles sheep. He's a hypochondriac. He needs therapy. I've been telling him to get help for ages, but he won't. He just sits for hours with his head in the *Home Doctor*."

"Must be doing wonders for your sex life."

"Practically nonexistent. He's too frightened to come in case the strain of it gives him a heart attack, and then if he does manage it he takes off the condom afterwards, looks to see how much

semen he has produced—in case he has a blockage somewhere—then examines it for traces of blood."

As a smooth method of changing the subject, Alison got up to
go to the loo. Anna suspected she was going to chuck up her
salad. When she returned, Anna sniffed for vomit, but only got
L'Eau d'Issy. "Listen, Anna," Alison began the instant her bony
bottom made contact with the hard Phillipe Starck chair. "I've
had an idea for a story I think just might be up your street."

Dan bought the first round of drinks in the pub and then went to
the can to feel his testicle. It was less than an hour before his appointment with the specialist. The pain was still there.

Almost passing out with anxiety, he sat on the lavatory, put
his head between his knees and did what he always did when he
thought he was terminally ill: he began to pray. Of course it
wasn't real prayer, it was more like some kind of sacred trade-
union negotiation in which the earthly official, Dan, set out his
position—i.e., dying—and demanded that celestial management,
God, put an acceptable offer on the table—i.e., cure him. By way
of compromise, Dan agreed that he would start going to synagogue again—or church, or Quaker meeting house, if God preferred—as soon as he had confirmation he wasn't dying anymore.

Mr. Andrew Goodall, the ruddy-complexioned former rugby fly-
half testicle doctor, leaned back in his leather Harley Street
swivel chair, plonked both feet on top of his desk and looked at
Dan over half-moon specs.

"Perfectly healthy set of bollocks, old boy," he declared.

Kissed him? Dan could have tongue-wrestled the old bugger.

"But what about all this pain I've been getting?"

"You seemed perfectly all right when I examined you. I strongly
suspect this is all psychosomatic, Mr. Bloomfield. I mean, I could

chop the little blighter orf if you really want me to, but I suspect that if I did, in six months you'd be back in this office with phantom ball pain. My advice to you would be to have a break. Why not book a few days away in the sun with your good lady? Alternatively, I can prescribe you something to calm you down."

Dan had stopped listening round about "psychosomatic." The next thing he knew he was punching the air and skipping like an overgrown four-year-old down Harley Street towards Cavendish Square. He, Dan Bloomfield, was not dying. He, Dan Bloomfield, was going to live.

With thoughts of going to synagogue entirely forgotten, he went into John Lewis and bought Anna a new blender to celebrate. One can only imagine that God sighed and wondered why he had created a world full of such ungrateful bleeders.

Anna got home just after four. Denise, her babysitter, had taken Josh and Amy swimming after school, so she would be bratless for at least a couple of hours—more if Denise got them sausages and chips at the pool. Anna decided to have a bath and a quick de-fuzz. All through the lunch she had been aware that she was having a bad pubic hair day. The sideburns on her inner thighs were reaching a density that would have done a woolly mammoth proud.

As she turned over Dan's knicker drawer looking for his razor, which he always tried to hide because whenever she used it she left it blunt and clogged up with leg hairs, Anna realized she was getting quite enthused by Alison's feature idea.

She'd said to Alison she wasn't sure if she had time to do it, which was a lie she always told features editors just in case they started taking her for granted. But she thought she probably would. She could never say no to work, in case the Alison O'Farrells of this world forgot who she was and never used her again. But more than that, while Alison was explaining the idea to her, she began to feel rather horny.

Alison had just received a preview copy of Rachel Stern's new book, *The Clitoris-Centered Woman*. Anna despised Rachel Stern almost as much as she despised polenta-eaters. Stern, an American, was one of a gaggle of beautiful Harvard-educated feminist writers, barely old enough to menstruate, who with their pert bosoms, firm arses and live-in personal trainers had the audacity to lecture the sagging, stretch-marked masses on how antiwrinkle creams, Wonderbras and cosmetic Polyfillas were a form of treachery against the sisterhood, or some such rot.

In her last book, *Dermis,* Stern had railed against cosmetic surgery. On the day of publication she had led a massive protest rally outside an L.A. clinic to launch her "Get a Life Not the Knife" campaign. Hundreds of East and West Coast academics, "educators" and writers—mainly svelte Stern look-alikes, but with a smattering of token uglies—turned up to yell abuse at the women going into the clinic. According to the *LA Times* the protesters even dunked one woman's head in a vat of liposucted fat, thoughtfully provided by a mole at the clinic who was sympathetic to the cause.

"Look, I know you can't stand the bitch," Alison had said, "but I reckon *The Clitoris-Centered Woman* is actually quite sensible. It's about infidelity and why women are more reluctant to be unfaithful than men. She says women don't go in for extramarital shagging because they feel they can only do it if they are actually in love with the guy, and being in love with two men seriously does your brain in, so not doing it in the first place saves all the hassle of whose heart you're going to end up breaking. Anyway, Stern says that all this needing to be in love in order to have an affair is crap and women are just as capable as men of having affairs purely for the sexual pleasure—hence the title. So affairs become no more than a bit of glorified pampering—like going for a manicure or a facial except you get an orgasm instead of your blackheads squeezing. Of course, the most difficult part is keeping it secret and not blurting it out to hubby."

"And don't tell me, she reckons we should all be into extracurricular rutting because it can really zap up your marriage . . . and what you want me to do is to go out and interview three slappers who make a habit of being unfaithful just for the sex."

"You got it. Two thousand words if you can. You've got loads of time—she's not due over here to launch the book until mid-July, which gives you about eight weeks."

Anna realized she had got so carried away replaying in her mind all this talk of adultery that she had been absentmindedly shaving her pubes for at least ten minutes and had left herself with little more than a Hitler mustache between her legs. As she rinsed Dan's razor in the bathwater and watched her hairs float on top of the white scum, it began to dawn on her that if anybody needed to become a clitoris-centered woman, it was her.